B... **T'...**

'A real page-turner, I lov[...]
B A Paris, bestselling author of *Behind Closed Doors*

'Tense, suspenseful and unsettling!'
Lisa Hall, bestselling author of *Between You and Me*

'Unsettling, insightful, evocative and poignant, Morgan's writing
is both delicate and devastating.'
Helen Fields, author of *Perfect Remains*

'A brilliantly creepy and insightfully written debut. I tore
through it.'
Gillian McAllister, Sunday Times bestselling author of
Everything But the Truth

'Totally engrossing from start to finish. A clever, clever book.'
Amanda Robson, author of *Obsession*

'Morgan's intense prose grips and thrills from the first page…a
terrific debut.'
S. R. Masters, author of *The Killer You Know*

'Atmospheric, dark and haunting, I could not put this book down.'
Caroline Mitchell, USA Today bestselling author

'Deliciously creepy, genuinely unnerving and incredibly
confident, *The Doll House* is the stellar first outing of a major
new voice.'
Catherine Ryan Howard, author of *Distress Signals*

'The definition of a page-turner… I had to remind

Phoebe Morgan is an author and editor. She studied English at Leeds University after growing up in the Suffolk countryside. She has previously worked as a journalist and now edits crime and women's fiction for a publishing house during the day, and writes her own books in the evenings. She lives in London and you can follow her on Twitter@Phoebe_A_Morgan. *The Doll House* is her debut novel.

The Doll House

Phoebe Morgan

ONE PLACE. MANY STORIES

HQ
An imprint of HarperCollins*Publishers* Ltd
1 London Bridge Street
London SE1 9GF

This paperback edition 2018
6
First published in Great Britain by
HQ, an imprint of HarperCollins*Publishers* Ltd 2017

ISBN: 978-0-00-832066-9

MIX
Paper from
responsible sources
FSC™ C007454

This book is produced from independently certified FSC™ paper to ensure responsible forest management.
For more information visit: www.harpercollins.co.uk/green

Printed and bound in Great Britain by
CPI Group (UK) Ltd, Croydon, CR0 4YY

To my family, for not being like this one.

Then

'Can we go now?'

I am tugging on Mummy's coat, my fingers clutching the thin black fabric of it as though it is a life raft. Mummy's eyes don't move; her gaze doesn't falter. It is as if I have not spoken at all.

Minutes pass. I begin to cry, small, quiet sobs that choke in my throat, sting my cheeks in the wind. Mummy takes no notice. I push my palms into my eyes, blotting out the last remnants of light in the shadowy garden around us. The darkness continues to fall, but still Mummy stares, glassy-eyed. She doesn't comfort me. She just stares. I bite down hard into the flesh of my cheek, harder and harder until I can taste a little bit of blood on my tongue. I'm trying to be quiet, trying not to make a sound. Mummy tells me that I shouldn't complain, that we're just playing the game. But it's too cold tonight, and I'm hungry. The chocolate bar I had at school is swirling around in my stomach. I don't think I'll get anything else tonight, not if we don't see them soon.

In the winter time it's always cold like this, but Mummy never lets us leave. In the summer time it's better, sometimes the game is almost fun. The garden is the best part, I like the way the grass feels against my knees, and the way the hole in the fence fits me perfectly, like it's been built just for me. I'm really good at getting through it now, I never even snag my clothes any more. I'm almost perfect.

Now though it's freezing and my hands are red, they burn like they're set on fire. I squeeze my eyes tightly shut and pretend that it's summer time, all nice and warm, and that I can feel the rays of sun on my back from where I'm hiding. In summer I get to see animals. They have rabbits in cages but I don't go near those any more. One time I did, I crept right up to the cage and put my fingers through the gap, touched one of the bunnies on his little soft nose. But when Mummy realised, she got very angry, she said I had to stay back in the shadows. She says the bunnies don't belong to us. So I don't see them any more, but I do get to see the little hedgehog that lives near the fence, and all the creepy-crawlies; the worms and the beetles that Mummy says I oughtn't to touch. I do touch, though. I push my fingers into the dirt and pick them up, lay the worms flat on my hand and watch them wriggle. I don't think they mind. It's nice to have things to play with. I'm usually by myself.

Mummy suddenly leans forward, grabs my frozen hand in hers. I can feel the bones of her hand against mine, clutching me tight. It hurts.

'Do you see them?' she says, and I open up my eyes, blink in the darkness. It's almost fully dark now but I look at the golden window, and I do see them. I see them all. My heart begins to thud.

1

Now

Corinne

The house is huge. It sits like a broken sandcastle in the middle of the lawn, strangely out of place amongst the remnants of construction, discarded hats and polystyrene cups left by over-caffeinated builders. I cling to Dominic's hand as we pick our way through the site. Two fold-up chairs are positioned mid-way across the lawn, their silver legs wet with cold condensation.

'Dominic? You're here early!' A man is striding towards us, hand outstretched. I let go of Dominic and step backwards, feel the immediate rush of anxiety as we disengage.

'You must be Warren.' Dom smiles, reaching out to grasp the bigger man's hand in his own. 'This is my girlfriend, Corinne Hawes.' He propels me forward slightly with his left hand. 'She's got the day off work so I thought I'd bring her along with me. Got a keen eye for a story too, so she might be of use!'

Neither of these things are exactly true. Dominic is a journalist; it's easy to twist the truth, blur the lines. He's good at it.

'Thanks for coming down,' Warren is saying, his voice loud and fast. 'We really appreciate the coverage.' Spittle connects the fleshy pouches of his lips, hangs horribly before separating itself into two sticky drops. He is moving as fast as he speaks, leading us both towards the house, raising a hand to builders as they walk past. The closer we get to the building, the worse I feel. It looms over us, white in the winter sun. There is something strange about it, something sad. It looks ruined. Forgotten.

'So, Dominic, Dom, can I call you Dom?' Warren continues without bothering to wait for an answer. 'Dom, the thing is, this building is going to be a beauty by the time we're finished with it. Yeah, it needs a bit of TLC, but that's what we're here for.' He looks at me suddenly and winks. I recoil. He reminds me of Dom's colleague Andy, the one who spent the entire Christmas party staring down my blouse, his eyes finding the gaps between the buttons on my chest. The memory makes me shudder. That man has never liked me since.

'Shall we start off with a few questions, I'll tell you what you need to know? Then you can take a few snaps, I know what you paparazzi are like!' Warren laughs. I want to catch Dominic's eye, share the horror of Warren together, but he's scribbling in his notebook, little squiggles of grey against the white page.

We sit down at the chairs, I feel the wetness of the cold plastic seep through my jeans. The sun hits my eyes and I close them momentarily; they feel dry, the tear ducts

10

emptied. Dom made me come with him today, told me I needed to get out of the flat. He said a week is long enough. He's right, I know he is. I just can't bear the fact that we've failed again, that another round of IVF has led to nothing. I feel empty.

'Our readers love a good backstory,' Dominic continues, and I find a glimmer of peace in the familiar rise and fall of his voice. 'Especially with a building as beautiful as this.'

'Well, let's see,' Warren says. 'Carlington House – this is what's left of it – was originally built back in 1792. It was designed by a guy named Robert Parler—'

Something shifts slightly in my brain, a bell of recognition.

'I know Robert Parler,' I say. 'Well, not *know* him, of course. I mean I know of him; my dad told me.'

Dom smiles at me, his eyes flashing over the notepad.

'Corinne's dad was an architect too,' he tells Warren, and I feel that familiar sucker-punch at the use of the past tense. It's coming up to a year since Dad died. I miss him every single day. I miss him more than anyone thinks. I'm grateful to Dom for not saying Dad's name – Warren will no doubt have heard of him and I don't want to have to hear him start to suck up to me. People do that when they realise who my father was – one of the most well-known architects in London, famous in the industry and beyond. But it hurts to talk about him, and I feel fragile today, as though I'm made of glass that might shatter at any second.

'Got yourself a smart little lady here, Dom!' Warren grins. His teeth are too big for his mouth; I spy a piece of greenery stuck in his gums. 'So, Parler does a grand job with Carlington and it passes through the hands of local landowners, the few that were wealthy enough. But then the Blitz rolls around, and we suffer some pretty major damage. Family living in it at the time, the littlest of their kiddies is found under the rubble nearly three months later. Three months, can you believe. Tragedy.'

Warren shakes his head, presses on gleefully. I picture tiny bones, birdlike under the aftermath of a bomb.

'So, the thing is, the place never had the chance to shine until years later, must've been around twenty years ago.' He pauses, stares for a moment at the house before us. I follow his gaze; there is a sudden movement, a shower of white dust spills from the collapsing roof. A trio of rooks fly out from the left-hand corner, shooting into the light, their spidery legs trailing behind them like stray threads in the ashy grey sky. One of them calls out, fleetingly, a short sharp cry that echoes in my chest.

'Anyway, eventually someone spotted its potential. Employed a whole new round of builders, started work again. By that time, it was owned by the de Bonnier family, you know, they were a big deal in the jewellery business? Very wealthy back then.' Warren sucks his teeth and raises his eyebrows at me.

Dominic, in the midst of writing, pauses and looks up. 'You've not been at this twenty years though, surely?'

'Of course not, Dom, of course not.' Warren laughs. 'My men are quicker than that! No, the de Bonniers hired a new company, started to do the place up. Made some good progress—'

'So what happened?' Dominic leans forward. His breath mists the air; I watch the cloudy white of it disappear into nothingness.

'Whole thing got abandoned.'

'Abandoned?'

'Yep. Story goes that some pretty deep shit went down between the de Bonniers and the architect firm. All turned a bit nasty. Lot of money lost, from what I understand. That's what it always comes down to, isn't it? Money.' He waves a large hand in the air, it comes dangerously close to my shoulder.

'So then of course, lucky us, we manage to wangle the deal and get the go-ahead to renovate. One of my biggest commissions so far, Dom, pays for the kids' school fees, that's what I always say. You guys got kids? Bloody rip-off these days. My missus says the little buggers are bleeding us dry.'

He turns his head towards me, I feel the heat rise in my face as his eyes meet mine. How can he say that? Doesn't he know how lucky he is?

'What kind of trouble went down?' Dominic asks, saving me from answering his question.

'Oh,' Warren wafts a hand airily. 'It was all a bit hush hush—' I receive another wink '—I'm sure we can find out for you though! But isn't that more your department?' He laughs, the criticism veiled.

Dominic inclines his head. I sense his annoyance and my heart beats a little bit faster.

'So who owns the house now?'

'Oh, it's being sold,' Warren says. 'Woman who owns it can't afford to keep it, that's why it's in the state it's in. Been left to rot, really. But someone's finally come forward to buy it, pumped a load of money in – not that I care where the money's coming from, as long as it's coming!'

Dominic winces. 'Right, right.'

13

Warren grins at me. 'I can show you the house, if you like. Any excuse to show off our work, that's what I always say.'

We are treated to a few statistics on Warren's builders before we all stand up and Dominic takes a couple of photos. I close my eyes when the camera flashes; I hate cameras. Dad always said he hated them too, but I don't think he did. He loved the attention, the limelight he used to get in London whenever he unveiled a new design. Flash. Flash. Dominic sees me wincing and touches my hair, asking if I'm all right, and I force myself to smile at him. The house surrounds us. I feel like it's watching me.

Warren leads us both around the back, to where a hole in the wall gapes brutally, exposing the half-finished rooms inside. I remove a mitten and run my hand over the sturdy stone, enjoying the cold sensation. It is an off-white colour, *argent grey*, I think, the paint number popping into my head, an old habit from my first gallery days. A spider drifts downwards, its legs moving quickly like tiny knitting needles, spinning itself towards the soft padding of my outstretched arm. Drops of water glisten on its silvery web.

As we wander through the garden, around the crumbling walls, I feel the building enveloping me, touching me with its feelers, pulling me in. Cold fronds of air creep towards me from the dark holes where the windows should be. I stare up at the highest window, wondering who lived here, what secrets this house has held. As I turn away I see it – a flash in the darkness, a white movement. A face. There's a face in the blackness, ghostly pale. I can see it.

I scream, put a hand to my chest and stumble backwards, my heart thudding.

'No!' I am saying, the words bursting out of my mouth before I can stop them. 'No!'

'Ssh, Corinne, ssh now, it's all right.' Dominic is there, holding me, telling me to calm down, it's just him, just the flash of his camera. Nothing to see. There is nobody there. He holds me against his chest and I take deep breaths, my legs shaking, cheeks flushing as Warren stares at me. My heart is thudding uncomfortably. I can't keep doing this, living on my nerves, panicking at nothing. Dom continues to stroke my hair and tell me everything is fine, and I know he's right but I can't help it, I keep picturing the sight: a face at the window, looking out at me, staring straight into my eyes.

*

I run a bath that evening while Dominic goes to buy dinner for us both. My discarded boots sit by the radiator, their insides stuffed with old newspaper. We always have far too much of it; Dominic keeps his old copies of the *Herald* stacked up in the hallway.

I sit on the side of the bathtub, my legs cold against the white enamel, and turn the page of a book called *Taking Charge of Your Fertility*. I'm trying not to think about earlier, the way I panicked at the house. It's not good for me, these bursts of irrationality. Dom thinks it's to do with my dad, the shock of his death. He's said as much too.

I flip the book in my hands over. It has a picture of a serious-looking woman on the back and a photograph of a baby in a pushchair on the inside jacket flap. I have been hiding the book from Dominic since I bought it on Amazon. I'm embarrassed by it, I suppose, because actually I don't really believe in any of this stuff, never have.

I saw the fertility book in Waterstones the other day and found myself hovering, looking around to see if anyone was watching me research ways to have children the way other people look up hobbies. I picked the book up, started to carry it to the counter, but the woman in the queue looked at me sympathetically when she saw what I was holding. I left the shop in a hurry, cheeks flaming, unable to bear her pity, but that night I found myself on the computer with my purse open beside me, typing in my bank security details and our address.

I have forgotten that I am running a bath until I feel the ends of my dressing gown getting wet against my skin. The water has reached the rim of the tub and is threatening to overflow. Swearing, I reach for the tap and turn it off, plunging my hand down into the wet heat to release the plug. The book falls from my lap onto the floor, landing with a dull thud.

Once the bath water has resigned itself to an acceptable level, I undress, my dressing gown pooling on the floor. My stomach is flat, white. I imagine it stretched out in front of me, like Ashley's was with Holly, and the hairs on my body stand up against the cold air, only relaxing as I slide into the hot water. I put my shoulders back against the enamel, feel the points of my shoulder blades flinch at the sensation. I lean down to pick up the book. I should be more open-minded. Perhaps it will work. After all, I am fast running out of options.

Around me, the water goes cold but I stay in the bath, letting my body relax. I used to have baths when I was a little girl, I've always preferred them to showers. Images of Carlington House keep surfacing in my mind; the way I screamed, the darkness of the windows. I need to get a grip. I've always been a bit like this. When I was a little girl, I was always thinking I saw faces, ghosts in the dark. There was never anyone there. Dad used to say I had an overactive imagination. 'Seeing the spooks again, Corinne?' He'd laugh, ruffle my hair. He thought it was funny, but actually it made me feel scared. Still. I'm an adult now, I ought to know better.

My mobile rings twice, a sharp trill followed by a thudding vibration that echoes through the silent flat, but I don't want to get out of the water just yet. It's probably my sister. As the sound of the phone begins again, I give up and sink my head under the water, enjoying the cold rush enveloping me, my hair floating up and around me like a dark halo.

The next thing I know, Dominic is shouting, his hands are underneath my armpits, slipping and sliding, and there is water splashing everywhere. The bath mat is bristly under my feet and the towel as he rubs it over me is rough. My teeth are chattering and my fingertips are prune-like. He has pulled the plug and the water is draining out, forming rivulets around the sides of the sodden paperback lying on the floor of the tub.

'Jesus Christ, Corinne,' Dominic says, and his voice is shaky.

2

13 January 2017
London

Ashley

Ashley shifts her daughter from one hip to the other so that she can bend to pick up the mail on the doormat. Holly lets out a cry, a short, sharp sound followed by a wail that makes the muscles in Ashley's shoulders clench. Every bone in her body is aching. Her hands clasp Holly's warm body to her own; her daughter's soft, downy hair brushes against her chest and she feels the familiar aching thud in her breasts. *Please, not now.*

She feels exhausted; even on days when she's not at the café it's as though she's on a never-ending treadmill of nappies and tantrums, homework and school runs. It's not as if James is around to help her; her husband has been staying at the office later and later, leaving early each morning before the children are even out of bed. He is pulling the sheets back usually around the time that Ashley is starting to drift off to sleep, having spent the night rocking Holly, trying to calm her red little body as she screams. She has never known anything like it; her third child is by far the most unsettled of the three. It has been nine months and still Holly refuses to sleep through the night; if anything she is getting worse. Ashley doesn't think it's normal. James stopped waking up at around the four-month mark, has been sleeping lately as though he is dead to the world. She doesn't know how he manages it.

Ashley had woken yesterday to find his side of the bed empty and the sound of the tap running in their bathroom. She had put her hand to the space beside her, sat there mutely as her husband gave her a brief kiss on the cheek and headed out the door. As he had leaned close to her, Ashley had had to fight the urge to grip his shirt, force him to stay with her. She hadn't, of course, she had let him go. Then she had been up, bringing Benji a glass of orange juice, placing Holly in her high chair, making coffee for her teenage daughter Lucy. On the treadmill for another day.

Working a few shifts a week at Colours café is her one respite, her only time when she is no longer a tired mother or a wife, she is simply a waitress. James had laughed at her when she decided to start working at the little café on Barnes Common, with the ice creams and the till and the tourists. He had been amazed when she insisted on continuing work a few months after having Holly, strapping her daughter carefully into the car and driving her across the common to their childminder.

'You don't need to now, honey,' he used to say, before giving her little pep talks on the latest figures of eReader sales, on how well his company was doing. She knows they don't need the money any more. But the waitressing isn't for the money – most days she even forgets to pick up the little tip jar that sits at the edge of the counter, ignores the dirty metal coins inside as though they are nothing more than

20

the empty pistachio shells that Lucy leaves in salty piles around the house. Ashley has always been happy to give up her publishing career for her children, but she craves this small contact with the outside world. The easy days at the café give her insights into other people's lives, a chance to be in an adult environment. Just a few times a week, when she becomes someone else, someone simple, leaves her daughter in the capable hands of June at number 43 and walks back to her car alone, her arms deliciously light, weightless. It isn't about the money.

June has been a godsend to Ashley in the last six months. A retired schoolteacher, she had been recommended to them a couple of months after Holly was born. Neither of them had been coping very well and the offer of a childminder seemed like a golden ticket, a chance opportunity that might never come again. Neither Benji nor Lucy had ever had a babysitter. Ashley had stayed at home all hours of the day and night, playing endless games of peek-a-boo and living her life on a vicious cycle of nappies and tears. Not that she'd minded at the time, not really, but now that she is older she finds her mind wandering, her energy limited. To be able to work in the café is bliss.

June is unwaveringly kind, and Ashley is overwhelmingly grateful to her for stepping in a few days a week. As far as she knows, the woman lives completely alone, has never had children of her own. Ashley can sense the sadness there, is happy to see the joy in June's eyes when she drops off Holly. Yes, June really has been a blessing.

Ashley has thought about asking Corinne to mind Holly, but she has the gallery, and besides, Ashley doesn't want it to upset her. Her sister's emotions are so close to the surface at the moment, spending all day looking after someone else's child rather than her own might have been too much.

It took Ashley seconds to make the decision last week. When Corinne had called with the doctor's news Ashley had gone straight to her laptop and transferred her sister the money for her final round of IVF, thousands of pounds gone with a wiggle of the mouse. Still, it's for the best. The money would only have been accumulating dust in their joint account. She hasn't told James yet, has barely had the chance. She can hardly tell him at midnight, when she is half asleep, trying to catch one of her half-hour bursts between the baby's cries and he rolls into bed next to her, pulls her towards him in the dark and wraps his arms round her stomach. There never seems to be the time.

'Are you worried?' her friend Megan had asked her last week. They had been sitting outside Colours café, taking a break from their waitressing duties, huddled against the cold with a pair of creamy hot chocolates.

'Am I worried?' Ashley had repeated the question out loud, the words misting the January air.

Megan had nodded, pushed her strawberry blonde hair behind her ears, tucked the ends underneath her purple wool hat.

'About what?' Ashley knew what her friend meant, had pretended not to.

'Well, you know.' To her credit, Megan had had the grace to look slightly uncomfortable. 'Why do you think he's staying late so much?'

'He's working, Megan,' Ashley had told her, and they had finished their drinks in silence, drunk them too fast so that the cocoa burned the top of Ashley's mouth and scorched the taste buds off her tongue. Megan had apologised later, put her arm around Ashley as they stood behind the counter together.

'Ignore me,' she said, 'I haven't had any faith in men since Simon left. James is one of the good ones. Don't worry.'

Ashley had squeezed her friend back, allowed herself the warm flood of relief. The feeling hadn't lasted. The hot chocolate she'd had coated her mouth, she felt the thick sweetness of it on her tongue, looked down at herself in shame and felt the bulge of her stomach, the way it pressed against her jeans since having Holly. It never used to.

In the kitchen, Ashley sets Holly down in her high chair, humming to her until she begins to quieten down. Holly's chubby hands reach out for the wooden spoon on the work surface and Ashley hands it to her obligingly, closes her ears to the noise of the daily drumbeat beginning, the sound of her baby hitting the spoon on the table. She begins to sift through the pile of mail, catches the edge of her finger on an envelope and closes her eyes briefly as a slit appears in her flesh. She is so tired; as she squeezes her hand she thinks momentarily how nice it would be to sink onto the sofa and blot everything out, just for an hour, just for five minutes. Three children have knocked the wind completely out of her sails. She thinks of herself as a child, and wonders at how well behaved she was. She and Corinne were good as gold, would spend hours sitting cross-legged in front of the big doll house their dad had made, playing endless games of families in the light of the big French windows that overlooked their garden, the sprawling green jungle that was home for so many years.

At fifteen, Ashley would never have spoken to her dad the way Lucy sometimes talks to James. She would never have wanted to let him down – the disappointment in his eyes if she came home with a less than perfect grade was always heartbreaking, though he'd always pull her into his arms and tell her it didn't matter. By contrast, Lucy can be so insolent, the harsh words fly out of her mouth like bullets. She apologises, of course, most of the time. Ashley has seen her curl up next to James, rest her head against his shoulder, put on her pink piggy socks so that she looks like a ten-year-old again. With Ashley she is closed off, on guard. Perhaps it's just a phase. Her friend Aoife's daughter had come home the other night with a shoe missing, vomiting up vodka in horrible swirls of sick. At least they are not there yet.

Ashley checks her watch. Ten to five. Her eyes meet Holly's, as though her daughter will speak to her, will offer some advice. Instead she smiles, a big, round-cheeked smile that makes Ashley's heart melt. Neither of them blink and the moment stretches out, and, just for a second, Ashley feels the rush of love, the energy she used to have. It is all worth it, the exhaustion, it is worth it for this. These moments. Then Holly's eyelids swoop down to cover her eyes and the moment is gone, lost. The kitchen is humming with everything still to do. Ashley has to pick Lucy up from the school bus in ten minutes, which leaves her about forty-five seconds to spoon some coffee granules into her mouth. She doesn't bother with the kettle and water ritual any more, there never seems to be time. Still, she'd never eat granules in front of James; it feels shameful, like a dirty secret. As she unscrews the jar of the coffee, the phone begins to ring; Ashley reaches for it automatically, using her other hand to dip a spoon into the brown granules.

'Hello?'

There is a silence on the other end of the line. Ashley listens, straining to hear. Being a mother always gives telephone calls a new level of anxiety: the children, the children, the children.

'This is Ashley?' she tries again but there is still nothing, just the steady sound of the house around her, the receiver pressed to her ear. Behind her, Holly gurgles, she hears the sound of a spoon hitting the floor. Ashley thinks of her husband, wonders where he is, who he is with, what he is doing right this second. There was a time when the only place he'd ever be was right next to her. She puts the phone down, crunches the coffee between her teeth. The taste is bitter in her mouth.

3

London

Corinne

'Are you sure you're going to be all right?' Dominic calls from the kitchen. He is standing at the sink, eating a plum for breakfast. The juice drips down his fingers, yellow rivulets running into the silver basin. I reach for my hand cream, rub it into the crevices of my palms, inhale the soft sweet smell of it.

'Yes. Yes, Dom, of course.'

'And you're going to the gallery today? D'you feel up to it?'

'Of course. Dominic, I'm not ill.'

He turns on the tap, rinses his fingers and shakes them dry. 'OK. Sorry. So we'll meet after work at the clinic, yes?'

I nod, he reaches for me and I lean forward to kiss him. He's dressed for work and he smells lovely; clean and fresh.

'Yes, sounds good. What are you working on at the paper today?'

He sighs. 'Alison's really on my case at the moment. She's insisting I get on with the Carlington House piece, says she's being hassled a lot by the owner. Cool place though, didn't you think?'

I stare at him. 'I thought it was kind of scary.'

Dominic smiles. 'Maybe a bit creepy. Weird to think of it abandoned for so long. I'm hoping there'll be time to start writing it up today. I've got a bit of a backlog at the moment, what with ...' He tails off.

I feel a flash of guilt. 'I know, time off. I'm sorry, I'm OK today. Promise!'

He shakes his head, folds his arms around me again, even though the clock is now showing nearly a quarter to eight and he's going to be late.

'Don't ever apologise to me, Corinne,' he says, the words urgent in my ear, his breath warm on my cheek.

We straighten up. There is a loud banging sound upstairs, the familiar noise of an electric drill gearing up. The people above us are extending their flat, I don't know what they're doing up there, they've been messing around for weeks.

'The fun continues,' Dominic says, rolling his eyes at me. 'I wonder whether they'll ever actually complete?'

'Go, go!' I say, and I adjust his blue tie, touch his chest. I don't really want him to, I don't want him to leave me on my own. He picks up a cooling cup of coffee from the counter, drains it and leaves the flat; the door bounces noisily on the hinges behind him as it always does, far too loud. The neighbours have complained several times, we ought to fix it.

After he's gone, I go back into our bedroom. I've got to get better at being by myself. My dad used to say being able to be alone is a skill; he told me his alone time was precious to him, something he cultivated in spite of all the parties and the attention, the people who wanted to know his name, where he got his ideas from, what project he was working on next. We used to have a photo of him propped up on the windowsill in the dining room – in it he's surrounded by people, his dark eyes flashing. He looks like he's in his element, but one night when I was a teenager he told me that all he'd wanted to do that night was be alone, away from the frenzy. I never would have guessed.

I take a deep breath. Perhaps I can find my element too, perhaps being alone is something I can learn to enjoy. The bedroom feels so quiet and still. The bed is made; Dom is good at things like that. He says we have to try to keep the flat tidy with it being so small. It is tiny, nestled in the tangle of streets between Finsbury Park and Crouch End, a two-room affair with a little bathroom leading off the kitchen. I love it; it's minuscule, miniature, fit for a pair of dolls.

I go to my drawers, the insides pretty with the embroidered linings that Ashley made for me. In the bottom drawer, a clump of black tights lies in wait, flecked with tiny specks of white tissue. The nylon feels dry and rubbery. I think about untangling the blackness and drawing the material over my legs, getting on the Tube and going to work, and all of a sudden the idea seems overwhelming.

I sit down, hugging my knees to my chest. The flat always feels even smaller when I am on my own, I don't know why. The absence of a child seems worse. I stare at the painting above the clock, the first picture I ever commissioned for the gallery. I brought it home three years ago, hung it proudly in the flat. The blue waves of the ocean, the bright red of a ship. It's beautiful. I used to love it, the way the thick paint glistened on the canvas, the hint of sunlight dappling the left corner. *Aurora yellow*, *cadmium red*. I know all the paint names, or I did. I used to recite them to Dominic when I got my first gallery job, spent hours hunched over the colour chart, making sure I didn't forget. That was a long time ago now.

My gaze shifts from the painting to the clock below and, as I watch, the crimson figures (*geranium lake*, paint number 405) flicker, rearrange themselves into new numbers, and that's when I realise that I have been sitting by the pile of black nylon for almost forty-five minutes.

It's too late to go to work now. I don't know where the time has gone. The hormones I am taking make me feel dopey, a wasp in a honey-jar. When I call the gallery, Marjorie sounds irritated and I feel bad. I'll go tomorrow, definitely.

I get back into bed, lie still for a while, listening to the sound of rain beginning outside, the steady drip drip drip of the pipe on the roof. The builders upstairs seem to have stopped for a bit, the quiet is nice. When I was little I used to go up to Dad's office and listen to the way the rain spattered on the skylight, hammered down hard so that it bounced off the glass. It used to make me feel safe, because the rain was outside and I was inside. It couldn't get to me.

There is a sudden sound, a little thud that makes me jump, and I feel my body stiffen, the muscles in my legs tense slightly under the sheets. *You're too jumpy, Corinne*, Dominic always says. *You exhaust yourself with nerves.* He's right about the exhaustion. I'm not sure I can help the nerves.

Eventually, I start to need the bathroom, so I ease myself out of bed, go out into the hallway. I've got to pull myself together, I know I have. I take a deep breath, peer at my reflection in the mirror. I need to keep hoping, I can't give up.

The tiles are freezing on my bare feet. The hallway is draughty; the front door has sprung slightly ajar. Occasionally it refuses to close properly; I've told Dom to fix it time and time again. I frown, step over a pile of yellowing newspapers, push my shoulder against it to make it jam shut, but it won't. I open the door again and try harder, but something is bouncing it back. I crouch down. Something is stopping the door from closing; something small jammed in the frame. I stare at it for a few seconds and then it comes to me; I know exactly what this looks like.

I bend down, pick up the small object, hold it carefully between my cold hands. Flecks of auburn paint flake off onto my skin, lying on my hands like specks of blood. How strange. It's a little chimney pot. It looks like the chimneys we had on our doll house when we were little, on the big pink house Dad built for us.

I stand there at the doorway, clutching the little chimney, and a small smile comes to my lips as I remember.

It was no ordinary doll house. Nothing Dad did was ordinary – I remember one of his clients telling him that over lunch, him regaling us with the story that evening, his eyes glowing with pride. 'Nothing by halves,' he always said, and he was always true to his word. Our doll house was almost a metre high, with pink walls and a blue painted door, a red-slated roof and four big brown chimney pots made of real terracotta. Each of the rooms was tiny, compact, perfectly formed. Dad was obsessed with buildings, and he'd spent months working on this one, a little replica of our real home that Ashley and I could play with. Whenever Mum would tell him to come to bed, rest his eyes for a bit, he'd shake his head. 'It's a challenge,' he used to say, 'and there's nothing better for you than that. I've got to get it right.'

He knelt on the floor with us on Christmas Day and showed us how it worked; the intricacies of the rooms and the stairways and the loft, and even when Mum came out with the Christmas pudding I wasn't drawn away. I became obsessed with finding miniature furniture, little rugs, curtains that I cut out painstakingly from scraps of white material I found in my mother's sewing box. And the dolls. Oh, the dolls. Dad brought them home for us, one by one, beautiful, smartly dressed figures that we positioned in the house: a long-skirted mother cooking in the kitchen, a baby in the miniature cradle, a father sitting in the little pink armchair stuffed with real feathers. Every time he went away for work he'd come back with another one. He got some of them from abroad, bringing them carefully wrapped in scarlet tissue paper to protect the china, regaling us with tales of the countries he'd been to as we pulled open the presents. His work took him further than any of us had ever been.

I haven't thought of the doll house properly for years, had always assumed Mum had put it in her attic with the rest of our childhood things. A lump fills my throat.

I bring the chimney pot up to eye level, twist it around so that I can see it from all sides. It is as tall as the length of my hand and as wide as my palm. As I stand in our doorway, I feel a pair of eyes on me and raise my gaze. A young woman is watching me, a dark-haired toddler in her arms, an empty pushchair at her side. I blush, pull my dressing gown more tightly around me, suddenly aware of my bare feet, the untamed hairs on my legs.

'Sorry!' she says. 'I just wondered if you were OK? You looked a bit upset.'

'Oh!' I say. 'Yes, yes, I'm fine, thank you. Just had something in the mail.' I smile at her, trying not to notice the way her child is clinging to her chest, its little hands clutching at her hair. She strokes its head absent-mindedly. She hardly looks old enough to have a baby; I hope she knows how lucky she is. God, of course she does. What's the matter with me?

'I'm Gilly,' she tells me, 'I've just moved in.' She gestures behind her to where the door to her flat hangs open and I see boxes, the edge of a packing crate.

'Welcome to the building,' I say, and she laughs. Something about the sound of it is familiar, as though I have heard it somewhere before. The way she gasps slightly, as though she hasn't quite enough breath to properly let go. She's smiling at me.

'Thank you, it's been a bit of a rocky ride so far but we're hoping to settle in here.'

'Is it just you and the baby?' I ask her.

She nods, looks down. 'Just me and the kiddy. Do you have any little horrors?'

I flinch, clutch the chimney pot tighter to my chest.

'No,' I say. 'No I don't. It was nice to meet you, Gilly.' She looks a bit taken aback but I try not to mind. I step back inside our flat and close the door. I can't be friends with another mother, I just can't. It's too painful. The gasping sound of her laugh niggles at me. I'm sure I've heard someone laugh like that before but I can't think

32

where – the thought slips away from me like the string of a kite that I can't quite grab hold of.

Inside, I prop the chimney pot on the table. I know it can't really be from the doll house, but it does look almost identical to what I remember, and even though the rational side of my brain knows it must be something else, it feels almost like it is a sign, a little spark of hope, a reminder of why I put myself through this every time. I want to cling to it, to cling to something. It's as if this being here is a message from Dad, telling me not to give up hope. I have wanted a family since I was a little girl. It will happen. I have to believe.

*

Later on, I leave to meet Dominic at the fertility clinic. As I dressed, I put the chimney pot into my pocket, gave it a lucky pat before I left the house. I can feel it bumping slightly against my hip bone; I like it, it feels like a little talisman, a good luck charm. If I do have a daughter I could dig out the doll house, give it to her as a present. One day. I feel bad for being abrupt with Gilly this morning. I know she can't help having kids, I know I can't behave like that. Maybe I'll knock on her door later, apologise.

Outside it is freezing. Minus two, the radio said. Strings of Christmas lights are still dotted around, twinkling stubbornly, even though it's past the deadline of the sixth. I can see my breath, misty particles floating in the air, glowing under the street lamps. It is already dark even though it has only just gone five-thirty. Despite the weather, I feel a little glow inside me, a swell of hope from the chimney pot cocooned in my coat.

I'm walking along the pavement by the park, past the playground, the empty swings hanging loosely in the darkness. Resting for the evening. A car speeds past, its headlights illuminate the tall, spiked tops of the park railings and I give a little gasp; someone is there, right beside me, I see a face hidden in the railings amongst the dark. My breath catches in my throat. Oh, God. I can't breathe.

Then the headlights swing by, the golden light throwing itself over me and I exhale; it's just the shadowy figure of a dog-walker, hurrying along towards the park exit and the gaping steps of the Underground. It's nothing, it's nobody. It never is.

I put my head down and keep walking, focusing on my feet clad in their little black boots. My heart rate returns to normal, I can feel my body calming down. I'm used to the feelings now – the immediate rush of anxiety followed by the weak-kneed relief. The cycle of it all.

It is a relief to see the double doors of the clinic glowing ahead of me. Dominic is waiting inside, looking at his watch, wearing the sky-blue scarf I bought him last Christmas. He looks so handsome. As I stare at him through the glass, I remember the times we used to meet after work, back when we first met; I'd sneak out early to see him, desperate to be in his arms. It was so exciting; it was like a drug. Somewhere along the way we lost that excitement, between the endless rounds of IVF and the money flowing out of our bank account like water through a sieve.

I walk a little faster, eager to get to him, to feel his arms around me. I slip my left glove off as I go, run my fingers

34

over the tiny chimney. As I enter, a couple push past me, hurrying through the door, and I catch a glimpse of young, bright eyes, hopeful red lips chapped with cold. An elderly woman follows them out, walking quickly with a slight hobble, grey hair falling across her face. She looks like a grandmother, a grandmother in waiting.

In the entrance room of the clinic we hug hello, I feel the relief of Dominic around me. We might not have the excitement, but we've still got each other.

'You OK?' he asks. 'Good day?'

I smile at him reassuringly and almost tell him about finding the chimney, but something stops me. I know he'll think I'm being silly. He thinks I cling on to the past a bit too much, to memories of Dad. So instead I say nothing, I feel for the chimney pot in the pocket of my coat and tell Dominic that my day has been fine.

'Miss Hawes?' The nurse appears and gestures to me. Dominic puts an arm around me as we enter a little side room. We sit down together on the green chairs, our thighs touching.

'IVF treatment can be a difficult process, Miss Hawes.' The nurse is smiling kindly at me. 'Corinne? Sometimes it helps to chat to others who are going through the process. We do have a support group that meets once a month? Would you and Dominic be interested?'

The nurse is looking at me expectantly, her face open, eyes wide. She means well, I know, so I smile back at her, even though tonight I will have more hormones pushed into me, will wince as Dominic injects me with bromocriptine, clomifene, fertinex. We can both recite the drugs as though they are our times tables.

'I think we're OK, actually. But thank you,' I tell the nurse, and then we start going through it again, planning the insemination. I force myself to keep cheerful, keep hoping, and I squeeze my hands around the little chimney pot in my pocket and imagine my dad smiling at me, telling me this is just another challenge. It makes me feel better, and I close my eyes and I wish and I wish and I wish.

Then

The windows of the car are misting up. Mummy has turned off her headlights so that our car sits in the darkness, hidden on the tree-lined street. Now that I'm almost eight, she talks to me more. She says if we're lucky though, the next time it's very cold winter time we might be able to get out of the car and go into the house. She says she's not sure yet, she'll have to let me know. I like talking to her, it's the best thing, except for I can't talk to her on her quiet days, because she hardly says a thing. On those days I have to talk to myself, make up the voices in my head, pretend there is someone else who will chat to me. Really I know it's just me but sometimes I can trick myself. I can pretend.

I'm seven nearly eight, I'm getting big, and I know I'm getting taller because on the nights when we sleep in the car my legs hurt more. They're hurting now, it's harder to scrunch them up small in the passenger seat. I draw shapes on the car window, circles and diamonds and swirly lines that tangle into great messy scribbles. I am bored. I want to go home. We have been here for hours.

'I'm hungry, Mummy.' I am hungry, my stomach is growling like a lion. There has been no food all day. Sometimes Mummy forgets. When there is no reply, I pull on Mummy's sleeve and eventually she gives me a bar of chocolate, squashed and warm but whole, bright in its wrapper. Yum. Just as I'm about to eat it, I am jerked forwards; the car is moving, we are on our way. Mummy is pressing her foot to the floor, glancing into the rear-view mirror, her eyes alive again. She still hasn't put the headlights on. The chocolate tastes old and a bit stale, but I don't mind, I eat it anyway. It's gone too quickly. I want more.

The car is moving very fast; the chocolate whooshes around in my stomach and I begin to feel sick. We bend in and out of streets, faster and faster, until suddenly we are stopping, Mummy is slamming her foot onto the brakes and our little car is screeching to a halt. Outside the world has become very dark, I can just about see the tiny silver stars if I tilt my head back all the way and look out of the window. The dashboard lights glow; their green and orange lines form a face in the reflection and I jump, startled by the way the features leap out at me. That finally gets Mummy's attention.

'What is it? Do you see him?'

'I see a face,' I say, and Mummy leans over me, right across my lap so that I can smell her hair, the strange sour scent of her skin. I hate the way my mother smells now. The girls at school tease me for it, they say that it's because she doesn't wash. I wash myself, I run myself baths in our little flat, fill the tub up until the water runs cold. I sit in them for ages, wishing I could be a mermaid and live underwater. I don't like the flat, I want to move back to the big house but Mummy says we can't. All our money is gone. The bad man took it.

4

Ashley

James still isn't home. Ashley has put Holly and Benji to bed and Lucy has stomped upstairs with her headphones in. The door to her room is permanently closed these days; Ashley knocked about an hour ago but got no response. Her fifteen-year-old daughter is surgically attached to her phone, the little buzz of it vibrates through the house, tailing her around.

She is in the kitchen, pretending to watch television, but her mind is on the big clock on the wall and all she can hear is the second hand moving, tick tick tick, and all she can think about is James, and *why isn't he home yet.*

The phone bill came in today. Ashley went through it late at night with a glass of red wine, hating herself all the way through. It was because of what Megan said, how she looked when they were sitting outside Colours. It made Ashley doubt herself. There have been three silent calls, now. Not a lot by anyone's standards, but two have been late at night, and she can't help but wish that just for once, James would be here, and she'd be able to ask him, she'd be able to see his face. Looking at the bill, Ashley tried to pinpoint the times of the calls, but all that shows up is private number. Obviously. Still, she has kept the records, stashed them in the drawer in the kitchen, the one that houses Benji's school projects and the million phone chargers that this family seems to need.

It isn't that she doesn't trust him. It isn't that at all. They've been married for almost sixteen years; Ashley knows him almost as well as she knows her sister. As well as she knows herself. It's just that there have been a lot of late nights, and he hasn't given her any explanations. She tries to think back, runs her mind over the last few months. When did his late nights begin? He was here when Holly was born, of course he was, he was up in the night with her for weeks on end while their newborn rocked and raged. The months afterwards are a blur, a sleepless, messy stream of tasks. At some point, they stopped doing them together.

Ashley takes a gulp of wine. Her fingers have left misty prints on the glass in her hand; she stares at them in the light of the kitchen. The gold band of her wedding ring glints and a shiver goes through her. What if it is a woman calling the house? They have all read the stories. If you've got a group of girlfriends, you're bound to know someone whose husband ran off with the secretary, someone who came home one day to find him in bed with the office floozy. Someone who let themselves go, became wrapped up in the children, looked the other way when her husband strayed. Ashley just never considered that it would happen to her.

God, listen to herself! She must stop this. She doesn't think he's having an affair, of course she doesn't. Not really, not deep down. She just feels unsettled, she feels that there's something not right, something that he's not telling her. And she hates it.

Ashley picks up a magazine from the side, flips through the pages to distract herself. The women in it are young, glossy. She thinks of her own eye cream sitting in the fridge. She'd given in, bought the anti-ageing stuff that her friend Aoife had raved about. Corinne had laughed at her, told her not to be so silly. She isn't being silly, she's being realistic. She's got four years on her sister, perhaps when Corinne gets to her age she'll be buying eye cream herself. She turns another page, winces at the bright pink heading. *New year, new you!* Should she be doing a January diet? She puts a hand in the waistband of her jeans, feels the indents the zips have left in her flesh. She doesn't know how other people do it, pop kids out then spring back to size. She's never been able to manage it, but perhaps she isn't trying hard enough.

She ought to give Corinne a call. Her insemination is coming up. *Insemination*. When Corinne first started the fertility treatments the word had made Ashley uncomfortable, conjured up grotesque images of cows and oversized pipettes. Now it trips off the tongue as easily as a hair appointment. Ashley sighs. Corinne has had to go through the process more times than anyone should have to bear. It makes Ashley's heart hurt. When Holly was born, Corinne had come to the hospital room, bearing a huge bunch of yellow balloons and a smile that looked as though it might crack at any minute. They had sat together on the bed, staring at Holly as she nuzzled Ashley's chest, nudged for the nipple. Ashley had pretended not to notice the tears in her sister's eyes, knew Corinne wouldn't want her to see.

Yes, she needs to call Corinne. While she's at it she should ring her mother too; Ashley worries about her, all alone in Kent, rattling around like a penny in a jar. Mathilde moved last year, barely two months after their dad died, said she couldn't face being there, surrounded by all his things. They had packed up the Hampstead house together, boxing things up, making endless trips to the charity shops, clearing room after room until at last the big house was empty, full of nothing but dustballs clinging to the floorboards. Ashley had stood for a moment in their old living room, her hand on the light switch, staring at the bare walls, the stripped shelves, the blank windows. Then she had snapped off the switch and closed the door, blinked back the tears that threatened to fall.

Mathilde was installed in her new place quickly, a small house in Kent with a gravel drive and double-glazing. It is better for her, really. Ashley should go and see her, take the children. If James can spare the time.

Ashley looks at the clock again. Ten to ten. Holly will wake up at about eleven, no doubt. Then again at twelve, one if she's lucky. She has finished the wine so she stands up, pours herself another, fills it to the rim. Her hand is shaking slightly and a droplet of wine hits the work surface, spreads rapidly across the wood. Ashley reaches for the sponge and, as she does so, the phone begins to ring. Ashley stares at it as though it's a bomb; the little red light flashing again and again. Then she remembers the children, sleeping upstairs, and she reaches for it, taking a big gulp of wine as she does so.

This time there's breathing. Quite loud, as though the person on the other end of the line might be out of breath. Ashley's mind pictures a horrible host of possibilities; women flash through her head in various states of undress, bosoms out, taut stomachs, lips pressed to the phone, wanting her husband. *Stop it, Ashley*, she thinks to herself, and she takes another sip of wine and says:

'Who is this, please?'

No answer. The breathing increases in tempo, and as Ashley listens, she thinks she can hear a sort of rattle, as if the person on the other end of the line is ill, or elderly. Perhaps it really is a wrong number. She is about to speak again when the line goes dead, and at that moment James walks through the door, his briefcase in his hand.

'You're so late,' Ashley says, and he immediately looks guilty. She feels sick. 'Where have you been?'

'I'm just working, Ash,' he tells her, and he comes forward, takes the wine glass and the phone from her hand, puts his arms around her waist. He nuzzles her neck. 'Mmm, you smell nice. Did I buy you that perfume?'

For a second she tenses, imagining the weight around her stomach, the soft cushion of her skin. She shouldn't have had the wine. He leans towards her, kisses her quickly on the mouth. She puts her hands to the back of his neck, feels the tiny hairs prickle beneath her fingers.

'You're always working, James,' she says, and she pulls back from him, looks into his eyes. They are grey, flecked with brown around the edges. She loves his eyes. 'Is everything all right?'

He isn't meeting her eyes. He runs a hand through his hair, the brown curls spring up beneath his fingers.

He looks so like their son when he does this, the gesture makes Ashley's chest tighten, just a little.

'Everything's fine, Ash,' he says. 'I'm sorry, I'm really tired. Did Holly go down OK tonight?'

Ashley nods. 'Yes. But, James—'

'Can we go to bed? Please?' He interrupts her, and she swallows. She stares at him, at the bags underneath his eyes, the wrinkles that are forming around his temples.

'Of course we can,' she says, and he looks so relieved that she can't face telling him about the phone calls, not just now. They troop upstairs to where the children are softly snoring. Holly's bedroom door is ajar, the end of her cot just visible. Ashley tiptoes past, holding her breath, but James forgets and the sound of his shoes on the floorboards cuts through the quiet.

'James!'

There is a pause. Three, two, one – the sound of Holly's cry spills into the corridor, as if on cue. As she goes to her daughter, Ashley catches sight of herself in the wall mirror. Her lips are dark red, stained with the wine.

5

London

Dominic

Dominic sits at his desk in the newsroom, gulps down his slightly burned tasting coffee as he prepares to start writing up his copy. He thinks of Corinne shading her eyes as she stared at Carlington House yesterday, of her small hands running over the derelict white walls. She was thinking about her dad, he knows she was. Richard looms as large in death as he did in life.

As he types up his notes, Dominic grits his teeth, remembering the way Warren leered at Corinne. He probably shouldn't have brought her along, but he hasn't wanted to leave her alone much since the doctor called. He pictures her lying in the bath, her eyes shut, the water cold. A shiver goes down his spine and he shakes himself slightly, pushes the thought away. She'll be all right, he knows she will. This is just a setback.

He works quietly until lunchtime, when a hand comes down, claps him on the shoulder. Andy, the court reporter, is grinning down at him, Cheshire cat-like.

'Stop slaving away over property stuff, Dom. I want you to meet Erin.' He gestures to a young-looking blonde girl standing beside him, who is holding her hands behind her back nervously. 'She started last week, while you were away. Erin, this is Dom.'

Dominic stands and shakes hands with Erin, noticing as he does so that he has a large black ink spot on his thumb, brilliant against the smooth white of his skin.

'Sorry.' He laughs, rubs at it with the fingers of his other hand. 'Comes with the territory, I suppose. Good to meet you!'

Erin smiles back. 'It's lovely to meet you, Dominic,' she says. 'I hope you don't mind but Andy said you guys were going for lunch together – is it all right if I join you? I've only just started and I don't know the area yet.'

Behind Erin's back, Andy winks at him and Dominic nods quickly.

'Sure, of course.' There's no point protesting. Erin is Andy's usual type; he has a big thing for blondes. In the five years that Dominic has known him he has never stayed with a woman for more than six months.

Dominic swings his chair around, pulls his jacket off the seat behind him and shrugs it over his shoulders. The three of them make their way through the newsroom to the lifts.

'What've you been working on this morning, Erin?' Dominic asks.

'God, it's a horrible court case. Mother accused of neglect. Claudia Winters?'

The image immediately flashes into Dominic's mind: a small woman, dark hair tied back off her neck, hand raised to shield herself from the lights of the media. She has been all over the papers. Extreme neglect leading to infant mortality. He swallows.

'See, this is exactly why I became a features man!'

'I know,' Erin says. 'It's not a nice one to start with. In at the deep end!'

They step into the lift together.

'How you finding it here so far?' he asks.

'Good, good, you know, still settling in. Everybody seems friendly.'

'Oh, yeah? Where have you come from?'

'Oh, I grew up in Suffolk if you know it, over by the coast.'

'Bit of a change from Finchley Road,' Dominic says. 'Lot less stabbings, I bet, although we'd all be out of a job without them.'

'Right.' She nods. 'I'm living in Tooting now, though, just got a flat.' She laughs. 'It's in serious need of decoration, bit of a shit-hole actually. Tooting seems a bit dodgy so far! Or maybe I just notice it more cos of the job. I'm still getting to grips with it all!'

'Takes a while,' Dominic says. 'You'll get there!'

They have reached the ground floor; he fumbles for his lanyard in his pocket but Andy dangles his own in front of his eyes.

'Honestly, mate, what are you like.' He grins at Erin, opens the door for her and guides her through, his large hand on her back. Dominic rolls his eyes and follows the pair of them out onto the high road. He can already tell what Andy is thinking, almost see the cogs turning in his brain. He never takes long to make his moves.

*

47

They make their way to the pub on the corner, the Hare and Hound. An abandoned Christmas tree sits outside it, next to a pile of empty beer cans. Pine needles blow along the pavement, dry and brown.

The three of them chat about Andy's court case. It's a drug deal; he says that today was the sentencing, he watched a nineteen-year-old girl go down for twenty years. Dominic shivers – he has always hated sentencings, hated seeing the look on people's faces when the enormity of what they'd done would crash down on them. Always too late, of course. Half the kids he went to school with are behind bars now.

'I hate sentencings, actually,' Erin says. 'So final, aren't they? Imagine being locked away like that. God, it would be awful.'

Dominic looks at her. She really is very young; she can't be more than a few years older than nineteen herself, mid-twenties at the most. It will still take a while for the edges to form. He's surprised they've started her on the Winters case, it's a high-profile job.

'Well, prisons are hardly prisons any more, are they?' Andy says. 'It's not as if they're off to Bedlam. Most of them have gyms attached.'

'I think gyms is a bit of an exaggeration,' Dominic says.

'Do you do any court stuff, Dominic?' Erin asks him. 'Or do you stick to the features?'

'I'm a features man,' Dominic says, 'I used to cover the court stories too, but it got a bit much. I just found it a bit depressing, really. All that horror. All those wasted lives.'

He looks down, feeling suddenly embarrassed, but Erin nods sympathetically.

'I know exactly what you mean. It gets you down, doesn't it?'

Andy interrupts, flexes his knuckles on the table. He's a big guy; Dominic can see the tendons in his arm straining.

'So, Dom, how's Corinne doing?'

Dominic shifts in his chair, pretending to be engrossed in a remaining chip congealed on his plate.

'She's … she's doing OK, man,' he says, although he is not sure that it's completely the truth.

'Corinne is my girlfriend,' he tells Erin.

'Beautiful name – unusual. Is that after anyone? Grandmother, or anything?'

'I don't think so,' Dominic says. He doesn't actually know, has never thought of it.

'Well, it's lovely,' Erin says. 'Have you been together long?'

'A while, haven't you, Dom?' Andy says, grinning at him. 'They're joined at the hip.' His chair has moved closer to Erin's, the tip of his elbow grazes her water glass as he spreads his arms across the table. Dom is reminded of an animal, a monkey asserting his territory. He's no idea why Andy bothers.

'Yeah, years now actually. She's great. We're very—' he bobs his head, awkwardly '—very happy.'

'Most of the time,' Andy says. Dominic ignores him.

'What does she do?' Erin says, and Dominic feels grateful to her for changing the subject.

'She works in a gallery,' Dominic says. 'Over in Islington. They do really well, a lot of nice pieces. She's very arty, talented, that sort of thing.'

'Do you live in Islington then?'

'No, we're Crouch End way,' he tells her, 'closer to the rough side.'

Erin sighs, dramatically. 'An art gallery though, wow. I always wished I could draw. The best I can manage is stick people.'

'Stick people, hey?' Andy asks. 'I like stick people.'

'Maybe I'll draw you some sometime.' There is a note of flirtation in her voice.

Dominic looks away from them both, traces a pattern on the tabletop. A bored-looking waitress who is hovering around behind the bar calls over to them.

'Can I get you anything else?'

'Just the bill, please,' Dominic says. He doesn't need to watch Andy start to make his moves. What right does he have to comment on Corinne? Just because she wasn't taken in by him at the Christmas party, wasn't won over by his charms like the rest of the female population, he seems to have got it into his head that Dominic is making a mistake. Well, he isn't.

They head outside, back to the office. Erin is going back to court after a quick briefing with the boss on the Claudia Winters case.

'She just doesn't seem to show any remorse, that's the thing,' she is saying. 'I mean, her daughter ended up dead! And Claudia sits in the courtroom like she's not even listening, like she's in another world. It's mad.'

Dominic nods. 'She's quite ill though, isn't she? I read somewhere that she had post-partum depression.'

Erin nods. 'Yes, but how far can you take that, you know? The blame has to fall somewhere.'

They reach the office. Andy holds the door open for them both. He places a hand on Erin's back as she enters the building and Dominic rolls his eyes. Poor girl. God knows he wouldn't want Andy homing in on Corinne. As a mate he's all right, but with women … Dominic rubs a hand through his hair and follows them into the newsroom, the clatter of keys quickly surrounding them, swallowing him up.

6

London

Corinne

I gave in and showed Dom the chimney pot when I got home from the gallery yesterday. But I was right – he didn't really understand.

'You know it's just a piece of pot, babe?' he said, and I could tell he wasn't properly paying attention because he was still focused on the news, reading the headlines as they streamed across the bottom of the TV. They were showing footage of that awful woman on trial for the death of her daughter – Claudia Winters. I don't understand how anyone could ever hurt their child. Anyone lucky enough to have one in the first place. There were pictures of her as she came out of the courtroom, the paparazzi lights in her face. Her head was bent. You couldn't see her eyes. The sight of her hunched body made me shiver.

Dom had his laptop out on his knee, he was meant to be writing notes on the property piece, the house we went to together. I dreamed about it last night, I dreamed I was trapped inside and when I woke up I was sweating, a cold sweat that drenched the sheets. I wish he'd write about something else.

'Yes, of course,' I said, 'but it looks so similar, it's weird. You'd have to see the doll house to know what I mean, I'll show it to you. I feel like it's a sign, Dom, like it's Dad reminding me that things will be all right.'

Dominic rolled his eyes as I knew he would, grabbed the end of my socked foot and wiggled it.

'Maybe.'

I smiled at him, put the chimney on the dresser, next to the photograph of my dad and my old set of paints.

I haven't seen Gilly today, I looked for her as I got home, checked to see if she was in. I've been trying to think why she sounded familiar, it's annoying me. But the front door was closed and I couldn't hear anything. I might knock tomorrow. I ought to be friendly.

When we went to bed, I lay awake for ages, burrowed my face into Dominic's back, breathing in his warm smell. My feet were cold so I pressed them up against his. It was only then I remembered that I needed to remind him to get the front door fixed. I'm sick of the draught in this flat.

I drifted off around two, and then when I woke up later I felt surprisingly strong and positive, as though a little window had opened in my head. The little chimney pot feels like the first sign of hope in a year, this horrible time since Dad died and the IVF all started.

So, I'm not going to let anything upset me today. I'm going to work, and I'm going to be productive. I make Dominic a nice filter coffee and get myself ready to go, choosing my clothes carefully. A red jumper, my purple earrings. Crimson coat. Triumphant colours. I knock on Gilly's door before I go to work; this time she's in, I can hear the child crying.

'Hi!' I say. 'It's Corinne, I live at number twenty.' I point at my front door and she nods, smiles. She looks a tiny bit guarded but I can't really blame her.

'I just wanted to apologise if I seemed a bit blunt the other day,' I say. 'I'm actually ...' I spread my hands. I may as well just tell her. 'I'm actually trying for a baby at the moment and it's been a bit ... tough so, so I reacted a bit weirdly when you mentioned kids. That's all. I'm so sorry!'

'Oh,' she says. 'Thank you for dropping by – please don't worry! I thought I might have offended you! I'm sorry to hear it's been rough. You'll get there.'

Her little boy crawls up to her, grips her skirt and looks up at me with big eyes. I swallow.

'Who's this?'

'This is Tommy,' she says, and she puts a hand on his head, ruffles his dark curls. The gesture gives me the same flicker of familiarity as her laugh did before, but the recognition is gone as quickly as it came. 'He's almost two. Listen, Corinne, it'd be lovely to chat sometime, why don't you pop round for a cup of tea one night? It'd be lovely to see you.'

I take a deep breath. Gilly's face is kind, her eyes are warm and there is something hopeful in her gaze. I can cope with this. I can be friends with a mum.

'That would be lovely,' I say. 'Thank you.'

We say our goodbyes, I wave at Tommy and walk off down the corridor, feeling absurdly proud of myself. I did it! She was lovely! I was lovely! It'd be nice to have a friend in the building; it'd mean I don't have to be on my own when Dom has to work. Besides, she could probably use a friend – it must be hard being a single mum at her age. Not that I wouldn't swap with her in a heartbeat.

At the gallery, it's freezing cold; our heating has broken and the pipes are frozen solid. Marjorie is refusing to close so I line up storage heaters and put them up to full power, brushing the dust off the bars with my gloved hands. I hum to myself, ignoring Marjorie's grumpy huffs. My appointment is this afternoon, and there's nothing to say that this time won't work, that we might finally get lucky. I have to believe.

My positivity floods through into my work and I sell an expensive painting to a businessman who wants to impress his wife, and a set of prints to a young girl who tells me she's just moved to South London, is redecorating her new flat.

'These are so cute!' she says, her voice bright and bubbly. She's very pretty, and blonde, and even though I am wearing my triumphant clothes I feel a tiny bit put out by her vivacity. Still, she buys the prints and I write down the sale, watching the numbers add up. It's my best day for a while and I sit a little straighter at the till, smiling at the shoppers as they browse against the thick waves of air being pumped out by the heaters. The gallery is only two rooms so it can look quite full on busy days like this.

At lunchtime I call Ashley from my desk. I'm keen to tell her about the chimney pot, see what she thinks. Maybe Mum has the doll house up in the attic; it would be fun to get it out when we're next visiting, show Lucy as well. I bet she'd love it. My sister answers quickly, sounding a bit out of breath as she always does these days.

'Hey, Ash,' I say. 'How's it going? You OK?'

I can hear the whirr of their dishwasher in the background. She sounds tired.

'I'm fine,' she says, then, 'Oh, shit! Hang on.'

'What's matter?'

There's a scuffling sound before she comes back on the line.

'Sorry, sorry. Benji keeps putting his crayons in the dishwasher and jamming it all up.' She sighs. 'I think he thinks I find it funny. He doesn't listen when I tell him to stop.'

'Get James to have a word,' I tell her. 'Lay down the law and all that.'

She snorts. 'Yeah, right. James is hardly ever here at the moment.'

I can hear something in her voice, as though there's something she's not saying.

'What d'you mean?'

She sighs. 'He's always at work, Cor. Like, always. I barely see him. He gets home from the office after ten at night, by which point I've usually worked myself up into a temper and gone to bed. It's getting worse and worse.'

Her voice breaks a little and instantly I feel bad.

'Oh, Ash, hey, come on. I'm sure he's just got a lot on. Is it a busy time of year, the post-Christmas rush or something? Is that a thing?'

She half laughs. 'I don't know, yeah maybe. I never really worked on the digital side of things like he does. But I just – I just feel like there's something more going on, Cor. Like there's something he isn't telling me.'

There is a beat between us. I know what she's thinking, but I don't think James is the type somehow. He's not the kind of guy to mess around.

'I had a phone call the other night too,' she says then. 'No one on the other end. James wasn't in, it must have been after ten. Second one in three days.' She gives a strained little laugh, and I know she's trying to reassure herself.

'Don't be silly,' I tell her. 'It'll be nothing to worry about. James is obsessed with you.'

There's a small silence, I can hear her exhale.

'Was obsessed, maybe,' Ashley says. 'These days he hardly notices me. Or the children. The other night Benji cried when I put him to bed. I think he prefers it when James does it. Says he's better at the story voices.'

'Ash, James works hard for you all. Seriously, you have nothing to worry about. Maybe the call's from abroad? You know, some stupid call centre or something that can't connect. Happens all the time.' I try to reassure her but I can hear the doubt in her voice.

'Maybe.'

'Seriously, Ash. Don't jump to conclusions.'

I can hear her moving what sounds like plates and mugs around, the clatter of the china.

'Hey,' I say, ready to distract her. 'D'you remember our doll house, Ash?'

'Of course! God, we loved that house. You especially! I don't know how Dad put up with us, making him play for hours at a time like that. I don't know any men who'd do that these days. Certainly not James, although I don't think Lucy's really the dolls type anyway. Not that I can work out what type she is at the moment.' She pauses. 'What made you think of that, anyway?'

'So, this is going to sound crazy,' I say, 'but I found something the other day, just outside the door of the flat – it was exactly like one of the chimney pots that Dad

57

built. I mean, it was probably something left over from the building work upstairs, but it made me smile – it looked so similar!'

'How funny,' Ashley says. 'I do that sometimes too. The strangest things will remind me of Dad – definitely buildings, anything like that – but other stuff, as well. Last week someone at the café ordered a hot chocolate and the way they ate their flake was just like he used to, all around the edges like a hamster. Funny.'

There is a pause.

'I can't believe it'll be a year in March,' Ashley says. 'Doesn't feel like it, does it? Almost a whole year since he died.'

I swallow. It's been a long year.

'We should visit Mum soon,' Ashley says, echoing my thoughts. 'She called me the other day and I feel bad; we haven't been for ages, I—Holly – no! Put that down!' Another pause and then she is back. 'God, sorry. She went for the fork.'

'We could go this weekend?' I tell her, trying not to picture her kitchen, the baby in the high chair, Holly's beautiful big eyes. 'Dom isn't working. Can you bring James along too?'

She hesitates. 'I hope so. I mean – yes, yes, of course he'll come. Hey –' She clears her throat. I imagine her giving herself a little shake. 'You will let me know how you get on this afternoon at the hospital, won't you? Keep me posted? And we'll go to Mum's at the weekend.'

I nod, before remembering she can't see me.

'Are you sure you don't want me to come with you, Cor?' she says. I hesitate. I know she's only being kind. I can't tell her that having her next to me makes it worse, having her fertile body beside me in a hospital makes me feel like I'm going to drown in grief and jealousy. I can't ever tell her how much it hurts seeing baby Holly, although sometimes I worry that she guesses.

'No,' I say. 'Thanks, Ash, but don't worry, honestly. I'll let you know how I get on. Promise. I love you, Ash. Most in the world.'

We hang up. 'Most in the world' is what Dad always used to say.

The afternoon is quieter. At around three o'clock I remind Marjorie that I need to leave early for the hospital.

'Can you just run and get us some more milk before you leave,' Marjorie instructs me. 'We've got a buyer coming in this afternoon for a meeting. I can't give him water.'

I force myself not to snap; she's always asking me to do things at the last minute.

'Sure.' I smile. Positive, positive.

In the off-licence there's a queue so I grab the milk and line up. I've got an hour until I need to meet Dominic at the hospital. The queue moves slowly forward; there's an old lady at the front, fumbling with her basket. The cashier catches my eye and rolls her own in apology.

As I push open the gallery's glass door, I notice the old lady a few shops down, staring through the window. She looks so lonely I feel a pang or sympathy, no, more than that, understanding. It's how I imagine I must look to the world sometimes, when the days are really bad. After the second round of IVF failed I used to wander around during my lunch hours, staring into space, no idea where I was going. She looks a bit like that.

I'm so distracted by her that as I walk across the polished wooden floor to my desk I don't see anything different at first. My desk is really the till and there are always things scattered around the computer and keypad; pens, Post-it notes, receipts and tags. But my eyes pick up on the object before my brain does, they linger on it, notice how it is laid across my keypad, carefully, deliberately.

This time the recognition is faster, the image pops straight into my head. It is small and blue, exactly as I remembered. A little door, broken off from its hinges, the edges of it sharp and splintered. I pause, look around the gallery. It is empty; the paintings stare back at me blankly, giving nothing away. My heart quickens in my chest and I pick up the door, lift it gently as though it might break. The wood is cold and slightly damp in my fingers, as if it has been out in the rain. The tiny golden handle is still there, glinting under the soft lighting of the gallery. It winks up at me as I stand at my desk, the milk forgotten on the side. I can remember Dad fixing it on, showing me how it actually turned on its axis so that the dolls could use it. I'd been delighted, had spent hours walking them through the door, into the house and back out again. In and out, in and out. That's what I did.

Marjorie comes in, frowns at me when she sees the milk abandoned.

'Has anyone been in here, Marjorie?' I ask her. My voice is a bit too high and my fingers are shaking slightly around the tiny door. It looks suddenly forlorn, as if it might have been torn from the hinges pretty roughly. I can't help it; I feel a tiny bit spooked.

'No,' she tells me. 'Don't think so in the last ten minutes. Why, who were you expecting?'

I'm too thrown to reply. How could this even get here? I think of the chimney pot at home. I must be wrong. It must be a coincidence. I haven't seen the house in years, we don't even know where it is. I'm imagining things, the way I do when I'm anxious. Marjorie is staring at me and I realise that I'm shaking my head; over and over from side to side as though trying to dislodge my thoughts.

'Oh, nobody,' I tell her. 'I'm not expecting anyone.' I put my hand to my forehead; it is clammy despite the cold. My brain is scrambling, filled with thoughts of Dad, of us sitting with the doll house, the door opening and closing. In my mind a parade of dolls come in and out, their dresses swishing between my fingers. Their faces are hidden beneath great swathes of hair.

'Corinne?'

'Sorry.' I take a deep breath. I need to pull myself together, get to the hospital on time. I make a big effort, force myself to push the thoughts of the past to the back of my mind. I pull open my desk drawer and place the little door inside, closing it into the darkness. There.

Then an idea occurs to me. I could find it. I could look for the doll house at Mum's this weekend. That way I'll know, I'll be certain that it's my imagination and nothing else. Besides, what else could it be?

*

Dominic is shaking his head. I walked to meet him at University College Hospital along the back roads, and now we're sitting in the waiting room, ready for the appointment. I've just finished telling him about the little door on my desk.

'I felt as though the chimney pot was a nice reminder,' I say. 'I know that sounds odd but I liked it, it was like a little good luck charm. But it's weird to find the door as well. Don't you think? Are you listening, Dom?' I tug on his arm, feeling like a child.

He doesn't believe me anyway, I can tell.

'Are you sure, Cor?' he says, frowning at me. 'I mean, seriously, why would it be there? It's probably just something Marjorie's left lying around. Come on!' He pulls me towards him, puts an arm around my shoulders and gives me a squeeze.

'I know you're feeling stressed out. You'll feel better when this is over, you know you will. We can go to Jubilee Café and get you a cup of mint tea. I think you're probably just projecting a bit, you're thinking about your childhood because of everything we're going through, and because the anniversary is coming up. That's all it'll be. All right?'

I smile at him uncertainly, pull out my hand cream and massage my hands, watching the cream absorb itself into the cracks. I try to stop thinking about the sight of the little door, try not to imagine it now, sitting in my desk drawer, pulsing quietly in the dark like a heartbeat. I might bring it home from work tomorrow, show it to Ashley at the weekend.

The nurse comes to get us and it is time. The insemination. My leg muscles contract, tighten in anticipation of the soreness. Funny how the memory of that goes away. Even if it is painful, I can always go again. I feel a surge of excitement as we walk down the corridor, and Dominic squeezes my hand. This could be it. This might be my chance to have a child, this might be the time that everything works, my body co-operates and it all slots into place like perfect clockwork. I can be a good mother. I just need the chance. I think of myself placing dolls in their cradles, rocking them gently to sleep in the miniature bedrooms of the house. The little blue door opening and closing, trapping them inside. I'd do anything to have a child of my own. Anything.

Then

*Today's a bad day. Mummy didn't seem to want to get out of bed
this morning, so I had to go to school without breakfast. All that
was left in the cupboard was her jar of pills, but she says she isn't
taking those ones any more. They looked almost like they could be
sweets and I was so hungry I almost ate one, but there was a big
sticky label saying not to and anyway the top was really hard to
open. So I had nothing.*

In Maths, my stomach growls and Toby Newton laughs at me.

*'Poor little rich girl,' he says, and I don't understand what he
means. It happens a lot after that though, as though it's catching
on, spreading like a disease through the school. They hiss it at me
in the corridors, whisper it as I walk past. I've started to just keep
my head down, focus on my shoes. I need new ones.* I'm not a
rich girl, *I want to say.* Rich girls have shoes without holes.

*Mummy says she'll buy me some, when she's feeling better. On
the way home today my feet got wet, the puddles soaked through
into my socks. When I get home she wants to go straight away,
she says we're going to do an all-nighter. I don't want to go. Not
tonight.*

*But she makes me. We get in the car and drive until we're
outside, and then we go round the back and hunch down in the
usual place. There are lots of stars tonight; I start to count them,
and for a while Mummy tells me their names but then the lights
in the house go on and she stops talking to me because she's
listening for them. After a while I give up trying to talk to her
and just listen too. Usually I get distracted, by the creepy-crawlies
or the scabs on my knees but today I sit further forward, right up
next to Mum. Her breathing is fast; she's pointing at something.*

'Do you see it?'

My eyes hurt from straining so hard but I stare at where she's looking and I do see it. My insides curl up and I have to look away. After a while, Mummy takes my hand in hers and strokes it, she pulls me close to her and gives me a little cuddle. It helps.

It's been Mummy and me ever since I was born. I think that's why Mummy is sad, and it makes me feel guilty. I try to be good, to do everything she wants. I go with her everywhere and watch when she tells me to watch and listen when she tells me to listen. But it doesn't make her happy. Some of the time it makes her angry, and most of the time it just makes her sad. Then I get sad too, and sometimes I feel cross because I just want her to be like the other mothers, all smiley and happy and like a normal mummy.

But we haven't got a normal family. Not any more. Mummy says we were going to have but that it got taken away. Someone else got it instead. When she says that it gives me a funny feeling inside, it makes me want to pull on the ends of my hair until the strands come out and it hurts a little bit. I did that a lot when I was younger but Mummy said I had to stop or I'd never be able to plait my hair like they do. I stopped after that, because their hair is lovely, it's the thing I'm most jealous of right now. I've seen them plait it through the upstairs window, I think they do it before they go to bed.

7

Kent

Ashley

Ashley gently shakes her son awake. The roads to her mother's house were horribly busy, and she has done all the driving. James is not here. She slips a hand into her cardigan pocket and brings out her mobile; has he even called yet? But of course, there isn't any reception at the house. Never has been. She'd bet on the fact that he hasn't rung anyway. Ashley sighs. She's eaten Minstrels all the way to Kent, dipping into the bag proffered by Benji. No wonder James isn't here; he probably doesn't want to be stuck with a fatso like her.

Ashley shoves her phone away, takes a deep breath and gently kisses Benji's still-closed eyelids. She'll have to put James to the back of her mind, but it's hard. Beside Benji, Holly stirs in her car seat. Her little fists are clenched by her sides. They have had to stop three times on the way, once to change her nappy, once to buy Lucy a magazine and once to get Benji the Minstrels. Every stop has been a struggle. Lucy has been quiet and unhelpful, Ashley is hot and tired from juggling all three children on her own. Without James.

Every time Ashley thinks of it she gets a little spurt of anger. She had pleaded with him to come but he had been resolute.

'Ash, I have to be in the office on Saturday morning. I'm sorry, I know it's not ideal but ...' He had tailed off, looked down at the floor. Lucy had come into the kitchen moaning about her shoes ('Where are they, Mum? I left them in the hallway. Why do you always move everything?') and the moment had gone, slipped away from Ashley like sand through her fingers.

'I'll meet you there, I promise,' James had murmured, planting a brief kiss on her forehead. She had reached for him, brushed the ends of his shirt as the jangle of his mobile pulled him into the next room. He had pressed it tight against his ear, turned his mouth away from her so that she couldn't hear what he was saying, or who was on the phone. She'd watched the back of his head through the glass window in the door frame, the way the muscles in the back of his neck stood tense and alert.

At least this weekend is an excuse to get away from the house. Ashley is not sure how many more nights sitting alone in front of the TV she can take, listening to the hum of the refrigerator and the ticking of the clock, waiting for Holly to start crying again. Lately, when Benji and Holly are sleeping upstairs and Lucy has retreated to her room, Ashley finds herself at a loss – not that there isn't anything to do, there is always washing to be done, surfaces to be wiped – but she finds herself alone, left with nobody to talk to. When this happens, she realises what is happening – she is missing her husband. Even in the marital home they have shared for years, Ashley is missing the man she married.

And she wants to know where he is. She has come to dread the little pangs of anxiety that ripple through her every time the phone rings, the places her imagination jumps to. There had been another call late last night, the needling sound of her mobile this time, jolting her awake just as she dozed off, alone in the double bed. She had stared at the screen. Unknown number. Sitting upright in bed, Ashley had pressed the phone to her ear. She'd said nothing, didn't want whoever it was to have the satisfaction of hearing her voice. After a few seconds of silence, she'd pressed end call, buried the little phone deep underneath the pillows, laid back down in the bed. In the morning the phone had been placed neatly back on their nightstand; James had smiled at her.

'You shouldn't sleep with it under your head. I moved it for you.' She had nodded, watched him leave the room, go straight upstairs to his office even though it was first thing in the morning and the children were all clamouring for breakfast.

His absences have shown no signs of stopping. She knows she ought to confront him but something is making her wait. She supposes it is hope; hope that she is getting things out of proportion, is misreading the signs. Once it's out there, she will have to deal with it. But how much longer can this go on? How can he not see how much she needs him?

When they reach Sevenoaks, Ashley hugs her mother tightly. She can feel Mathilde's bones through her top, is shocked by how skinny she has become. Ashley worries that her mum spends too much time alone. Even though the house is small it still seems too big for one person;

Ashley is taken aback by the emptiness of it each time they come. And the gap her dad has left in the family looms larger whenever the three of them are together.

'It's so good to see you, Mum.' It is; she smiles at her mother, breathes in her familiar scent of cleaning products and freesias. Mathilde reaches for Holly, buries her face in her neck.

'How is our little one? Oh, your grandad would have loved you so much.'

Ashley feels a twist of sadness. When Holly was born, a part of her had wanted her to be a boy, another Richard. The letters of her father's name had hovered around her head in the terrible weeks between his death and Holly's birth, as though waiting to latch on to something else, to reassign themselves. But Holly is Holly. And her father is gone. He would have loved her to distraction. Ashley knows he would.

Benji runs forward into the house, screaming excitedly for Dominic. Lucy follows, the white buds of her earphones trailing after her, her mobile buzzing in her hands.

Corinne is curled up like a cat on the living room sofa, her dark hair tied back from her face, fiddling with the gold bracelet on her wrist. She's wearing jeans and a pale blue jumper, she looks somehow younger than her thirty-four years. Dominic is by her side. He grins at Ashley.

'Great to see you, Ash!' He pulls her into a hug and she embraces him warmly. She has always liked Dominic, he is so down-to-earth, good for her sister. Ashley leans down to kiss Corinne, cupping her face in both her hands affectionately. Her sister looks thin; as Ashley hugs her, she feels Corinne's body jerk slightly, as though she is nervous.

'Hi, Ash. Where's James?' Corinne asks.

Ashley's face flushes slightly, she feels suddenly alone in the crowded room. 'He's working, coming down tomorrow,' she says, keeping her voice light. 'We drove all the way. Well, I did, no "we" about it. I've had more takeaway coffees than I care to think about and the car's covered in Minstrels.'

Dominic laughs and is interrupted by a small body hitting his knees.

'Benji, my little man!' He swings him upwards; Benji giggles delightedly and launches into a description of the book he is reading at school, which is all about space. Ashley has heard more talk about the solar system in the last two weeks than she has about anything else.

'There are loads and loads of planets, and stars, and even things called black holes that suck things up!' Benji announces proudly.

'I'm not sure they actually suck things up, Ben,' Dominic says.

Ashley smiles wryly at him and sits down next to Corinne, who is pulling at a stray thread on the sofa, worrying the cotton until it snaps.

'How are you, Cor?'

'Yeah, I'm OK,' Corinne says. She circles her gold bracelet around her wrist. 'Where's the baby?'

'With Mum. She's changing her nappy for me, bless her.'

There is a pause. Ashley clears her throat. 'Work good?'

Corinne hesitates. 'I wanted to talk to you,' she says. She glances around the room. The expression on her face is odd. Ashley nods, surprised at the sudden tension.

'Do you remember I told you about the little chimney pot? That looked like it came from the doll house?'

Ashley nods, frowns. 'Yes. Did you hang on to it?'

'Yes,' Corinne says. 'But … but I also found something else, the other day.' She takes a breath and looks over at Dominic, lowering her voice. 'Ashley, I found the little door, the front door of the house. It was on my desk at work.'

There is a silence. Ashley reaches up, rubs her own shoulder blades, feeling how tight the muscles are. She'd love a massage. James used to massage her shoulders when he got home from work, sit her down at the kitchen table and knead her shoulders gently, trace words across her back that she had to try to guess. That hasn't happened in a while.

Benji crashes into the sides of her legs and Ashley puts out a hand to him absent-mindedly. She shouldn't have let him have sweets in the car, he will be buzzing for hours.

'Ash?' Corinne is looking at her.

'Sorry, sorry. You found a door?' She repeats her sister's words, stalling for time. 'What did it look like?'

Corinne reaches down, rummages in the brown handbag sitting by her feet. Ashley stares as she pulls a small piece of wood from her bag. It is painted blue, with a little gold piece sticking out of it, what looks like the remainder of an old nail. Corinne holds it in her palm, flat against her skin. Ashley blinks.

'What do you think? It's exactly the same as the door that Dad made. Don't you remember it?'

Ashley stares at the object for a few seconds. Is she missing something? It looks like a piece of wood that is probably full of splinters; best not let Benji near it. Corinne is still staring at her expectantly; she closes her eyes, tries to think. If she is honest, the details of their doll house have long slipped away from her, overtaken by the hundreds of toys she has bought

71

her own children over the years, hours and hours spent in hellish department stores every Christmas.

'I mean … I don't really think it looks familiar, Cor, to be truthful,' Ashley says. Her sister pauses.

'You don't?'

'Well … it looks to me like a piece of wood. Why would it be from our doll house? Neither of us have seen that in years. I mean, I suppose it might look similar? I can't properly remember. Benji! Will you stop!'

Her son is tugging on the sleeve of her cardigan, anxious for attention. His little face crumples when she snaps at him and she instantly feels terrible. Corinne doesn't say anything, closes her hand around the object and puts it back into her handbag. Ashley wishes for the fiftieth time that James were here.

She tries to change the subject.

'How did you get on at the hospital? What did they say? That's what I want to know!'

Corinne lights up. 'It went well! God, I can't thank you enough. We will pay you back, you know that right?'

Ashley waves a hand. 'Stop, please. I'm more than happy to give it to you. We aren't using it for anything.' She grips her sister's hand. 'I'm keeping everything crossed for you. It's going to work this time, I know it is.'

'Mummmm.' Benji is back, hopping from foot to foot in impatience.

'Come on,' Ashley says to her sister. 'Come find Lucy, she's been dying to see you.' She stands, grabs Benji by the hand and gestures to Corinne to come into the kitchen, where Lucy is sitting at the table with her grandmother, their heads huddled together. Beside them, Holly is happily blowing bubbles, the saliva forming domes around her rosebud mouth. Ashley smiles at the sight of them.

'I can't understand this, my dear,' Mathilde is saying, bent forward over Lucy's iPhone. 'What does this mean? How did you do that?' Lucy is laughing, explaining something to her and Mathilde is shaking her head in bemusement.

'These gadgets! I don't know, it all seems very odd to me. Why don't you just talk to people in real life? What's wrong with that?'

'I do, Grandma!' Lucy rolls her eyes. 'This is different, it's more fun. Look—'

They both glance up as Ashley and Corinne enter the room and Lucy grins at her auntie. Ashley feels a pang as Corinne greets her daughter. They have none of the tension that exists whenever Ashley tries to connect with Lucy. Corinne is wonderful with her.

'What you looking at, Luce?' she asks.

'Oh, it's nothing,' her daughter says, immediately flicking her eyes back down to her phone. Ashley tries to ignore the hurt that blooms in her chest.

'Instagram?' Corinne asks. Ashley blinks. She wouldn't know Instagram if it slapped her in the face. Her sister has pulled up a chair next to Lucy and is peering over her shoulder, swiping the little touch screen and giggling at something on the phone. Ashley sighs. Even though there is only four years between her and Corinne, she suddenly feels very old.

Her mother shrugs her shoulders at her.

'They've lost me. Come on.' She puts a hand on Ashley's shoulder. 'Help me start the dinner. Where's that husband of yours? Not working again?'

8

Kent

Corinne

Maybe Ashley is right. Perhaps it's nothing to do with the doll house at all. I keep telling myself that as we eat our dinner, spooning great chunks of meaty lasagne into our mouths. Benji has spilled his orange squash; I can see tears forming in his eyes, his cheeks puffing out with the delicious fat of small children. They've put Holly down upstairs, in the little cot at the end of the double bed. She looks like she's grown again; every time I see her she is more and more alive, more and more of a person. It's amazing to watch. Amazing and heartbreaking all at the same time. I don't see the children as much as I ought to; I know I could make the hour and a bit journey to Barnes more often than I do, but seeing them is always so bittersweet for me, even though I love them all to bits. It hurts that they aren't mine.

Mum's fussing around us all; she is constantly reaching for a J-cloth, her yellow rubber gloves, mopping up imaginary dirt. She doesn't know what to do with herself any more, without Dad. The sight of her fussing makes me want to cry. I squeeze her arm.

'Sit down, Mum,' I say. 'This is really delicious. Enjoy it with us.' She looks at me and I smile encouragingly. In the last year, she has looked older every time I've seen her, has shrunken into herself like a creature retreating to its shell. Gone is the woman Dad used to call his princess, replaced by a fading shadow. I remember the way he used to look at her; like she wasn't real, like he couldn't believe his luck. Whenever he used to get back from an evening in the city she would light up at the sound of his key in the door and the minute he saw her he would circle his arms around her waist and nuzzle his face into her hair. It made Ashley and I giggle and blush behind our hands. 'All I've wanted to do all night is be home with my princess,' he'd say, and Mum would roll her eyes, tap him on the arm. ('Your father loves being centre of attention,' she told me once. 'He needs it, it's his fuel.' Secretly I always thought she was wrong – what Dad needed the most was us.)

Mum smiles back at me, the lines around her eyes deepening. Her hands twist a tea towel back and forth, the cotton catching on her dry hands. The only thing she seems to love now is seeing the children; her face lights up whenever Lucy and Benji are around, and she cuddles Holly so tightly sometimes I'm scared she might break.

'Mum,' I say when she's finally sat down, the tea towel to one side. 'I wanted to ask you something.'

She looks at me, her brown eyes slightly rheumy over the rim of her glass. I'm not drinking, but Ashley and Mum are sharing a bottle of white. Lucy has been angling for a glass for a while but Ashley hasn't given in yet. Lucy keeps taking pictures of our meal, adding retro filters, zooming in on the flowers on the table to take a close-up. She holds up her iPhone proudly, shows me the photos each time; it makes me laugh as she tries to make Mum's lasagne look arty.

'I wanted to ask about Dad's things,' I say to Mum, 'I've been wondering what happened to them all.' I can feel Ashley and Dom looking at me but I push on, ignoring them. 'And I've been thinking a lot about the doll house we had, you know, the one he made for us. Do you know where it might be?'

There's a pause. I hear the scrape of cutlery on plates, but apart from that the room seems to take on a strange kind of silence which I could be imagining.

'They're all in the loft, my love,' Mum says then, and she smiles at me, a quick, nervous smile. 'The doll house is upstairs. It's packed away, though, so it's tricky to get to. You didn't need it for something, did you?'

'No, no,' I say, because she looks panicked, her face is sort of blotchy and I don't want to make her worry. She seems so frail; although she's only pushing sixty-five, her hair is completely grey now and her hands are wrinkled, dotted with brown liver spots. Dad's death has aged her; I know it has. I suppose it's aged us all in way.

'Did you know that one day we're all going to be sucked into a black hole?' Benji has stopped crying and is holding a piece of lasagne aloft, speared on his fork in front of his face. He zooms the pasta around, dances it in front of Dominic's eyes.

'Black hole, black holeeee,' he cries, and obediently Dom opens his mouth and eats the forkful, his cheeks bulging slightly with the effort. Benji laughs, and everybody's attention is focused on him, but I look over at my mother, who is looking down at her plate, picking at her fingers, pulling at the skin of a hangnail so that the flesh around her nails shines red in the overhead lamp. She's lost in a world of her own, and I can't help but feel that there's something she isn't saying.

*

The house is quiet. Holly has been crying but she is silent now, her wails extinguished by Ashley's gentle voice. Dominic is sleeping beside me, his mouth partially open. The sound of him snoring fills the room. Carefully, I ease myself away, lift up the corner of the duvet. I'm going up to the loft. I've got to find out, I've got to just check.

There is a thin sliver of light emanating from Lucy's bedroom. I pause on the landing, catch sight of myself in the mirror, dressed in my old navy pyjamas that Dom bought me last year. My hair is standing on end. Dad used to call me his little scrubbing brush, he'd put his hand on my head and rub my hair until it puffed up like bristles.

The loft is at the end of the corridor. I walk carefully and quietly, trying not to wake Holly up, my feet tightening against the cold wooden boards. At the little stairway that leads up to the loft, I clamber upwards to the door, my mobile clutched in my hand, ready to activate the flashlight function.

The first thing that strikes me is how much junk my mother keeps up here; piles and piles of our old things, schoolbooks belonging to Ashley, boxes of clothes bursting at the sides. I can see the purple trail of my old tie-dye trousers poking out from behind a ream of Sellotape, catch sight of a box containing what looks like our old artwork. Misshapen clay lumps gleam in the dark.

My eyes begin to adjust to the darkness, and I make out more and more of my things, stacks upon stacks of boxes with my name on, boxes with Ashley's name on. I reach for one of mine; pull off the masking tape and open it up. Just my old shoes, small pairs of trainers that wouldn't even fit Benji. I start to open more boxes, another and another. Books, clothes. My old ballet things, a little plastic box full of sparkly nail polish. I was terrible at ballet, pretty good at manicures. There's a collapsing old art project I made in year four, I don't know why Mum's kept it.

I want to find the dolls. Beatrice was my favourite; she wore a red velvet dress and had long brown ringlets. She was beautiful. She must be here somewhere. There is a sudden sound, a scrabbling noise behind the walls, that makes me jump and catch my breath, pressing my hand to my heart. It must be an animal, a rodent hidden in the walls.

As I stare around, something starts to become clear to me. At first I think I must be wrong and I begin to lift things up, push things aside. I find Ashley's crumpled Brownies outfit, all our Christmas decorations. The red and green baubles glint in the flashlight. Something dislodges itself and a stack of old magazines starts to topple; I peer at them, expecting Dad's back issues of *Architecture Today*, but they all look like Mum's, fading copies of *Women and Home*. I'm trying to be quiet but my heart is beating a little too fast, my movements becoming quicker, frustrated. I don't understand it. I must be wrong. Nothing of my father's is up here.

There are no boxes, none of his clothes. And after a further twenty minutes of searching, there is no doll house anywhere. It is as though it never existed.

9

Kent

Ashley

Ashley's mouth feels dry, fogged with wine. Holly has been surprisingly quiet in the night; she was up at two and again at four, but apart from that she has slept. The silence feels dreamlike, unreal. Ashley reaches across the bed for her mobile. Seven a.m. The numbers stare back at her. There are no missed calls and she feels something inside her loosen, relax a little. She dials the Barnes house. The phone rings and rings.

James doesn't pick up; she ends the call, lies staring at the blank face of her mobile. Yuck. She needs to brush her teeth.

The bedroom door creaks open and she lifts her head. Her sister enters the room and Ashley immediately scoots over, bunching up the covers under her chin, making room for Corinne. She looks worried, as though she hasn't slept much.

'Budge over, will you?' She glances into the cot. 'Hol asleep?'

Ashley nods, moves further along the bed, pulling back the duvet to let Corinne in. Her hair tickles Ashley's shoulder as she wriggles in next to her and they turn towards each other, lying face to face like they used to when they were girls.

'You all right? It's really early. I thought you were Benji wanting juice.'

Corinne frowns. 'It's the hormones. My schedule's messed up; I can't sleep, and when I do, I have nightmares. And I can never get comfortable.' She sighs, shifts so that her back is to Ashley.

'Oh, poor you.' Ashley reaches out and rubs her sister's back, feeling the proximity of the bones through the skin. When they were small she used to run her palm up and down Corinne's little spine, count the humps as her sister slept beside her. It was fun sleeping in the same bed, cuddling up like sardines in a tin and drifting off to the sound of their parents chatting downstairs.

'How's the gallery going now? Did you get that new commission?'

Corinne rolls over, spreading her arms out until she is flat on her back, staring at the ceiling. She reminds Ashley of a snow angel, the type they used to make in the Hampstead garden when they were children. Their dad had shown them how to throw themselves backwards, spread their arms wide, enjoy the cold thud of the ground beneath them.

'No. Not yet, anyway. I mean, I hope I do.'

'Has Marjorie mentioned it?'

Corinne shrugs. 'On and off. She's not my biggest fan at the moment. I need to pull my socks up.' She says the last phrase in a forced matronly voice and they both laugh.

'There's a new woman moved into our building,' Corinne says. 'Gilly something. Quite young, younger than me. She's got a little boy, a toddler, she's on her own.'

Ashley waits.

'I'm going to try to be friendly to her,' Corinne says. 'I have to, don't I? I can't be rude to people just because they've got what I haven't.' She looks as Ashley as though for approval, and Ashley feels a rush of love for her sister.

'Oh, Cor. Yes, of course you need to try. But don't beat yourself up. It's normal that you feel this way, really, it is.'

Corinne nods. 'I know. But I can't give in to it, I've got to keep trying.'

'You can do it,' Ashley says. 'You always were a determined person. Remember when we were little? You wouldn't take no for an answer.' She smiles. 'Dad used to call you his little dictator.'

Corinne laughs. 'God, I'd forgotten that.'

The alcohol from the night before is making Ashley's heartbeat fast and irregular.

'I can't get hold of James,' she tells Corinne. 'I tried him just now and he's not answering.' She tries to keep her voice light.

'Probably asleep. Or already on the way? I thought you said he was coming down anyway?'

'I did. He's meant to be. Said he had to work.'

'Well, then, he's working! Don't worry, silly billy.'

Ashley feels a bite of irritation. She swallows down her feelings, picks up her mobile and dials again. The line takes a while to connect and when it does it clicks on to their automatic answering machine.

'James, Ashley and the children are unavailable to take your call right now. Please leave a message and we'll call you straight back!' Her own voice shrills out at her. God, she's chirpy. She pulls back the covers, swings her legs out of the bed.

'I should go and check on Benji. Want some tea?'

'Just hot water, please.'

Ashley stands up. She is gasping for a cup of Earl Grey. At thirty-nine, she can't drink wine like she used to in her twenties. Not without consequences, anyway. As she leaves the room, Corinne says her name.

'Ashley?'

Corinne's voice is high, as though she is unsure of what she is about to say.

'What's the matter?'

She turns back towards the bed. Corinne sits up, pulls the quilt tight across her knees. There are bags under her eyes, purple in the dimmed light of the bedroom.

Corinne stares at her for a few seconds as though about to say something, then seems to change her mind.

'Nothing,' she says. 'Nothing. I'll see you downstairs.'

'You sure?'

'I'm sure. Sorry.'

'OK. Let me know if Hol wakes up, will you? Watch her for me.'

Ashley pulls the door to and goes down the corridor, pausing at the doorway to Benji's room. She has done this ever since he was born: stop outside his door and listen to the rise and fall of his breathing. She holds her own breath as she listens. God knows what would happen if she couldn't actually hear him.

Ashley retrieves the tea bags from her mother's cupboard. She hopes Corinne is all right; her sister is prone to getting things out of proportion, seeing significance in everything even when there is none. She panics easily, always has. The doll house is a typical example. Their dad's death hit Corinne particularly hard, Ashley knows it did. Perhaps the fertility treatment has brought the feelings to the surface.

She goes over to her mother's landline and dials her husband again. The phone rings and she is about to give up when James answers, his voice sounding gruff.

'James? Are you OK?' A spurt of worry grips her heart and she presses the phone to her ear, listening for another voice in the background. Is there someone there, is there somebody with him?

She waits, counts to three. Perhaps she is imagining it. The phone can distort. She takes a big gulp of tea.

'Are you coming down today? Everyone wants to see you. We'll probably go for lunch.' Ashley can feel herself holding her breath.

James clears his throat and when he speaks his voice sounds more like himself. The energy leaves her suddenly and she has to lean against the counter. What is the matter with her?

'I'll be on the next train.'

Ashley remains in the kitchen after they hang up, holding the phone to her chest. Her friend Megan's voice filters through her ears, *Are you worried, Ashley? Ashley, are you worried?*

Then

I don't tell anyone what we do any more. I did once, when I was younger, when I was just little, I wrote about it for my school project. The title was 'What I Did at the Weekend'. It was in art and design class and the teacher asked us to draw a picture of what we did on our Saturday and Sunday. But it wasn't just a normal drawing, we were allowed to use all different materials. That means paint and glue and felt-tip pen. Mrs Sanderson said I could do whatever I liked and so I picked up all the shoeboxes from the corner of the classroom, the spare ones from when we made bug boxes, and I started to build a house.

I used Sellotape and Pritt Stick (although that didn't work very well) and I put the boxes one on top of the other, because the house we go to is quite big. Then I added in windows for us to look through and a door, although we aren't allowed to go through that yet but Mummy says we will one day.

It looked really good, everyone said so, even that boy Toby who is mean to me. So that means it really was good. The teacher asked me if that was my house and I said yes, yes, it is my house, and then I had to go to the toilet and I felt a bit sick because I knew I had told a lie. Mummy says lies are what adults say and I felt scared then because I thought I must be becoming an adult. I don't think I want to be an adult. They're not very nice to each other. I wrote down a story to go with the picture, but then when the teacher saw it, she crossed it all out with a big red pen, she said I had to learn the difference between making something up and telling the truth. I was telling the truth though. It's just that no one believed me.

I told Mummy what had happened and she was cross, she told me that what we do is our special secret and that I haven't to tell anyone ever again. She didn't hit me or anything, she never does that, but she looked at me like what I had done was really serious and so I felt frightened. I turned my face against the wall but she spun me round, her hands digging into my shoulders, and she put her face all close to mine and she said that I must never tell anybody because if I do we will get into big trouble, both of us, and especially her and if she is taken away then nobody will look after me at all, because she's sure as hell the only one doing it now.

'Sure as hell' is what she said. I've never heard anyone say that before but I don't like the sound of it. I kept my mouth zipped shut the rest of the night, zip zip zip. Nothing came out of my mouth at all. Next time at school I'm going to say we went to the beach, because that's what Natasha next to me always does. The teacher will think we're friends, which is another lie. But at least that won't make Mummy cross.

Sometimes I think it is all my fault, that I'm not a good enough child for Mummy. That she wants a different one, a better one, a daughter with longer hair or a nicer face. I feel all sad when I think that, and I try extra hard to be good. I don't complain when we visit the house three nights running, I don't cry when she forgets to sign my reading book, I don't make a fuss when the dinner is cold fish fingers again. But none of it makes a difference, she still talks about it all the time, about how badly her life has turned out. She asks the air sometimes, she says, what did I do to deserve this?

Once I asked her if she meant me, deserve me, and then she looked a bit sorry and she gave me a cuddle. She smelled a bit funny but for once I didn't mind.

'No,' she said, 'That's not what I mean. I just wanted better for you, that's all. For both of us. I still do.

I want that too, but I don't know how we're going to get it.

10

Kent

Corinne

I don't know why my mother lied, but I do know that the doll house isn't in the attic. I keep looking at her, trying to catch her eye, but it's as though she is avoiding me; she is constantly doing something, talking to Ashley, playing games with Benji.

I can't shake the kernel of worry in my mind, the possibility that the things I've found – the chimney and tiny door – really are from the house. That someone has left them both for me to find. What I don't know is why. It makes no sense. I don't know why someone would do it, I don't know who would do it, or what on earth it would mean.

Did Mum throw Dad's things away without telling us? Maybe they made her too sad. Has she forgotten where they are, is that it? I try to think of the last time I saw his stuff. I remember packing everything away after the funeral, but it is all a bit of a blur. Ashley guided me through most of it, her stomach stretching out before her, walked me past the row of well-wishers as though I was a zombie. It was just before Holly was born. I close my eyes for a second, remembering the sadness of the day. Dad had a mahogany coffin, a wreath of yellow daffodils. Lots of people came – people from the architectural scene, designers, all of them singing his praises. 'Highest of the high-flyers, your old man,' one guy said to me, and I felt the praise warm on my skin in spite of my grief.

Mum really struggled; I think of her face, almost hidden by her big black hat. She had been almost completely silent for the whole day. Maybe she did find it too hard keeping his things. Even as I try to rationalise, I can't shake the feeling that she knows more than she said last night.

'Corinneeeeee!' Benji is tapping his fork against my arm. There's a smear of mashed potato on it but I don't mind. I ruffle his hair and feel Dominic watching me from across the table. I catch his eye and smile. His cheeks are red from the cold outside and his hair's a bit messy. He looks gorgeous.

We're at a pub in the Kent countryside having lunch; it's all very rural, surrounded by open fields. I keep seeing burly men who look like they've come straight from a hunt; it's a far cry from our tangle of streets in Crouch End.

James arrived about an hour ago. He seems a bit strained and he's been sipping at the same pint for ages. I watch him lean over to prise Lucy's fingers away from her mobile phone. I need to remember to thank him for the money.

I spot my chance when he eventually goes to the bar to get more wine for Mum and Ashley.

'I'll get you a lemonade, Luce,' I say. 'You can Instagram the bubbles.' I smile at her, ignore her scowl and follow James up to the bar. The barman isn't looking at us, his attention caught by a pretty blonde girl who's asking him to mix her a drink. She's twirling her plait flirtatiously, putting the end to her lips, confident in that way I have never understood or mastered. Her tinkling laugh travels. I touch my own hair self-consciously.

'James,' I start, and he turns towards me. His eyes look a bit bloodshot and I smile. 'Late night?'

'Me? God no, no, just working, you know how it is. I wanted to come up yesterday but I was just swamped.'

'Oh, poor you,' I say. 'Ashley's told me great things about the digital world, though, seems like it's all really taking off. eBooks are all the rage right now.'

He's not really listening to me; his eyes are scanning the bottles of whisky behind the bar. The barman has finally spotted us and stands waiting, PDQ machine in hand.

'Pint of Amstel, please, and a bottle of the Merlot,' James says.

'And a lemonade,' I add and the barman nods.

'Listen, James, I just wanted to say thank you,' I say quickly. I can feel the heat rising in my face. 'It's so kind of you to help us, and I want you to know that we will pay you back, and we are so grateful. It means such a lot to me and it's our last hope.'

He turns to face me, looks confused. 'Sorry, Cor … you've lost me.'

I lower my voice. 'Well, we went to the hospital last week. For the last round of IVF. And I wanted to thank you for the money you lent us.' I swallow, praying that I don't have to repeat myself again.

The barman places a dripping pint in front of us.

'The money … oh right, sorry, Corinne, of course,' James says, and he reaches out and touches my hand. Thank God for that.

I smile, relieved, and pick up Lucy's lemonade. As I walk back to the table I think I can feel his eyes on my back, watching me as I weave through the people, past the dwindling fire. I wonder what he is thinking, whether there is any truth in Ashley's worries. When I look back at the bar though, unable to bear the sensation any more, James has gone, his pint still sitting on the wet wood. I scan the pub, feeling jumpy, but all I see are families engaged in conversation. No one is remotely near me.

I sit down next to Dom, take a big bite of my roast and try to relax. 'So, Dominic,' Mum says, 'tell me, how is the paper going? I've been trying to read the online version but our internet wire is terrible here.'

'You don't need a wire, Grandma,' Lucy says, rolling her eyes. 'I showed you before.'

'I'm sorry, darling, forgive an old lady,' Mathilde says. 'Perhaps you'll show me again when we're home?'

Dominic smiles. 'It's fine, thanks, going really well,' he says. 'I've just started work on a property piece – a big Georgian house on the outskirts of London. Massive place! Corinne came to see it with me, didn't you, Cor?'

I nod. The image of Carlington comes to my mind, the strange atmosphere, the way my hand felt against the stone. The dark windows. The empty rooms. The face at the window. I shiver.

Dominic is still talking.

'We're featuring it in the spring property round-up. Got the tip-off from a company called Wells and Duggan. Impressive building, or it will be anyway.' There is a clatter; water spills from Mum's upturned glass out over the table.

'Wells and Duggan, did you say?'

Dom nods. 'Yep, that's right. Here, let me get you a napkin.' He reaches out, starts to blot the table.

Ashley leans forward, her wedding ring tapping against the wine glass in her hand. 'Ooh, sounds wonderful. I love Georgian buildings.'

James reappears suddenly, slides in beside Ashley at the long table. He picks up his beer and takes a long drink, the tendons in his neck stiff. He looks very pale. My sister's eyes follow his movements, track the liquid as it slides from hand to throat. The blonde girl at the bar laughs again and I see James look at her, see my sister notice.

*

Dominic squeezes my hand as we walk back out to the car park. I've just put hand cream on and he laughs.

'You use too much of that stuff!'

He's probably right, but I like it. It calms my nerves a bit.

'OK? Enjoy your chicken?' he says, and I nod and squeeze him back, his hand warm in my own. I am so lucky to have him. I know he'd never hurt me. But then, I still don't think James would hurt Ashley.

'Time for a quick walk? Burn off those roasts?' Ashley suggests and I nod yes, say I'll just grab my hat and gloves from out of the car.

'Can you get me my scarf, please?' Dom asks, fastened to the spot by Benji, who has hold of his leg and is talking about aliens, and I laugh and catch the keys from him as he throws them across the gravel.

I'm about to open the passenger side when something catches my eye. At first I can't work out what it is, I think it's a piece of clothing lying on the bonnet, but when I lean closer it hits me. The shock of it is awful; I recoil from the car, bile rising in my throat.

'Dominic!' I shout. 'Dominic!'

I look over to the group frantically, they're not paying attention to me. I cry out again, backing away from the car, and Dominic looks up, sees me and begins to come over, breaking into a run when he sees my face.

'What is it?' he says. 'What's the matter?'

I'm covering my mouth now, I can see passers-by staring at me, families emerging from the pub, making their way to their cars.

'Look,' I say. 'Look!'

Dom steps forward, swears loudly when he sees what is lying on the bonnet of our car.

It is a rabbit. Dead, one of its eyes hanging slightly out of its skull, its mouth open in a frozen scream. The underside of it is matted with blood, its paws lie limply against the bonnet. It looks like it has been hit by a car.

'Jesus,' Dominic says. 'Why the hell is this on the bonnet?'

'I don't know!' I say. 'I don't know! I just came to the car and it was here, someone's put it on our car! It's horrible, oh God, it's so horrible.'

'Slow coaches slow coaches!' Benji is running towards us, eager to begin the walk, and Dominic puts out an arm to stop him seeing the car. But it is too late.

'Yuck! What's happened to that bunny?' Benji asks, screwing up his face and sticking out his tongue. 'It's dead like in science.'

'Yep, yep it is, mate, OK, but not to worry, be a good lad and run back to your mum now,' Dominic says. 'You guys start without us, we'll catch you up.'

Benji pulls another face, rolls his eyes. 'Can I look at it?'

Dominic shakes his head. 'No, mate, come on, go back to Grandma. We'll be along in a bit. Do us a favour will you and tell them we're just having a quick chat.'

Benji runs off, skidding his shoes along the gravel of the car park as he goes, making racing car noises. Dominic sighs.

'What a sick thing to do, put it on the car like that. Poor creature. Leave it to me, I'll get this cleared up. What a bloody mess.'

I am shaking, my eyes fixed on the poor rabbit's face, half squashed by the force of whatever hit it.

'Why our car, Dominic? Why this?'

He shrugs, shakes his head slowly. I don't know how he can be so calm. 'I don't know,' he says. 'You didn't see anyone?'

'Nobody.'

He grimaces. 'Could be a practical joke, I suppose, or more likely some local weirdo.' He glances around the car park. There are a group of men coming towards us, all clad in wellies and waterproof coats, laughing and jostling each other as they make their way into the pub. 'Or someone protesting – people in the countryside are always against something – the badger cull, fox hunting. The amount of roadkill.' He puts an arm around me, I am shaking.

'It's all right, my love. It won't be anything personal – think about it, who do we know living out in deepest darkest Kent? No one. Except your mum of course, and somehow I don't think she's behind this.' He smiles at me, trying to make me laugh. 'Whoever did it was probably too scared to pick one of the fancy BMWs round here. Chose the scruffy car that looked as though its owners weren't bothered!' He sniffs. 'You go on, join your family. Don't let it upset you, my love. I'll speak to the landlord of the pub too, report it. I bet you'll find there's been a spate of this kind of thing.'

My eyes flit across the car park. There are a couple of other cars: James's Golf, a little red Mini and a dirty white camper van with the number plate loose. One of the waitresses is emptying a big barrel of bottles in the alley by the pub, the green glass smashing loudly. As I watch, two women come out of the restaurant area, both groaning and holding their stomachs as though they've eaten too much. A man with a little terrier holds the door open for them, smiling broadly. They look like mother and daughter.

My heart is beating fast through the thickness of my coat and I try to be logical, keep my gaze away from the poor bunny lying on the car. The sight of its bloodied fur makes my legs feel weak. Dominic is right – nobody knows us in Kent, nobody even knows we're here.

Dominic has opened up the car, is looking for a plastic bag. The rabbit lies prone in front of us, its stiffening body a dark shape just in front of the windscreen. We used to have rabbits in Hampstead, two pet bunnies. Bertie and Nosie. They belonged to me and Ash.

I put my arms around Dominic, wanting his warmth and security. I don't want to go on the walk without him. I look back at the car, at the bunny's splayed legs, the way its skull has smashed in on itself. The poor thing wouldn't have stood a chance.

11

Kent

Ashley

They are walking down the hill from the pub when James pulls Ashley over to one side. They lag back so that the group edge in front of them, Mathilde pushing the pram. Corinne and Dom are still by the pub; Ashley doesn't know what is taking them so long. James grabs her sleeve and says he's got to talk to her. Now.

'Well all right,' she says, in a joking sort of voice because the Merlot has gone to her head a bit and she's just happy that he's here, and they are all together, the five of them; she isn't on her own, watching TV and waiting for the silent phone to ring.

Ashley tucks her hand inside the pocket of James's jacket to join his own and puts her face close to his like a mock detective. Perhaps if she pretends as though everything is OK it really will be.

'What's up, mister?' The look on his face is very serious and suddenly she feels a tiny bit sick. She pushes her tongue over her teeth, hoping they're not stained from the red wine. Her heart begins to thud. Is he going to tell her? Is he going to tell her there's another woman? Not now. Surely he wouldn't do it here, in front of the children. Would he?

'Did you give Corinne and Dominic money?'

There is a pause. Ashley blinks.

'Well, yes, I lent her money for their final round of IVF. You know they'd run out. I told you, and I wanted to help. Sorry, I should have mentioned it but you've been so busy and I didn't think you'd mind. You don't, do you?'

'Jesus.' He exhales.

Ashley pulls her hand from his pocket and takes a step backwards, confused. 'What's the matter? I was only being kind.'

'You should have discussed it with me, Ash,' he says. 'Or at least mentioned it. For fuck's sake.'

Ashley stands on the hill, staring at him. She can feel tears prick the backs of her eyes.

'The only reason I haven't told you, James, is because I never bloody see you! You're never at home! You're always at work! If that's what they're calling it these days.'

James looks shocked. 'What's that supposed to mean?'

'You know what it means.' All of a sudden she feels exhausted; the energy leaves her body and her arms drop down to her sides. The rest of the family are a way ahead but they can probably hear her, screeching like a banshee. How humiliating.

'I don't want to discuss this now,' she says, in a low voice, and she turns on her heel and walks fast to catch up with the children, ignoring her husband as he calls after her. How dare James make her feel guilty? It's not like he runs it past Ashley every time he uses money from their account. And it's hardly as if she was using the cash for a selfish reason. James loves Corinne. They have talked about her fertility struggles, lots of times. Just last week he was saying how much he felt for them both. How can he mind her using the money for such a good purpose?

Ashley runs a little so that she is alongside Benji, scoops her son close to her. The tip of his nose is dribbling a little in the wintery wind and she whips out a tissue before he can wipe it on his coat, glad she came prepared.

'Auntie Corinne found a dead rabbit, Mummy,' Benji says. 'It's dead like in science.'

'Oh, did she? Well, yes, you do get that sometimes in the countryside, Ben,' Ashley tells him, and she zips up his coat where it has fallen down, tucks his hat more tightly on his little head. He starts gabbling on about the rabbit but Ashley isn't listening, tunes her son out as she thinks over James's reaction. She's never seen that side of him before, has never had him down as someone anything other than generous.

'OK, Luce?' she calls out to her daughter, who has her arm through Mathilde's and is walking on ahead, one hand on Holly's pushchair. Her daughter looks back at her, gives her a rare smile. Ashley feels momentarily better. Maybe James is just tired. He will have to come round soon. She has never thought of her husband as a selfish man. Why on earth would he mind her giving away money when he is doing so well?

12

Corinne

'Don't you think it's weird?' I say to Ashley and Mum. I've just finished telling them about the rabbit, the poor dead creature now lying in a makeshift grave on the countryside verge. Dom and I buried him together, while the others were walking. I didn't know what else to do, I couldn't bear the thought of the poor thing stuffed in a bin, left to rot amongst the rubbish.

'To find it on the car like that? I mean it wasn't just on the ground, someone had actually picked it up and put it on the bonnet.'

'Awful.' Mum nods. 'Really horrid. Poor thing, and poor you. What a dreadful shock.' She takes a long sip of her tea. 'Mind you, you do get some queer folk around here, country people with all sorts of ideas about the way things should be run. There's always some protest or other going on – when they started the badger cull you heard a lot of talk of this kind of thing – activists leaving dead animals in public places.'

We're sat in front of the fire, the flames crackling in front of us. I watch the colours dance – orange, red, gold.

The image of the mangled rabbit keeps surfacing in my brain, its broken limbs, flattened ears. We reported it to the people who own the pub, they said they'd be on the lookout for anything suspicious.

'Has it happened here before?' I asked the barman, trying to keep the panic out of my voice, but he just frowned and said he didn't think so before getting caught up in a row over a pint with too much head.

I don't know what else we can do. I can't stop thinking about it, the way the poor creature's jaw was frozen open, his staring little eyes. I used to love our pet bunnies, with their soft pink noses and glossy brown fur. They're such gentle creatures. We had them for years, I used to run home from school to play with them, bring them in the house with me when Mum and Dad weren't looking.

Lucy is horrified by it when she finds out.

'Why would someone do that to a poor little rabbit?' she asks.

'It was probably an accident, Luce,' Ashley says. 'It's roadkill, a car ran it over without meaning to. Some horrible person just wanted to put it where it could be seen, that's all, probably to make a point. Let's try to forget about it, shall we?'

Her voice is tight, tense. I glance at her. There's something wrong between her and James, I can tell. I think they've had a row.

13

Kent

Corinne

We leave the next morning, early. I slept badly, dreamed of our old Hampstead house. I was in the garden, near the rabbit cages, waiting for Ashley to find me. We were playing hide and seek. I waited and waited but she never came, no one did. I stayed hidden in the trees for hours, until it got dark, and then nobody could hear me calling out for help. I woke up mid-shout, my mouth wide open, and Dominic jolted awake beside me.

'Corinne? What's the matter?' He touched my arm. 'God, you're freezing.'

'Bad dream,' I mumbled, lying back against the pillow. Cold sweat dampened my body, pooled uncomfortably on my stomach and the back of my neck. The anxiety didn't go away, it stayed with me as we got up, had breakfast and packed to go back to London. I was jumpy, catching my breath at the slightest thing, the smallest sound.

Mum wouldn't meet my eye properly at breakfast when I asked her again about Dad's things. I know she's lying to me, but I don't know why. The thought careers round and around in my head, making me clumsy, distracted.

I hug Ashley hard as we leave, tell her to ring me any time.

'Will you come outside with me for a sec?' she whispers, and I nod and follow her out into the garden, our feet crunching on the gravel that surrounds the house. We keep walking onto the grass, which is wet with condensation. Ashley doesn't say anything until we're right at the bottom, near where the fence meets the field. Plumes of smoke rise from the building across the meadow, spiral into the sky like grey ghosts. I stare out over the grass, at the hedgerows criss-crossing the countryside. Someone out there put that rabbit on our car. Someone scraped it off the road, positioned it where they knew I'd see it. The thought makes me feel sick.

'What's happened?' I ask her. 'What's going on with James?' She won't meet my eye. I know she hates looking upset, hates showing weakness. She's always been the same, ever since we were children.

'I think James might be having an affair.' The words come out in a rush, and I can see how hard it is for her to say them. Her cheeks are red, as though she doesn't even like admitting to the thought. I focus, try to choose my words carefully.

'What makes you think that, Ash?'

She's crossing and uncrossing her arms like she does when she's uncomfortable.

'I confronted him last night – you probably heard, sorry – about why he's been staying so late at work, why he's hardly been home in the last month. He didn't have an answer, he just kept evading the question. He looked really shady, Cor. He couldn't reassure me, just keeps saying it's stuff in the office, stuff he needs to sort out. I can't see what on earth could be so important though, that's the thing. He's always been so successful, I can't see why …' She trails off, pushes her toe into the damp ground, creating furrows with the tips of her shoes. She takes a deep breath.

'And I keep getting these phone calls. Late at night, someone breathing. To the house and to my mobile. I think it's a woman. Every time his mobile rings he jumps for it, takes it in the other room like some sort of spy. He never used to be like this, Cor. He didn't. I just—'

Her voice breaks and I reach out, put my arms around her and rub her back. Her tears dampen my shoulder. We stand there in the grass for a long time, holding each other, the dew seeping through our shoes.

'Anyway.' She pulls away from me, sniffs, wipes her nose on her sleeve. 'God, look at me. I'm so sorry, Cor.' She squeezes my hand. 'Call me when you get back to London, won't you? And keep me posted. When are you going to take the first pregnancy test?'

'They say I can try next week,' I tell her. A bubble of hope grows in my chest even as I say the words, but I gently push it back, feel a flash of guilt that I could be distracted when Ashley is so upset.

She nods. 'OK. Keep me in the loop.' We turn to go back to the house, where Dom is waiting with the car.

'Oh, and, Cor, don't worry about the doll house, will you? It's in the attic, you heard Mum. We'll get it out one day for your little one.' She holds up her hand, crosses her fingers in the air. 'But seriously, I think this stuff is just your imagination. I really do. And try to stop thinking about the poor rabbit.' She smiles at me. 'Remember Bertie and Nosie? How old were we when we had them?'

'Five,' I say. 'Dad bought them for us. Well, I was five, you would've been older. We had them for years and years.'

Ashley nods. 'We loved them.'

*

It's only early afternoon but I want to go to bed. I am tired, the journey back from Mum's has wiped me out and the whole weekend has hardly been the relaxing break I needed. Far from it.

Dominic has to go into work, it's Monday so the paper is on deadline. I've booked the whole day off, so I tell him I'll just go home and see him later. He drops me off with my keys and I wave as he drives off to the office. There's a little dead bird lying on the corner of our road, a pigeon with its feathers flattened. It looks like it's been dead for days. I lift my eyes upwards, away from the matted mess on the pavement. At least this one isn't plastered on our car.

I'm looking forward to snuggling up with a cup of lemon hot water. I've been drinking lots of it, doctor's orders. The thought of the doctor jumps my mind to next week. I'm going to take a pregnancy test on the first recommended day, perhaps one before? There are so many tests now that say early results. I'm not sure I can wait much longer.

'Corinne!' It's Gilly, she's coming out of the lift behind me, pushing her pram. She's got no make-up on; it makes her look younger than ever.

'Hi!' I say. 'How're you?'

'Exhausted,' she says. 'I've just about finished unpacking, but it's been a slog. Fancy a quick cuppa? I'm about to have one myself.'

I hesitate. I'm keen to get into bed and lie down but I promised myself I'd be friendly. I could just have a quick drink; it might take my mind off things.

'Sure,' I say, and I help her get the buggy inside, put my bags down at the foot of her stairs. She sits me down at the table in the living room, it is small and round, Tommy's high chair is next to a couple of wooden stools. There are beads for him to play with attached to the front, the remains of a yogurt pot stuck to the little tray. I perch on one of the stools gingerly.

'Earl Grey all right?' she calls to me from the kitchen.

'Have you got decaf?' I ask. 'I'm not meant to have caffeine, you know, because of the baby stuff.'

'Oh God, of course, sorry. And I'm sorry about the mess! Ignore it, please. How was Kent?'

I look up. Did I tell her we were going to Kent? I must've done.

'It was — it was OK thanks,' I reply, not wanting to relive the horror of the rabbit all over again. To distract myself, I look around her sitting room while she makes the tea, taking in a couple of hastily unpacked books, the small pile of toys that I guess belong to Tommy. They haven't got much stuff. It looks like they moved in a hurry. She's started to make the place homely though; there is a row of pot plants on the windowsill, their leaves straining towards the sunlight, and one or two photographs framed on the sideboard. One of them catches my eye and I lean forwards, frowning.

'Gilly?' I call out to her, and she pops her head back into the sitting room, a carton of open milk in her hand.

'Yes?'

'Is this you and your husband?'

She nods. 'God, I didn't even put that out. Tommy must have hoiked it from the boxes.' She comes into the room, picks up the photo and turns it over, places it face down.

'Sorry. That's Ben – he's my ex-husband now. That was us on our wedding day. Can do without it staring me in the face! Two ticks.' She disappears into the kitchen again and comes back holding two mugs of tea and a little plate of biscuits on a plastic pink tray.

'Hobnob?'

She offers me the plate and I take one.

'I didn't mean to pry about your husband,' I say, but she's waving a hand in the air, dismissing my apologies.

'Oh, God, don't worry about it. Water under the bridge.' She sips her tea. 'These things happen.'

'I'm sorry,' I say.

She shakes her head at me. 'Don't be. Honest. We're better off.' She smiles. 'I worry about Tommy, but you know, what can I do. Better to be apart than bring him up in a household full of arguments.'

'What happened?' I ask, and then feel rude – the question is too personal. It's been so long since I've relaxed in female company like this that I worry I've forgotten how to be. She doesn't look bothered, takes a big bite of her biscuit and crunches thoughtfully.

'Money,' she tells me, 'That's what started it. Isn't that always the way? Well, money or a woman, I suppose.' She sighs. 'It wasn't really his fault, actually.' She looks down at her biscuit plate, then back up at me. There is a sudden sharpness in her gaze as our eyes connect and I look down at the tabletop, feeling a tiny bit uncomfortable.

'I'm sorry,' I say. 'That's awful.'

She sips her tea again, her gaze softer now. 'Yeah, well, it was for a bit. He just lost it, you know, couldn't keep it together, terrible mood swings. I'd tell him it wasn't his fault but he wouldn't listen … It ate away at us, as these things do. We just fought all the time. Maybe we got married too young. Me wanting to get away from my mother.' Something flickers in her eyes and I push the plate of biscuits towards her. She grins at me. I want to ask her more, find out what happened with the money. I open my mouth but she shakes her head, begins to speak again before I can.

'Hey, look at me going on. Sorry! Really, it's OK now. Tommy sees him, from time to time. But I wanted a fresh start. Hence—' She gestures at the room. 'New place.' She frowns. 'It's a bit bare, isn't it? I don't really have much stuff of my own. Need to get down the shops.'

I shake my head. 'It's a lovely flat. I like your plants. Where were you before?'

'Oh,' she says, 'all over, really. We lived in Camberwell when we were married. What about you? Have you always been a North London girl?'

'I grew up in Hampstead,' I tell her.

She raises her eyebrows, smiles at me. 'Fancy. Lucky you! Hampstead is gorgeous.'

I shift slightly on my stool, feeling embarrassed. I always worry about sounding privileged, whenever I mention Hampstead the reaction is the same. She's looking at me over her tea, thoughtfully. I feel a splash of panic; I don't

105

want her to dislike me, not now, not now I'm making friends for once.

I try to change the subject. 'So, since your husband … has there been … is there anyone else on the scene?'

Her face brightens and she leans forward. I breathe a sigh of relief, feel my stomach muscles unclench. It feels fun to have this kind of chat, it's been ages since I've talked to a friend like this. A lot of my old friends have stopped calling, given up on me when I never called them back. I let the IVF take over everything, I know I did.

Gilly is blushing, just a little, and I squeal.

'Tell me!'

'No, no,' she says. 'It's nothing really – it's, well, we'll see.' She lowers her voice. 'He's with someone else, actually. At the moment.' She bites her lip. She reminds me of a teenager, suddenly, furtive behind the bicycle sheds. 'I know what you're thinking, you're thinking I'm awful, but it's not like that, really it isn't. He's trying to leave her. He's a good guy, bit older than me.'

I swallow. I don't know what to say. I can feel my face tightening with the effort of trying not to look shocked, my mouth contorting weirdly as she leans forward, covers her hand with mine. 'Oh, please don't go thinking I'm some sort of hussy! I've never done this before in my life! Nothing's happening, not really, not until he leaves. I've told him it can't.'

I drink the rest of my tea, feel the hot liquid trickling down my throat. Gilly looks worried, as though she knows I don't approve. I don't really know what to think about it, to be honest – the thought of infidelity has always seemed so alien to me. But, saying that, she seems a nice enough girl. Woman. I try to be open-minded. I suppose things do get complicated. I've been with Dominic so long that I can't remember what it's like to be on your own. Maybe this guy really loves her.

After a while, I start to feel really tired so I thank Gilly for the tea and say she'll have to come to mine next time.

'Definitely!' she says, looking relieved. 'It's lovely to know a neighbour. Have a good evening, won't you.'

I give her a kiss on the cheek and say goodbye, walk down the corridor to our flat. I can't help wondering about this man she's seeing – someone who wants to take on a young mother and a child that isn't his? I wonder if he already has children, has babies. I think of Holly and remember my sister, her worried face in Mum's garden, and I feel a bit sad. People's lives are so messy. Is there ever an excuse to stray?

When I get in, the flat feels strangely warm, which is odd because I'm sure we turned the heating off before we left; Dom is annoyingly strict about things like that, but I'm more forgetful. Still, at least I don't have to shiver my way to the bedroom. I put on my comfiest socks, the ones Ash bought me last year, and go to the bed. Without the distraction of Gilly, everything comes back; I think about the poor dead rabbit splayed on the bonnet, about Mum telling me the doll house is upstairs. Perhaps a sleep will do me good, give my thoughts a chance to clear. Then I can think rationally, work out what to do. I stretch out my hand to pull back the covers, stop deadly still as I see it. My stomach churns.

It's there on my pillow. A little wooden rocking horse, painted yellow with a brown saddle and a flowing mane of hair. Its teeth are bared, big and white, and its eyes are huge in its head, one on each side. It's miniature, the size of my fist. I freeze, stand totally still as my breath catches in my throat.

This time I'm not imagining things. I back away from the bed, spin around to stare at the room. My heart racing, I check the kitchen, the hallway, the bathroom. Nobody is there. I find my mobile, dial Dominic, my fingers stumbling over the buttons so that I have to start again twice. No answer.

I return to the bed, pick the little horse up with shaking fingers. It stands on wooden rails, I know if I put it down it will begin to rock, backwards and forwards, backwards and forwards. I remember the day Dad gave this to me. It was my eighth birthday. I'd saved his present till last, seen all my party guests off with cake and balloons. The horse was wrapped in brown paper and Sellotape. He had carved it himself. We put it in the nursery of the doll house, the baby's room. I can remember it as clear as day.

I run to the windows, check that they're all locked tight, which they are. The house is deadly quiet and I can't help it, as I pace around the rooms I start to cry a little, ugly hot tears that spill down my cheeks. *What is going on?* Someone has been inside this flat, has touched our things, walked across this room. I'm sure of it now. I know this horse is the one Dad gave me. I know it is. Someone has got our things, and someone is making sure I get them back.

Then

I've only seen the bad man once. He gave me a coat with a blue furry hood. I wish I could properly remember but I can't, all I can remember is the way the material felt between my fingers, soft and warm. I've still got it, I wear it all the time but Mummy says it's getting too small for me, that I look ridiculous. Once she said that and I cried, and then she cuddled me. I think she felt sorry. After a while I realised that she was crying too, and then I was a bit annoyed because she'd made the blue furry hood all soggy and wet. She took it away from me to wash it and I was scared I wouldn't get it back, but I did. She told me not to get used to that though. She said often when you're a grown-up, things go away and you don't get them back. You never get them back. I put my hands over my ears when she said that because I don't want it to be true.

Anyway, I don't want to think about that now. Mummy has made me a nice dinner tonight. It's on the table for me here, all red and yummy looking. Pasta with tomatoes and cheese, my favourite. She says she's sorry that she has been mean lately and that she is going to try harder. She doesn't eat any pasta herself, but she eats from her little blue bottle, one, two, three little pills. She says these ones are to help her be better. To care less.

I frown at her when she says that. I don't want her to care less, I want her to care more. I want her to care about me more, but I want her to care less about him and about them. I'm not sure she'll ever do that.

I start eating my pasta, the cheese tastes funny in my mouth, it sticks to my teeth. She's watching me.

'You know I didn't used to be like this, don't you?' she asks me. I freeze. I don't know what to say.

'I used to be different. I used to be like them. But when someone does this to you, it's hard to forgive. It makes you different.'

I still don't say anything.

'One day you'll understand,' she says, and she has one more pill, a little white one which she drinks with a glass of water. 'One day you'll want to help me.'

I still don't say anything. I don't know what she means.

After dinner, Mummy has to lie down in her bed, which means we don't go to the house. I sort of miss it, but I don't tell her that. I miss the bunny rabbits and the crawly worms and the rustle of the trees around me. Sometimes the rustles sound like whispers. The other day one of the bunny rabbits was out of its cage and I held my breath to see if it would come near me, but it didn't. I watched the way its ears twitched in the wind; I think maybe it knew I was there.

While Mummy lies down, I run myself a bath and get in, feel the water swallow me up. I put my head underneath the surface and blow bubbles, pretending to be a deep sea diver like we learned about at school. I'd like to be a deep sea diver, I think. I'd explore all the oceans and see all the fishes, and Mummy couldn't grab me and the bad man couldn't upset her and the money wouldn't matter because you don't need money in the sea. Everything is free.

14

Deadline day at the paper is always horrendously busy, and he has so much left to finish. His head is full of Corinne, how jittery she was on the car ride home from Mathilde's. Every time he'd looked at her she was staring at him anxiously, tapping her fingers on the side of the window like she does when she's nervous. When she's got something on her mind. He knows the incident with the rabbit was horrible – Christ, it freaked him out a bit too, but he knows she will latch on to it, think it is something more sinister than it is.

He had stared at the poor creature as they covered it with soil, wondered about who would go to the trouble of doing something so morbid, so macabre. He hadn't wanted to overreact so had tried to keep calm, even though the sight of it on his car like that had been unsettling to say the least.

Andy is making himself a coffee in the tiny kitchen, spooning granules into his Arsenal FC mug with the faded red logo emblazoned on the side. He looks rough, his chin stubbly, his eyes slightly bleary.

Dominic claps him on the shoulder. 'Good weekend?'

He looks up, shakes his head, a smile forming on his face.

'Late one last night.' He winks, jerks his head in the direction of the lower bank of desks, where Erin's blonde head is bent over her computer.

Dominic groans. 'Already?'

Andy holds his hands up in a gesture of mock defence. 'Hey, what can I say. She didn't seem to mind.'

The kettle clicks; he pours boiling water into his mug, slurps it quickly without bothering to stir.

'How's things with you? Had the morning off?'

'We went to my mother-in-law's. Only just got back.'

Andy snorts. 'Since when have you had a mother-in-law? Something you forgot to mention?'

Dominic frowns. 'No, well.' He shrugs and looks down, thrown a little. 'You know we're not … married, yet, but you know, whatever, we've been together so long we may as well be.'

'So why aren't you?'

'What?' Dominic feels a flash of annoyance. He wishes Andy would stop with the Corinne jokes.

Andy is raising his eyebrows, grinning like a Cheshire cat. 'Don't worry, mate, you don't need to tell me. Wouldn't catch me going down the whole ball and chain route.' He winks again and nods at Dom. 'I'm just winding you up, mate, you know I am. Jesus. Relax!'

Dominic looks away, out across the newsroom. He sees the peeling walls, the empty desks, the gaps that haven't been replaced. The only reason he and Corinne are not married is because they can't afford it; all the money they have has gone on IVF. He has always imagined that they will marry, in the future, has pictured the day in his mind. His mum wants them to, is always on at him about it. He doesn't think she realises how much a wedding costs these days.

'We will get married,' he says to Andy, 'we're not all of the wild oats variety. Go easy on the new girl, hey? She looks about twenty. Even for you, that's young.'

Andy stiffens slightly, as though Dom's words have touched a nerve. Dominic ignores this, reaches for the kettle, starts to refill it for himself. He feels his friend's eyes on his back for a moment, but by the time he has turned around Andy has gone, is making his way through the newsroom to his desk. He passes Erin's chair without stopping, and Dominic winces when he sees the look on her face. *And so it starts again. Another one down.*

Later in the morning, he passes Erin on the stairs. She looks a bit lost, slightly forlorn.

'Hey,' he says. 'How're you? Getting on OK?'

'Oh, Dominic,' she says. She looks relieved to see him. 'Sorry, I must look silly – I've got to go out on a job and I don't know where the cameras are kept. Are they around?'

'You'll get used to it,' Dominic says. 'This place is a bit of a shambles. Alison keeps talking about getting organised, but, well …' He shrugs, shows her to the cupboard where the reporters' cameras are stored. 'What's the story? Anything good?'

She takes one gratefully. 'Thanks, you're a lifesaver. It's the Claudia Winters sentencing today. I'm hoping to get a picture of her when she comes out. They think she might get life. You know she has another daughter too? Older. It's her I feel sorry for.'

113

Dominic shuts the cupboard door.

'I didn't know that. God, poor thing. Mother banged up and her sister dead, Christ. Rather you than me!'

Erin smiles at him. 'You really are a features guy. In a good way. What you working on today?'

'I'm trying—' they thread their way through the newsroom, back towards the desks '—I'm trying to write up a piece about Carlington House, a mansion just outside London. Alison's a bit obsessed with it. It's a big Georgian building that was damaged in the war, the owners are paying God knows how many pounds to fix it up again. Nice houses always attract readers though, especially round here. Sounds like there could be a bit more to it, as well. More interesting than the usual rich kids showing off their flats.'

'Oh?' She looks interested.

'Yeah, but I've lost my notes. I haven't finished writing it up and I need the boring stuff – dates, names, you know.'

'I do.' She smiles at him. 'Well, I'll leave you to it, then – you write your Georgian piece and I'll go try to snap some seedy shot of this woman.' She grimaces. 'See you later. Hope you find your notes!'

As she leaves him, Dominic catches Andy's eye from across the room. He is staring at them head on, not bothering to look away. Dominic stares back. What's the matter with him? Surely he can't be jealous. He's only talking to her!

He ignores Andy, begins to rummage through his desk, turning his drawers inside out. He can't remember the name of the architect that Warren had been going on about, or the date the house was built. He could try

Corinne, but he doubts she'll remember – that was the week they'd had the awful phone call from the doctor about the last IVF. She hadn't been herself.

Dominic sighs, cursing himself for being so careless. He will have to get in touch with Warren. He digs out the number, grits his teeth as he is placed immediately on hold.

'Dom? Dom, my man, how are you?' Warren's voice booms down the phone and Dominic winces.

'Hi, Warren, how are you? Sorry to call like this …' Dominic hesitates, he doesn't want to admit that he's lost his notes, it makes him sound foolish and underprepared. He decides to get straight to it.

'I was wondering if you could just remind me of a few details on the Carlington property? I missed a couple things the other day.' He tries to sound cheery, flippant, no big deal.

Warren laughs. 'You journos, what are you like! I said to my missus, I don't think the hack that came to visit had even heard of Robert Parler, but his little lady had. How is the lovely Corinne? Pretty thing you've got there, Dom, bit quiet mind, 'cept for when she screams, of course.' He chuckles. 'Still, feel free to bring her along next time, you know what they say about the quiet ones!' He guffaws to himself.

Dominic clenches his hand around the receiver. 'If I could just check a few facts, please, Warren?'

There is a woman's voice in the background, and a scuffling sound.

'Here's a thought, Dom, why don't you pop back over this afternoon? I've got the owner with me here today. Says she'd love to see your pics now the house is being

115

sold. Something to hold on to, I guess.' He lowers his voice. 'Poor bird can't afford to keep the place afloat. She's getting on a bit too.' He raises his voice to a normal level. 'Then you can firm up your notes, can't you. Sound good?'

Dominic hesitates. If he leaves now he can be there in half an hour and perhaps if he gets the owner involved it will get Alison off his back, which is always a bit of a bonus.

'Great, sounds good,' he says.

Dominic grabs his bag. On his way out, he hears the sound of laughter, the high tinkle of the work experience girl on the website team. Andy is leaning over her, grinning, and she is twirling a strand of hair around her fingers. The bright blonde of it glows in the office lights.

*

The imposing white ruins of Carlington House stare down at him, the sun behind slanting through the clouds, giving the building an ethereal glow. It doesn't look like much progress has been made, the windows are still black holes, the left side of the building is crumpled in on itself.

Warren sees him at once.

'Ah, if it isn't Dominic! Resident hack. Welcome back, welcome back. Just can't get enough of the place, can you? Now, as promised, here's the lady you need. Mind how you go with the old dear.'

Dominic groans inwardly at Warren's exaggerated grin. He can imagine him as one of the kids who went to the private school near where he grew up, the ones he and his friends crossed the street to avoid. The man is as up himself as they were.

Warren waves at a figure standing over near the house. She is walking slowly towards them; as she comes closer, Dominic realises how elderly she is, she is older than he'd expected. There is a slight lean to her walk, her body slopes a little to one side. When she reaches them though her eyes are clear, bright specks in her face. Dominic smiles at her.

Warren steps forward. 'Dom, this is Ms de Bonnier, current owner of Carlington, soon to be released! Pleasure to have you stop by, as always.' As he says this, Warren catches Dominic's eye, raises his eyebrows sarcastically as though the woman cannot even see him. Dominic feels a pang of sympathy for her but she is still smiling; if Warren has upset her she doesn't show it.

'Ms de Bonnier, Dom is the writer from London, from the *Herald*.' Warren makes his voice even louder and Dominic cringes inwardly; the woman is elderly but she's hardly senile. He doesn't have to talk to her as though she is a child.

'Dominic, hello.' The woman smiles, extends a hand to Dominic. It is small and dry, her fingers thin. There is no wedding ring.

'Good to meet you,' Dominic says. 'Amazing house. Readers are going to love it.'

'I hope so.' She looks up at the house. Her voice is soft, there is something sad in her eyes as her gaze flickers over the ruin. He sees her taking in the disrepair, the overgrown garden, the dust clouds that rise every time the builders make contact with the walls.

'I'm sure Dom here would like to ask you a few questions, check a few facts, if that's all right with you?' Warren butts in.

Ms de Bonnier glances at him, then back at Dominic. 'Are you here alone, Dominic?'

'Yeah,' Dominic says. 'I just wanted to have a very quick chat,' he adds. 'I can't stay long.' He is keen to reassure her, dispel any fears she may have about the press. Over the years he has become accustomed to it; no matter how innocent the story the public seem to panic, as though their distrust in the press is inherent in them, something deep inside which cannot be disproven.

'A quick chat is fine,' she says, looking at her watch. Her wrists are thin, fragile looking. 'I have to be somewhere soon but I can give you a bit of background. I appreciate you coming down.' She looks at Warren. 'The men know what they have to do.'

She turns away from Warren, begins to move slowly towards Dominic's car. Dominic almost wants to take her arm like he used to with his grandmother, there is something about her that makes him want to help her, to reach out. But she reaches his car, leans against the bonnet, taking a deep breath and briefly closing her eyes before opening them again and turning to look at him. Her gaze is clear.

Dominic clears his throat. 'So, Ms de Bonnier, sorry to stop by like this, I did come the other day and I think we're going to get a nice feature out of this. Got some great photos.' He smiles, trying to sound encouraging. 'It must be wonderful, having somewhere like this to call home. You've owned Carlington for … how long?' he asks.

She looks at him, opens her mouth briefly and closes it again, as though deciding what to say. For a moment she closes her eyes, tilts her head back. The lines in her neck are deep grooves in her flesh.

'Too long, really. Years now.'

'And I understand you're selling up?'

She smiles at him, puts a hand to her throat and pulls her coat around her a little more tightly. 'I can't afford to keep it, I'm afraid. I've never been able to afford it. It has to sell.'

She shifts slightly on the bonnet and winces, quickly. Dominic wonders if she is in pain, and if so, how much. As if reading his thoughts, she reaches down into a small black handbag at her hip and extracts a packet of tablets, popping two of them into her hand and sliding the remainder back out of sight. Dominic catches a glimpse of pink, the hint of a prescription label. He wishes he had some water to offer her, pictures the white pills growing warmer and warmer in her hand.

'It's a stunning place,' he says again, feeling awkward at her visible discomfort. 'It must be hard to let it go.'

She looks up at the building, gives a deep sigh.

'I used to think it would be. But I haven't lived here for years, you couldn't live in this place. It's a ruin. When it fell into disrepair I couldn't afford to pay, and now … I should have sold it years ago. I should never have been so weak.'

She breaks off. Dominic is horrified to see a shine to her eyes. Is she crying? He clears his throat, looks away to where the builders are scattered on the lawn. He thinks of Corinne, wonders what she is doing. She has always been good with elderly people; elderly people and children. She is one of the most caring people he has ever known.

'This place has to go.' Dominic looks back at Ms de Bonnier and her mouth has changed, it is set in a firm line, her lips pressed tightly together as though she is forcing herself to hold back emotion. 'It has to go,' she repeats.

'Finally. There's no reason to hold on to it any longer.' She pauses, swallows and looks back at Dominic. 'The de Bonnier family, don't tell me Warren hasn't told you, for I won't believe it,' she says, and laughs, a sad sort of laugh that sends a pang of sympathy to Dominic's heart. 'It's his favourite namedrop,' she continues. 'Loves throwing it into conversation. My father was a very wealthy man. Still, at least he's doing a good job on the house, although I can't say much for his personal skills.' She smiles at Dominic as though they are conspirators and he can't help but grin back.

'No, fair comment,' he agrees. She shifts again, as though she cannot get comfortable, and reaches her left hand up to her mouth, quickly swallows the two pills that have been nestling awkwardly in her hand. Dominic wonders what they are for – whether it's more than the usual gripes of old age.

'Arthritis,' she says, popping one into her mouth and grimacing. 'Excuse me.'

'I'm sorry,' Dominic says awkwardly, but she lifts her shoulders.

'Comes with my age, that's all.'

There is a beat of silence between them. Dominic clears his throat and is just about to speak when the woman opens her mouth.

'So he didn't tell you?' she says. She reaches up, touches her neck, feeling for something underneath her jacket. Dominic imagines a necklace, hidden beneath the layers. His own grandmother used to wear a silver cross, her fingers perpetually feeling for it like a touchstone.

'This house nearly ruined me.'

For a moment Dominic thinks he has misheard. There is a pause. The house seems to grow larger, burn more brightly behind them, a white backdrop to their conversation.

'You want a story? I put my heart and soul into doing this place up. I thought I was doing the right thing, that I'd do the de Bonnier family proud.' Her voice has taken on a funny edge, the words coming out of her mouth as though she is dredging them up from inside her. Dominic notices that her slender frame is shaking slightly, small tremors that she makes no effort to stop.

Dominic frowns. He isn't sure what to say, is taken aback by her sudden emotion. 'Sorry, I don't follow you – what ...'

She is looking away from him. He waits. She adjusts her coat, tightening the black belt around her waist. Her shaking frame is horribly thin beneath the wool. Dominic wonders whether she ought to be here.

'Ms de Bonnier ...' he starts, but she is placing her hands on either side of her, pushing herself upwards, her black boots hitting the gravel of the driveway.

'What does it matter, anyway. I'm a silly woman, I'm sorry. Ignore me, Dominic. What's done is done, isn't it? I've got to get on, I'm afraid. I hope your piece turns out well.' Her voice has become flat, the spark of emotion dying as quickly as it reared.

She is standing, now, staring at the house.

'I'm sorry, Dominic,' she says again, turning back to look at him. Her hair is blowing slightly in the wind, grey strands escaping into the white air. 'I'm sorry for being like this, I can't imagine it's what you were expecting.' She half laughs and Dominic feels another twist of sympathy. 'I'm just disappointed, that's all. This house could have been magnificent. Still, we don't always get what we want, do we?'

Slowly, she turns away from him, winds her scarf more tightly around her neck, leaves him where he is and heads in the direction of the house. One hand goes to her hip, as though it is hurting her, and Dominic imagines her features twisting in pain, the joints inside protesting as she walks. He remains leaning on the bonnet of the car, stunned by her behaviour. What was that all about?

Out of the corner of his eye, Dominic sees Warren turn and start to walk towards him and he hurriedly hops back into the car, starts up the engine. The car coughs then roars into life. He isn't in the mood to talk any more, is perplexed by the owner's reaction, her sadness when she spoke about the house. He imagines having to give up the flat he and Corinne share and shudders – he would hate it. It is their home, the home they have built together. He peels out of the drive, fumbling for his mobile as he does so. The battery's gone. Shit. A car screams past him and he slams on his brakes; he hasn't been concentrating and has veered too far across the highway. Dominic shoves his phone back in his pocket and rubs at his face. He needs to get home in one piece.

15

London

Ashley

When they get back from Mathilde's, Ashley sees there are dirty dishes left out and coats on the floor, which doesn't help her bad mood. The car journey was spent in near silence, punctuated only by Lucy on her mobile phone, Holly's minor tantrum and Benji's endless chatter about rabbits.

'The bunny was all yucky and red,' he told Lucy. 'All mangled up with one eye popping out, urgh.' He had pulled his eyelid down, revealing the red rim of his eye. Ashley snapped at him.

'Benji! That's enough. You'll hurt yourself. Stop it now, please.'

James goes straight to his office when they get back, leaves her in the house with it all to clear up, muttering something about finishing off a report due in Tuesday morning. Ashley bangs around the kitchen irritably, scraping congealed food into the bin, clearly the remnants of James's dinner before he came to Mathilde's. There is an abandoned glass with it too, she lifts it to her nose briefly and sniffs, the sharp scent of whiskey hitting her nostrils. Quickly she sinks both plate and glass into the hot water, submerges them in the bubbles, starts scrubbing fiercely.

As she scours, the telephone begins to ring. Ashley pauses, her hands covered by yellow Marigolds, the sink steadily filling with more water, multiplying the bubbles. Ring, ring. Clearly no one else is going to get it.

Her hand is slippery and wet on the white plastic. She has left the tap running.

'Hello?'

Nothing. Then breathing, slow at first and then faster, and the sound of laughter – unmistakably a woman's. Ashley feels her stomach go cold, as though her insides have turned to ice.

'What do you want?' she says, and her voice sounds ridiculous even to her own ears. 'Who are you? Why do you keep calling?'

There is still the laughter, and the rushing sound of the kitchen tap. The water is rising in the sink. Ashley feels something inside her break and before she knows what she is doing she is shouting into the phone.

'Do you want my husband? Is that it? Is that what you want?'

The plastic of the phone is threatening to splinter under her hand. The laughter continues, and suddenly Ashley is sobbing, tears are rolling down her cheeks, and her breath is coming hard and fast. In the back of her mind she knows she has to stop, she knows the children might hear, and just as she is thinking this the line goes dead. Ashley stands for a second more, stock-still with the receiver in her hand. Drips of water slide down her wrist and pool on the kitchen floor. Above her, she hears the sound of Holly beginning to cry.

Ashley puts the receiver back in its cradle, goes to the sink and turns off the tap with a shaking hand. Tears slide steadily down her cheeks. She removes her gloves, folds them neatly on the side, and goes to the foot of the stairs. Benji's voice floats down to her, punctuated by the sound of his video game. She has given up trying to ban it, is too tired to resist.

'Mummmm,' he shouts. 'Holly's crying! Mummmm. Baby's crying. Hellooooo?'

'I'm coming,' she says, but instead of replying to her son she whispers the words to herself, under her breath, trying to make herself go up the stairs. The wails continue. She listens for a few seconds, then puts her hand on the banister and starts to climb. Holly's room is on the right. Ashley goes left, down the corridor, to the second set of stairs. As she climbs, the wails get softer.

James's office is in the loft. When she gets there, the room is completely dark, sodden brown leaves cover the glass of the skylight and the overhead bulb is off. She hardly ever comes up here, can't remember where the switch is. Ashley puts her hands out in front of her, grabs the side of James's desk and feels for the mouse of his computer. She wiggles it and the screen jumps to life; a green glow illuminates the room.

Slowly, she sits down on the swivel chair, puts her fingers on the keyboard. They rest on the letters. Ashley has the sensation that they are not part of her at all, as though she is removed from her body, watching herself from above. Holly's cries come to her faintly. She should go to her. She has to go to her baby.

Her fingers begin to type words. *Ashley. AshleyandJames. Benji. Lucy15. Holly01. Parkway. JamesThomas. London.* Nothing works. Sweat dampens her shirt and she feels her upper lip moisten. She can see her own face reflected oddly in the computer screen, her hair standing strangely on end. The screen stares back at her, the cursor blinking. She feels as if it is mocking her. Frustrated, Ashley slams her elbows onto the desk, puts her head in her hands. *Think. Think.* The drawers. She slides her hands down, grips the handles of James's desk drawers, slides them open. It is still dark in the room, she bends forwards, peers at the piles of paper inside. Bills. Receipts. She squints at them in the half-light, her eyes scanning over the numbers, feeling more and more cross with herself. Why hasn't she kept a better eye on things? What kind of head-in-the-sand wife is she, blindly ignoring the bank account, trusting James with it all?

She keeps looking. More papers, the trailing cord of an iPad charger. What looks like one of Benji's drawings, a picture of a house, wobbly lines connecting windows, doors, a chimney. It is surrounded by a green square of a garden complete with white-tailed rabbits, a yellow cat and an almost-circular football. The crayons are faded, as though the drawing is old.

'Mum?'

Ashley's body gives a huge jolt, as though she has been electrocuted. Heart thumping, she slams both drawers shut and spins on the chair, is met with Benji's round little face. He looks upset, his lower lip is wobbling. She puts a hand to her chest, takes a slow, deep breath.

'What is it, my love?'

'Mum,' Benji says, 'I can't find Lucy.'

'What do you mean?' Ashley says. She presses the erase button to remove her latest attempt at guessing James's password, stands up and takes Benji by the hand.

'Holly's crying too,' Benji says. 'She won't shut up. What are you doing in Dad's room?' He follows her down the stairs.

'Nothing,' Ashley says. 'Just looking for something.'

'For what?'

'Nothing, Ben,' she tells him. 'Just something boring, that's all.' Why is it her children are so inquisitive? She squeezes her son's little hand, goes to Holly's cot and lifts her daughter out. She is hot, her face a mess of tears. Ashley feels a wave of guilt; what is the matter with her, leaving her baby to cry like that? Benji peers worriedly at his sister.

'Is she OK?'

'She's fine, Ben. She's just little. You were like this once!'

'Was I?'

'You were. Now what do you mean, you can't find Lucy? Isn't she in her room?'

Ashley taps on her daughter's door before pushing it open, snapping on the light. It is empty, the bed a mess of sheets, discarded clothes all over the floor.

'Luce?' Ashley calls. Her voice echoes around the house, bounces back at her. Holly is silenced by the sound, her little face stares into Lucy's empty room. Benji grips Ashley's skirt.

'We were playing,' he says. 'We were playing hide and seek but she's gone, I can't find her. I told you. I can't find her, Mum.'

Ashley frowns. She isn't worried; her daughter has been moody recently, is probably bored of entertaining her little brother. Still, it is cruel of her to do this to Benji.

'Lucy!' she shouts again, but the house is quiet. Her daughter's room has a funny smell, sort of stale. Ashley is never allowed in to clean any more. She feels a flash of frustration. When did she become a mum that followed her children's demands, instead of them doing what she asked?

'Come on, let's go downstairs,' she says. 'We'll find her.'

'I think she went out,' Benji says then, and Ashley stops, stares down at him. Holly reaches up, grabs at her neck.

'Ouch, stop it, Hol. She went out? When?'

'I don't know,' Benji says. 'I was counting to a hundred, and I got to eighty-nine and she said she was going, ready or not, and then she put on her coat and those pointy shoes you don't like. I know, because I looked through my fingers. I thought she'd come back but she didn't, and I didn't go out of the gate because you said I was never ever to do that because we might get hit by cars and be deaded.' He starts to cry then, hot little tears that trickle down his cheeks. 'Like the rabbit. You said, don't go out to the road "under any circumstances". That's what you *said*.' His cries become louder, snot begins to dribble from his nose.

Ashley sets Holly down and pulls him to her, strokes the top of his head. His little heart is thudding away. Where the hell is James when she needs him?

'You're right, Benji, I did say that, and it was very naughty of Lucy to go out without telling me,' she says. She closes her eyes and tries to keep calm, tries not to worry. This is typical teenage behaviour, she knows it is. She'll probably be back very soon, she's probably gone to meet Sophia from school, but Ashley wishes she knew where her daughter was, and she wishes it weren't quite so dark and cold outside, and she wishes most of all that James were here.

16

London

Corinne

I'm waiting for Dominic. The door is tightly shut, and I'm sitting in the kitchen, clutching the little yellow rocking horse in my hand. I don't know where else to go. I don't even want to go to Gilly's, she'll think I'm mad already. Or her lover might be there.

Every sound makes me jump out of my skin. Outside, the wind is howling; there's a storm coming, the radio said. Rain spatters against the windows, the sound echoing in the empty flat. When I was little I found the sound of rain comforting; now it feels like a threat.

He's late home from work. When it gets to seven, I call him again, but he isn't picking up, I get his voicemail. He could be driving, I suppose. The roads will be slippery; I don't want him to crash.

I put the horse on the side, get up and go to the window. A sudden clatter of sound hits me in the face and I start, propel myself away from the window as though something has touched me. But it hasn't – it's pebbles, dashing against the panes. Someone is throwing stones at our window.

My heart begins to jump. I look around the room, as though someone is going to appear, someone is going to help me, but of course I'm alone. Totally alone. The sound comes again; I see little grey stones rise against the glass, fall back. I strain my ears, and then I hear it, a shouting. Someone is shouting my name.

'Corinne! Corinne!'

A huge surge of relief hits me. It's Dominic. He's outside the window. It's just Dom!

I run forwards, yank up the sash. A gust of wind grabs the ends of my hair, lifts them up around my face. Water splashes my cheeks, the rain is coming down hard. I peer into the blackness of the night; try to see him on the street below.

'Dominic? Dom? Is that you?'

I run downstairs, my heart bumping in my chest. I push past an old woman who is bringing in her shopping, call out a rushed apology and fumble with the downstairs latch, open the door to the building and let him in. He is dripping wet, rainwater trickling from the ankles of his trousers, his shirt dark and sodden.

'God, sorry Cor,' he says, 'I've lost my keys, what a fucking moron. It's pissing it down out there.' He sniffs, shakes his head from side to side like a puppy. He seems oblivious to the fact that I've been scared half out of my wits. I stare at him, the rain pelting down behind us. I feel shaky, slightly sick.

He doesn't notice.

'Sorry I'm late,' he says when we get back upstairs. He kicks his soaking shoes off at the front door and goes to the fridge, opens the door and grabs a piece of salami from

130

within. 'Work was busy, my phone died and then I spent ages trying to find my keys in the office. Dunno what I've done with them, I'll have to get a new set cut tomorrow. Christ, look at me, I need to get changed.'

He takes a big bite of salami and leaves the kitchen, a trail of wet footprints in his wake. Did he not see my missed calls? I hear the sound of the shower being switched on, then him singing the theme tune to *Breaking Bad*, tone deaf like he always is.

I look behind me, at the kitchen counter where I left the little rocking horse. My mouth falls open. It isn't there. The surface is empty. The wooden horse has gone.

Then

One of the teachers talked to me today. Not in our classroom, on my own. In her special office. I didn't really like it in there, it smelled bad. Musty and old. I wanted to be out in the playground, in the fresh air. Still, at least this way I didn't have to worry about people not playing with me.

She crouched down so that she was looking right into my eyes, so that we were on the same level. I stared at the lines on her face, they're like Mummy's only worse. I think she's really old.

'Is everything all right at home?' she said to me. I could feel the hotness starting in my cheeks but I took a deep breath, pictured a nice blue swimming pool, which is a trick I taught myself for when I start to blush. It's really useful for when people ask you questions.

'I know – Dad's not around at the moment, is he?' The teacher smiled at me, tipped her head to one side. I think she was trying to be nice but I remembered how Mummy's hands felt digging into my shoulders, ouchie ouch, and so I zipped up my lips and I shook my head from side to side.

'If there's anything that's making you unhappy, I'd like you to tell me,' the teacher said, and I shook my head again, harder this time, and I pressed my lips together like they were stuck with superglue.

Then I realised she actually wanted me to speak so I unstuck them and I said:

'Fine. Everything at home is fine. Thank you.' And I gave her my best smile. And then I felt good, because I had got away with it. That was the best feeling; it lasted all the way through the day until I got home. Like a secret I had locked inside me.

132

When I got back to the flat, Mummy was sitting in front of the mirror, and there were loads of bottles and tubes in front of her. Like in art class. She said that it's time to get serious, and she started painting her face. Make-up. Red lips and dark eyes. I thought she looked lovely. I told her so but she just looked sad. I think I was annoying her so I went to play in the sitting room but after a while it got boring. I'm always on my own.

They aren't on their own, the people in the other house. We visited tonight and I saw them, very quickly, and they looked really happy and as though the game they were playing was a lot of fun. They were all sat together around a big table. He was there, he was laughing. The girls are older than me, their hair is long and their clothes look more grown-up than mine. I asked Mummy if she thought they might like to play with me and she laughed. It wasn't a happy sort of laugh though, it was a mean sort of laugh, and her painted red lips opened wide so I could see her teeth. I didn't like it. It made my tummy hurt.

17

London

Ashley

Lucy gets home at ten. By this time Ashley has tried her mobile over twenty times and is pacing the kitchen floor, her heart in her mouth. James is on his way back; Ashley managed to get hold of him about an hour ago and he said he would come straight home.

When her daughter falls through the door, Ashley feels a whirlwind of sensations: overwhelming relief, joy and anger. The combination makes her legs weak. She grabs Lucy by the shoulders, feels the slender bones beneath her fingers.

'Where the *hell* have you been?'

Benji is watching from the top of the stairs, his fingers in his mouth. Ashley buries her face in Lucy's hair for a second then pulls back, stares at her daughter. With a shock, she sees the way Lucy's eyes are out of focus, her skin blotchy. The smell of tequila hits Ashley, acidic and unpleasant. Lucy lets out a giggle, shortly followed by a hiccup. She's drunk.

Ashley tells Benji to go back to bed, brings her daughter into the living room and sits her down with a glass of water. Her skinny legs fold underneath her like Bambi.

'I need to know where you've been, Lucy,' she says. 'The reason we allowed you a key is not so you can go out at all hours without even telling me where you were going. I have no problem with you seeing your friends—'

Lucy giggles. Ashley isn't even sure if she is listening. She hates having to do this alone. Where the hell is her husband?

As if on cue, his key is in the lock and James walks in. Relief crashes over his features as he sees Lucy.

'Thank God for that! Jesus, Luce, you've had your mother all worried. You OK, Ash?'

Ashley stares at him. Anger pulses in her fingertips.

'Am I OK? No, James, I'm not OK! I've been worried sick about our teenage daughter for three hours and you swan in here, ludicrously late as usual, back from "work"—'

She is interrupted by a retching sound; Lucy is doubled over, strands of spittle dangling from her mouth, heading towards the cream of the living room carpet.

'Stop shouting,' Lucy says suddenly, her voice groggy. She lifts her head up from the floor, her eyes focus on her parents. 'Don't feel good.'

'No, I'm sure you don't, young lady,' James says. 'Are you going to tell us where you think you've been?'

Lucy smiles. Her mouth is smudged slightly, red lipstick filters into the skin around her lips.

'She told me not to tell you.'

18

Corinne

I wake up in the night, my body jerking. I can't relax, can't lie here knowing someone has been inside. I haven't told Dom anything yet, I didn't want to sound mad. He'll think I'm talking rubbish. But I can't keep still.

'Dominic,' I hiss. 'Dom! Wake up!' I shake his bare shoulder, he grunts and turns over in his sleep. I reach over, switch on the little bedside lamp. 'Dominic!'

This time he hears me. He opens his eyes blearily, puts a hand up to shield his face from the light.

'What time is it?' He squints at the clock and groans. 'God, Corinne, what are you doing? What's the matter?'

'Dom, please, listen to me for a minute. We need to get up, I need to look for something.'

He's still half asleep. I sit up straight and he yanks the duvet up so it's covering his face. 'Go to sleep, Cor, please. I've got work in the morning, I need to rest. Do whatever you need to do tomorrow, please, babe.'

I wait, stare at the hump of his back. He reaches out, switches off the light and tries to pull me close to him. I wriggle away. Fine. If he won't help me, I'll do it myself.

I grab my phone and flick on the flashlight. Leaving Dom asleep, I search the flat for the little rocking horse, turning out the drawers in the kitchen, shaking out the sofa covers, rummaging through the pile of clothes lying by our bed. Dominic thinks I'm going mad, and maybe I am. I can't understand how this happened; it was here, it was right here on the kitchen surface. I had it in my hand! I only left the flat for a few minutes, to let Dominic in. Could somebody have got inside? *Is someone hiding inside?* No. The thought feels as ridiculous as it sounds, plus, despite my efforts, I can find nothing out of place, nothing looks touched. I think of hands turning our door handle, fingers running over the surfaces. I feel cold, as though I cannot get warm.

I pace around the flat, go from room to room like an animal on the prowl. The doors and windows are tightly shut. I hear a faint sound, it sounds like a baby. I think of Gilly getting up in the night, soothing her child, stroking his forehead. Outside it's black, the moon shines into the kitchen, highlighting the blank work surfaces. I feel as though I am the only person awake in the world. There's a sudden cry outside; a horrible keening sound, and my heart leaps. I look down onto the street, see the flick of a fox scuffling round by the rubbish bins, the burnt orange of its tail just visible in the moonlight. It's scavenging. I know I won't be able to get back to sleep.

I go back into the bedroom, snap on the big light. Dom shifts and groans, but this time I ignore him. I feel jittery, wired. Why should I have to go through this on my own? If he thinks I sound mad, tough. I've got to tell him.

He sits up in bed, and I tell him about the rocking horse. He looks completely confused, his hair sticking up on end.

'Babe, I don't know what you're talking about,' he says. He's got that tired, grumpy look but I keep going, sit opposite him on the bed so that he can't lie back down.

'I'm telling you, Dominic, it was here! A little rocking horse, the one Dad bought me for the doll house when I was a child. I promise, I had it, someone put it on my pillow. Someone has been inside this flat.'

He's shaking his head. 'So you're telling me somebody came in, put a horse on your pillow, and then came back and took it away again? This isn't *The Godfather*, Cor.' He snorts to himself at his stupid joke and just for a flicker of a second a tiny bit of me hates him for not taking me seriously.

I swallow, trying not to snap at him. 'I don't know,' I say, 'I don't know where it's gone. I know how it sounds, but someone is threatening me, Dom. Think about it – think about the rabbit on our car. It was dead, Dominic. Killed. Think about what that might mean!' I break off, push the palms of my hands into my eyes. I want to go back to sleep, I want to wake up and all this have been a nightmare. I reach out and grip Dominic's hands, try again.

'I don't know why and I don't know who, but it's frightening me, Dominic. Please, try to listen, try to understand!'

He puts his arms around me, kisses me on the forehead.

'Shh, shh,' he says. 'OK, OK. Let's think this through. Who has all your dad's things now, who would have access to your old doll house?'

'I don't know!' I say. My voice is coming out high and squeaky. I hate whoever is doing this, whoever is playing games with me like I'm their little puppet on a string. Because somebody is. They must be.

'I thought Mum did,' I tell him, trying to stay calm. 'Last I knew they were in the attic, but they aren't— '

'How do you know?'

I pause. I'll have to tell him. 'I looked for them. When we were at Mum's.'

'You looked for them? When? Why didn't you say?'

'When you were asleep, I got up one night. I didn't want you to think – I thought you'd think I was being silly.'

Dominic exhales, runs a hand through his hair.

'Christ, Cor. You snuck up to the loft in the middle of the night?' He puts his head in his hands. 'Come on. Are you going to be roaming around the flat every night from now on?' He shakes his head. 'You loony!' He smiles at me; he's joking, he isn't taking me seriously.

'Dominic!'

'OK, OK. Sorry.' He holds up his hands. 'Look, do you want me to be honest? I think you're just panicking, you're thinking too much about the baby stuff, you're getting things a bit out of proportion. That's all. The dead rabbit – I know it was horrible, I do, but it wasn't a personal attack, babe. You heard your mum – sometimes that kind of thing happens in the country, it's just nutters! Nobody even knows us in Kent. And I'm telling you, no one's been inside the flat. Don't you think they'd take something a bit more valuable than a little wooden toy?!' He sighs, runs a hand through his hair. 'I mean, how would they even get in? Unless—'

He breaks off. I jump on it.

'What? Unless what?'

'Well …' He looks down at the bedclothes sheepishly. 'Nothing, nothing. I just … well, all right, I probably ought to find my keys. That's all. I've lost my keys, I mislaid them at work the other day, which you know, so yes, technically we ought to change the locks. But come on! I've probably dropped them, and they don't say our address on anyway. I'm not worried, Cor. And you shouldn't be either.'

He tugs on the end of my hair affectionately.

'Please, my love, stop looking so panicked! I think you need to take a test. I think that's what this is all about, really I do. Take a pregnancy test soon and we'll get it over with. And when we find out, well, we'll cross that bridge when we come to it. At least we'll know.'

He sighs, nudges me with his legs. 'I have to go back to sleep. You should too. Please, keep calm. Come here.'

He kisses me softly on the mouth. I hang on to him, not wanting him to turn out the light. I feel like I'm going completely mad.

19

London

Ashley

'She? Who is she?'

She is staring at her drunken daughter. Lucy is smiling strangely. Her head lolls forward onto her chest and Ashley sighs. She looks at James.

'This is pointless,' she says. 'I'll put her to bed.'

Together they half drag, half carry a comatose Lucy up the stairs to her bedroom, where Ashley undresses her gently, eases her out of the black leather skirt and replaces it with her daughter's purple pyjama shorts. She didn't know Lucy even owned a leather skirt. It is tiny, would barely fit one of Ashley's thighs these days.

How has she got so drunk? She thinks of her friend Aoife, saying the same thing about her own daughter. Perhaps it's not so unusual at fifteen, perhaps they have just been lucky up until now. Ashley feels a flash of her old worries; she'd had Lucy young, and for a while after she was born she'd felt a nagging sense of unease, as though motherhood was a job she wasn't quite qualified for. The feeling had dissipated over the years, but at times of uncertainty it rears its head. She tries to think back to herself at fifteen – was she drinking by then? Their father always warned them off it, told them horror stories about people whose lives had been ruined by alcoholism. ('No one ever got where they needed to be by becoming a lush. I didn't get where I am by drinking beer in a park, believe me.') As a teenager, the stories had scared Ashley senseless.

She told me not to tell you. Ashley thinks of her daughter saying the words, of the red lipstick blurring into her skin. She doesn't usually wear that colour. Who is *she*? Someone from a new group of friends? Something to do with boys? Ashley likes to think she knows most of her daughter's friends, is acquainted with their mothers through the high school. Lucy turns over in her sleep, emits a low groan. Ashley clears a space on the side table next to the bed, pushing aside a packet of chewing gum and a little pile of coins. She places a glass of water and two paracetamols down so Lucy will see them when she wakes and tiptoes from the room, back to where her husband is waiting downstairs.

'I'm sorry you had to deal with that, Ash.' He looks utterly exhausted, dark bags circle his eyes. 'Who d'you think she meant?'

She shrugs. 'I don't know. She never mentions anyone to me any more. I mean, if it was one of the girls from school why wouldn't she just say? I can't say I like the idea of whoever it is, she can hardly be a good influence, can she?'

'I suppose not,' he says. He sinks down heavily on the sofa, rubs his eyes with his hands.

'Work busy, then?' She wants to see what he will say.

He looks immediately uncomfortable. 'It's a … it's a bit of a nightmare. Do you mind if we don't talk about it for now?'

'Were you at work, James?'

He looks up. 'Not this again. Of course I was at work! Where do you think I've been, out on the town?'

As he speaks, she hears it; the slow, steady whine from upstairs. Holly is crying. They stare at each other. The sound gets louder and louder, more and more intense.

'I don't know what's the matter with her,' Ashley says. 'She's getting worse.' A headache stretches itself across her temples, she feels teary. Holly's crying increases.

'I'll go,' James says, and he exhales, sighs as though she ought to be grateful, she ought to thank him for this one sacrifice, this one occasion when he will see to his daughter. *Their* daughter. Ashley puts a hand to her forehead, thinking of herself hunched over his computer screen, tapping madly at the keys, rummaging through his drawers. She hates this. She hates it so much.

'James, I don't—' Ashley is about to say more when there is the unmistakable sound of vomiting from upstairs, the sound of liquid hitting the floor. Seconds afterwards, the crying gets louder.

Ashley groans. 'I'll go.' She leaves her husband sitting in the living room, his head in his hands, his back bent over like that of a much older man. Upstairs, she bends over her daughter's cot. She is burning up, her face a screaming ball of tears. Her little body is twitching, her legs jerking under the covers. Why is she so upset? It seems her nightmares are getting worse, she is finding it harder and harder to sleep for more than an hour or two at a time. Shouldn't it be getting easier? It did with Lucy and Benji. Ashley strokes her daughter's little face, murmuring to her. It is her baby's eyes that frighten her;

they are big, staring. If she didn't know better Ashley would say they look terrified.

'What are you dreaming, my love?' she whispers, and she lifts Holly up, puts her over her shoulder, rocks her gently until at last the sobs begin to quieten down.

*

The next morning, Lucy's skin is green. Benji is fascinated by it, if not ecstatic.

'An alien! Mum, look! Look at Lucy's face. She's an alien!'

'Darling, stop it,' Ashley says. 'Lucy's fine, she's just not feeling very well is all.' In spite of everything, she stifles a smile, turns away from Benji to pour milk into his cornflakes.

Lucy groans. 'I think I'm going to be sick again.'

Ashley is biding her time, waiting until her daughter feels better. There is no point questioning her when she is in the grip of her first real hangover.

'Now, Daddy's taking you to school today so be good, won't you, Benji,' she tells her son, placing the bowl of cereal in front of him. 'I'll be back when you get home this afternoon.'

'Lucy.' She turns to her daughter, who is sitting motionless in front of a plate of untouched eggs. She is still wearing her pyjamas. Ashley has not got the heart to make her go to school and there is another part of her, a part she doesn't want to admit to, that is worried about what people will think if she sends her daughter in reeking of alcohol. She can't imagine the response would be good.

'Lucy, drink lots of water, please. Make sure Holly doesn't cause a racket, check on her, please. She's been crying a lot lately – if she starts, call for Dad. And ask him for some more paracetamol if your head's bad. I think there might be some Alka-Seltzer in the bathroom cabinet.' She pauses. Lucy is silent. 'We'll talk later. I've got to get to Colours. If all else fails, go back to sleep.'

Ashley ruffles her son's hair, bends down to kiss Holly, picks up her handbag and goes to the foot of the stairs. James is up in the study. He has miraculously agreed to work from home this morning, Ashley has to do her shift at the café. Megan has covered for her more than once and she doesn't want to appear rude. Besides, there is a side of her that wants to get out of the house, wants to immerse herself in the easy world of Colours, away from her hungover daughter and her unreachable husband. She has had so little sleep, the kitchen feels too tight, as though it is closing in around her like an elastic band.

'James? James, I'm going! Come see to Holly!' she shouts. She is met only with a grunt. Ashley is about to call again when she hears the phone start to ring. Her heart skips a beat.

'Phoneeeee,' Benji says through a spoonful of cornflakes. 'Phone, phone, phoneeeee.'

James appears at the top of the stairs. Ashley stares up at him. The phone continues to ring but nobody reaches for it.

'I'm going to work,' she says, 'Benji needs to get to school, make sure he takes his reading folder. OK? And you can drop Holly off at June's around lunchtime; I've told her to expect you around twelve. I'm going to make an appointment at the doctor's for Hol, make sure there's nothing wrong. Lucy's having a day at home.' She pauses. 'Think you can manage all that?'

Ashley can feel her children looking at her, can almost sense their surprise at her tone. She feels her cheeks getting warm but ignores their stares, keeps her eyes focused on James. He nods.

'Sure. Of course. Have a good morning at the café.'

There is a brief pause; the phone stops ringing and the kitchen falls silent. Holly gurgles. James sighs. Ashley makes a split decision; she slings her bag over her shoulder and swiftly clicks open the front door. James is a grown man. He can handle the children, and he can handle the phone. As she walks away down the street she can hear the shrill of the telephone start up once again from inside the house, before the sound is replaced by the tap of her own footsteps, taking her further and further away.

Then

I'm so bored! I hate being by myself all the time. I hate not having proper toys to play with. I hate not having a Dad who will pick me up and swing me around like Jenny at school's does, or a brother who will ruffle my hair and give me stickers to trade. I hate not having a sister who will share her gel pens or a dog that will jump up at me when I get home from school. People on the TV have those things. And so do the people at school. All I have is Mummy, and most of the time she doesn't even like me.

Today, she took me to the house first thing in the morning, really early, even before school. She said she hadn't been able to sleep, that she was scared something might have happened at the house. She said she had to know something important. I wriggled through the gap in the fence, but I was so sleepy, I still felt like I was in my dream. I looked up at window number three (that's what I call it anyway) and saw him with her, and she looked the same as she normally does. I said that to Mummy.

'Not different?' she asked me. 'Not bigger? Rounder?' She gestured to her own stomach, made a curving shape. 'Did she look like that?'

I shook my head no. 'She looks the same as always, Mummy.'

I think that was the right answer; Mummy took a big breath as though she had been holding it, then she took hold of my hand and said she'd make me a special breakfast before school, because I had been such a big helpful girl. We had eggs and soldiers. It was nice, but then when I got home from school in the afternoon, she left me on my own.

I really didn't like it. The flat felt too big for me even though really it's small, it felt like it was swallowing me up. I tried playing a game by myself, going into the different rooms and counting the furniture, counting the lights, counting everything. None of it worked. I felt frightened.

She put on a lot of red lipstick and said she was going to him. I watched her in the mirror, her hands were a bit shaky like an old person. She made her eyes look all sparkly and put her hair up in a clip.

'This is how I used to look,' she told me. 'This is why he fell in love with me.'

I asked her how long she would be and she told me she'd be as long as it takes. I don't know what that means. I don't know why we need him to be here so badly.

It's been three hours now and I'm getting hungry. The fridge smells a bit funny when I open the door. The flat is so quiet. I think about their house and I wonder what they are doing. At least they're together. I wish I was there. I can't stop thinking about the playground, what happened yesterday at school.

Someone asked me at break time if my mummy has a boyfriend. I didn't know what to say so I waited a bit.

They asked me again. It was Natasha from class, she was twirling a strand of hair around her fingers and she looked at me sideways, like she was trying to catch me out.

'She has an old boyfriend,' I said eventually. 'He's going to be her boyfriend again soon. He's going to come back to us.'

I was repeating what Mummy said so I knew it was right, but it didn't seem to satisfy Natasha, she covered her mouth with her hand and giggled. The sound pierced through my ears, made me want to run, burrow my way through the hole in the fence and stay very very still. I've started to feel safe there now, it's weird. I used to hate it but now it's the place I sort of feel at home. Even though I know it's not our home, not really, it's theirs, but still I like the feeling of being there, down in the grass, looking at the warm golden windows, seeing them all safe inside. Last week I found an old tennis ball resting in the grass, all soft and soggy like the air had gone out of it, but I slipped it in my pocket and took it home with me. Mummy doesn't know. I like it, it's like a little bit of them with me in my room.

'Oh yeah?' Natasha said. 'And when is this old boyfriend going to come back?'

'Soon,' I said. 'He wants to come back. He wants to come back very much.'

She was still laughing. I knew there was something wrong with what I was saying but I didn't know what. I could feel my cheeks getting hotter and hotter and suddenly I felt it, a flash of anger, a little spark of rage that lit up inside me and started to burn.

'Why are you laughing?' I asked her, and she just carried on, higher and higher, louder and louder. I clenched my fists into balls at my sides. My fingers all started to hurt.

20

London

Corinne

In the morning, Dom wakes up late. I can tell he's annoyed with me for going on at him all night. I sit on the side of the bath, watching him shave quickly. He swears as the razor nicks his skin.

'Shit!' He glances at me, meets my eye in the mirror.

'I'm sorry!' I say. 'I've said I'm sorry, Dom. It's not like I had a great night's sleep either.' I'm so tired that my eyes hurt.

He drinks his coffee too fast, gulps it down and hands me the cup. 'I've got to get to work.'

I must look upset because he relents a bit, sighs. 'Sorry,' he says, 'I'm just tired. I know you're stressed out – I know you are. But you've got to try to stop worrying, Corinne. Nobody is out to get you.' He leans in, kisses me. I taste the coffee on his tongue.

'Give me a call if that rocking horse decides to show itself, OK?'

I don't answer. He thinks it's a joke. There's a tiny piece of tissue paper stuck to the blood on his cheek where he caught himself with the razor but I don't tell him, just say that I'll see him later on. The door bangs shut behind him and I get up from the table, go over to it and slam it again, slide the silver bolt all the way across. I'm not taking any more chances.

When I'm sure Dom's gone down the stairs I search the flat again, one more time, kneel down on the floor and check under the cupboards, under the fridge, behind the sofa. My eyes meet nothing but dust.

I go to the dresser, pull open the first drawer. My fingers catch on staples as I push paper aside, then my hands grasp wood. I pull out the little blue door and the chimney. There is a sharp pain in my index finger and I yelp and wince; my finger has caught on the nail sticking out of the little door. I drop everything, close my other hand around the cut but not before a few drops of blood have fallen onto the dresser, bright scarlet pinpricks that soak into the wood. I stare at them without blinking until my eyes begin to tear. The cut deepens, I peer at the skin, see the white folds of it parting to reveal the pink flesh beneath. I ignore it and pick up the objects again, twist them from side to side, hold them to the light. Then I shove them back into the darkness, pile newspaper on top of them, pushing them down and down into the black.

I sit down at the kitchen table, racking my brain. I think of finding the little chimney lying in the doorframe, seeing the blue door on my desk. I screw up my eyes, picturing the last time I saw the doll house, in our big living room with the French windows. Someone must know. There is somebody out there who knows where that house is.

I pick up the phone. Enough is enough. It's time to call my mother.

21

Ashley

She's made a doctor's appointment for Holly for this afternoon. Ashley rings June, tells her she will come collect Holly a bit early.

June sounds concerned. 'Is everything all right?'

'Yes, yes,' Ashley says. 'Nothing to worry about, just a check-up, I think she seems a bit unsettled. James will drop Hol off around lunchtime but you don't mind if I come pick her up early, do you?' She pauses. 'I can stop at the shops for you if you need. Can I get you anything?'

'That's fine,' June says, and her voice sounds a little strange, taken aback. Ashley worries she's offended her by suggesting a shop-run, she doesn't want June to think she is treating her as someone who is too elderly to make it herself.

'I mean, I'll be passing the shops, that's all,' Ashley says, but June says no, she has everything she needs.

Halfway through the Colours lunchtime rush, Ashley is cutting two extra-large slices of coffee cake for a pair of women when she feels her mobile buzz in her pocket. She pops a small sliver of cake into her mouth and immediately feels guilty, as though the waistband on her jeans has tightened within seconds.

'Excuse me,' she says, laying down the knife and slipping to one side, motioning to Megan to finish serving them. She watches the women nudge each other and make eyes at the creamy slabs of cake.

'There goes my diet!'

She smiles to herself and presses the phone to her ear. The smile vanishes as the voice of Benji's headmistress cuts through the happy warmth of the café, telling her to come collect her son *right this instant*.

Ashley bridles, feeling as though the bossy headteacher has spat at her, and puts on her best regal voice, an old speciality of her mother's.

'What *exactly* seems to be the problem, Mrs Armitage?' she asks.

'I'm afraid we've had a bit of an issue in class today,' the head says. Her voice is nasal, slightly smug as though she's enjoying making the call. 'Benji got a bit angry in his Maths lesson, Mrs Thomas. He's not usually a violent child but …'

Ashley swallows. Why is the bloody woman dragging it out?

'Yes?' she says. She can feel Megan looking at her worriedly from behind the café counter.

'Well, I'm afraid Benjamin kicked another little boy named Oscar,' Mrs Armitage says. 'In the left shin. As I'm sure you understand, this kind of behaviour is not tolerated in the classroom, or anywhere else for that matter. We've had a word with Benji, of course, but I feel it would be best if you could come to collect him. The other little boy is really quite upset.' She sniffs disapprovingly.

Ashley sighs. *Oscar.* The name conjures up a vague image of a snotty-looking child prone to major parts in the Christmas plays. She bets he's milking it.

'Mrs Thomas?'

'I'll be there straight away,' Ashley says, gritting her teeth. It is very unlike Benji to be badly behaved.

She hangs up and gestures to Megan, who is halfway through cutting a slice of pecan pie.

'Megs, I'm so sorry, that was the school. I've got to go get Benji, seems he's been acting up.' She pulls a face but Megan waves a hand.

'No worries, Ash. Kids come first! I think I can cope with cake and coffee.'

As she drives to the school, Ashley's mobile vibrates again. She glances at the screen. Unknown number. Her chest tightens. The screen lights up and goes dark, lights up and goes dark. Ashley's fingers grip the wheel. She isn't going to answer. Her eyes are not on the road, they slide towards the mobile lying on the passenger seat and a car horn blares at her. She jumps, looks up to see a big Range Rover roaring past, the blurry outline of a middle finger raised at her through the window. She has to concentrate. The mobile stops vibrating, lies silently beside her, as though its job is done.

At school, thoughts of the phone fly out of Ashley's head as she hurries along the corridors to where her son is standing. Benji is contrite, red-faced, in the hallway outside the teacher's office. His laces are undone, and his little white shirt is untucked. Ashley feels her heart melt, tries and fails to administer a disapproving face. She crouches down and brushes the strands of hair from her son's eyes. He will not meet her own, looks steadfastly at the linoleum floor, his dark eyelashes curled against the fullness of his childish cheeks.

'Hey,' she says, softly, keeping her voice light. 'What's up, buddy?'

The door behind her opens and Mrs Armitage steps out. Ashley, squatted on the floor, sees the black court shoes and nylon tights appear next to her and rises hurriedly to her feet, placing a hand on the top of Benji's tousled head. The teacher makes her feel instantly inadequate.

'Ah, Mrs Thomas.' The head's mouth is set in a thin, straight line, her lips almost invisible. 'Thank you for coming in. I'm afraid I'm going to have to ask you to take your son home for the day. I think it's best he settles down outside of the school environment.'

Ashley straightens up, wishing the hemline of her blouse didn't have a smear of cake on it. Standing in front of the teacher, she feels a wave of humiliation, and is horrified to find her throat flushing red, embarrassment making her whole body feel hot.

There is a tug on the bottom of her shirt and she looks down into her son's large eyes. He looks helpless and she feels a pang of sympathy shoot through her. Ashley takes a deep breath, tries to compose her thoughts. She takes Benji's hand firmly in her own, gives his damp palm a little squeeze.

'I'm very sorry there's been trouble, Mrs Thomas,' she says. 'I do hope Oscar is recovering. I'll speak to my son at home and find out what's the matter. I have to say—' she glances at Benji '—I can't really imagine my son doing this unless provoked.' She raises her eyebrows, tries to keep her voice calm.

The head's face is horribly smug. 'I'm afraid there's no excuse for violence, Mrs Thomas.'

'No, of course not,' Ashley says. 'I wasn't suggesting there was.'

There's a pause. Clearly the head isn't going to back down.

'Well.' Ashley gives her son's hand another squeeze. 'We'll be going home now.'

'I do think that's best, really,' the teacher says, looking down at Benji as though she is looking at a soon-to-be criminal rather than a small boy with a plaster on his knee. 'We'll see Benji tomorrow when he's calmed down a bit.'

They walk out to the car in silence. Ashley waits as Benji buckles up his belt, his little hands fumbling with the red and black lock. She starts the ignition and holds off until they are a few roads away from the school before gently asking her son what happened.

His face is blotchy; she can tell that he is still angry. He mumbles something incoherent under his breath, and she slows the car down so that she can hear him over the noise of the accelerator.

'Ben, I can't hear you. What?'

He mumbles again.

'Benji, I can't hear you if you have your hand over your mouth. Tell me what the matter is, please.'

'Oscar said a bad word about Lucy,' he says.

Ashley frowns. 'What kind of bad word?'

Her son shakes his head, playing with the seat belt. Ashley stares over at him, the way his hair curls around his ears, the childish swell of his limbs. She thinks of the drawing she found in James's desk; faded colours, imagination on the page. He is just a child. He is her baby. How can he be in trouble?

'I don't want to say.'

'I'm giving you permission, Ben. Just tell me, please.'

He looks at her and his rosebud mouth forms the word 'slut', in a half-whisper, accentuating the 't'. Ashley can't help herself; she gasps in surprise and her foot catches the brake pedal. The car jolts.

'Sorry.' She puts her hands quickly on the steering wheel, in the ten and two position, steadying herself and the car. Benji's cheeks are red, his voice is wobbly and small.

'I didn't know what it meant but he said it in a mean voice so I kicked him. I'm sorry, Mummy.'

His eyes are very big and wide. She feels sick.

'It's OK, Benji, but you mustn't ever use violence, even when people say very bad things like that. OK, you promise me?'

He nods.

'I don't want you to ever use that word either, Ben, OK? And you aren't to tell your sister about this. What that boy said was silly and it wasn't true. So the best thing to do with people like that is to ignore them. OK?'

'OK.'

They continue to drive in silence. Ashley's head is spinning, her heart is hammering uncomfortably in her chest. How can an eight-year-old even know this word? And, more importantly, how does an eight-year-old boy know anything about her daughter?

She glances at her watch. James will have gone to work. They may as well call at June's now, Holly's doctor's appointment isn't far off and maybe they can be seen early.

As they pull into the driveway, Ashley notices another car sitting beside June's little Renault Clio. The other car seems oddly too large, out of place among the suburban gravel. She parks, unfastens, hurries to June's front door.

When June opens the door she looks flustered. Ashley stands back slightly, embarrassed.

'Sorry, hi, June. I had to grab Benji from school a little early as it turned out so I thought I may as well collect Holly now too, take her to the doctor's like I mentioned earlier. That OK? How're you?'

'Of course, of course,' June says. 'Sorry, dear, I just wasn't expecting you this minute. Holly's just down for a nap, I'll get her.'

The door remains half closed as June disappears into the house. Ashley hovers on the doorstep, trying to peer inside.

'Shall I … shall I come in?' she calls.

In seconds, June is back, Holly in her arms, wrapped in a fleecy purple blanket with her Frozen socks on.

'Here we are, she's been a very good girl today. I hope all goes well at the doctor. All right then!'

'Thanks, June. Is there someone here?' Ashley asks, taking her daughter from the older woman's outstretched hands. Usually she'd be inside, sometimes having a quick cup of tea at June's kitchen table, but today it's as though she can't wait to be rid of her.

'No, no, well, just the plumber.'

'The plumber?'

'Yes, I've been having some trouble with the heating, that's all, silly me, it's probably just a case of flicking a switch but I can't seem to get it right! The chap's upstairs now, having a quick look.'

'Oh, I'm sorry,' Ashley says, 'I hope you're keeping warm enough!'

'Don't worry,' June says, 'Holly's been lovely and tucked up all afternoon, she's not got a chill on her. That's not what you're at the doctor's for, is it?' She looks so worried that Ashley feels bad, she reaches out to touch June's arm.

'Oh, no, June, I wasn't suggesting it's anything to do with you! I was meaning I hope the heating gets fixed for yourself!' Ashley says. 'If you ever need anything doing round the house just let me know and I can send James over. I know he wouldn't mind helping you out. You do such a lot for us, with Hol.'

June smiles, the creases around her eyes deepening. Ashley thinks how pretty she must have been when she was younger. She has a sudden urge to take June's hand; she hates to think of her being cold in the house.

'That's very kind,' June says, and she reaches out, chucks Holly gently under the chin. 'It's a pleasure looking after this little one. I'm sure the man will get the heating sorted in no time. I'd better go take him some more tea – I'll see you on Thursday. Let me know what Doc says.' She has kept the door half closed for their whole conversation, and now she begins to push it to. Something in her movements seems jittery, nervous, but Ashley cannot work out whether she is imagining it or not.

'Thursday,' Ashley repeats, nodding, and she is about to say more when the front door of June's terraced house shuts firmly in her face. For a second she and Holly stand on the doorstep, her daughter's heartbeat thudding against her own. Then there is a beep; Benji is leaning on the car horn. Ashley turns back to her car, noticing as she does so

159

that Holly's nappy is warm and wet. She feels a pang of dismay. June is usually so good with Holly; perhaps she's been distracted by the plumber. Ashley kisses Holly on the forehead; June is right, she is very warm. Not cold at all. She'll change her nappy when they get to the surgery.

Benji's face back in the car reminds her of everything all over again, all of it hitting her like a punch to the gut. *Slut. Slut. Slut.* The word reverberates in her head as they drive to the doctor's, so loudly that Ashley is almost surprised her children cannot hear it too.

'What are we doing?' Benji says.

'I've got to take Holly in to see the doctor quickly,' Ashley tells him. 'Do you want to come in? Or wait in the car?'

'Car,' Benji says, and he leans down in his seat, pulls his Game Boy out of his pocket. Ashley pulls the car into the doctor's car park, noticing as she reaches for the handbrake that her hands are shaking. Inside, she unfastens Holly's nappy, changes her daughter quickly. Her face is warm, her eyes large in her face.

When they are shown in to see the doctor Ashley feels a bit silly. Is she being a fussy mother?

'What's wrong with your little one?' Doctor McPherson has been treating their family for a few years, Ashley likes him. He is calm, efficient. Everything you'd want in a doctor.

'Oh, well, I don't think it's anything much really,' Ashley says. 'It's just … it's just she has these… well, I think they're nightmares. Proper screaming fits, and I know all babies cry, of course they do, but this just, well, it feels different. She exhausts herself, almost every night, and she has this

160

look on her face, as though she's scared, as if she's seeing something I can't.' She gives a little laugh. 'Sorry, that probably sounds like rubbish.'

'Not at all,' the doctor says. 'Let's have a look at her.' He places Holly on the bed and examines her, Ashley biting her lip behind him.

'Does she move around, when she cries?' the doctor asks. 'Almost as though she's having a fit?'

'Yes!' Ashley says. 'It's horrible actually, she looks as though she's in pain.'

He nods. 'And you say you notice her eyes?'

'They stare,' Ashley says. 'Like she can't see me, like she's seeing something else. I don't know.'

'How long has this been going on for?'

Ashley tries to think. 'I don't know, maybe – six months? It didn't happen when she was very young, when I had her full time. We take her to a childminder now, just a few times a week.'

'Hmm.' Doctor McPherson looks up at Ashley, adjusts his glasses on his nose. 'I don't think it's anything to worry about. Night terrors, most likely. Have you been doing anything out of the ordinary? Has she met anyone new, done anything different?'

Ashley shakes her head. 'No. The only people she's ever really with are me, June and the children. And James. When he's around.'

The doctor narrows his eyes. 'Is everything OK at home?'

Ashley nods, horrified to find that her eyes are beginning to blur. She can't cry here. She has to keep it together.

Sensing her discomfort, Doctor McPherson hands Holly back to her, turns his back to wash his hands. Ashley breathes in her daughter's comforting smell.

'The only thing I would say,' the doctor says as he dries his hands on a blue paper towel, and Ashley's ears instantly prick up. 'The only thing is that she seems a little floppy, a tiny bit on the lethargic side. I don't think it's anything to worry about, as I said, I think it's probably a very basic side effect of being up all night. She's exhausted herself, most likely.' He pauses, looks at Ashley over his glasses. 'What I might do is a little blood test, nothing major, just to rule everything else out.' He sees Ashley's face and raises a hand in the air, smiling. 'Please, Mrs Thomas, I must reassure you that I'm only covering all bases because we have to. I think your daughter is absolutely fine. We can take a quick sample now and have the results in a week or so.'

Ashley swallows. She hates the thought of her baby being tested, of a needle piercing Holly's flesh.

'OK,' she says. 'OK, if you think that's best.'

'I do.' Doctor McPherson smiles. 'If you take Holly through to the nurse room next door, one of the practitioners will be with you to quickly take a sample. For now, though, I'm going to prescribe some medicine, nothing major, just to try to help her sleep through,' the doctor says. 'For your sake as much as hers. You must be exhausted.'

He scribbles down a prescription, hands it to Ashley. 'And just keep an eye on her, check she isn't being exposed to anything she shouldn't – I don't know, your son's videogames, your daughter's phone – anything out of the ordinary. But I should think Holly will be fine. Night terrors are fairly common. Try not to worry.'

Ashley nods and smiles, thanks the doctor. Holding Holly tightly, they go through to the nurse room. The nurse is jolly, chattering to them almost without pause as she readies the needle, her hands encased in white gloves. Ashley closes her eyes as the nurse slips the needle into the pale flesh of Holly's tiny arm, counts to five in her head. Holly cries, the sound breaking Ashley's heart. Ashley cuddles her close as soon as it is over, stroking the top of her head until she calms down. She knows she's being silly – the doctor hadn't really seemed worried. They will have the results soon. It is always best to be thorough. She picks up her handbag and heads for the door with Holly, her mind racing, then collects the little bottle of medicine from the pharmacy outside. Her heart is beating fast. Has her daughter been exposed to anything odd? She doesn't think so.

Back in the car, Benji looks up. He looks contrite. She drives them home, hangs up Benji's coat and his red reading folder and tells him that he can play outside and she will make him some squash. She lays Holly down upstairs, pulls the covers gently over her little frame. Her daughter snuggles in against her pillows, her little face calm. Her eyes are closed, the lashes sooty against her skin. Ashley's heart swells with love. Thank God it is nothing more serious. Night terrors. That's what he said. She repeats the words to herself, trying not to think about the needle piercing Holly's soft baby skin.

Lucy is lying on the sofa, asleep, with a blanket thrown over her legs. She looks so young; mascara from the night before is smudged around her eyes and there is a half-drunk glass of water by her side. Ashley doesn't really want to wake her, needs her daughter to sleep it off so that she can get some sense out of her, find out what possessed her to get drunk last night and do God knows what.

She isn't sure what to do. She wants to call James but he's left a note by the key bowl saying he is at work this afternoon, surprise surprise. Why is it he is never here when she wants him?

The thought of her daughter being used as playground gossip makes Ashley's blood boil, makes her want to tear up to the school like a madwoman. She doesn't know where this Oscar creature can have heard such a thing, can only assume it is through the older teenagers; the high school is across the road from the primary. Lots of siblings attend both, she imagines news travelling like wildfire.

Ashley sees in her mind the mothers whispering in the playground, their glossy lips parted like birds' beaks, *Is everything alright at home? It's just, we've heard* … She sees a glimpse of Benji through the window, kicking a deflated football across the garden, the sad shape of it bouncing across the fence. He looks up at her and Ashley waves at him quickly, forces a smile onto her face. At the sight of her, he brightens, runs to the ball and kicks it into the air. She loves him for defending his sister.

Ashley takes a deep breath, tries to think. She has to speak to Lucy. Can she probe Benji for more information? A burst of anger bubbles up inside her. How did they ever find themselves here, at this point?

She thinks again of her son's little face repeating the horrid word and her stomach churns. Ashley's body moves as though she is a puppet on a string, up the stairs of the house, and then her hand is on Lucy's doorknob and she is pushing open the solid white door. There are posters tacked to the wooden panels, and Blu-tack marks where their corners have peeled upwards. She isn't sure what she is looking for when she bends down and pulls out the drawers underneath Lucy's bed. They are stuffed with clothes, hastily crumpled skirts and shoes with dirty heels, a pair with the nails poking through the bottom. They need to be re-heeled or thrown away. As she searches, she thinks to herself that this is the second time in a week that she has rummaged through drawers that are not hers. What is the matter with her? Doesn't she know her family at all?

Sitting on the bed, she moves her hand mechanically towards her daughter's bedside drawers, trying to ignore the feelings of guilt. Bottles of nail varnish are lined up on the top of the drawers, red, pink, gold. Her iPhone charger trails across the floor.

Carefully, Ashley reaches out, opens the top drawer of Lucy's bedside cabinet. She has no idea what she is looking for. In moments like this, panic starts to creep at her insides; she is younger than most of the other mothers, maybe she doesn't know what she's doing, doesn't know what's normal. She pushes the thoughts away. Inside the dark of the drawer, Lucy's contact lens case sits neatly with a bottle of solution. The green and white plastic eyes look at Ashley, unblinkingly, accusingly. She slams the drawer shut and makes herself leave the room and walk back down the stairs. Her daughter is still sound asleep on the sofa, her breathing slow and steady, her lips parted in an unconscious pout.

22

London

Corinne

I'm taking Mum out for dinner. I told her on the phone that I'd like to meet her in London today and treat her to a meal. She sounded good, like she was happy to hear from me.

She got the train into Blackfriars and we met at the station, found a quiet little French place just off Farringdon Road. Mum's always liked French food; she and Dad used to eat it all the time. Not that I'm trying to bribe her or anything, but I want her to feel comfortable.

'This is a lovely choice, darling,' she says, and she smiles at me. Is it my imagination or does she look nervous?

I give the waiter my name and Mum gives a sad smile.

'I always used to put everything under your father's name, you know,' she says. 'People recognised it, sometimes. Quite often, actually. Richard Hawes. Gave us a certain gravitas, especially in London. Where people knew his work. He liked it, he liked the recognition.' She paused. 'I had a call from the Royal Institute of British Architects the other day, they want to host a memorial dinner for him on the anniversary. Black tie. Fundraiser for cancer. They invited me of course, but I just … I just don't think I can face it.

I squeeze her arm; the action hurts my finger where the little nail ripped into it. I've wrapped a plaster around it but the blood keeps seeping through, drying around the edges. I pull at it anxiously.

'Don't worry,' I tell her, 'we can have our own dinner that night. Just us. But it's good that they're honouring him, Mum.'

We are shown to a little table near the window, a red and white clothed affair boasting a candle stuck into a wine bottle. The menus are leather-bound, several pages long. I've no idea what to get and to be truthful I'm not that hungry. Mum debates for a while then gives her order, pointing to the words rather than attempting the pronunciation.

'Give it a go, Mum!' I joke, and she blushes slightly, embarrassed.

'Your dad always did it for me. He liked to.'

Perhaps this is my chance. I need to be careful, I don't want to upset her.

'Mum,' I say, 'speaking of Dad, how are you feeling?'

She looks down at the tabletop. 'Oh, I'm all right,' she says. 'Not too bad. Soldiering on, you know.'

I nod. I do know.

'You know we are here for you, don't you, Mum?' I say. 'Me and Ash. I know we don't see you as often as we'd like but we're only a short train ride away, you know that. Lucy and Ben loved seeing you the other weekend, so did I. It was really lovely.'

I pause. 'Apart from the rabbit, of course.'

Mum reaches out, touches my hand. 'I feel awful about that, really I do. What a horrid thing to happen

167

on your visit. Thank goodness Dominic sorted it all.' She sighs. 'And your sister didn't seem in very high spirits, did she?'

I squeeze her hand. 'It's not your fault, Mum! Ashley will be OK, she and James will work it out.' I mentally cross my fingers as I say this, because the truth is, I don't know if they will. She'd never forgive him if he really was having an affair, I know she wouldn't.

Mum's figure looks so small across from me, in the busy restaurant she nearly shrinks into the background. She used to be such a presence, when we were little, she was so elegant, so put together. Her once-blonde hair is ashy grey, she never even wears lipstick any more. It's as though she's fading away.

'Anyway,' I say, 'I really … I've been meaning to ask you, Mum, and I know I mentioned this before, but I could do with finding out what happened to all of dad's stuff. And I really do want to know where the doll house is.' I swallow.

She's fiddling with her fork, running her fingers up and down the prongs. The waiter interrupts, bustles over with a basket of bread.

'This looks delicious,' Mum says, and she smiles at me across the sawn-off slices. I can almost feel her willing me to let it go, change the subject.

'Mum?' I say. 'Mum, it's me. It's Corinne. If something's happened to dad's stuff – if you've lost it, or you can't remember where it is – please, you can just tell me! I won't think any less of you!'

There's a beat. I panic slightly, worry that I've gone too far. I don't want to sound like I'm accusing her of being senile, or something.

'Corinne,' she says, and she puts a hand to her head, palm to forehead like you would to a poorly child. 'Corinne, please. I don't know why you don't believe me. It's all at home, it's in the loft. It's under a lot of stuff, that's all. There's an awful lot of junk up there. I haven't got round to sorting it out. Why do you need to know so badly?'

She looks up at me. I stare back at her. French music plays overhead, *sur le pont d'Avignon* … I can't believe she's lying to me again. I don't want to tell her what I've found. I'll sound mad.

'Mum!' I say. 'Listen to me, I—'

'Duck à *l'orange*?' The waiter appears, interrupts me with a smile and two steaming white plates. We sit in silence as he places the meals down in front of us. I flash him a tense smile.

'Corinne—' Mum says, and I hold my breath, thinking she is about to tell me the truth, but then I see her eyes flick behind me, see her look out of the window, and the change in her expression is like nothing I have ever seen before.

She looks terrified. She looks like she has seen a ghost.

23

London

Corinne

My heart jumps. 'Mum!' I say. 'Mum! What's the matter?'
I wheel around in my chair, follow her gaze out to the
street. There's nobody there, nothing out of the ordinary,
just the wet London pavements and a couple of men
in suits, striding towards the Underground with their
briefcases. I twist back around, grab my mother's hand.

'What's going on, you look terrified. Did something just
happen?'

My breathing is fast and I try to control it. But I've
never seen Mum look like this. It's horrible. She hasn't said
a word; her face is as white as a sheet.

'Here,' I say. 'Here, Mum, have some water.' I slide my own
glass across to her and she picks it up, takes a sip. I can see that
her hands are shaking, the glass clinks slightly against her teeth.

Slowly, she lets out her breath in a long whoosh.

'You OK?' I say. 'What was all that about?'

Her head is bowed, she's looking down at the table.

'Mum?'

She lifts her head, and I see then that her eyes are shiny
with tears. When she speaks, it is in a whisper.

'I'm sorry, Corinne. I'm so sorry, my darling, but I've got to go. I have to get home.'

Before I can speak, Mum is pushing back her chair, grabbing her handbag, threading her way through the busy restaurant. I push back my own, jump to my feet and follow her, calling her name, not caring about the fellow diners.

'Mum! Mum? Will you just stop!'

She turns to me at the door. I catch her arm, breathing hard from the adrenaline.

'What are you doing?' I say. 'We're supposed to be having dinner!'

'I'm so sorry,' she says, and she puts her arms round me, her thin little arms, and I smell the scent of her perfume, the freesia scent that clings to all her cardigans. She hugs me tight and then she whispers in my ear, her breath tickling the skin on my neck. 'Please let me go, Corinne, I'll call you in the morning. I promise.'

'What? No! Mum, you can't just run off!'

'Please, Corinne,' she says. 'I'm sorry I just can't – I can't cope with being here. It's too much – the crowds, and being without your dad, I can't do it.'

Her face is white, her eyes red. I stand in front of her, staring. Her eyes are pleading.

'I'm not trying to be difficult, my darling, I just … I feel overwhelmed, here, I have to… I have to get out.'

'Oh, Mum,' I say, 'come on. If you really want to go then at least let me call you a cab? I can take you to the station.'

She shakes her head at me, pulls a shawl around her shoulders. I put a hand on her arm but she turns away. I have no choice but to do as she asks. I gaze at her retreating figure, my thoughts spinning in confusion.

171

'Please ring me, Mum!' I call desperately after her retreating back. 'I'll worry!' She raises a tiny hand to me, I see her wedding ring shine in the darkness and then she is gone, swallowed up by the crowds on the street.

The waiter appears at my side.

'Will Madame be wanting the bill?'

Then

It's my birthday today! I woke up feeling happy, but when Mummy saw me she got sad. She'd bought me some presents, a big badge and a balloon that stayed in the air the whole time, and she said she was going to make a cake as well. But then her eyes started to look all funny, like they were made of glass, and a tear came down her cheek. She reached out and stroked my hair, and she said she can remember the day I was born and how happy she was, and how after that everything started to go wrong.

So that means it is my fault that we're like this. I couldn't eat any of my birthday cake after that. We ended up throwing it away. Then I felt guilty about that too. I could have saved it to feed to the animals at the big house. I hate my birthday.

The next time we go there, one of the cars is gone. Mummy says the older one is going to live somewhere else now, because she's getting married. When she says that word, her lip curls up at the top and her cheeks suck in, like she's eating a lemon, yuck. I wonder if I'll ever be a married person. I hope not. I don't think I'd like it.

After that, we go somewhere new, somewhere we've never been before. All around us are offices, we are right in the middle of London. Mummy says I'm old enough to come into the city now. It's a Saturday, the weather is warm. I want an ice cream but Mummy says not yet. We go to some of the shops and Mummy says I can have whatever I want, which she never normally says, so I quickly grab a teddy bear and we're just about to go to the dolls section when suddenly she grabs me by the hand and tells me to move. I'm about to argue with her but then I see him, he's over on the other side of the shop, at the counter where you buy things. I look around but I can't see the others. Maybe he's buying presents for them. Just for one second, I let myself imagine – I imagine that he's remembered my birthday, that he's buying me a surprise present and any minute now he'll turn around and give me it. But then I tell myself not to be so stupid. He doesn't care about my birthday. Nobody does.

Mummy stares at him, and her grip on my hand gets tighter and tighter until I want to scream out but I know that I mustn't. I did that last time and it wasn't good. We have to be quiet, we always have to be quiet, that's our special thing. We're hidden behind a row of teddy bears but I can see his hands at the counter, and he's buying things for a baby. Little pink socks and a tiny white hat.

So we follow him. In and out of the crowds like usual, keeping our distance. All I can think about is how I had to put down my toys, my teddy and my dolls, how I never got to have them before we had to leave. We're going to a big office building, all shiny with glass windows that make the sunshine bounce back into my eyes, bright bright bright, so that I have to screw them up tight. We stop on the corner, watch him wave a black card in front of the doors and step through them. Like magic.

'Mummy,' I say, pulling on her hand, 'can we go back to the shops after? Please?'

I don't think she hears me. We don't go back. I never get the toys.

24

London

Corinne

Mum rings me early the next morning.

'I'm so sorry, darling,' she says. She tells me again that she'd been feeling really unwell, had found coming to London last night too hard. Being there in the restaurant had reminded her of Dad, of the places they used to go together when he was alive.

'I know it's silly, Corinne, but it hasn't been easy,' she says. 'I miss your father so much … perhaps being in London just brought it all back. I don't know, I'm holed up in Kent on my own and I just … I felt suddenly like I had to get home. London is so busy. The feeling was a bit … overwhelming. I was never as good at all that as your father. All that hustle.' She clears her throat. 'I suppose it was a bit of a panic attack. I'm so sorry.'

She apologises again and again, says she'll give me the money for our uneaten meal.

'It's OK, really,' I say, but she insists, tells me she feels terribly guilty.

'You do understand, don't you Corinne?' she says, and then I have to say yes, of course I do, because how can

I tell her that I don't really believe her, that I don't think she's telling me the whole truth?

When I told Dom all about it he stayed calmly in the centre of things, as he always does.

'Maybe she was upset, though, Cor,' he says. 'She hasn't been to London in a while, has she? I guess there are a lot of memories.' He pauses. 'Or was it something to do with the food?'

'No!' I say. 'We didn't even get to eat anything! It was something she saw through the window, Dom, I'm sure of it.'

He looks sceptical then, and I feel a little pang of dread. Is he going to start doubting every single thing I say?

'Have you thought about taking a pregnancy test yet?' he asks me, and I tell him that I'll do it this week, that I'm going to do it as soon as I can. And I am. I'm going to get one today.

I see Gilly as I'm walking out of our building. She looks harassed, she's on her own, Tommy isn't there. Her mobile phone is pressed to her ear, and she's gesturing a lot, waving her other hand in the air as she talks. I don't know if she's seen me. I wonder if she's talking to the man, the man who's going to leave his wife. She looks up suddenly and sees me; I wave awkwardly, not wanting to intrude. She makes a 'one-minute' gesture and crosses the road towards me, hanging up the phone as she does.

'How are you?' I say. 'That looked a bit intense.'

She rolls her eyes. She looks like she might have been crying and her hair is all messy, scraped back in a bun to show her wrinkle-free forehead.

'Oh, I'm fine, fine,' she says. 'Just, you know. Bloody men! It's my birthday, actually, and I'm trying to get Ben – my ex – to take Tommy, but …'

'Oh!' I say. 'Happy birthday! I didn't realise. Have you got anything special planned?'

She shrugs. 'Well, not any more, I've got Tommy. Anyway, sorry, it doesn't matter, I hate my bloody birthday as it is. Better off staying in. But how're you? Any news?'

I smile at her. Why not tell her? 'Actually, I'm planning to do a pregnancy test today,' I say, and she grins at me, gives me a little hug.

'Oh, Corinne, that's wonderful news. I'll be thinking about you. Let me know how you get on.' I tell her I will, and then her phone begins to ring again, a sharp, incessant sound that pierces through the air.

'I'll let you go,' I say, and I leave her standing on the street outside our building, the phone against her ear. I look back once and she's still standing there, her mouth pressed to the mobile, her eyes on me. She waves, gives me a big thumbs-up. I wave back, and she smiles, keeps talking into the phone. Her eyes look like they're still fixed on me but I must be imagining it, she's just staring into the middle distance, staring at nothing at all. I feel a pang of sympathy for her; I wonder why she hates her birthday. Maybe it reminds her that she's on her own. *But she's not really*, I think to myself, *she's got a child*.

*

It's a rainy Thursday and the gallery's been relatively quiet for the last hour or so, Marjorie's leaving me alone. It is a relief to be there, away from the flat, from the increasing sense of unease I feel within its walls. I know part of me is avoiding being at home. I keep thinking the little horse is going to turn up at any second and I almost wish it would, so I can prove it to Dominic.

The clock reaches one. There is a Boots on the high street, five minutes from the gallery. I can be there and back in my lunch break. As I head for the pregnancy aisle, I think of how often I have done this before, of the mind games I play with myself; if I can get to them in an even number of steps, it will work. If I can hold my breath all the way to the till, it will work. If, if, if. This time I force myself not to. I select the blue and white packet, then take two more for luck.

Sixty pounds. I hand over my debit card. We've waited long enough and I won't be able to do anything until I know. The price no longer even makes me swallow. I put the pregnancy tests in my pocket. I'll do it tonight, when I'm with Dom. I feel on edge. When I get back to the gallery, I scan my desk, but there is nothing there, nothing out of the ordinary. Could Dominic be right? The cut on my index finger thrums. I put a new plaster on this morning, threw the wet curl of the old one into the bathroom bin. The skin on my hand is white, softer, as though it is dying. I think of the objects I have found in the last few weeks: the chimney pot, the little door, the tiny rocking horse. I have seen them all with my own eyes, I have felt them in my hands. I wish someone would believe me. At this stage, anyone would do.

I spend the afternoon in the little side room of the gallery, where the lighting is soft and warm. When I first started here I loved this room, used to come in here with my morning coffee and rearrange the paintings, making different displays every time another one sold. The lighting makes all of them look beautiful. The effect of it is sometimes soporific but today I feel alert, aware of every tiny sound. My brain won't switch off, it is whirring over and over my mum's face in the restaurant, her eyes staring out of the window.

I know she is very sad about Dad, and I suppose coming to London would make things hard. But to leave like that? In the middle of our meal?

I try to concentrate on the work, give my thoughts a rest. I arrange a stack of landscape prints on the far wall, trying to angle them so that the light catches the colours, reds and golds depicting autumn trees. Cornsilk gold, currant red. I touch the print, feel the ridges of the brushstrokes under my fingers. They're beautiful. The trees remind me of our old garden in Hampstead; Ashley and I used to play hide and seek for hours, dart away amongst the trees while our parents counted to twenty. When the leaves fell down we'd gather them up, make life-sized birds' nests and sit in the middle of the dry orange piles. In the wintertime we made snow angels, fanning our arms out in the powdery snow, Dad laughing, showing us how to throw ourselves onto the ground so that it didn't hurt. The memory makes me smile and for a minute or two I lose myself in the pictures, in the nostalgic pull of our childhood. We were happy, weren't we? Maybe we had it too good, maybe the amount of luck you get in one lifetime is finite.

'Corinne?'

Marjorie calls me and I have to go to the till, put the memories aside. I remember when I first began at the gallery, I used to get lost in thought staring at the paintings, wondering about the artists behind them. I'd research them all obsessively, and after a while I felt like I could see their personalities shining through the paint. I was that close to it all, before the IVF began. I loved it.

Still. Things are different now. Art and the gallery are no longer my top priority. I leave bang on time at five o'clock and start home, the pregnancy tests bouncing against my side. I know I shouldn't get my hopes up and I'm trying not to, really I am, but I can't wait to take one.

Just as I round the corner to Finsbury Park, I feel the sharp pain of a stone inside my shoe, and bend down to adjust my boot. As I straighten up, I feel a strange sensation, a prickling feeling. Leaves rustle behind me and I spin around, clutching the Boots bag in my pocket between my fingers. My heart begins to thump. The street is quiet; a couple stroll past, their hands in each other's back pocket. I see an elderly woman coming towards me; moving slowly, her stick tapping on the pavement. She shuffles past, head down. I think she's one of our neighbours but I don't say hello.

The space directly around me is empty, save for sweet wrappers blowing in the wind.

'Hello? Hello? Is there anyone there?' I call out, feeling foolish. I swallow hard. The giddy feelings are vanishing; I feel suddenly alone. I can hear the traffic from the main road, the horns of taxis and the hiss of buses. A police siren cuts through the evening, wailing and fading. There is a loud bang behind me – my heart leaps and my legs go weak, as though they are made of water. A rubbish bin has blown to its side; the wooden barrel rolls on the tarmac and litter spills out; the rotten curl of a banana skin, the bright orange of a can.

A group of men around my age are approaching, dressed in dark office clothing. Four of them, bundled up against the cold in scarves that obscure their faces. They jostle each other, smiling and laughing. As they get closer, I feel an irrational burst of panic uncurl itself in my chest. I am sick of feeling scared.

Without thinking, I break into a run. My feet grow wet as I sprint through puddles, but I don't stop until I am outside our flat, bent over, panting and wheezing. I put my key in the lock with shaking hands and go to slam the door shut behind me. It bounces back in my face and I force my entire weight against it in frustration. There is a tight pain in my chest and my eyes are stinging. The lock finally catches and the door shuts. Outside the flat the wind roars, defeated.

*

Dominic has come back early and cooked us a meal. The smell of it pricks my nostrils. I'm glad not to be alone in the flat and I stand in the hallway for a moment, amongst the old newspapers, trapped in the midst of their headlines. I make myself take deep breaths, in through my nose, out through my mouth, in through my nose, out through my mouth, counting to three in my head.

As soon as he smiles at me I can tell he feels bad for not believing me earlier. He has had a new key cut; I see the silvery new one is lying on the dresser. I feel a flash of frustration. He said we should change the locks completely.

'Dom,' I say, 'I wanted the locks changed. Not just a new key.'

He pauses, looks up from the stove. 'What?'

'I think we should have the locks to the door altered. So that nobody can get in. Remember, I asked you?'

'Corinne,' he says, 'come on. There's nothing to worry about – there really isn't. I don't think anyone's been inside this flat. The only people who can get inside our house are already in it.'

He smiles at me. I stare back at him.

'Us, you ninny. There's no one else getting in.'

I smile weakly. He's put the stub of a candle in the centre of the table, its flame casting a ring of light on the wooden surface. For a moment the fire seems to circle around us both, joining us together. *The only people who can get inside our house are already in it.*

I watch him start to scoop together a salad dressing, mixing mustard with pools of olive oil. He looks up at me again, smiles. I can't see his eyes properly, the lids flicker down over them as he mixes the leaves together, turning the spoon over and over rhythmically.

I wriggle past him to the tiny bathroom, the Boots bag tucked under my arm. This moment suddenly feels so private and I am not sure I can handle my own hope, let alone his too. So I don't tell him about the tests, don't tell him that this might be it. I don't say anything at all.

The tap is dripping; cold water circles the plughole. I turn it off with a shaking hand. I tug down my jeans, fumbling with the buckle, and pull out the first box. In my fingers, it hums as though alive.

I unwrap the blue packet, biting the plastic with my teeth. There is no need to read the instructions, I know them by heart. *Step 1: Remove the test stick …* Reaching

182

underneath myself, I awkwardly push the stick into the warm liquid, trying not to think of all the times that I have done this before, have tensed my legs and prayed for a miracle. Afterwards, I lie the stick flat next to the tap, my eyes slipping to the display window even though it's way too soon, and then I pull up my jeans and pants, put down the toilet lid, then sit back with my eyes gently closed. *Breathe in through my nose, out through my mouth, in through my nose, out through my mouth.*

The minutes tick by. I wait, thinking about the park, the horrible sensation that there was someone behind me, following me back here. There can't have been, can there? My thoughts feel slippery, elastic as the seconds slide by. I didn't actually see anyone, did I? I just felt it. It isn't enough. It isn't proof. I wish he'd had the locks changed. I wish he'd done as I asked.

I open my eyes and stare at the white face of my watch, tight on my wrist like a talisman. One more minute. I wanted my father's old watch after he died, a big brown face with tiny golden hands, held by a navy strap. I used to try it on, parade around the house in it as other girls wore their mother's high heels. It was far too big for me but I loved it, whirled it around my tiny wrist like a spinning fairground wheel. I asked Mum about it after the funeral, but she told me that it must have been lost, that she hadn't seen it.

'Corinne! Dinner is served!' Dominic calls in a silly posh voice.

I sit on the toilet, my underwear tying my ankles together, my head in my hands. I think suddenly of my father last year, sick and exhausted, pulling me towards him in the hospital, clasping my hand between his own. Had he been wearing the watch then?

'I'm sorry, Corinne,' he had said, and I had leaned over him, puzzled.

'What for, Daddy? What for?' Instead of an answer there was the drone of the monitor flatlining, and the shouts of my sister and the white figures that appeared around the bedside. That was the worst day of my life.

Thirty seconds.

I shut my eyes again and wish as hard as I ever have in my life.

When I open them, the stick shows two blue lines, one faint and struggling, but there. Undoubtedly there. I stare at it for a few seconds and my eyes fill and the lines blur and I can't believe it, and then I scream, a high-pitched yelp that causes Dominic to come running to the bathroom, spilt olive oil on his shirt. I can only keep yelping, my breath coming in short blasts, as the look of panic on his face disappears when he sees my grin.

'I'm pregnant, Dominic! We're pregnant,' I cry, and he is grabbing me and we are dancing, hitting the toilet wall with the palms of our hands, slapping the wallpaper in excitement.

He never washes the oil from his shirt, keeps it instead in the back of the wardrobe, a dirty talisman. The day we finally got pregnant. I forget about the silvery key lying on the dresser, I forget my annoyance that he hasn't changed the locks. I forget everything. *I'm pregnant.*

25

Corinne

The first thing I want to do, after I have called Ashley with the news, is go to visit Dad's grave. He is buried near Hampstead Heath, near the house where we grew up. I need to tell him. I need him to know. He'd be so happy. I am so happy! For all of Thursday evening, it is as though the fear I've been feeling over the last week seems to die down, just as Dominic said. We have dinner together and go to bed early, lie like spoons with my stomach between us. For the first time in ages, I sleep properly, right through the night. I forget about Mum, I forget about the rocking horse, I forget about everything. All I can think about is that I'm pregnant, that there is a tiny scrap of life inside me. At last. *Stay safe, little one.*

When I call Ashley on Friday morning, she screams down the telephone. I can hear her voice get all teary and then I can feel myself going, emotion shaking in my voice.

'I've got to be careful,' I tell her, 'I know I have, and I still need to have the blood test at the doctors but I'm pregnant, Ashley. I really am. And it's down to you, we could never have afforded IVF again on our own. Thank you. I mean it.'

She ignores my thanks, goes unusually quiet.

'How are things with James?' I ask then. I'm a bad sister. I should have asked before.

She sighs. 'I'm not sure. This week hasn't been great.'

'Are you OK?' I say gently.

'Yes, I'm sorry, this is your time. Ignore me.' She sounds on the edge of tears and I swallow.

'Come on, Ash, just tell me. Is it James? And your, well, your worries?'

'No, yes, oh, it's everything. But it's not specifically that, whatever that is.' She huffs a fake laugh and I hold the phone a little tighter. 'James hasn't told me anything and I had another phone call the other day, this time in the morning and I know it was a woman. She was laughing, there was laughter coming down the phone.'

The way she says it gives me a little shiver. 'Laughter?'

'Yes. It made me feel sick, I got—' she lowers her voice '—I got a bit paranoid then. I … oh God, I'm embarrassed even telling you … I tried to get into his computer.'

'Ashley!'

'I know.'

'I really, really don't think he'd do this to you, Ash,' I tell her. 'You just need to speak to him.'

'I was going to ask him this week,' Ashley says, 'but Lucy came home drunk, I mean really, really drunk. She could hardly stand. It's the first time that's ever happened, it was horrible.'

'She's a teenager, I guess.'

'I know, but. She's usually fairly sensible, or so I thought. I think she must have gone out with someone older, someone new to the school. I'm going to try to get more out of her.'

I don't know whether to tell Ashley about seeing Mum or not. I haven't told her about the little rocking horse either. When I say the sentence in my head, it sounds absurd. She didn't think the little door looked like it was from the doll house, did she? It sounds like she has a lot on her plate already. I don't want to make it worse.

'Benji was sent home from school as well on Tuesday,' Ashley says, and she tells me about the child in the playground calling Lucy a slut. I gasp.

'Ash, that's awful! You need to have it out with her. ASAP, I'd say.'

'I know,' she says, 'I know I do. And that's not all. The doctor thinks Holly's having night terrors. She's up screaming nearly every hour, I can hardly close my eyes. They did a blood test as well, said she seemed a bit floppy … I don't know what that means, he said he reckons its exhaustion, from her being up all night. We get the results in a week or two, they said. But he only did it to be thorough, I think.' There's a pause. 'It's night terrors, he said.'

'Shit, Ash. You're having the week from hell. I'm so sorry!' I desperately want to be there with her, to give her a hug. The urge is so strong it feels almost uncomfortable. 'I'm sure the doctor is right, though,' I say. 'If it was something more serious they'd have told you on the spot.'

She sighs loudly; I can hear the air of her breath crackle through the phone. 'I hope so. Anyway, God, you don't need to know all of this right now. Your news is amazing, Cor, it's wonderful. The best.'

'Forget about me,' I tell her softly. 'Just try to stay calm and get to the bottom of what's going on with Lucy, I think. It's so unlike her.' And it is, I really can't imagine her behaving like that, but then I don't live with her, I suppose. The teenage years, what a nightmare. I roll the words around in my head, they feel so alien, but perhaps one day I'll be able to say them to a stroppy teen of my own. The tiny glimmer of hope, as small as the tiny bundle of cells inside me, flares softly. My flash of excitement is followed quickly by a wave of guilt.

'Is everything else OK?' Ashley is asking.

Feeling caught out, I stutter slightly before replying. 'Yes, sure. Why?'

'You seemed a bit worked up the other week at Mum's; I mean, I know what happened with the car was horrible, but apart from that. Are you feeling better now?'

I take a breath. One thing is for certain; I can't burden her any more right now. Not after she's told me all that. *If I find something else*, I think, *if something else happens then I'll tell her.*

'No, I'm fine! I think it was just the nerves with the treatment and the wait. I let it get the better of me, I guess.'

'And the wait's over!' Ashley says, and I can hear the smile in her voice.

'I should do some more tests, and we need to wait to see the doctor, but maybe, Ash. Maybe it is.'

*

On Friday afternoon, I tell Marjorie I've got another appointment and instead I get the bus over to Hampstead. Every time the bus jolts I put my hands to my stomach. Already people feel like they're too close to me, to my tiny precious load. I stare out of the window as we pass the BBC building, towering on the side of the road.

I wipe the glass with my fingers so I can get a better look. It was one of Dad's greatest projects. Ashley and I went with him to the site a few times. I must have been around eleven, Ashley just turned fifteen. There were a lot of problems with the stairs, I think – my father said the details of stairs are one of the hardest aspects of any building.

'They take up twice the amount of time as anything else. Bit of a nightmare, though you wouldn't guess. Look, see these joins? See how smooth they are?' He got down on his hands and knees after supper once and showed Ashley and I how the three storeys of our house worked and the levels slotted together, crawling around for hours like an excitable bear. When he made us the doll house, the stairs were exactly the same, a miniature replica of our own family home. 'What can I say?' Dad laughed. 'I'm a perfectionist.' I caught him looking at Mum, as if for approval, and she beamed back at him, eyes shining with pride.

We got the Tube together at the start of the BBC project; my father spent the journey looking over his plans one more time. He spread his blueprint out across his knees, adjusting and tweaking the diagrams with the black marker pen he always carried in the upper left pocket of his jacket. I remember eating a Kinder egg on the train, which melted all over my hands, meaning that the director of the BBC ended up incorporating smears of milk chocolate into his design. Dad told me I'd only improved it.

The building itself was an old redbrick, a Grade II listed monastery which Dad told us used to be home to the monks of Whitefriars. After that, whenever we visited I imagined white-clad men walking around, heads bowed, when in reality all I ever saw were blue overalled construction workers who drank endless mugs of tea and smoked roll-up cigarettes out of the half-finished windows.

One day, Dad took us right to the top of the building. There was a thunderstorm, and Ashley was scared. She hid under the tarpaulin which was covering the door frame, but I stood out in the rain with my father, looking out across London.

'You can see the whole city from here!' my father shouted, his voice straining above the noise of the water on the roof and the rolling grumbles of the sky. He was smiling, his eyelashes flecked with the rain. 'The builders told me this wouldn't work, this rooftop, but we proved them wrong, didn't we?' He pulled me close to him, and we watched as a flash of lightning illuminated London, the towering buildings, the slick black of the Thames. I felt as though I'd helped design the building, then, as though we were a team.

'Why did they say it wouldn't work?' I asked and he shook his head, frowned down at me through his glasses, the lenses now speckled with water droplets.

'Doesn't matter,' he shouted, 'what matters is that I was right!' He grinned again, the frown gone, and, as lightning hit the sky again, I felt a rush of something strange, something like fear. Then he pulled me underneath his arm and we joined Ashley under the protection of the blue plastic.

We visited the building a couple more times after that day, watching it expand until it stood proudly with the

BBC branding emblazoned on the bricks and hundreds of dark-suited men and lipsticked women striding up and down the halls where the monks used to walk. I was so proud of it; I showed it to Dom when we first got together.

Just after Dad died last year, I went and stood round the back of this building, underneath an old archway that had been turned into a bright green fire exit with a flashing white light. I put my hand against the bricks and tried to breathe. It felt as though there was water inside my brain, a great tidal wave of grief threatening to take me under, pull me into the riptide. I held the wall and made myself fill my lungs in and out, in and out, imagining the air seeping into my brain and making space above the water. It helped. I stayed there, sodden, as the rain poured down around me, until I realised there was a car parked opposite with someone inside, staring at me through misted-up windows. I must have looked crazy, I guess.

I put my face up against the glass window of the bus now, one hand on my stomach. It's a wonderful building. As we bump on up to Hampstead, I imagine my father's big square hands examining the bricks, casting an expert eye over the way the cement solidified and the red stone stacked. I smile. Dad feels more alive to me in those auburn walls than he does in the stone of a grave. London slides past me in a blur of colour, as the windows steam up it begins to look like a cloudy painting, a sea of greys and greens.

The cemetery is a nice place, actually, just down the hill from the heath, not far from our old home. I haven't been since before Christmas. For a while I found it really difficult to see the grave at all. But now, now it is different. I want to tell him my news.

After the bus lets me off, I push open the iron gates and make my way through the graveyard. It is deserted, the little pathways empty. It's well kept, the plots are expensive.

The gravestone is right in the middle of the plots, surrounded by oak trees. Their branches hang over me, blocking out the blue sky. I kneel down, my jeans soaking up the cold of the grass. My eyes are closed, my hands clasped together.

'I'm pregnant, Dad. I'm going to have a baby.' I whisper the words as though they are magic, imagine him grinning down at me, scooping me up in his arms like he used to when we were children. Ashley and I would vie for his attention like magpies, would run to greet him at the door whenever he got in from work. Looking back, I think it made Mum jealous.

I kneel silently for a few minutes. The air around me is still, I can hear the distant cry of birds, the rustle of a squirrel. I feel peaceful, a wonderful, rare sense of calm, the first time I've felt like this in weeks. My hand moves over my stomach. I hope it's a girl in there.

I open my eyes, lift my gaze up to Dad's gravestone and it is only then that I see it, see the word that has no place on the silvered stone.

Richard Hawes, 1949–2014. Architect, husband, father. They are the same words I have stared at for months. But someone has added to the list. Staring back at me, scrawled in glaring black paint is the word 'LIAR'.

It's been written in messy capital letters, scrawled across the stone. The letters glisten, as though the paint has been freshly applied.

I can't help myself; even though the cemetery is deadly quiet I open my mouth wide and I scream. The sound echoes, pierces the air. Birds flutter from the trees around me, darken the sky with their flapping wings.

I scrabble to my feet, stumble backwards. I can't take my eyes off the paint, the angrily slashed letters defacing the grave. My foot slips on the wet ground and I almost fall over. My heart is racing; I spin around and look up and down the cemetery. The gloom of the afternoon is closing in, the sky casting an eerie light over the spires of the church that overlooks me. For a minute I think I see a flash of something in the corner, near the railings, and I start towards it but then the movement is gone, there's nobody there.

I fumble with my phone, desperate to call Dom, but there's a crack of a stick and so I begin to run, my footsteps trampling carelessly over fresh mounds. As I reach the huge black gates, I turn around, stare back at Dad's grave one more time. The church bell above me begins to toll and I can't stay any longer; I've got to find Dominic. I race through the gates, launch myself out into the road. There is the screech of brakes, high and urgent, and as the headlights swing over me all I can see is the word, flashing through my head: *LIAR, LIAR, LIAR.*

Then

It's time. We're going inside.

Mummy has been waiting for this, she tells me, and she checks her watch until it reaches half past six and that's when we know that they've gone. Spain, she says, and when she says it her lip curls up as though Spain is a horrible place, which is strange because I know Spain is nice, we did it at school and it looks hot and sandy and lots of fun. They've gone on holiday there and I'm jealous. I can't tell her that though.

So this time when we drive to the house like usual, we don't have to park far away, we can park almost right outside, where their car usually goes. There aren't any cameras, Mummy says, the house is too old and he didn't want to ruin it by having messy wires installed.

Mummy knows where they keep the keys, she says she does anyway. We go up the driveway and it's really weird, as we're walking up I feel different. I feel taller, better, smarter, as though this could be my house, my home. As we get near to the doorway, Mummy takes my hand and squeezes. I squeeze back. I feel excited.

We get inside and oh my God, they have SO MUCH STUFF. I run my hands over all of it, it's not even dusty like our house is sometimes. Mummy says she thinks they have a cleaner. We don't have a cleaner. Our flat isn't really very clean, especially on bad days when we don't wash up.

She goes upstairs to the bedrooms but I stay in the living room, looking out into the garden. It's so big. That's where I normally am, but I don't think they ever look out like this and see me. It's funny being on the other side, it makes me giggle. I can't see the hole in the fence but I can see the tree where the tennis ball was, and I can see the rabbit cages, and the little bank of flowers that surrounds the house that we never go near.

I stare out at the garden for a while, and then I turn into the room, look at all the things they have on the walls. Some of them are pretty and some of them are a bit boring, like you see in museums or maybe in the high school. There's a corner with a lot of books in, and I pick up a couple to look at, turning the pages in my hands. They feel heavy. They're mostly full of drawings. Then something catches my eye, and I stop looking at the books because wow, it's there. The best thing I've ever seen in my life, the thing I dream about. It is amazing.

I accidentally drop one of the books on my foot, but it doesn't even barely hurt because I am so excited! I run across the room to where it sits, pink and amazing, standing on a table against the back wall of the room. I've never seen it up close before, I've only seen it through the windows. They don't play with it much any more, they're too big, but sometimes I see them looking at it, touching the top of it with their fingers. I reach out and touch it. Just like them. Wow.

*

I wish we'd never gone inside the house. Everything is worse. Now I know what's in there, I have started to dream about it, I dream that I am inside, running through the rooms, round and around in circles that never end. The house seeps into my thoughts every night so that when I wake up I get a horrible feeling, a sad monster in my tummy because I'm not there. I'm here. On the outside.

Mummy says we can't go back into the house, not while they're there. I told her all about the doll house, how the stairs really *look like stairs and the little bath really looks like a bath and the chimneys really look like chimneys. I spent ages last night telling her about it, she was listening at first but then she got a funny look on her face, all twisted up and cross. I thought she was cross with me and I started to get worried but then she put her arms out and she gave me a cuddle, a big one like she does when she's all happy and OK.*

'You'll get a house like that, my darling,' she tells me, and I bury my head in her clothes and I believe her. She's my mum. What she says comes true. Most of the time, anyway.

26

London

Ashley

Lucy has been subdued for the last few days. Ashley hasn't told James what Benji said, has been waiting for the right moment since Tuesday. If it ever comes. Corinne's news is the only good thing that has happened all week; Ashley is so happy for her, it makes her heart want to burst. She can only pray that nothing goes wrong. If she believed in a God she'd beg him.

The children are back in school and her husband is in the office. Ashley slept well; Holly had had a spoonful of medicine before she went down and managed to sleep solidly from two to six, almost a record. Ashley's limbs felt different when she woke up, more rested, lighter. She had lifted Holly from her cot in the morning, tried to work out whether her body seemed floppy, whether there was anything unusual in the way her daughter's little frame lay against her chest. She is still waiting to hear back from the doctor.

James rose at six this morning, Ashley woke to the sound of him closing their bedroom door. She had called after him and he'd come back to kiss her.

'Sorry, Ash, I didn't want to wake you is all.'

She had watched him leave. The expression on his face had reminded her of Benji, standing outside the headmistress's office. She had recognised it instantly. Guilt. He looked guilty. And he'd looked awfully at home sneaking out of a bedroom. How many times has he done that before?

As Ashley was hunting for Benji's trainers ('Football Friday, Mum!'), there had been another call, another silent line. She'd listened for several minutes, ignoring her son's increasingly desperate shouts about needing the shoes with the bright red laces. Nothing. Just silence, and another blocked number, like the one the night Lucy went missing.

Ashley had retrieved the trainers from behind the sofa, hustled her children into the car and driven them to school as though on autopilot. One of the mothers had waved at her at the school gates, beamed at Ashley through the window of the car but instead of stopping Ashley had pretended not to see, put the car into reverse and twisted the wheels away. She doesn't want to talk to any of them. Instead, she goes to June's, holds Holly tightly to her chest before passing her over. Her daughter's body feels warm, solid. Ashley thinks of the doctor's words again. Is she floppy? Ashley cannot tell, feels the familiar sense of worry begin to grip her heart. The lightness she felt this morning has evaporated; she feels tense, her body coiled like a spring. What kind of mother is she that she can't work out what is wrong with her baby? She doesn't want to let go of Holly, is suddenly overwhelmed by a desire to keep her close, safe in her arms, far away from the future world of gossipy schoolrooms and silent phone calls that haunt Ashley's thoughts.

When June opens the door her face immediately looks concerned.

'Oh, my dear, whatever's wrong?' She is wearing a red and white apron and the sight of her is suddenly so comforting that Ashley wants to cry. She swallows, stands on the doorstep. June reaches out and wordlessly lifts Holly from her arms.

'Come here, there now.' She lifts Holly onto her hip, gestures to Ashley. 'Why don't you come in for a quick cup of tea? You look like you could use one. Yes, she does, doesn't she?' She says this last part to Holly who gurgles happily, spreads out her tiny hand so that it rests against June's shoulder.

'Oh, really, I'm OK,' Ashley says, feeling embarrassed, but June shakes her head.

'You don't look OK, excuse my saying so. Come in, come have a sit-down for five minutes. I bet you're exhausted.'

Ashley looks at her watch. She is due at Colours in twenty minutes but the thought of sitting down with someone who is not going to judge her, someone who has been so kind to her daughter over the last few months is very tempting. One cup of tea won't hurt.

'Thanks, June, that would be great actually then,' she says, and she follows the older woman into the house. It is comfortingly warm inside; Ashley allows her body to relax at the kitchen table while June bustles around with the kettle, pours steaming mugs of tea into blue china cups. Holly has gone very quiet, sitting in a high chair with blue and white beads attached to the front. The sides of it are decorated with painted birds, swallows that dart up the chair legs and swoop across the bars at the front. Ashley frowns.

'That's a beautiful high chair, June,' she says. 'Goodness. It's gorgeous.'

June's back is to her, Ashley can see her fingers unscrewing a carton of milk.

'Yes, it is lovely, isn't it?' she says. 'It used to belong to a friend of mine, I mentioned I'd been looking after Holly and she brought it round for me the other day. Kind of her.'

'Very,' Ashley agrees.

'How did it go with the doctor the other day?'

'He thinks it's night terrors,' Ashley says. 'Nothing too serious. I've got some medicine for her, actually – here.' She reaches in her bag and hands the little bottle to June. 'Could you give her a spoonful before she goes to sleep? Just one.'

'Of course.' June nods, hands Ashley a mug of steaming tea. She sips it gratefully.

'They also said she needs a blood test,' she tells June, cupping the mug to try to reassure herself. 'But it seems like a precaution really, that's all.'

'I see,' June says. 'Well, best not to worry, I'm sure if it was anything serious they'd have said.'

'Yes,' says Ashley. 'That's what my sister said too. I'm probably worrying about nothing.'

'Oh, we all do that.' June smiles, takes a seat opposite her. 'Oof. I can't sit down without making some sort of noise these days. That's what old age does to you!' She sips her tea, then stands again and goes to the side cabinet, rummages before coming back to the table with a small packet of pills. 'I can feel my joints creaking when I bend my knees,' she says, popping the tablets onto the table and swallowing them with another mouthful of tea. 'How's your sister doing these days, anyway?'

'Oh!' Ashley smiles, almost spills her tea as she puts the mug down on the table. 'I didn't tell you! She's pregnant. Isn't it wonderful?'

June clasps her hands together. 'Oh, my dear, you must be over the moon for her. Poor love, how long has she been trying for now? I remember you saying it'd been a while.'

'Since before Dad died,' Ashley says. 'I'm thrilled for her. She'll be a wonderful mother.' The warmth of the tea relaxes her. June brings out a plate of biscuits and she helps herself, ignoring the way her shirt is clinging to her hips. She's got enough to worry about.

'And how is James?' June asks. 'I saw him when he dropped off Holly the other day, poor man looked a bit flustered.'

Ashley feels the biscuit she's just eaten churn in her stomach.

'Actually … actually I'm not sure,' she says.

June looks at her questioningly.

'I don't know what's going on with him at the moment,' she says, the words blurting out of her mouth before she can stop them. 'I never see him, he's always at work, and there have been these phone calls …' She trails off. The older woman is looking at her sympathetically.

'What do you think?' Ashley asks. She can hear the edge of desperation in her voice and is embarrassed by it, but she has a sudden urge for the older woman's opinion, wants somebody to reassure her. 'Do you think I'm jumping to conclusions?'

There's a small pause. Ashley can hear the ticking of the clock, the hum of June's boiler. She focuses on a stray biscuit crumb on the table, trying not to cry.

'On the contrary,' June says. She looks intently at Ashley, reaches one hand out across the table to her. Her fingers clasp Ashley's, they are warm and soft. When she speaks, her voice sounds different from usual, more serious, with more of an edge. 'I know I'm a silly old woman, Ashley, but I've lived a long life and believe it or not I have known a few men in my time. And if what you say about James's behaviour is true, then I think you need to be careful. And be prepared.'

*

When Ashley finally gets to Colours, the shift is busy. June's words are going round and around in her mind, she cannot concentrate. She appreciates the woman's concern – it sounded as though the words meant something to her, and in recent months they have grown close, in a way. Afterwards, she'd patted Ashley's hand and offered her another biscuit, which she'd accepted gratefully even though her stomach felt like it was churning.

Ashley sighs, trying to focus on the café. The weather is a little warmer than it has been and everyone has come outside, breathing in the crisp February air, admiring the lake in the middle of the common, the sprigs of blossom that have started to appear on the trees.

She serves cup after cup of coffee, focusing on the process: the hiss and steam of the machine, the powdery chocolate heart shapes they shake onto the top of the drinks, the quick exchange of coins from hand to hand. Megan keeps glancing at her oddly. She is being quiet, she knows.

At three o'clock, they wipe down the surfaces, turn away the last of the tourists. Ashley can see her reflection as she shines the coffee machine. Her face is pale and drawn.

'Out with it, Ash.' Megan leans on the counter, takes the J-cloth out of Ashley's hand. 'Come on, I think that thing is clean already. You all right? You don't seem yourself.'

Ashley hesitates.

'Come on,' says Megan. 'Why don't we go have lunch? Just a quick bite, there's that pop-up street food place that's just opened. We could even have a sneaky glass of wine; you look like you could use one. It's Friday, after all. Weekend rules apply!'

Ashley gives a half-smile. Megan bats her eyelashes at her.

'How can you resist my winning stare?'

Ashley relents, rolls her eyes at her friend. 'OK. Just a quick one then. Let me just stop at a cashpoint. That place is too trendy for debit cards.'

She pulls on her scarf. Megan links her arm as they cross the road to the bank. At the cashpoint, Ashley inserts her card, drums her fingers on the little counter as she waits for the screen to load. Is June right? Should she be prepared for the worst? She once read a book about a woman whose husband was having affairs all over the village – everybody knew but her. The thought makes her feel sick.

She thinks of Corinne, Megan, the mums at school. What if they all know? What if nobody wants to be the one to tell her?

'Busy today,' Megan says, interrupting Ashley's spiralling thoughts. 'Did you see that blond guy who ordered the latte from me just now? I thought he was a bit of a fox.'

Ashley laughs a little, in spite of her mood. 'You always think everyone's a bit of a fox.'

'Do not!'

The machine is beeping. Ashley frowns, takes her card back as the machine spits the plastic out. She squints at the screen. There's a message flashing up: *insufficient funds.*

'Oh, for God's sake.'

'Well, OK, maybe I do a bit then. But he was a fox! Seriously, he was gorgeous. Did you see his eyes?' Megan's giggling now.

'No, it's not that. This ATM's broken is all. Hang on, let me try the next one.'

Ashley tries a total of four ATMs. By the fifth try, Megan is looking a bit uncomfortable.

'Hey, Ash, I can treat you, no worries. Let's go.'

Ashley swallows. She feels a bit sick. She's tried Lloyds, Santander, HSBC. They cannot all be wrong.

'Actually, Megs, I'm just going to go inside,' she says, gesturing at the double doors of HSBC. 'Just want to find out what's going on. Sorry about this. You get on, don't worry. We can have lunch next week.'

In the line for the counter, Ashley tries not to panic. There is something wrong with the card, that's all! It is their joint account, she uses it all the time. Of course there is money in there, lots of it. Besides, she'd only been trying to get out a twenty. She turns the little piece of plastic over and over in her hands, trying to ignore the niggling thoughts building up in the back of her mind.

'I'm sorry, Mrs Thomas.' The man speaking to her from behind the glass pane is softly spoken, she has to lean forward to hear what he says.

'But it appears this account has been emptied. You've got – let's see … ten pounds and forty-nine pence left. Did you want to retrieve that now?' He taps at the keyboard, glances up at her expectantly.

Ashley rests her forehead on the little window, not caring that the man is now looking at her strangely.

'It's … I didn't take that money out,' she whispers. 'There must be some mistake.'

The cashier nods. 'No, that's right, it was removed by the other account holder. A Mr James B. Thomas? I'm guessing he's your husband?'

27

London

Corinne

I can't breathe. I ran all the way from the cemetery to Dominic's office, feeling as though there was someone at my back the entire way. I am covered in sweat and my hair is falling over my eyes, blocking my vision as I dart in and out of the traffic that piles up around Finchley Road. A taxi beeps its horn at me and I see the driver gesticulating angrily but I don't care; I've got to get to Dom.

Gasping in the reception, I tell the woman on the front desk that I need to see Dominic Stones at the *Herald*.

'Is it for a story?' she says in a bored voice, tapping her red-painted nails on the desktop.

'No!' I say. 'Tell him it's Corinne, tell him it's important. I really need to talk to him right now.'

She looks unmoved by my flustered state, but picks up the phone and dials. I wait, doubled over. Spots dance before my eyes. Fear grips my stomach as I realise I could be putting the baby at risk; stupid, stupid, stupid.

'Ah, I see,' the receptionist is saying, 'OK, OK. Thank you, that would be great.' She replaces the receiver and smiles at me with pink plasticky lips, gestures to the big leather chairs against the wall.

'Have a seat, someone's coming down for you.'

'Someone?' I say. 'I don't want someone, I want Dominic! He's my boyfriend.'

She's about to reply when the door to the stairs opens and a young girl comes out, clutching a notepad. She's got a look of sympathy as she comes towards me; I feel her taking in the stains on my kneecaps, the red blotches on my face.

'Corinne?' she says cautiously. 'Corinne, are you OK?'

'Where's Dominic?' I ask her. 'He's a reporter here, he works on the fifth floor.'

'I'm so sorry, Corinne, Dominic's actually out on a story at the moment, I thought I'd come down to get you instead so you're not left on your own. Oh dear.' She pauses as tears fill my eyes. 'Poor you, what's happened? Here, sit down.'

She gives the woman on reception a little nod, a not-to-worry gesture, and eases me down onto the chair, puts a sympathetic hand on my arm.

'I'm sorry,' I say, 'I'm so sorry. God, how embarrassing.' I try to wipe my face with my sleeve and she wordlessly hands me a tissue, perfectly white. I take a deep breath, blow my nose. The sound is ugly. She doesn't seem to mind, she just smiles at me and touches my hand. The gesture is comforting, her skin is soft and warm.

'Why don't you come upstairs to the cafeteria on the roof?' she asks me. 'Come on, we can get you a cup of tea and wait for Dom to come back. I'm sure he won't be long. He's just gone out to do an interview near King's Cross this afternoon. He had to step in for someone at the last minute I'm afraid. People drop like flies this time of year! We call it the February flu.'

My hands are shaking badly; I press them to my thighs. My jeans are stained with mud from the graveyard. I picture the gravestone. LIAR. Who would do that to Dad? And why? How long has it been there for?

Thinking about it brings a fresh round of tears to my eyes and I turn away, hideously embarrassed in front of this lovely girl. She must think I am totally insane.

'I'm sorry,' I say again, 'I've just had some … I've just had some bad news and it's… it's shocked me a bit. I wanted to see my boyfriend, I had something to tell him. Sorry, I'm sorry to be like this.'

'Hey, hey,' she says. 'Come on, we all have our moments! Especially us girls! I hope it's not anything that a cuppa won't fix. Or they do a wicked hot chocolate too, it might help for you to have some sugar. If you've had a bit of a shock.'

I look up at her.

'OK,' I say. 'If you could point me in the direction of the café I'll wait there for Dom, if that's all right.'

'Don't be silly,' she says, and she gives my shoulder a little nudge as I stand up. 'I'll have a hot choc with you. Give me an excuse to get away from my desk! You're a blessing in disguise! The news is dire today. Here, I'll take that.'

She takes the soggy tissue out of my hand and throws it into the bin in the corner of the room. I feel humiliated, in spite of how sweet she's being.

'Thank you so much,' I say, and I follow her up the stairs, feeling the eyes of the receptionist on my back. My breathing starts to slow slightly; I'll sit down, wait for Dominic. He'll be here soon.

Then

The day she tells me, I go sit by myself down by the canal. I stare at the water, the green algae that coats the glassy surface of it like a trap. She tells me that I'm old enough to know now, that I deserve to know the truth. But I wish she hadn't told me. It makes everything hurt. It's like everything has changed. I can feel the hurt rising up in my stomach, like bile, and it's coming up in my throat and then I lean forward over the dark water and vomit. Strands of it dangle down towards the blackness. I stay like that for a bit, pitched over the side of the canal, thinking about it all, about him, and just for a minute I think about what it would be like to just keep leaning forward, further and further, until my body slips away from the cold concrete of the bank and into the darkness, underneath the algae. Would she care? Would anyone?

*

I didn't lean forward into the water. I leaned back, I went home, carried on. Like a good girl. But now that I know, everything feels different, and every time I walk past the canal my thoughts are the same. Mum says she always wanted to tell me, was always going to tell me, she says she was waiting for the right time. I'm in high school now, she thinks I'm old enough to understand.

'It's for the best,' she said. 'Now you know how I feel.'

Secretly, I think she only told me so that she wouldn't have to be the only one who knew. Like it is a gift she has given me that I don't really want. Sometimes, I forget for a bit, like today at school when we got put into our new form groups for year seven, I was thinking about that and who I wanted to be in form with and I wasn't thinking about what Mum told me at all. But then I remembered, and it felt as though I was finding out all over again.

That happens in the mornings too. I wake up at home, and the windows are all misted and frosty and the air is seeping through the sides, and I re-remember everything and then I don't want to get out of bed because my stomach feels sick and twisty. I think about them and I wonder if the air is coming through their windows and making them cold, but somehow I know that it isn't. Then Mum comes in and says I need to go to school, and I feel like I hate her then because this is all her fault.

I dream about them almost every time I close my eyes. I wake up in the night, covered in cold sweat, the bedclothes twisted around my legs. I picture their faces, the curves of their lips, the strong swoop of their noses. Then I picture their living room, imagine if I got to play with what's inside. It's all I can think about.

We drew portraits in art class yesterday. Miss Brown showed us how to draw lines across an oval shape to mark out where the eyes and nose go. She says I'm quite good at art, she says I might have a talent for it. I don't really know what that means but she smiled at me so I smiled back and showed her my drawing. We had to look at our own faces in the mirror; the eyes are much further down than you think they ought to be. Last night when we went to the house I screwed up my eyes really hard and stared at his face, noticing how far down his eyes are, trying to remember his features exactly so that I can draw them later. There was a baby in the house today, I could see its pram and when they opened the windows in the living room I could hear it crying. I think it's a girl.

When we eventually got home, Mum didn't want to talk to me, so I went and stared in the bathroom mirror for ages, looking at my own eyes, listening to the drip of the tap and the shouts of the neighbours upstairs. The walls of our flat are so thin. You can hear every argument, every cross word. If I listen carefully I can sometimes hear crying from upstairs, but I don't know who it is.

28

London

Dominic

The newsroom is busy today but Dominic doesn't care. He's almost bouncing as he walks. He hopes Corinne is feeling just as excited; she'll be in Hampstead now, telling her dad the good news. He knows it helps her to talk aloud to the headstone, pretend her dad can hear. Lots of people do that, don't they? In nine months' time they'll be able to take the baby up there. The baby! He is grinning to himself as he threads his way through the desks to Alison's office.

He isn't sure what to do about the Carlington House piece. It is due today so he's typed it up as sparingly as possible, leaving out the de Bonnier woman's strange additions. He has thought about her a lot, the sadness on her face as she stared at the ruins, the way her features twisted in pain as she walked. Part of him wants to investigate, the journalist in him wanting to push and pull until the story unearths itself, falls out of her like vomit, but somehow he can't bring himself to put her sadness to the page. Andy would say he has gone soft, and perhaps he has; he can no longer stomach the secret horrors of the world, the dark underneath full of corruption and fraud, murder and neglect. He just wants to write features. Nice and easy. Nothing to shock. Besides, the woman is elderly, the last thing they need is to be seen as taking advantage. Dominic shudders; there had been letters, two years ago now, drip-fed through the mail to the newspaper – poor handling of an inquest, inappropriate conduct by reporters leading to the untimely suicide of another member of the deceased's family. The Warrington case. They don't want that again. The press upset people, they make people do funny things. Poor woman was found floating in the canal, unable to deal with the reports in the papers about her mother.

Dominic plans to run his write-up past his boss, see what she thinks he ought to do. *Always cover your back.* The new rule of conduct for a modern-day journalist. Alison's office is much nicer than the rest of the newsroom; she has a pine table and an old-fashioned desk lamp, a stark contrast to the rest of their cheap MDF desks and harsh white bulbs. The door is partially open; Dominic hesitates. She can get a bit funny if people don't knock, a few junior reporters have got on her bad side by barging in uninvited. Still, he's not a junior now, is he? Alison likes him as much as she likes anyone.

He taps lightly on the door with his knuckles, is about to push it open, his eyes on the piece of paper in his hand. Suddenly he hears Alison's voice: low, almost a whisper. He pauses, one hand on the doorknob. Why is she talking so quietly? She sounds pissed off. Dominic is just about to leave it, come back later when he hears his own name.

'I sent Dominic, didn't I?' Alison is almost hissing the words. He strains his ears, cannot hear a response. She must be on the phone. Dominic frowns. He is curious now, piqued by his own name. Has he done something wrong? He mentally runs his mind back over his recent features. Have they been sloppy? Late?

Alison's talking again, but her voice has taken on a different tone, sort of pleading.

'We had a deal,' she is saying, 'I thought we had a deal.' There's a pause. Dominic hovers.

'Well that's not my fault, that's yours!' Alison's voice is louder now, annoyed. 'I don't know why—' She breaks off. 'OK. Well, I don't know why she didn't go with him then. I don't know why you care so much, but I did what you asked, so—'

There is silence. After a second, Dominic hears the sound of the receiver being put down, the squeak of Alison's leather chair as she leans back in it. What the hell was all that about?

He is still holding the piece of paper with the Carlington House copy on it. He clears his throat, knocks firmly on the door and goes into the office. Alison doesn't look up when he comes in, is sitting with her head in her hands. Her brown hair is usually perfectly coiffed but she's clearly been running her fingers through it.

'Alison? Hi, sorry to interrupt, I just wanted to check some things on the property feature, I know it was quite urgent,' Dominic says. He puts the paper on the desk, slides it towards her. He coughs, feeling awkward. She doesn't say anything.

'So I wanted to just check with you – I've had to keep it fairly short as the owner seems a bit …'

Alison finally looks up at him, as though she's seeing him for the first time.

'It doesn't matter, Dom,' she says. 'Thanks though. You can just leave it on my desk. I'll look at it later.'

Dominic hovers in front of her desk. Surely if it was something to do with him she would bring it up now? He doesn't really want to admit he was eavesdropping, that would not go down well.

He hesitates, glances at his watch. It is late, almost five-thirty. 'OK, thanks then,' he says. He turns around, pulls the door to behind him and heads back to his desk. He wonders what that conversation was about. Hearing the editor-in-chief say his name makes him nervous, but he can't think of anything that he's done particularly wrong. Perhaps she's talking about someone else.

Erin comes up to him as Dominic reaches his desk. He hasn't seen her all afternoon, has been chained to his desk with the Carlington piece, stopping work only once to grab a Twix from the vending machine in the corner.

She looks surprised to see him.

'Shit, Dominic! I thought you were out this afternoon!'

'Nope,' he tells her, 'right here!'

'Oh, God!' She puts a hand to her eyes. 'I've just been upstairs with Corinne – she came to see you but I couldn't see you at your desk so I told her you were out on a job. Andy said he thought you'd gone to cover Paul on the King's Cross piece?'

Dominic frowns. Why would Andy have said that? 'No, I was with Alison earlier but I haven't been out. Did you say Corinne's upstairs?'

Erin nods. 'In the café. I bought her a hot chocolate, bless her. She seems a bit upset about something. You'd

214

better go up. I'm so sorry, I'd have come and got you ages ago if I'd known you were here.'

'Don't worry about it,' he says, quickly grabbing his jacket. 'Thanks for taking care of her! I'll go up now. Did she say what was wrong?'

Erin shakes her head. 'No, I'm sorry. I hope everything's OK.'

Dominic takes the stairs two at a time, his heart beating fast. Why the hell did Andy say he was out on a job? Has he really got such a problem with Corinne that he'd go that far? Jesus, it's pathetic. There are enough women boosting Andy's ego without his girlfriend needing to be one of them. He looks at his watch. It is gone five-thirty, now. The stairs seem to rise up before him, as though they are multiplying, they are never-ending. He moves faster. Sweat pools beneath his collar.

29

London

Corinne

Dominic hasn't come up to the café. I wait and wait. An hour passes. An hour and a half. Every minute that goes by feels twice as long.

At five-thirty the cleaner tells me they're closing.

'But I'm waiting for my boyfriend, he works in this building, he works downstairs,' I say.

The blonde girl from Dominic's paper was so sweet and apologetic, she said she had to get back to her desk after we'd had a hot chocolate each and shared a gingerbread man, though I couldn't eat much.

'I'm so sorry, Corinne! But look, I bet Dom will be back soon and I'll grab him as soon as he gets in, tell him to come meet you up here. OK?'

'Thank you so much,' I say, and I smile weakly at her. Although I feel calmer, more in control, I don't really know where else to go, I don't want to go home to the flat alone. So I stay huddled up in the cafeteria, wrapped in my big scarf, waiting for Dom to come up. I've tried his mobile, several times. He's probably got it on silent, he often does when he's working. Still, I wish he'd check it occasionally.

I realised after she'd gone that I'd been rude, hadn't even asked her name. I can't think straight. She talked to me, I think, but I wasn't really listening, just drinking my hot chocolate and trying to keep calm, picturing the horrible sight of Dad's gravestone, the flash of black paint smeared across it. That awful word.

I should have thanked her properly, she seemed to know exactly what I needed and just talked to take my mind off things, like you would to a child having an injection. She didn't pry, didn't make me tell her what was wrong. She chattered to me about what did I do, and did I have a family, and how lovely Dom is. Apparently they work together, she started as a court reporter at the beginning of the year. She's been working on the Claudia Winters case, the woman who got life imprisonment the other day.

'It was brutal,' she tells me, 'It got to me a bit. That poor daughter of hers. Left all alone in that house.'

I nod. 'Dominic hates things like that, it's why he does features.'

'He's a real diamond, that one,' she said to me, munching on the leg of the gingerbread man. 'You're lucky.'

I'd smiled weakly back at her, pushed the rest of the biscuit towards her. She didn't seem to mind that I kept glancing at the door, she just kept me calm, kept me talking – where was I from, was I always arty, did I like living in London? She'd only just moved here, was still getting to grips with the city.

'You'll be fine,' I told her. 'You'll love it in the end.'

She'd raised her eyebrows, slurped her hot chocolate. 'I hope so!'

Then she paid for both our drinks and told me to take care of myself.

'Don't worry,' she said, 'I'll make sure Dom comes up as soon as I see him. Promise.'

'Miss.' The cleaner is in front of me, hands on her hips. 'We're closing the cafeteria. I'm sorry, but you'll have to leave.'

I get up to go, and that's when he comes in. He looks as though he's been running.

'Corinne! What are you doing here?'

I can't speak, I'm so relieved to see him. The cleaning lady stares at us as I fall into his arms, cling to his shirt. *Liar. Liar. Liar.* An image comes to my mind, suddenly, of my mother clinging to my father, just like this. She'd been crying too, and he'd held her tight, close to his chest, her head tucked under his shoulder like mine is now. The memory makes the tears come faster, my ribcage seems to strain under the pressure of what I'm feeling and my knees buckle slightly. Dominic is saying something, and his voice sounds panicked, he wants to know what's wrong, but I'm so exhausted and scared that I can't form the words properly. All I can do is hold on to him, standing here in the newspaper café, while the light fades outside and the cleaning lady switches off the lights, one by one, until we are standing there in the darkness, surrounded by chairs on tables, the only sound the drip drip drip of the cafeteria tap.

Then

He came round today. He actually came to our flat. I couldn't believe it. Mum told me not to come down so I stayed at the top of the stairs, peering through the banisters. It felt like I was in prison.

I could hear them talking and then it got louder and louder, they started really shouting, and I put my hands over my ears because it felt really frightening. I don't always like Mum but I don't want her to cry. It went on for a while and I was just starting to think that I would have to go downstairs when there was the sound of the front door slamming, then silence.

'Mum?' I yelled, and I took my hands away from my ears and ran down our staircase. There was no one in the flat. I reached up and opened the front door, she hadn't locked it, and then I saw her in the street. She had no shoes on, her hair was blowing everywhere. There were tears and snot running all down her face and her hand looked as if it was bleeding. I looked around for him but he wasn't there, he was over on the other side of the street, getting into a car. I only saw the back of his head, the shine of his waxy coat. Mum didn't even hear me calling to her, she just stood there, crying and shaking in the cold. It was horrible. I looked around and I saw them, all the faces at the windows on our street, staring out at Mum, shaking their heads and drawing the curtains. They don't like her. They don't like me.

30

London

Ashley

Ashley's handbag hits the floor with a thump as she deposits it by the front door. She heads straight to the loft, doesn't bother knocking on James's door. He's home for once so she is just going to ask him, she's going to find out what's going on. Enough is enough. The bank had been absolutely humiliating. Ashley had stood in front of the cashier for a few seconds, let his words sink into her brain. *That account has been emptied.* Then she had turned around, walked blindly out of the bank, all the way home, as if in a trance. All she can hear is June's words in her ear: be careful, and be prepared. Her heart thuds. Sweat coats her underarms.

Ashley turns the door handle and barges into the room. Nothing prepares her for what she sees inside and, despite herself, she lets out a gasp.

Her husband is crying. Big, fat tears slide down his cheeks, seep into the collar of his crisp blue shirt, and his broad shoulders shake as he sits in front of the computer screen, the page before him filled with digits.

Ashley has only ever seen her husband cry three times in their whole married life, when each of their children were born. In a few seconds, she is beside him, holding his shoulders, her throat contracting in total, instant fear.

'James!' She shakes him slightly and his hands go to her waist. His tears continue and Ashley strokes the top of his head, trying to be gentle, but her mind is racing and she just wants him to tell her, to come clean.

'James,' she says. 'I know about the money. I went to the bank. Enough. You have to tell me now. You owe me that, James. Please.' Her voice breaks.

His face is buried against her stomach, a hot mass, and she holds his cheeks and pulls him away from her so that she can look into his eyes. He can't look at her, and as she realises this, Ashley feels as though her heart is breaking inside her chest, because she can't believe this is it, that he's really done it, he's betrayed her after all these years. It must be a woman. He's spent all the money on some woman. He's leaving her. She knows it, can feel it in her bones.

'I need you to calm down, James,' she says, and her voice is low and steady now, at odds with her scrambling insides. 'Let's go downstairs, we can talk this through.'

She wipes her own eyes, lets go of him and heads for the stairs, leaving him up there in the half-light, waiting for him to follow.

In the empty kitchen, Ashley goes to the cupboard and finds a bar of dark chocolate. She pulls apart the silvery foil and crams the cold pieces into her mouth without tasting them properly, they lodge in her throat, her stomach too knotted to eat. James's footsteps come up behind her. She braces herself, interlocks her fingers behind her back. *Be prepared.*

'Let's sit down,' she says, and suddenly she feels absurd; like all of this is happening to someone else, like she's watching it in one of the bad television shows that Lucy likes. They sit at the table with the clutter of phone chargers and soup stains and Benji's pencil drawings. He has been drawing the solar system but the planets are outsized: a tiny Jupiter cowers next to a towering Earth. Alien figures dot the surface of the sun, rainbow coloured. Ashley puts a hand to her chest. Her heart is beating so fast she worries it will stop altogether. In her mind she suddenly begins to see a roll of images, as though on a video – her and James getting married, him standing before her in the church, them laughing together at a party, her younger self screaming when he asked her to be his wife. She can't bear it. She will have to bear it.

'Ashley,' he begins. She takes a deep breath, looks him in the eye. She'll deal with it. She'll deal with it. She. Will. Deal. With. It.

'Ashley, I made a mistake.'

The ceiling is crashing in, coming down towards her. Her mouth is dry. It is how she knew it would be.

'OK,' she says, and she doesn't know where the word has come from, she cannot feel the tips of her fingers. She can't bear it. She loves him.

He can't look at her, his gaze flits away and he hangs his head. 'I lost Parkway Publishing a deal, a big deal in America. The eReaders cannot be sold in the States, I got the figures wrong, created a backlog of money that the company can't clear. Daniel is … well, Daniel's fuming.'

She stares at him, her mouth open, her mind frozen.

'I've tried, Ashley. I've spent the last few months in meetings, begging Daniel for a chance, trying to persuade him to let me keep my job,' James says. 'It's why I've had to work so much, it's why I've been taking phone calls all the time. I offered to try to make up the company shortfall. I've had to use our money.'

His face is drawn; there are purple pockets underneath his eyes. 'I've just been trying to sort it out, and I didn't want to tell you unless … unless I had to. I didn't want you to be ashamed of me.' His voice breaks, but he takes a deep breath, carries on.

'It's not … certain, yet, what's going to happen, but it means that I … that we've … it means we've lost a lot of money, Ash. I'm so sorry. I hired a lawyer last month to help me, to try to get us out of the loophole that meant we lost the deal. It was expensive. God, I'm sorry. It means that … it means that things don't look good. For me, I mean. For us.'

Ashley stares at him. The dark chocolate tastes bitter on her tongue. The silence stretches out between them, broken only by the ticking of the clock on the wall.

After a few minutes, she finds her voice. She almost wants to laugh. It is so not what she had been expecting.

'James,' she tells him, 'I thought you were having an affair.'

He stares at her. He looks shocked, upset. 'Ashley!'

'I did, James, I'm sorry but I did. You've been acting so strangely, and you're never here, and—' She breaks off. 'The phone calls.'

'What phone calls? I told you, I've had to be on the mobile whenever the office call.'

'No.' She shakes her head. 'Not that. The phone calls to the house, to my mobile phone. I've had what, four, maybe

223

five, prank calls. From a woman. I thought they were for you.' She stares at him, frowning. 'And I had another, two days ago, and she was laughing, the voice on the other end was laughing at me. It was horrible. I wanted to tell you but then Lucy … Lucy went out.'

James is looking at her, bewildered. 'Nothing to do with me,' he says, his words oddly defensive, as though he's forgotten what he's just told her. 'Perhaps they're just prank calls. Why didn't you tell me?'

'I was scared to ask,' Ashley says. 'I thought … I was so sure you were … and I couldn't stand to hear it. I thought maybe if I ignored it for long enough it would go away.' She dips her head, stares at the tabletop. Heat floods her cheeks. 'I suppose they must just be prank calls. If you're not—'

'God, no!' he cuts her off, shakes his head, looks so sure that in that moment Ashley cannot doubt him.

She puts a hand to her head. She feels foolish now, a wave of embarrassment comes over her as she recalls herself screeching into the telephone. Can they just be prank calls? Is her husband telling the truth?

'How could you have thought that of me, Ashley?' James says, and he suddenly looks so hurt that Ashley starts to feel awful, because she doesn't know really, she has let herself get carried away, she knows she has. This is James, this is her James. Her husband. *Oh, thank God.* She leans forward, puts her head in her hands. James touches the top of her head.

'I'm so sorry, Ash. I'm sorry I didn't tell you, but I was – I am – so ashamed. I don't know what we're going to do. It's why I panicked, you know, at the weekend. Because of the money you gave to Corinne. It was … it was the last bit of money we had.'

224

31

London

Corinne

Dominic wants to go out for dinner. He drives me home from his office, trying to cheer me up the whole way. He makes jokes, touches my knee, says he's happy I came to meet him at work. I have to tell him about the headstone. I can't find the words. He chatters on, he's like a monkey. He thinks I'm upset about Dad, that the cemetery has made me sad. If only that was it.

'Come on, Cor. It's the best news. The very best news. We're going to be parents. At last. Christ, I think it's only just sinking in.' He turns to look at me, taking one hand off the wheel to touch the side of my face. 'Your dad would want you to be happy. You know he would.'

When we get home, he jumps in the shower, comes out all wide-eyed. His cheeks are flushed. When he puts his arms around me, he smells of minty shower gel and toothpaste. My stomach is between us. Just for a second I think of how happy I could be, how happy I would feel if we were a normal family, if all these horrible things weren't ruining it all. I feel like the moment I tell him, I'm ruining things, spoiling the happiness for us both.

'I've booked us a table,' he says, 'at Daphne's in Holborn. You ready for dinner?'

'I … Dominic, Dom, I need to tell you something.' I don't want to go out for dinner, right now it's the last thing I feel like doing.

'OK, OK, but the reservation is for seven – tell me over dinner?' He grins at me, puts on his nicest blue shirt. I watch as he fastens up the buttons, so capable, so in control. Not like me. Reluctantly, I splash cold water onto my face, smear foundation across my cheeks. On the street outside he flags down a taxi.

'Special occasion. Let's travel in style.'

In the taxi, I catch sight of myself in the rear-view mirror. I look awful; I think of the beautiful blonde girl at his office today and cringe inside. I don't want to go to a fancy restaurant looking like this. Why is he being so over the top?

'Is everything OK, Dom?' I ask him.

He turns to me and kisses me. 'It's more than OK. Isn't it?'

I put my hand on the car door, feel the lock snapped shut between my fingers. Dominic sees me and reaches out his hand to take mine, holds it tightly between his own. My eyes stay fastened on the lock.

The restaurant is gorgeous, all twinkly lights and crisp white tablecloths. The waiter pulls back my chair for me and I sit down, feel the tension in my shoulders lift slightly.

'Dom, listen. The reason I came to your building earlier is because I went to the cemetery, I went to Dad's grave.'

'I know you did – how was it? I was just about to ask. I wanted to give you a chance to calm down.'

He smiles at me, grips my hand across the tabletop. *Calm down*. He doesn't mean it how it sounds, I know he doesn't. He looks so handsome tonight that the feel of his hand makes my breath catch slightly in my throat. I take a deep breath, and tell him about Dad's headstone.

'Fuck,' he says, shaking his head at me. 'Cor, that's horrible! Don't worry, OK, we'll clean it off, we'll go sort it out. It's probably a bunch of vandals. Teenagers with nothing better to do.'

I can't eat my meal; the waiter's brought over a beautiful plate of scallops but my stomach is in knots.

'I don't think so, Dom, I don't think it's kids,' I say. 'Why would they choose that word? Why would they write liar? Dad didn't lie about anything. I feel like … I feel …' I drop my head against my chest. The restaurant feels wobbly, as though the walls are closing in around me. I force myself to look up. 'There's been a lot of weird stuff happening, Dom. I know you think I'm making it up—'

'I didn't say that!'

'But I feel as though – I feel as though I'm going mad. It's such a horrible feeling. Like my mind's playing tricks on me, and it's getting worse. That rocking horse …'

He keeps looking at the scallops, I can tell he wants to start eating.

'Eat,' I say. 'Come on, just start. I'm not hungry.'

There's a long pause. I can feel myself holding my breath, waiting for him to speak. Eventually, I can't stand it any more.

'Dom? Say something, for God's sake. Tell me what you're thinking.'

'I thought you'd be happy,' Dom says then, and his voice sounds so disappointed that I can't bear it. 'Aren't you? We're going to have a baby, Cor. A *baby*.'

'I know!' I say, my voice rising. I don't want him to be cross with me, I can't bear this, I can't bear ruining things between us. I'm gabbling at him now.

'I know and I am, Dom, I'm so happy about that, of course I am, but please, will you just listen to me about this? There's something not right. There's something funny going on, and I think it's to do with my Dad. It's something to do with the doll house.'

'Corinne.' Dom looks at me hard. 'Corinne, your dad is ... well, he's dead. He's not here any more, and I know it's hard, I know how hard the last year has been for you but—'

The waiter's in front of us, filling our water glasses. I smile at him tightly, try to say thank you but it comes out as a whisper.

Dominic exhales, puts his hands flat on the tablecloth.

'Cor. Look. I love you to bits and I don't want to lie to you. I think maybe ... I think maybe you ought to go see someone. You've not been yourself lately, and I think perhaps it's all just getting a bit much, you know, with work and the baby and everything we've been through with the IVF. It might help if you talked to someone. A professional, I mean.'

I stare at him. Is this what he thinks? Is this what I need? I think of the little yellow rocking horse, clutched in my hand. Gone the next minute. Is Dominic right? He is the person I trust most in the world, whose opinion I count on. Does that mean I can't trust myself? I don't know any more.

'Maybe you're right,' I say, and my eyes are starting to fill with tears for the hundredth time today. I put my hands across my stomach. Dominic gets up, comes over to my chair, ignoring the stares from the waiters.

'Shh,' he says, 'Shh, Cor. Come on, we'll sort this out, we'll get you right. I promise. Shh, my love.' He puts his arms around me, rocks me back and forth as though I'm a child. I cling to him like a woman drowning. Because isn't that what I am?

At home, he makes me a drink while I get into bed, pull the covers up to my chin like a child. I feel pathetic, small. When he comes into the bedroom there's something else in his hands. I sit up.

'Found this on the doormat,' he says, 'We must have missed it when we came in. Addressed to you.' He throws me a little Jiffy bag, my name is scrawled across the top. No stamp. 'Here you are, here's your hot water.' He puts the mug down next to me, starts getting undressed, but I'm not concentrating, I'm holding the little parcel in my hands. My heart is beating fast.

'What's wrong?' he says, and when he sees my face he actually rolls his eyes.

'Oh, come on. Here, I'll open it. It won't be anything bad.' He's annoyed with me, I can tell, or frustrated at the very least.

He sits down on the bed with me, rips open the Jiffy bag in one quick motion. My breath catches in my throat. I clutch his hands.

'Dominic!'

'What?' he says. 'What's so bad about this?'

It is a little rocking cradle, made of wood. Inside it are a pair of little pink bootees, fit for a newborn, and a handwritten note. *Congratulations*.

32

London

Ashley

Colours is dead on Monday. Ashley has been with the children all weekend while James stayed in the office. On Saturday night he'd come home at eleven. She'd left him dinner out on the stove, tried to make conversation with Lucy as the four of them sat around the kitchen table, Holly banging her spoon on the surface. Her older daughter had been moody, non-committal. It was almost a relief to put her on the school bus this morning.

There is a wind up today and the streets of London are quieter than they usually are; she supposes the weather is keeping people indoors. She drives to June's house, kisses Holly on her little rosy lips.

'You be a good girl for me, won't you?' she says. She has been, the last few nights have seen her sleep almost through, waking up only twice and crying a little, different altogether from the roaring screams of before she started the medicine. Ashley hopes to start weaning her off it, but is scared of going back to the nights of no sleep at all. The chance to sleep is just so tempting, so delicious.

June is a long time coming to the door. Ashley hesitates on the doorstep, checks her watch. She'll be late if she doesn't go now.

'June?' she calls through the letterbox, hearing her voice echo back at her through the flat. No reply. She checks her watch again. Holly begins to mewl, little cries that get louder and louder. It's cold, beginning to rain, the first drops falling onto the dark blue of Ashley's coat. She tugs Holly's little hood further over her face, protecting her daughter from the water.

'June?' She rings the bell one more time, knocks on the door. Nothing. Has she got the days mixed up? Ashley sighs. Probably. She feels as though everything is running away with her, as though she is losing her focus. June is most likely expecting them tomorrow instead. Ashley looks down at her daughter, who clings to her a little tighter. Her fingers latch onto Ashley's coat button. Ashley is on her own at the café today, Megan is off. Perhaps she can just bring Holly along.

Ashley straps Holly back into the car and drives to Colours, making a mental note to call June later in the day to confirm the schedule. As predicted, the café is very quiet. Ashley places Holly on the counter at the back, feeds her quickly and stands with her while she gnaws on one of the plastic spoons they use for stirring the takeaway coffees. She rests her chin on her palm. On quiet days there is no need for more than one waitress, she has the café to herself.

'We'll be OK, won't we, Holly?' She touches her daughter's hair. Holly smiles at her, calmer now. Ashley stares into her blue eyes, thinking of her father. They are so like his. She wishes he could see his third grandchild, could see how gorgeous she is, how lucky Ashley has been. She touches the tiny needlemark bruise made by the blood test.

'You're such a brave girl,' she says to her daughter, kissing her on the forehead. 'You're going to be just fine, aren't you, my love? The doctor is going to tell us that you're just fine.' Holly gurgles and blinks. Ashley smiles. Perhaps she ought to bring Holly to work more often; her presence makes the café seem brighter somehow, warmer. No doubt James would have something to say about that though.

Ashley's mind is still reeling from his confession. She has thought about it all weekend. She is overwhelmingly relieved that he is not having an affair, of course she is, but she cannot believe that he has been so foolish as to lose their money without telling her. All of it. And none of it explains the phone calls.

'You're a little busybody, Ashley Hawes,' her father used to say to her, ruffling her hair and grinning. 'Always wanting to know what's what.' On occasion, people have been less kind; the words 'control freak' have been thrown at her more than once.

But this is different. This is her husband! This is their money, their savings. Their life. How can she not want to know what's going on?

Ashley has never once regretted giving up her own career to have Lucy while James's took off. She had been an assistant in the publicity department of Parkway Publishing after graduating from Manchester, enjoyed a couple of years of long lunches with the media followed by afternoons spent huddled over her desk, surrounded by books and paper. It had been fun. James had begun working as a digital executive a few weeks before the office summer party, where they had bonded over the overly pretentious canapés that tasted like mush. One of Ashley's pink plastic earrings (she'd liked them at the time) had dropped to the floor and he'd stooped, picked it up, spent the rest of the evening by her side while they drank cheap wine that tasted far too sweet.

Their first date was three days later at a shellfish restaurant, just after Ashley turned twenty-three. She had been overwhelmed by his interest, at five years her senior he made her feel special, like she was someone important. She remembers trying to match his opinion of her, to live up to expectations. Ashley had tried to dip her fingers daintily into the water bowl in the restaurant but ruined it by getting hot melted butter all down her white halter neck, leaving an embarrassing stain. James had made eating the shrimps look easy, splitting the pink shells and popping the insides into his mouth in one fluid motion. Ashley remembers watching him crush the plump bodies between his teeth and feeling weirdly impressed.

They had dated for nine months before Ashley found out she was pregnant. At the time, it hadn't seemed to matter; her dad had made the odd comment about how young they were, and asked gently if she'd thought properly about her career, but Ashley had been over the moon; although she was nervous, having babies was all she'd ever really wanted to do. James had been fantastic, and they'd got engaged a week after finding out. It had seemed hopelessly romantic at the time. She used to think everything James did was near enough perfect. Now she isn't sure.

She runs through options in her head, pulls herself back into the present. They could take out a loan from the bank. Appeal to James's company to let him stay on. She doesn't know the ins and outs of what Daniel has told him, how close to the wire this whole thing is.

Another thought is spiralling through Ashley's mind.

She could get a proper job.

Ashley stares around the tiny café, at the little tables with their vases of flowers, at the sugar bowls sitting jauntily on the red and white cloths. She looks out of the window at the grey square in front of her. Dry leaves skitter round and around. They make her feel dizzy. Beside her, Holly taps her hand on the counter, smacks her lips together. As she stares at her, Ashley notices there is a smear of mashed banana caught in her blonde hair.

She lets herself imagine for a second what it would be like to return to work – back in an office, wearing clothes free from the muck of children. She thinks of Benji's sticky fingers, printing peanut butter on her dress. Of Lucy scowling at her across the dinner table, annoyed because Ashley has dared to tidy up her shoes. Her life has revolved around motherhood for so long. It might not be so bad. It might even be alright.

'Excuse me?'

Ashley jumps; she hasn't been paying attention and there is a customer at the counter. The girl's hair is windswept, her black leather jacket is spotted slightly with water. Ashley realises it is raining; great drops hit the window of the café.

'Sorry!' she says. 'I was miles away. What can I get for you?'

'Just a coffee, please,' the girl says. 'Black.' She smiles at Ashley and gives a little shake, like a dog dislodging water from its back. 'Horrible out there now.'

'Yes,' Ashley says, 'We've had hardly anyone in all day. Everyone's tucked up at home!'

'It's a shame,' the girl says, 'I'm only in Barnes for the night, just visiting my mother. We were hoping for a bit of sunshine on the common! Oh, who's this little munchkin?' She bends forward to Holly, strokes one of her little feet which are dangling towards the floor.

Ashley smiles. She loves it when people pay attention to her babies. Well, as long as it's the right kind. She could have done without the headmistress paying attention to Benji.

'This is Holly,' she says. 'The childminder's gone AWOL so I had to bring her in. She's my youngest.' She serves her the coffee, hands it to her with a smile.

'She's adorable,' the girl says. 'What beautiful eyes! Aren't you a cutie? Aren't you?' She is bending over Holly, who clearly likes her; she is smiling gummily, blowing bubbles like she does when she is excited. 'She's lovely,' she tells Ashley.

'Oh, thank you,' Ashley says. She strokes Holly's head. She shouldn't get so frustrated with it all, really. She is so lucky to have her baby girl.

'You take care now,' she says to the girl. 'Enjoy your night in London!'

'Oh, I will,' she says. 'Bye bye, Holly! Bye bye!'

She takes a sip of her coffee, gives Ashley a half-smile. As she turns to leave, there is a huge thunderclap and the wind roars; one of the wooden chairs positioned out on the square tips over, lies helpless on the ground.

'Oh well!' The girl laughs, turns back to grin at Ashley. 'Atmospheric, I guess. Thanks for the coffee.'

The door swings to behind her and she is gone. Ashley watches her pick her way across the square, clutching the coffee to her chest. Holly giggles, the sound echoing in the empty café. Ashley reaches out, rubs her daughter's back absent-mindedly, moving her hand in little round circles. She is thinking about Lucy.

Her elder daughter has been even more closed off than usual since the night she got drunk. Every time Ashley walks into the room she is on her mobile, giggling at the screen, tapping away while ignoring her family. Ashley has tried to corner her, talk to her alone, but each time she does so she is met with irritation or, worse, total disdain.

She looks at her watch. School will be about to finish. The storm is worsening. Colours has barely had five customers all day.

Ashley makes a sudden decision. She will go to the school, go pick her daughter up. She can catch her at the gates, make sure she's OK. Perhaps they can talk on the way home in the car. It doesn't really matter if she shuts up Colours early, just this once.

'Come on, Hol,' she says, and she scoops her up, fastens on her little coat again and zippers it to her daughter's chin. She takes a cloth, wipes around Holly's mouth; the skin is wet from where her daughter has burst saliva bubbles onto herself.

As she grabs her car keys from where they lie on the side, Ashley's fingers graze the little tip jar full of coins. Her eye is drawn by the colours, the silver and gold glinting out at her. Half the tips are her own, of course, but she usually just ignores them, leaves them all for Megan. Today, Ashley feels a shiver go through her as her fingers reach into the jar, pick out several pound coins before she really notices what she is doing. Ashley shoves the coins into her pocket and leaves the café, locking up quickly behind her, feeling as she does so an odd wave of guilt, as though somebody is watching her, as though somebody is judging. Holly's breath is warm against her neck.

Then

Now that I'm older, I walk home from school by myself. Some of the girls in my year have been talking to me recently, I think they're trying to be nice to me. I'm not sure. Mum always tells me that I haven't to trust anyone, and sometimes I think she's right, and sometimes I don't know.

Sometimes I think about what my life would be like if none of this had happened, if I had a normal family, and people who loved me, and things to play with. It makes me want to scream. If it's very late at night and I can't sleep, I do scream. I push my face really deep into the pillow and open my mouth as wide as it will go and yell at the top of my lungs. If I get tired I just have to think about them all in the house all over again and then I can feel the anger building up inside me, and I scream and I scream to let it all out. Sometimes I fall asleep with my mouth wide open, mid-way through a scream. It leaves a big oval mark on my flat white pillow. Mum says I could suffocate one day if I'm not careful.

I was walking back from school today and I saw a group of the sixth form girls all clustered together by the bike sheds, and one of them looked just like her. The prettier one with the darker hair. Then I started to think about what she might be doing and I suddenly wanted to see. It isn't fair for me not to know, to be the one who is left out.

So I changed my walk home and instead I walked to their house. I pretended to Mum that I was going to Natasha's, which is a joke because she doesn't even talk to me any more, not even to be mean. Instead I went to theirs. It took me quite a long time and when I got there my back was hurting from the way my school bag was digging into my shoulders, and my feet had blisters from where my shoes had rubbed. I didn't care though;

I was just happy that I had got there. I went to the hole in the fence but I can't really fit through so well any more, so instead I walked around to the front of the house, where the bushes meet the road. In the summertime, those bushes have flowers on, little pink buds that dart out from the green. But it's only just March so everything still looks kind of brown. He was there, he must not be working. I could only see a little sliver because they'd shut the curtains but I could see his body flickering past, quick flashes of his shirt. I imagined what would happen if I just knocked on the door, introduced myself. What would he say? Would he still recognise me?

I was just about to turn around and go back when I heard them. Voices coming towards me, up the road. It was the mother, walking with one of them, the one who didn't get married. I think she's his favourite. Maybe that's why he wants to keep her at home. They were laughing at something, and her hair was swinging down her back, plaited and tied with a shiny band a bit like the one I wanted the other day but Mum wouldn't buy me. I panicked, I didn't know what to do, Mum says we aren't ever allowed to let them see us. So I ducked my head down and I ran, ignoring how much my shoes were hurting, I put my head against my chest and gripped the straps of my rucksack and ran full speed down the lane. My breathing was funny and my chest hurt but I got away, I escaped before they saw me. When I got home, much later, the insides of my shoes were all stained with blood. I couldn't really feel much pain though, which is weird because both of my ankles were rubbed completely raw. Nothing seems to affect me much these days. I'm getting tough.

*

Last night, Mum and I stayed up talking, but I didn't tell her about going to the house on my own. I didn't need to. I'm halfway through high school, nearly an adult, I can deal with things differently. She let me have a glass of wine with her and it was nice, it made me feel like she liked me, like I was a proper grown-up who she could talk to and be friends with. The wine was red, dark, it stained my lips like cherries. The people at school don't drink red wine, they drink brightly coloured bottles and gin mixed with soda. It's sophisticated to drink red wine.

Mum sat me down at the table and she told me everything again, and she explained why we had been doing what we do all this time. After I'd finished the wine she gave me a little bit more, just half a glass this time, and after a bit I started to enjoy myself. Being with my mum, talking like a grown-up. It was good. I felt like I was being taken seriously, I wasn't an annoying child any more. Mum said she never thought I was an annoying child but that she knew when I was little that I couldn't have understood everything. She said she hopes I do now. She hopes I realise what we have to do.

The more Mum tells me, the angrier I get. She tells me about all the things he said, the promises he made. I can tell it makes her sad but it makes me angry. It's as though she's lit a fire underneath me and it is starting to burn, hotter and hotter, brighter and brighter. It gives me something to focus on when life starts to seem a bit grey, it gives me something to think about when the men on the streets stare at me, call things after my back. I hate it when they do that, I hate the way they look at my body. I didn't choose to look like this. I don't know where this body has come from. I feel like one of the dummies we used to draw in art class when I was younger, all long limbs and awkward angles. I feel like I don't belong to myself.

Mum says she's glad I can understand more now. We go to the house together the next week. I can't fit through the fence but we sit in the car outside on the street, headlights off like usual. It's just the two of them living there now, but the girls visit a lot. I saw them all the other day, another perfect family arriving in their big black car. I watched them all get out, unfold their legs and slam the doors behind them, pop pop pop like matchsticks falling out of a box. She's pregnant again, she looks as if she's about to burst. The sight of her stomach is like a knife in my heart. No doubt he'll love this one as much as the rest.

I'm just watching when there is the sudden sound of a siren behind us, a flash of blue lights. I duck down straight away and Mum puts the keys in the ignition, her foot on the ground. The engine roars. The lights dance over us, blue diamonds in the darkness. My heart beats so loudly that I almost vomit, I want to open the car window to let fresh air in but we don't want to draw any attention to us. I have to take deep breaths, in through my nose and out through my mouth, while Mum drives us away around the corner. We stop the car on a side street and sit for a while in the dark. There is silence for a moment. I swallow.

'He wouldn't call the police,' Mum says. 'It's too risky for him.' She says it a couple of times, almost to herself, as though she's trying to make herself believe it. Then there is a roaring sound and we both look up. The blue lights are speeding past again, and my heart jumps to my throat, but it isn't the police. It's an ambulance.

33

Corinne

I cannot make Dom understand. He says that somebody sending me a congratulations gift is hardly a threat, he thinks I'm being mad.

'It's sweet, Cor,' he says. 'It's just a token gesture, isn't it? Maybe it's Ash? Or your mum, or what's her name, the girl you've made friends with over the way?'

'Gilly?'

'Yeah. Maybe she wanted to give you something nice. I mean, come on. It says congratulations. I hardly think we can take that to the police. Someone's congratulated me on my pregnancy!' He puts on a silly voice, gives me a cuddle. I glare at him.

'It's the cradle,' I say. 'We had a cradle like this when we were young. In the doll house.'

He throws his hands up in the air, I can feel the frustration coming off him. 'Corinne, those things are ten a penny. Come on. Get your coat on, it's cold outside. Got to keep warm for the baby.' He rubs my stomach, kisses me gently. 'I love you,' he says. 'Please trust me.'

We're going to go to the cemetery this afternoon, to get Dad's grave cleaned up. Dom still thinks the graffiti is probably just kids and that they'll have done it to several headstones, not just Dad's. I didn't think to look at the time. Last night I picked all the little objects up and placed them in a carrier bag, tied the plastic handles tightly. Closing them all in. Evidence. In my head it is my evidence bag, should I ever need one.

I don't know whether to call Ashley and let her know, but then I don't want to upset her if there's no point. She'll hate the thought of the grave being graffitied as much as I do. And there's no way I'm telling Mum. If she can't cope with being in a French restaurant, how can she cope with this?

So I've left it, haven't broached the subject. I called to tell her about the baby, of course, and she was delighted, she was so happy for me. I couldn't really spoil the moment.

'Corinne?' Dom is calling me, he's at the front door, jangling his keys in his hand. They're still bright and new looking, on an anonymous silver ring – whoever's got his old keys has the pleasure of his scruffy old football key ring. Lucky them.

'You go down,' I say, 'I'll meet you at the car. Just getting my scarf.'

I hear the front door slam and wait a few seconds before following him out into the hallway. I can hear his footsteps going down the stairwell, and quickly I cross over to Gilly's flat, raise my hand to knock on the door. I've got to ask her, I have to know whether it's a present from her, a genuine congratulations gift. I know it isn't. She might have seen someone else near the flat. That envelope had been hand-delivered.

I knock twice, trying to be quick, jiggling my foot nervously. I'm scared Dom will reappear at any point, tell me not to be so silly. She doesn't answer. I can hear the faint whine of some sort of toy inside the flat, one of Tommy's wind-up things. I'm about to knock again when the sound of Gilly's voice cuts over the toy.

'How many times do we have to go over this? I have told you, Ben, we need to let it go. You need to let it go.'

I freeze. Her voice is high; she sounds younger than ever. Stressed out.

'I already know that! You already know that! But I am not prepared to lose any more money, or time for that matter, on this *sodding* architecture firm and what they did. And I can't believe you're dragging this up again.' There is a pause. My heart is thudding.

'You know what, Ben? Go fuck yourself.'

I jump, slightly, the word is shocking in her voice, I've never heard her swear like that before. Another pause and then crying, the wail of Tommy starting up, seeping out into the corridor where I am standing.

'Jesus.' The word is softer, Gilly sounds like she is right on the other side of the door. Panicking, I turn away, stuff my hands into my pockets and head down the stairwell, not wanting her to find me hovering outside her front door.

'What took you so long?' Dom says, and I tell him my scarf got caught as I shut the front door.

'Sorry,' I say. 'Let's go.'

244

In the car to Hampstead I am silent. I wanted the chance to talk to Gilly but she sounded so angry, so upset. Her words turn over in my mind. *Architecture firm.* I wonder who it was, who she means. It sounds as though they really screwed her over. My dad used to talk about that sometimes, about small companies who set themselves up then defrauded their clients, or did a half-job on an expensive project.

'Cutting corners,' he used to say. 'Except it's usually a lot more than that, and it's people's lives. When you're messing with someone's home, you're messing with their family, their life.' He'd smile at me. 'You know what they say. Home is where the heart is.' It was where his heart was, in spite of the pull of the city, the attention and the accolades. I knew that his heart belonged with us. But perhaps it's not the same for everyone.

I wonder what had happened to Gilly?

'You look tired,' Dom says to me, jolting me out of my thoughts. I blink, rub my eyes with the back of my hand. I haven't been concentrating.

'I'm fine,' I say, and give him a tight smile. I put a hand on my stomach, feel the tiny swell, invisible to probably anyone but me. I can't stop thinking about the little bootees, stuffed into the cradle. Someone knows about the baby. Someone's been watching.

It's starting to rain very slightly, drops splatter the windscreen and Dom turns on the wipers. We're halfway up Finchley Road when I suddenly remember the girl in his office.

'I forgot to tell you, Dom, when I came to meet you at work on Friday I met one of your colleagues. She was nice.

I was really upset, you know, about Dad, and she was really kind to me. I didn't get her name but I wanted to thank her.'

'Oh, that's Erin,' Dom says. 'She told me she saw you, actually – a mix-up. I'm glad you weren't on your own, anyway.'

'Yes, she was lovely,' I say. 'God, she must think I'm mental. I was really upset.'

'Understandably so.' He reaches out, touches my leg. His hand is warm through my jeans. 'Guess who's got his eye on her, though?'

I stare at him. 'Not Andy?'

Dominic nods grimly.

'Yeah. To be honest, I think he's done with her already. Moved quick, you know what he's like.' Dom's eyes are on the road, flicking the indicator as we swerve round the roundabout.

'Poor thing.' I give an involuntary shiver. I think of Dom's Christmas party last year, Andy staring down my blouse. I could feel his eyes on me for the whole evening, even when I was stood next to Dom. Sleazy doesn't even begin to cover it. He's hated me ever since, I think. Not that I care what he thinks of me. I know he doesn't like me being with Dom. Thinks I hold him back. Hold him back from what?

'She's so young, though!' I say.

Dom nods. 'I know. I tried to tell him, sort of, but hey, since when has he listened to me?'

'True,' I say. 'That's true. At least you tried.'

'Do you mind if we catch the last of the football?' Dom asks, and I shake my head no, turn to look out of the window as the noise of the commentator fills the car. The shower has stopped and the sun is coming out from behind the clouds, lighting up Hampstead, making the pavements sparkle.

The gates to the cemetery loom up before us. It looks much less threatening with the sun out, with Dom at my side, but still there is a little tug in my stomach, a twist of fear. As Dom cuts the engine I reach into the back for the bucket of cleaning stuff we brought with us: scrubbers, gloves and white spirit.

'Let's do this,' Dom says. He switches off the radio and grabs my hand as we walk to the graveside. For a moment as we walk, the instinct comes over me to turn and run, flee from the cemetery and what is inside. But his hand is tight around mine. I can't.

It looks awful. The sight of it shocks me all over again – the black paint is so harsh, so brutal. Dominic whistles under his breath as he sees the black letters, dark and foreboding against the pale stone. He glances at me, I think he's mainly relieved that I wasn't making it up. I'm relieved too, because for a moment, I wasn't so sure. Since the rocking horse disappeared I have started to doubt myself, more and more, double-check my thoughts almost before I think them. I hate it.

We kneel down, start to scrub the stone together. The paint comes off fairly easily under the chemicals and I start to feel a bit better. I run my hand over Dad's name, trace the letters with my fingers. He doesn't deserve this. He was the best man I have ever known.

'It's almost the anniversary,' I say softly.

Dom nods. 'End of the month. I know.'

'Sometimes it feels like yesterday.'

'Is your mum going to come up?'

'I hope so,' I say. 'She finds it really hard though – well, you know what happened last week. Apparently they're holding a memorial dinner thing for him too, at the Royal Institute of British Architects. Over in Marylebone. She doesn't want to go.' I glance at him. He nods. He doesn't think there's anything strange about Mum's reasons for leaving London the other day.

'But she said she'd try to come see us, visit the grave together. You might have to go get her, actually,' I say, and he nods. 'And Ash will be here. I'll get daffodils, hopefully it'll be more like spring soon.'

Dom looks at me. 'You might even be starting to properly show.' He looks excited.

'I'm not sure it'll happen that fast, Dom!' It won't; I'm only a few weeks gone.

I stare at the grave. I so wish my dad hadn't missed this, had lived to see me pregnant. He'd have been so happy to have another grandchild, someone else to love. Family meant everything to him.

Dominic puts his arms around me. I breathe slowly into his chest. I try to be calm.

'I love you,' I tell him. 'I'm sorry I've been so on edge, I'm sorry I got so upset the other night. You're probably right about it all.' I pause, swallow. 'I know I'm a bit … difficult to be with at the moment. I do know that.'

He tips my head back, kisses me on the lips.

'Don't be daft,' he says. 'No need to apologise. I'm sorry if I seem frustrated. But I do think you ought to think about what I said. Especially as the pregnancy continues. We want to make sure you're feeling … up to it.'

'Of course I'm up to it!' I pull back. 'Dominic!'

'Sorry, sorry.' He holds up his hands. 'You know what I mean, Cor. You'll be an amazing mum, you know that. I know that! But you've got to stop worrying. You've got to keep calm.' He pauses. 'Or I'll start to worry about you, and then we'll be the worry family!' He tickles me under the chin, moves his fingers down to stroke my neck. 'No one wants that. So just think about what I said. Come on.' He puts his arm round my waist and steers me away from the gravestone, back towards the car. I think about my evidence bag, the growing pile of objects hidden in my drawer.

As we leave, I glance back over my shoulder, at all the other graves. They stand still and silent in the grass, like little blank faces, watching me leave. Not one of them has been marked at all.

34

Ashley

Ashley stands in front of the high school, by the row of poplar trees that guard the street like willowy soldiers. Her car keys are clutched tight in her hand, the cold metal indenting her skin. Holly is sleeping in her arms; the day at the café has wiped her out. She is still at the stage where new environments, new people are all exhausting to her – they excite her, and then they tire her out. There is no sign of Lucy yet. Somewhere inside, she knows that perhaps this is a mistake, that she is trying to catch Lucy out. In what, she doesn't quite know.

Still she stands, shifts her feet back and forth in the cold. The storm has died down but the pavements are wet and the wind is still up. Her eyes are strained, fixed on the big gate, darting occasionally to the side exit, the double doors next to the slightly leaning bike sheds. It is six minutes past four; four minutes until the final bell. She imagines the screech of it inside, the simultaneous sighs of relief, her daughter carefully placing books back into her bag. They'd bought her a new rucksack just this Christmas, a dark red leather one with thin, rope-like straps. A world away from the badge-studded satchel she carted around before.

Ashley wraps her arms more tightly around Holly, grips her against her body. Lucy's drunken eyes flash in her mind. Has her daughter really grown up this fast? Is Holly going to be the same?

She isn't sure what she is looking for when the stream of teenagers begins. They pour past her too quickly; she sees flashes of badly dyed hair, triangles of ties. The smell of cigarette smoke reaches her nostrils. A group of boys pushes past her, kicking at a stray stone on the concrete, jostling each other with their shoulders. She squints at them, feels a rush of nausea as she imagines them crowding around her daughter, imagines Lucy's arms around their necks, her tongue in their mouths.

'Mum?' All of a sudden her daughter is in front of her. She looks confused; Ashley sees the momentary flicker of concern pass across her face like a shadow.

Ashley looks closely at her daughter. Lucy is wearing more make-up than usual. Her lips are slick with gloss, eyes spiked with mascara. Around her neck is a scarf Ashley hasn't seen before, it is bright yellow, almost fluorescent. She feels as though she is seeing Lucy through a fairground mirror – distorted, too bright. Close, but not quite there.

'What are you doing here?'

The words are accusatory; Ashley feels guilty.

She takes a deep breath.

'Got the afternoon free. Thought I'd save you the bus trip. Come on, let's go home. Good day?'

'Is Hol OK?'

'She's fine. She's just tired out. June wasn't in earlier so I had to take her to Colours with me.'

Her daughter stares at her for a few more moments, tips her head to the side in a surprisingly adult gesture. Finally, she seems to accept it, shrugs, falls into step beside Ashley as they walk to the car, their footsteps tapping away from the school. As they reach the car, Lucy turns around, stares back at the gates, scans the grey pavements. She reaches up, pulls the yellow scarf tighter around her neck, ducks her head into the back seat. She doesn't answer Ashley's question.

In the car she is quiet, reaches out to put the radio on. As the pop song fills the car, Lucy's face brightens.

'Hey, it's Ryn Weaver!' she says, 'I love him.' She lifts her iPhone aloft, pulls a silly face and snaps a picture of herself, giggling and tapping the screen. Immediately the phone pings back and she gives a little snort of laughter at some unknown joke.

'Did you just take your own picture?' Ashley asks, but it is as though the joy that came over her daughter's face disappears when her mother speaks, vanishes with the click of the iPhone camera. Ashley sighs. They aren't getting anywhere.

James comes home earlier than usual. Ashley is halfway through making a tuna pasta bake, her daughter's favourite. She has never claimed to be above bribery. The steam from the bubbling pasta is making Ashley sweat; the kitchen smells overpoweringly of fish. Benji wanders in, crinkles up his nose and asks for a Jaffa cake, which Ashley obligingly fetches from the cupboard, hoping he will give her a little time alone with James.

'Back early for once,' she says to her husband. He looks drained.

'Tricky day. We got the lawyers into the office, I've been in a meeting with Daniel all afternoon. It's gone to the board; they'll make a decision within a week.' He shrugs, spreads his palms out. 'I've done everything I can.'

Ashley stops stirring the pasta, puts down the wooden spoon. Perhaps this is her moment.

'James,' she says, 'I was thinking today, while I was at the café – I was thinking that I might go back to work.'

She hadn't meant to come out with it quite so quickly but she's started now, she may as well finish. He stares at her. She picks up the spoon again, stirs the pasta a little bit faster.

'Ash, no – that's not what I – you shouldn't have to— '

She interrupts him. 'Please, listen. I know nothing is certain with your job yet, so this might not need to happen, but isn't it something to think about? We'll need an income, James. If you lose this job.'

He starts to protest but she pushes on. 'I'm perfectly qualified, and Benji is at school until four every day anyway; Lucy can look after him until I'm home in the evening, which would only be at around six. Holly can go to June's, you know she's glad of the money and she's perfectly capable. As long as we get the schedule right!'

She hesitates. What she plans to say next is not quite true, but who is to say that it might not become so? Given time, it might.

'I'd like to, James. That way we'd have a safety net, we wouldn't have to worry about giving anything up. It might … it might be good for me.'

There is silence in the room. It is broken by Lucy. She clatters into the kitchen in a pair of black high heels, her lips a dark slash of red. Her top is lacy, half see-through. The yellow scarf she had on earlier is tied around her waist like a belt. Ashley stares.

'What on earth d'you think you're wearing?'

Her daughter doesn't look at her, isn't paying attention. She rummages in her handbag, pulls out a tube of scent, squirts her wrists. The smell is strong, musky. Sexy.

'Lucy!' Ashley forgets the pasta, steps towards her daughter. James reaches out, tries to touch her hand, but she jerks away from him. 'Lucy! Your dinner's here! Where are you going?'

Her daughter finally turns, looks her in the eye. The expression on her face is one of disdain. Her eyes are dark, heavily kohled.

'I'm going out, Mum. Don't wait up for me.'

The door slams.

Ashley splutters.

'What was that! *Don't wait up for me*. She's fifteen years old and it's a Monday night for God's sake! Go and stop her, James, will you!'

James is already on his feet, pulling open the front door. Ashley sinks down at the kitchen table. James has more sway with her daughter, Lucy will listen to him. There is a sudden sizzling noise – the pasta on the hob is boiling over, hot water gushing from underneath the lid.

Ashley gets to her feet, removes the pan lid and turns down the little flame. Frustration brims in her chest; that conversation with James did not go well. She runs her fingers through her hair. She can hear Benji banging his hands on the bottom step, tapping out a drum beat like he always does. The sound is going to wake Holly up, she knows it is. She'll want feeding. Ashley's breasts begin to ache. Suddenly she wants to curl up in a ball and hide from it all, open the cupboard and step right into the darkness. She is exhausted with trying.

The front door bangs and she looks up, expecting her daughter. She takes a deep breath, forces herself to stay in control. They need to sort this out, nip Lucy's sudden swerve into rebellion tightly in the bud.

But her daughter is not there. James stands in the kitchen, has the grace to look ashamed.

'I couldn't catch her,' he says. 'She got into a car.'

Ashley is instantly awake. 'What? Whose car?'

James shakes his head. 'I don't know.'

35

London

Ashley

'How could you have let her get in?'

Ashley is pacing up and down outside their house. The street is deserted, the moon illuminates James's face.

'I didn't have a chance to stop her!' James says. 'God, Ash, come on! It's not like I did it on purpose, it's not like I said, "Oh hey, Luce, get in the stranger's car, have a double on me!" I mean—' He stops, exhales. 'Look, let's just calm down. Let's go back inside, Benji needs to go to bed. We'll work out what to do.'

'Was it a boy? Just tell me, James, did it look like there was a boy driving? Oh God.' Ashley can feel her voice rising, becoming a wail. She cannot stop picturing Benji's little mouth, his eight-year-old lips forming the word 'slut'. Who is her daughter with?

James puts his hands on her shoulders and she leans her head forward, bangs it against his chest. A moan escapes her.

'Shh, I'm trying to think.' He screws up his eyes. 'No, honestly, Ash, I don't think it was. I mean, it was hard to see because she got in so quickly but I'm pretty sure it was a girl behind the wheel. OK? All right?'

'Well.' Ashley sniffs. 'I hope you're right, is all. I don't want her going off with some older guy.'

'I'd kill anyone that touched her,' James says. His face clouds with anger. Ashley feels his body tense up, his muscles contract. 'Christ, when I think of myself at that age … if I find out she's been with some loser, I mean it, I'll go for him.'

Benji's figure appears at the open doorway of the house, lit up in the hallway light. He has his little blue pyjamas on, a book in his hand.

'Dad? Mum?'

'Coming!' they shout in unison. James puts a hand on her back and they hurry inside the house.

'What are you doing?' Benji looks confused. Ashley strokes his head, goes to the noticeboard, dials a number.

'Diane? It's Ashley, Lucy Thomas's mum. I'm sorry to bother you so late – it's just, I was wondering if Lucy's at yours?' She tries to laugh. 'She's gone out, and my husband forgot to ask where, so I was just checking if she and Sophia—' There's a pause. James is glaring at her but she ignores him.

'OK. OK, right. I see. All right, Diane, thanks. Yep, I will. Sorry again. Speak soon.'

She hangs up.

'She's no idea. Sophia's at home, she's right beside her.'

'OK,' James says. 'OK. Anyone else?'

Ashley rings through her phone book. Nobody has seen her daughter.

'Who did she say she was with the other night?' James rubs a hand across his temples.

'She didn't. She wouldn't tell us, remember?' Ashley sits at the table. James has made tea but it's cold, a film of milk congealing on its surface.

'Do you think we should call the—'

James shakes his head. 'Give it till eleven. She got in voluntarily, Ash, I promise you that. There's no point calling the police yet. They won't come out.'

She nods, tries to believe him even though her insides are screaming at her.

The phone rings. They both jump for it; James picks up.

'Thomas residence.'

Ashley stares at him, her heart thumping. 'Is it her?'

James is silent, frowning.

'Hello? Who is this?'

The hairs on Ashley's arms stand up. She feels a pulse of dread. Even before he speaks, she already knows what her husband is going to say.

'No one there.'

Then

After it happens, things are quiet and strange in our flat. The tension that has been building seems to have broken, have snapped like a thread. There is nothing we can do any more. I can't work out if I am sad or not. I can't work out how I am meant to feel. Mum lies down on the bed, face down against the pillow. I hover in the doorway, offer to bring her things – tea, water, her pills. She never answers. After a while I give up, go back into my bedroom and stare into the mirror, hating the way the red acne has dotted my forehead, the way my breasts strain against my T-shirt. I skip school for a few days, float around the flat like a ghost. It's almost graduation but I don't care about that. It's too hard to concentrate on school work, on anything else but what's happening. I want to go to the house, see how they are. My legs hum with the desire to go.

After a week, she gets up. She takes a shower, staying in there for ages until I start to panic that maybe she's drowned, slipped over accidentally on purpose. But she comes out, her hair dripping down her neck, her eyes bright. She wants to go to the funeral but I don't know if I do.

Eventually we do go, we sit at the back, dressed in dark clothing. Mum has a hat on, a fancy-looking one she bought years ago. She says it's from before, from her old life. I wear my black dress, the one that's too tight around my chest. I keep my arms crossed the whole time, and we both keep our eyes fixed on them. They're all crying. They're allowed to cry. I look at Mum and she is biting the inside of her cheek, puckering the flesh. I imagine the inside of her mouth filling with blood, the salty iron taste of it trickling onto her tongue. There are lots of people there, and speech after speech. I stare at the photograph of him, looming large at the front of the room. His eyes stare back at me. This must be the only time he's ever looked at me properly. Now that it is far too late.

I stare at the other people in the church, the men in their suits and the women weeping into hankies. None of them know. A slow burn starts in my cheeks, spreads its way into my heart. I shouldn't be here, skulking at the back, trying to be invisible. It isn't fair. We slope out after it's over, don't hang around for the wake. I am shaking a bit, I feel all shivery and weird.

*

Things are changing quickly now. After the funeral, Mum and I went for a walk, we walked across the heath. Her arm was linked through mine, tightly, like a rope. She's so thin these days, even thinner than usual. She's been back to the doctor's, she told me, not that new doctor she hated but her old one, the one that understands her a bit more. She's got a new prescription, packets and packets of little white pills, then another paper bag full of blue ones too. She's been different recently, but I don't know if it's because of the funeral or because of the tablets. She's getting up on time, washing her hair. More in control. Like she's got a purpose. Although things are easier when she's like this, a part of me can't help but feel sad – she had a purpose all along. Me. But that didn't jolt her awake in the same way as this has.

As we walked across the heath, she told me what she wants to do. I nodded along but she stopped walking and looked at me. She put her hands on my shoulders, her fingers digging in. I'm almost taller than her now, as if she's shrinking.

'You do understand how important this is, don't you?' she said. I stared at her. The wind whistled past us, scattering her hair in

its wake. The way she was talking to me made me feel angry. Of course I understand. I'm not a child any more.

It's better for Mum and I to be apart, I know it is, and she knows it too. Easier. Quicker. We'll be more efficient that way. When I say goodbye to her a few weeks later, I put my arms around her little body; she is older now, of course, and she feels flimsy beneath my hands, as though she might break. His death has shocked her. She's lost a lot of weight. I told her so but she looked pleased with herself, said it's a side effect of the pills. Then she said something else under her breath that I couldn't hear properly, but it sounded like, 'he always liked me thinner'.

'You know what to do, right?' she asks me on the day I leave, when she hands me the heavy bag, and I ask the same question back at her. She stops, looks at me.

'You really have grown up, haven't you?' she says, and then she starts to close the door and I walk off down the driveway with the bag, my fingers around the new phone in my pocket, stocked with the numbers I need. I turn back when I get to the road, and I see her there, standing in the window, a ghostly silhouette highlighted against the dark glass. As I watch her, she raises a hand up to the window, spreads her fingers out against the glass in a wave. The image of it stays in my head as I go home to my new flat, make my way up the stairs. There are lots of flats in this building; I stare at their closed blank faces, thinking about the people inside. There are neighbours next to me, across from me. I need to be careful. I let myself in using my brand-new key and put the bag of things on the side, peek inside one more time, remembering. It's a shame, really.

I make a phone call before I go to bed, but just one. No answer. I think about ringing again but decide not to. I can't stay up all night. Tomorrow is a big day. I need a good night's sleep.

36

London

Corinne

I can't stop thinking of Dom's words at the gravestone. 'We want to make sure you're feeling … up to it.' What does he mean, *up to it*? I'm capable of being a good mother. More than capable. Aren't I?

Dom and I order a takeaway when we get back from the cemetery.

'OK with Meat Feast?' Dominic says, brandishing the red and green menu in front of me. We're sitting together on the sofa and I know he's trying extra hard to be nice after the graffiti. I know I shouldn't, but I feel a shimmer of satisfaction that the word shook him too, seeing it emblazoned there like that. LIAR.

'Can we get a side?' I say. I'm starving hungry. I need to eat properly for the baby. 'Maybe pizza isn't the best idea,' I say then, feeling a pang of concern. 'It isn't very healthy, is it?'

'Aw come on,' Dom says, 'let's treat ourselves!'

He orders a big bottle of Diet Coke and extra garlic bread, putting on a silly Italian voice to the pizza guy on the phone. As he's on the phone, I slip into the bedroom, open my drawers and stare at the evidence bag. I open it up, even though I told myself I wouldn't. I stare at the tiny cradle, the little bootees. I know they're not from Ashley, or from Mum. I know what their handwriting looks like. I'll ask Gilly tomorrow morning.

'Corinne?' Dominic is calling me. 'What are you doing in there?'

I shut the drawer hurriedly and return to the living room, sit down with him on the sofa. My fingers feel tacky from the plastic bag. He puts his arms around me, lifts my legs so they're lying over his lap.

'So, Alison was weird at work on Friday,' Dom says. He tells me that he overheard her saying his name, something about a deal. He's fiddling with a strand of my hair, twisting it round his fingers.

'Maybe it's a drug deal,' I say.

Dom laughs. 'Yeah, right. Alison strikes me as just the type. Not.'

'Money-laundering?' I suggest. 'Good old-fashioned s-e-x?'

'That's more likely, I reckon,' Dom says, and he stops looking worried and starts kissing me, his lips warming the side of my neck. It feels nice. I feel a flash of pride. See? I'm up to it, I'm coping. I'm fine.

There's a knock at the door and I jump, my body shuddering slightly against Dom's.

'It's the pizza!' he says. 'Nothing to worry about. Here, I'll go.'

I blush, annoyed with myself. 'I know,' I say. 'Don't worry, I'll get it.'

I stand up and go to the door, my heart beating a little too fast. I have to get a grip. I have to calm down. Outside

I pay the delivery man, take the hot cardboard box from his gloved hands.

'Cheers,' he says, and I'm about to shut the door when I see Gilly behind him, standing in the doorway of her flat, holding Tommy by the hand and saying goodbye to a tall guy in a dark coat. I hesitate, curious. Is this her new guy? Then I see him reach down, scoop Tommy up in a hug and I realise it must be his dad, her ex. Ben something? The guy she was arguing with on the phone.

The man turns to go and I catch a glimpse of his face, sharp features, balding hair. The sight of him next to Gilly gives me a jolt of familiarity. I know them from somewhere, I know them as a couple. Then all of a sudden it clicks – I've seen them before. I've seen them in my dad's office. Three or four years ago, now, it must be – I was hanging around waiting for Dad, we were going out to lunch, and they were in a meeting with him, finishing up. He introduced me as they left – 'Corinne, this is Gilly and Ben McIntyre, guys, this is my daughter.' We'd exchanged pleasantries, they'd left and we'd gone out to La Forienta for lunch. The memory is complete, a tiny moment, but that's it – that's where I know her from. Her gasping laugh, her movements. I've met her once before, I've met the both of them. They did business with my dad.

37

London

Ashley

The doorbell rings. Lucy wouldn't ring the doorbell.

Ashley's face is ashen. She stares at James. He puts a hand on her shoulder.

'I'll go.'

She follows him to the door, hiding behind his body as though it is a shield.

The policeman is tall, with tired eyes. Ashley feels her body begin to give as she sees him, feels her husband's strong arms grab her shoulders.

The policeman raises a hand.

'Mr and Mrs Thomas, there's no need to panic. Your daughter's with us.' He looks down at his notepad. 'I know what people think when they see us at the door. Your daughter's safe. But —' he clears his throat, looks serious '—that's not to say that she's in a very good state.'

He gestures to someone behind him, and a policewoman comes forward, out of the darkness. Ashley, still in her husband's arms, gives a little gasp.

Lucy is slumped in the woman's arms. Her eyes are closed, there is mud on her legs and her shoes are missing. Her bare white feet dangle in the darkness.

James immediately steps forward, picks his daughter up as though she is a doll. She looks tiny in his arms, Ashley sees how fragile her limbs are, how small her body is. She is only fifteen.

'We found her on the street,' the policeman says.

There is a silence. Ashley's brain is full of white noise.

The policeman clears his throat. 'Would you mind if we came in?'

Ashley suddenly comes to.

'Of course,' she says, 'Of course you can come in.' The shape of the words feels weird in her mouth.

She brings them both inside while James tends to Lucy. Her hands shake as she shuts the front door, leads them into the living room. She feels like she might throw up.

'She was lying on the corner of Caledonian Road, all the way across town. Near the traffic lights. Mrs Thomas, do you know who your daughter was with this evening?'

Ashley shakes her head. 'She went out,' she says. Her voice sounds odd, unfamiliar, as though her ears are filled with water. 'She told us she was going out and then she got into a car. I thought … I thought it was with friends.'

'Well,' the policeman says, 'that's as may be, Mrs Thomas, but if I were you I'd have a second look at who your daughter's friends are. We had the medics come out to the scene already, before we brought her home – we would've called but it took us a while to find any ID on her. Anyway, they've checked her over, and it's reasonably tame – a combination of cannabis and a huge amount of alcohol.'

He glances at the policewoman, who is sitting beside him on Ashley's sofa.

'You're lucky she didn't have to have her stomach pumped.'

James comes back into the room, puts his arms around Ashley. She hasn't realised she is still trembling until he presses her quivering hand within both of his own.

He nods at the police, shakes the man's hand. 'Thank you for bringing her back, Officers.'

It feels like a movie; Ashley wants it to be over.

'You found her on the street?' James says. 'Whoever she was with just left her there?'

The policeman nods. 'You say you think she was with friends?'

James sighs, runs a hand through his hair. 'I mean, I'm not sure – she definitely seemed like she wanted to go out, she knew the car was picking her up. It certainly wasn't forced.'

The policewoman smiles sympathetically at Ashley. 'Best thing to do is talk to her tomorrow, when she comes round,' she says. 'She will be all right, she's just had far too much for one little girl. I can see you guys are concerned and you should be, but what's probably happened is her friends panicked when she got too drunk and left her because they just didn't know what else to do.' She sighs.

'You'd be surprised, I know it sounds harsh but it happens more often than you think, with very young teens. They're hopelessly inexperienced and, like I say, they panic. The thing is to make sure your daughter is with people you trust – people who are going to look out for her. I'd make sure she chooses her friends more carefully in the future.'

'But we don't know who she was with!' Ashley says. She feels terrible, like the worst mother in the world. Above them, Holly begins to cry.

The policewoman nods. 'I appreciate that, but, as I say, best thing to do is talk to your daughter in the morning. Let her sleep it off. At the moment, there's not really a lot we can do. But—' she gets to her feet, as does her colleague '—if you have any more questions once you've spoken to her, feel free to give us a call.' She hands Ashley her card. 'We'd best be off. Talk to us if you need to, but most of all talk to your daughter.' She smiles at Ashley. 'Sounds like you're needed upstairs.'

Ashley takes the card. It feels cold in her fingers.

Later, in bed that night, she turns her face to the wall, stares into the blackness. Her husband reaches out for her but she stiffens, moves away. Her mind is spinning.

James is losing his job. She is losing Lucy. Are they going to lose each other too? The darkness feels like it is closing in on her, she cannot stop picturing the moment James opened the door, the moment she saw the policeman. It is surely every parent's worst nightmare.

She can hear James breathing next to her, knows he is not asleep. His breathing is too shallow, too light. Ashley imagines her daughter, dressed up in a bar, hanging on the arm of some boy. *Slut*. The word is horrible, poisonous. She doesn't believe it. They haven't brought Lucy up to be like that. She tries to think of the last time she really talked to her daughter, had a proper conversation that didn't end in a rolling of the eyes or a snappy retort. Her mind comes up short, she draws a total blank.

Is she really such a terrible mother that her own daughter has become a stranger? Is this how it will be when Holly is older too? Ashley thinks of her baby's big blue eyes, imagines them sharper, spiked with mascara, looking the other way. She feels tears prick her eyes, turns her face into the pillow. She hasn't had a career, not like Corinne, not like her father with his passion and his creativity. It was always the thing she felt most insecure about – if she isn't a good mother, what is she? She has always prided herself on being there for her children. She'd thought being a young mum to Lucy would mean she could understand her daughter, would keep them on the same wavelength. All she'd wanted was to be as good a parent as her own were to her. A tear rolls down her cheek. It is almost exactly a year since her dad died; the anniversary is on the twenty-sixth. Ashley thinks of him on the day Lucy was born, of the glisten in his eyes as she handed the baby to him, passed her over as she lay recovering in the hospital bed.

'You'll be a terrific mother, Ashley,' he had said to her, and the pride in his eyes had stayed with her all night, that first sleepless night when she had held Lucy to her chest, her baby girl, her daughter. He had drawn Lucy to his chest, stroked the tiny wisps of hair on her head. 'I wonder what you'll grow up to be, little Lucy,' he'd whispered, and Ashley had smiled sleepily. Her dad was so ambitious, so driven, and now his granddaughter would be the same.

What would her dad say if he could see her now? Ashley shudders, because actually she knows what he would say. He would be ashamed. In the next room, Holly begins to cry again. The sound stabs at Ashley's heart like a knife. *Not good enough. Ashley, you're not good enough.*

38

London

Dominic

He is worried about Corinne. The night of the scallops is just part of it. Lately, she has seemed more and more on edge, and it is beginning to prick at him, little jabs of fear. She'd been OK at the weekend but he worries about her on her own, how she is without him there. He'd thought they were having a nice night with the takeaway, but after the food arrived she seemed to go down, kept looking at the dresser, darting little glances at the photo of her dad. She is just so up and down. And how can she possibly take the congratulations gift as something more sinister? The whole thing just seems absurd.

He doesn't want to upset her by suggesting again that she visit a psychiatrist, really he doesn't, but he's got to be honest, hasn't he?

She seems like she's losing the plot.

He knows she has always been a worrier. But this … this feels different. This feels like something else.

'Morning, Dom.'

Erin is smiling at him, carrying a steaming mug of tea past his desk. 'How're you doing? Good weekend?'

He spins his chair around, is about to lie, spout off the usual 'Good, thanks.' Something stops him; her head is tilted to the side and she's smiling at him, and suddenly he is overwhelmed with the urge to just be honest, to stop having to skirt around the truth. Sugarcoat everything.

'It was …' he hesitates. Why not tell her the truth? 'Actually it was a bit fraught.'

'Oh no,' she says. 'Sorry, Dom. Is there anything … well, what was wrong? I'm here, if you want someone to listen.'

'Thanks,' he says. 'Thanks, that's really nice of you.' He looks up, sees Andy watching them. Erin looks up, catches Andy's eye hopefully. He doesn't smile, lets his gaze wander over to the work experience girl, linger on her blonde hair. Dominic sees the blush spread over Erin's cheeks. She dips her head quickly. He can sense her discomfort, feels a pang of sympathy. She deserves better than to be picked up and put down by bloody Andy.

'If you want to pop out for a quick drink after work, that might be nice?' he says to her, trying to distract her from Andy's obvious loss of interest.

She hesitates.

'We don't have to,' Dominic says. 'Just thought it might be good to get out of the office for a bit. That's all. You can fill me in on your court cases, how you're getting on.' He smiles at her. He doesn't want her to feel that the whole paper is as bad as Andy, and she looks as though she could use a friend. To be fair, he could too – it would be nice to sit and have a quick beer somewhere, chat about something other than doll houses and graffitied headstones for a bit.

'Sure,' says Erin, looking relieved. 'That'd be great. Thanks, Dom.'

He rings Corinne at lunchtime. She's in the gallery, sounds quiet, a bit subdued.

'Everything OK?' he asks her.

'Fine,' she says. 'Everything's fine. You?'

'Yep, good,' he says. There's a pause. Why does it feel as though there is a distance between them, a slight awkwardness?

'Listen—' he clears his throat '—I thought I'd pop out for a quick drink tonight, after work. If you don't mind?'

'Of course,' she says. 'No problem. You go.'

He is relieved. 'You sure?'

'Yes! It's fine, Dom. I might go round and see Gilly. Come on, I'm OK. I don't want you to worry about me. It makes me feel … it makes me feel ridiculous.'

He grins, tucks the phone under his chin. 'You're not ridiculous, Cor. I love you. I'll see you back at home a bit later.'

'OK,' she says. 'Have fun with Andy.'

There is a beat.

'Thanks, I will,' he says, and he hangs up the phone quickly, trying to pretend that he didn't hear the tremor in her voice. He hasn't lied, has he? He just hasn't told her the whole truth.

39

London

Ashley

In the house the next day, things are quiet and strange. The policewoman's card sits on the kitchen counter, out of place amongst the usual wash of dishes and crumbs. Ashley brings Lucy a bowl of yogurt with a honey L laced on top, as though she is a child again. She and James sit together on their daughter's single bed, take it in turns to ask questions.

At first, Lucy will not answer. She turns her face away from them, pulls the duvet up to her chin. Ashley feels helpless. She glances at James. Time for a different tactic.

'Lucy,' she says. 'Lucy, I need you to be honest with us. I'm going to be straight with you, now—' She takes a deep breath. 'I didn't want to tell you this, Luce, but it looks like I'm going to have to. I've been getting reports about you from the schoolyard which, to be quite frank, are making my blood run cold, and you're my daughter, and I need to know what's been going on. I'm not trying to be the enemy, Luce, believe it or not.'

That catches her attention. Lucy pushes the duvet away from her head, sits up slightly in the bed.

'What does that mean, "reports from the schoolyard"?'

'Lucy.'

'What do you mean?' She glances between them, her face looks confused now, and a little bit frightened. 'Mum? Dad?'

Ashley sighs. 'The other day I was called to school to take Benji home because he kicked a little boy in the playground.'

Lucy swallows, rolls her eyes nervously. 'So?'

'So, the reason he did that was because this little boy had been going round telling people that his big sister is promiscuous. His fifteen-year-old sister.'

She doesn't say anything.

Ashley puts her hand out and touches the side of her daughter's face. She flinches, then her muscles relax suddenly and she starts to cry, hot, panicky tears that trickle onto the duvet.

Ashley puts an arm around her, James finds Lucy's foot under the covers and gives it a squeeze.

'All right, Luce, all right,' he murmurs. 'Now please, are you going to tell us what happened last night?'

Lucy looks at them. Mascara trails down her cheek.

'I can't … I can't remember. I can't remember what happened.' She lets out a sob. 'I can't remember anything at all!'

Ashley and James look at each other. Gently, Ashley explains.

'You were brought home by the police, Luce. They found you on the street, without your shoes. Alone. Your "friends" were nowhere to be seen.'

She pauses. Her daughter's eyes are huge in her head; she can tell this is all new information to her, that she really cannot recall the night.

'You'd been smoking,' Ashley continues. 'I don't know if that's something you've done before, Lucy, but I'm telling you now—' she glances at James '—I'm telling you now that it's going to stop. I won't have cannabis in this house.'

Lucy nods. Her face is very pale.

'The police said you were lucky not to have had your stomach pumped,' James says. 'I want to make sure you understand what that means, Lucy – if you'd had any more alcohol you'd have been in the hospital, connected to a machine designed to empty your stomach. Clear enough?'

Ashley puts a hand on his arm. Lucy looks terrified already, there's no point frightening her more. Her daughter is scared enough.

When they have finished telling her, Lucy begins to cry again. Ashley strokes the back of her hair, feeling it crispy from last night's hairspray. She rocks Lucy gently, as though she is a five-year-old who has spilled Ribena from her Tommy Tippee. It is so nice holding her daughter close, it feels like it has been a long time.

James brings them both tea with two sugars, extra sweet the way Lucy likes it. Ashley has a moment of doubt – perhaps they should be angry with her – but her daughter looks so young, so very very young, that she cannot bear it, she just wants to find out what happened and make sure that nothing like it ever happens again.

She had been plagued by it all night. Visions of Lucy on the street like a broken doll, abandoned and alone. Prey

275

for God knows who. At four in the morning, James had turned on their bedroom lamp.

'I can't sleep.'

'Me neither.'

He'd paused, turned to face her, put a tentative hand out to touch her hair. 'I'm so sorry, Ashley.'

She'd waited, let him speak.

'I'm sorry I haven't been better. I'm sorry I couldn't stop Lucy from getting in the car. I'm sorry I've let you down with the money, I'm sorry I didn't tell you from the start. I promise I will do from now on. I'll keep you informed of everything that happens in the office. When Daniel makes a decision about me, whatever it is, I'll tell you. I mean it. And if you want to go back to work, we'll talk about that too. I'll speak to Daniel. And we'll go from there.' He swallows. 'Won't we?'

Ashley looks into his grey eyes, the ones she has looked at for sixteen years, ever since he approached her at a too-hot party, complimented her tacky pink earrings and tight silver dress.

She'd pulled him towards her, held him as they lay together, as their children lay sleeping in the neighbouring rooms.

Ashley's family is so important to her. She has to fight for it, and they have to fight together; she and James.

'We have to get to the bottom of Lucy,' she had told him. 'We have to sort this out. I never want to go through a night like that again.' She'd paused. 'We'll work things out,' she said. 'Both of us. I'm always here, James. As long as you're honest with me.'

From 5 a.m. they'd slept, curled together like spoons. Two hours later, they'd gone to wake their daughter.

276

'Please, Lucy,' Ashley says now. 'Can you tell us who you were with, who you went out with? Dad saw you get in the car.'

Lucy sighs, her narrow shoulders shaking. There is a bowl by the side of her bed, she has vomited twice already.

'I was … OK, look, but you can't get angry with me, OK, Mum? Dad? You promise you won't shout?'

Ashley feels James tense beside her. She knows what he is thinking, knows he is imagining some spotty eighteen-year-old pawing Lucy, pushing his tongue down their daughter's throat. She shudders, tries to keep a neutral expression.

'Lucy, I've told you, neither of us are mad. We're upset, and we're worried. We need you to just be honest with us.'

'I met this girl,' Lucy says.

Ashley and James both pause. Ashley is holding her breath without noticing, she tries to exhale discreetly. She isn't sure what her daughter is saying; neither is James, he suddenly looks awkward, is fiddling with the corner of the duvet.

'Not … not like that,' Lucy says. 'I met this girl, she's … I thought she was really cool. I don't … I don't know why— ' She stops, closes her eyes. 'I don't know why she would have left me.' It comes out in a whisper.

Ashley can feel tears prick her own eyelids, reaches forward to take her daughter's hand.

'Shh, shh,' she says. 'Who is this girl, how do you know her? Is it someone from the school?'

'No,' Lucy says. 'No, she's a bit older, she's different. She likes me, she said, and we … I don't know, we had fun. We went out together, she told me I was cool. She told me she'd get us into new places, the places everyone wants to go to, you know – The Garage, Salvador, Fabric. The clubs the girls at school can't get into.'

'Fabric?' James says.

'It's a nightclub, Dad.'

'So you went out with this girl? When?' Ashley says.

Lucy nods. 'Yeah, a few times over the last couple of months … I … I told you I was with Sophia. I'm sorry.' She covers her eyes. Ashley sees that her nails are bitten to the quick, purple rags on the ends of her fingers. 'She's great, Mum … I mean, I thought she was. She's really fun and pretty and looked out for me, you know, made sure I was OK. I don't know why she left me like that.' She looks as though she's going to cry again. Ashley feels fury building up inside her, realises her hands are clenched into fists.

'Where did you meet this girl?' James says.

'All right, well, look I told you not to get annoyed.' Lucy looks nervously at Ashley, who attempts to give a reassuring smile. It is hard, through gritted teeth.

'Just tell us.'

'I met her through the internet,' Lucy says.

James puts his head in his hands. Ashley pushes her palms into her eyes.

'On Instagram,' Lucy says, 'It's a photo-sharing app, it lets you put up pictures, it's great. Everyone uses it.'

'I don't,' her parents say in unison.

Lucy rolls her eyes, gives a weak smile. Her skin is deathly pale. 'That's because you guys are old.'

'OK, OK,' Ashley says. She doesn't want to lose track of what her daughter is saying. 'So you met this girl through Instagram? How?'

278

'She started commenting on my photos,' Lucy says, and in spite of everything Ashley can hear the pride in her voice. 'Liking them, little things like that. It started around Christmas, I guess, and then we started chatting, you know, just in the Comments section, and she said she was coming up to London and that we ought to meet for a drink. She likes Ryn Weaver, just like me. She said she might be able to get us tickets.'

'And did she?'

Lucy looks down. 'No. But she was so nice, Mum, really she was. She didn't even seem that much older. She just liked me, she said I was fun, I reminded her of her sister. That's all it was. I suppose – I suppose the drink stuff got a bit out of hand. I'm really sorry. I'm really really sorry.'

James leans forward. 'You understand how serious this is, don't you, Luce? That your mother and I had to watch you be carried into this house by a policewoman last night? At fifteen years old?'

Lucy looks at him. 'I know.' Her voice is small. 'I'm so sorry, Daddy.'

'Promise me you won't see this girl again?' Ashley says. 'And you know you're grounded, right, you're not going anywhere for a while. Is that clear? And you're not having that phone either.'

She reaches out, retrieves Lucy's iPhone from where it lies tangled in the bedclothes.

James takes it from her. 'You shouldn't sleep with the bloody thing so close to your head, Lucy.'

Lucy protests. 'Dad! That's my phone!'

'Tough,' Ashley says, 'If you need a phone I'll give you my old Nokia. Nothing wrong with that.'

Then

I'm in the building, watching him leave for work. All smiles. Yeah right. Sometimes I really wonder how anyone can ever trust a man. I mean, really trust them. I know I couldn't. I don't understand why people do, I've never seen evidence that we ought to. It must be hard being like the girls, so trusting, even until the end. But they haven't seen what I've seen, they haven't endured what I've had to endure. They float above me, safe and warm and untouched, and I am down here on the ground, a rat scrabbling to keep up. Sometimes I think no matter what I do, even if all of this goes to plan, I'll never be able to change that. It's too deep within me, I'm too far gone.

The worst of it is the tedium, the endless little irritations. The new flat is noisy; you can hear everyone in my building but I try to tune them out. It's mostly bearable, but occasionally I feel so anxious and frustrated that I have to excuse myself, go to the bathroom, lock the stall door and scream into my hands like I used to with the pillow when I was a little girl. I put my left hand tight across my mouth so that the sound can't escape and I scream and I scream. When it's over I feel better, lighter. I can keep going. Keep playing. I'm still in the game. Even if no one thinks I am. I look at my watch, circle it round my wrist. The leather burns against my skin. Come on, come on, come on.

I reach into my bag, crouch down by the front door. I think of my mother. She has sounded so much stronger recently, our plan has brought her back to life. I don't want things to go back to how they used to be. An image flits across my mind, of her staring silently at me across the kitchen table, her hair lank, spilling into her eyes. This is for her. This is for both of us.

40

London

Dominic

At around six o'clock they meet at the lift.

'Phew,' Erin says, 'long afternoon. I could use that drink!'

Dominic falls into step with her as they wander out onto the high road, away from the office. 'Tell me about it.' He loosens his shirt, it feels tight around his neck.

'I know a bar just off Abbey Road,' Erin says. 'It's meant to do really good beer.'

'Are you a beer drinker?' He is surprised.

She laughs. 'No, but I know it's important to men. Or so Andy said, anyway.'

'You still seeing him?'

She shakes her head. 'Hardly. Don't think he's interested. Think I might have been a bit on the side.' She shrugs, but Dominic notices the flicker that moves across her face and feels a jolt of anger towards his friend. When is he going to learn to stop shagging around? Dominic suspects never.

In the bar, Erin has a glass of white wine while Dom decides on a Peroni. Erin offers to pay but Dominic waves her card away, sticks them on his debit card. The bar is warm, full of tired city workers ordering pints, unbuttoning collars, loosening ties, knocking back the alcohol to relieve the stresses of the day.

They sit opposite each other at a table in the middle of the bar.

'So,' Erin says. She smiles at him warmly, takes a sip of her wine. 'Mm, nice. Better than the stuff they serve at my local. Why was your weekend so fraught? I mean,' she adds hurriedly, 'you don't have to tell me, I just thought you might want to talk about it.'

Dominic frowns, takes a sip of beer. He hasn't drunk for a while, mainly in solidarity with Corinne; it feels vaguely illicit.

'Well,' he says. 'I'm just … I'm a bit worried about Corinne, I guess. That's all. She's very … she's a bit tense at the moment.'

'Is that work stuff?'

'No.' He looks down. 'It's more than that. It's … She sees things, imagines things that aren't there or reads too much into things that are. Or seems to, anyway. She has these theories about her dad, he passed away last year, and I think it's because of the fertility stuff—'

'Oh?'

He breaks off, hadn't meant to mention it.

'D' you guys have kids? I didn't know.'

He swallows. 'No, I … No. Not yet.' Dominic feels suddenly silly, being so furtive. She is pregnant, isn't she? He has seen the blue line of the test. Why must he be so careful all the time? Why shouldn't he be happy?

'We've actually been trying for children for a while,' he says. He sips his beer, feels his shoulders relax a little.

'Oh? I have a relative who's trying for a baby, they're doing IVF. Have you ever tried it? Sorry—' she claps a hand over her mouth '—that's so nosy of me! Ignore me, please.' She reaches out, touches his arm by way of apology. 'Can't take me anywhere, that's what my mum used to say.'

She seems genuinely embarrassed. Dominic shakes his head.

'No, no, it's fine,' he says. 'Actually, we've done IVF four times. Been a nightmare.' He swallows, takes a deep breath. 'But actually we've just – we've just got pregnant.' He doesn't know how to phrase it, the words come out awkwardly. 'Corinne got pregnant, I mean, it worked.' It is the first time he has said the words out loud and he feels a sudden rush of tears behind his eyelids. He bends his head slightly, embarrassed.

'Oh my God!' Erin beams at him. 'That's amazing! Congratulations! Dominic, I'm so happy for you! Wow. You must be over the moon.'

He grins, sheepishly, and takes another slug of Peroni, the liquid pleasant on his tongue.

'Do you know if it's a boy or a girl?' Erin asks.

'No, not yet, we've only just found out. Early days, still.' He clears his throat. It feels odd to be talking about it. He hasn't thought about the gender of the baby; it seems hardly to matter. What matters is its existence; a living creature made by him and Corinne.

'I bet Corinne is so excited!' Erin is saying.

Dominic smiles – she seems very happy for the pair of them. It's nice to have someone be excited.

'So you think it's all to do with that?' Erin asks. 'The hormones and stuff? I can imagine it's very stressful.'

'Yeah,' Dominic says. 'Yeah, I guess so. I mean, I don't know. Her dad died, like I said, almost exactly a year ago now, and it affected her quite badly. And lately she's, well, she's been thinking about him a lot, become a bit obsessed with remembering her childhood. That sort of thing.'

Erin is nodding. 'I suppose it's because you guys are going to be parents. Must bring it all back up. Besides, a year isn't long, the feelings are probably still fresh.'

Dominic nods, thinking. 'Yes, I think you're probably right. Something horrible happened – some fuckers scribbled on her dad's headstone, when she went to see it – and it really upset her. Like it would.'

Erin widens her eyes. 'God, how awful. I'd be upset too!'

He shrugs. 'I suggested to her the other night that perhaps she ought to see someone, you know, a professional.' He glances up at Erin, feels as though he wants somebody's approval.

'Not a bad idea,' Erin says. 'There's no shame in asking for help if you need it. Mental health is a serious issue.'

'Very wise.' He breathes out, smiles at her. 'Talking of which, I heard Claudia Winters got life?'

Erin nods. 'Yup. That woman won't be coming out for a very long time.'

41

Corinne

I've been avoiding Gilly. I know I'm being silly, I know I am. But the thought has made its way into my mind, turning around and around until I want to scream. *This sodding architecture firm and what they did.* The words I heard her screaming down the phone come back to me, over and over. I know they came to Dad's office, her and her husband. So … the thought refuses to go away. Can she have been talking about him, about my dad? Every time I think about it I feel uneasy, as if the air around me is tightening, closing me in. I run my mind back over the encounter with them, over and over. I can remember Dad reaching out, shaking their hands, Gilly's smiling face as I was introduced to her. They seemed like a nice couple, very loved-up, one of those young pairs who are always touching each other – a hand squeeze here, an arm around there.

I can't believe I'm even having these thoughts. Dad didn't do any dodgy dealings, he can't have done, he wouldn't have. But I know it's her, I know they're the couple I saw in his office. Maybe they came to Dad afterwards, or beforehand. Got a quote and went elsewhere. As soon as I have the thought I feel a rush of relief – yes, that's it, it must be. I almost laugh – I can't believe I've let my thoughts get so carried away. They came to Dad to get help fixing the mess the other firm made, that's it. I force myself to think about something else, to stop being ridiculous. My dad was the last man on earth to get involved with anything like that – it's just a coincidence, that's all. He won't have been the architect she meant. I'm sure of it. *Snap out of it, Corinne.* I feel in my pocket for the thing I've been holding all afternoon, my fingers diving in and out of my coat as though I'm checking it's still there, as though I can't quite believe I've got it. As though somebody might take it from me. It's my first scan.

It was today, almost a year to the day since Dad died. It's March and the hospital grounds were full of crocuses, their bright little heads poking up through the grass. I smiled at everybody even though I was nervous in case they found something wrong, but in the end it was wonderful, magical even. It sounds so silly but I loved the whole thing, it felt so exciting to be there for a good reason, so different from the endless consultations and failed IVF inseminations. They tested my blood and then the nurse said, as I'd had so many problems in the past, did I want an ultrasound now? I'm only six weeks and three days (I never thought I'd live my life counting in days, now every one means so much) but she advised trying to do one early, that with IVF there can be a chance of complications. The egg could be in the wrong place.

I hesitated – really I wanted Dom with me. I'd never pictured having my first glimpse of my baby all on my own. But now that I was there I didn't want to have to wait, and the nurse was really sweet, she held my hand all the way through as the doctor did the scan and gave me a hug when we saw the little image on the screen, all funny and grainy. It doesn't look like anything yet, not really, but I was so excited and the nurse printed me out a few copies specially so I can show Dom, send one each to Ashley and Mum.

It felt so lovely and safe at the hospital, in the clean white room. It felt as though nothing could touch me. When she showed me the little bundle on the screen and I saw the tiny dark cells, the little flashing light of my baby's heartbeat, for a moment I was invincible. I forgot all about the words on the gravestone, the things Dominic said at dinner, and there was just me and my baby, so far healthy and safe. It's amazing that this tiny little group of human cells is inside me, curled up underneath my jeans. I pray the next eight months go quickly.

Dom's gone for a drink tonight with Andy. He's forgotten about the appointment but I'm trying not to mind, he's been under lots of pressure at work with the Carlington House feature, and at home, with me. When he rang I hadn't the heart to tell him off for forgetting, and a little part of me wants to prove it to him – see, I can cope! I've been to the hospital on my own, I've seen our baby's heartbeat. I can be a mother. I can't bear him to be frustrated with me, especially not now with the baby on the way. So I left it, told him to have fun. Andy though, yuck. He makes me shiver. Still, I guess it's different for men. So long as Dom doesn't pick up any of his bad habits then I'm happy.

I get off at my stop, start to walk to the flat. I stick to the lit streets, don't take my usual shortcut. Even though I'm feeling excited, happy about the baby, the closer I get to the flat the slower my footsteps become, and it starts creeping back to me; images of the little horse rocking on the side, the cradle through the post, the horrible feeling that someone had been in the flat. I want to stay locked in the nice white hospital room for ever, where nobody can hurt me.

I think about what Dom said at the restaurant. Does he really think I should see a professional? I hate that he thinks that. It makes me feel so weak, so inadequate. I want him to be proud of me, I don't want him to worry.

I'm going to try harder. I'm going to be really calm, and rational. I run my mind over all the little objects I have found over the last six weeks. They're all still in the evidence bag, hidden beneath a mound of my underwear, deep in the drawer inside their plastic bag.

I rang Mum when I came out of the hospital, told her all about the scan.

'Oh Corinne, I'm so happy for you, and Dom,' she said, and her voice sounded teary. I told her the scan would be in the post. It was on the tip of my tongue to ask her one more time about the doll house, but she started telling me about when she first got pregnant with me and I just hadn't the heart to question her again.

'Maybe she really has forgotten about it,' Dom said when I mentioned it to him again. He's getting sick of me asking, I can tell. 'She's getting on a bit now, Cor. These things do happen.' He'd grimaced at me. 'Hope I never get old.'

I'd smacked him on the arm. 'A little sensitivity would be good, Dom!'

'Sorry. Sorry.' He'd given me a hug. 'I didn't mean it like that. I just mean, it could very well be that she's just forgotten where it is and doesn't want to admit it. It could be anywhere. I'm sure if I asked my parents to dredge up the crap I played with as a kid they wouldn't be able to. When I went to uni they turned my room into a gym! Couple of charmers.' He'd grinned at me, flexed his muscles. 'Why do you think I've got such a good body?'

Maybe he's right. It was such a beautiful, beautiful house. But that doesn't mean I want it back in bits.

As I enter our building I remember my resolve, think of the scans in my handbag and feel hopeful. Everything is going to be OK. I'll show them to Dom when he's back, and until then I'll … well, I'll start the dinner, or something. Make something nice. Show him how capable I can be.

When I get upstairs, there is a figure outside our front door, crouched down low to the ground. I freeze.

Gilly stands up and turns around. 'Corinne!'

'What are you doing?' I say. My voice comes out a little oddly, too high-pitched. I swallow, telling myself not to be silly, although my heart is jumping in my chest and my face feels flushed, as though I've done something wrong, as though she can see what I'm thinking.

She's wearing a bright green coat, clutching a biro in her left hand. She grins at me and comes over.

'I was just leaving you a note! Didn't think you were in so was going to pop it through the door – just saying it'd be lovely to get together soon! I've been meaning to come see you. How did it go with the, you know?' She gestures at my stomach and I can't help it, I break into a smile.

'I've just got back from the hospital,' I say, and her face falls briefly but I put out a hand. 'No, no, it's nothing bad – Gilly, I'm pregnant.'

For a second something flickers across her face, but before I can work out her expression it has changed again, and she's smiling. I must have imagined it, she's beaming, she looks so happy for me. It's lovely, and as I look at her I feel a bit better – she's so nice, she won't have been talking about Dad. It'll be nothing to do with him, nothing to do with me. She pulls me close and we have a little hug outside my flat; she smells comforting, familiar. Suddenly it hits me – she smells like my sister. She smells the same as Ashley.

She must have felt me stiffen because she pulls back. 'You OK?'

'Yes,' I say. 'Yes, sorry, it's just you're wearing the same perfume as my sister does, took me a second or two to place it.'

She laughs. 'Dior,' she says, 'Gift from my new man, actually. Like it?'

I nod. 'Smells lovely.'

She grins. 'Can only hope I'm the only woman he's buying it for, right?'

I nod, smile weakly. She turns as if to go and I hesitate. She's right in front of me. I am so sick of worrying, I've got enough to think about without this as well. I could just ask her.

'Gilly,' I say. 'I – I don't want to be intrusive and, well, this probably sounds mad, but I – I overheard you on the phone the other day.'

The expression on her face changes slightly, hardens. I take a deep breath. I've started now, I have to keep going. Even if she gets annoyed.

'You heard me on the phone?'

I nod. 'Yes, I was – I was about to knock on your door, I wanted to talk to you, and I heard you on the phone talking about – well, talking about an architecture firm.'

There is a pause. My heart is hammering. What am I going to do if she mentions Dad? I haven't thought any further ahead than asking her, seeing what she says.

She's sighing, shaking her head. 'Oh, Corinne. I'm sorry you had to hear that – it's just, the subject gets me really wound up. It's the reason we divorced, in the end. We lost so much money and my husband just … well, he couldn't cope. Wanted to get lawyers in, sue the bastards. I wanted to leave it.' She blows out her cheeks. 'He still won't let it lie.'

I swallow. 'I'm so sorry, that must have been awful.'

She nods. 'Oh, God, it was. Bastards. They're still doing business, you know. Company called Seymour Sheppard, based over in Holland Park. God knows how many other lives they ruined, how much money they're scamming people out of as we speak.'

I stare at her, weak with relief. 'Oh God,' I say. 'I thought …'

She's staring at me. 'You thought what? Are you OK? You're white as a sheet.'

'Nothing,' I say. 'It's nothing. Sorry, I … well, I recognised you, actually. My dad was an architect, and I think you once came to his old office, in Hampstead, you probably don't remember. But it came to me the other day, when I saw you with your ex, I realised where I'd seen you before and then I got it in my head that maybe… maybe it'd been my dad's firm, you know, the one you dealt with. But it wasn't. It obviously wasn't.' I try to laugh. 'I'm just going quietly mad.'

She tilts her head to one side, frowning.

'God, I'm sorry,' she says, 'I really don't remember – how odd. But no, Seymour Sheppard, big firm in West London, that's who we went with in the end. We got quotes from quite a few people though – your dad must've been one of them. How funny!'

'Yes,' I say, 'yes, it is. Goodness, I'm so sorry you went through all that, Gilly. And I'm sorry for bringing it up again now.'

'Don't be daft,' she says, 'It doesn't matter a bit. I'm just glad it wasn't your old man – that could've made things a bit awkward!' She laughs, the gasping sound. 'Now you ought to get yourself inside, put your feet up. God knows you'll be doing none of that once the baby arrives!' She smiles at me and I nod, give her a shaky grin and say I'll see her soon. She hurries off to the stairwell.

I stare after her for a minute, stupidly relieved. All that worry for nothing. She must be telling the truth – why would she lie? I fumble for my keys, shaking my head. I think of her crouched down by the flat door, the expression of surprise on her face when I told her I was pregnant. She didn't know. She couldn't have sent me the bootees. I knew she hadn't. Why would she?

I put my key in the lock and go into our flat. I snap the kitchen light on and stick one of the scans straight on the fridge, fasten it with a little red heart magnet so Dom will see it straight away. There. Perfect.

I turn around, start running through the cupboards in my head, trying to think of something good to make, filling my brain with a chatter of options to stop my thoughts from spiralling. Risotto? Pasta? A nice curry? Tomorrow night Ashley and Mum are coming to London and we're going out for dinner somewhere near the cemetery, so it would be good to use up the leftover peppers in the fridge.

Pleased, I get the chopping board out, reach for a knife. My fingers meet air. My best knife is gone. Did I leave it in the sink? Dom was supposed to do the washing-up last night.

I go to look, and at first glance I don't even see the worst of it.

I see a doll, lying in the stainless steel basin, her dark brown hair spread out like a fan around her head, her smooth plastic skin perfectly pale, her red lips painted beautifully. It's Beatrice, it's got to be. She was my favourite when I was a little girl. Dad brought her back one night in a big gold package, tied up with a bow. The sight of her is so familiar that it brings a hot rush of tears to my eyes and before I can really think what I'm doing I reach forward, pick her up, and it's then that I see.

She's been cut open, her red velvet dress has a gaping hole in the middle, right across her stomach, right where her womb would be. The cut is deep and dark; when I part the folds of her dress I see that it goes all the way through to the other side of her plastic body. I scream loudly, drop her back into the sink. I slowly back away from the kitchen, my heart bumping in my chest. My brain is filling up with panic; the walls feel as though they are hemming me in. I spin around, my eyes darting around the room. Empty. What the hell? I need Dominic, but he isn't here, I'm all alone, and so I turn and I run from the kitchen, and I slam the bathroom door behind me, closing Beatrice in.

42

Dominic

Dominic feels a little bit drunk. He is still sitting in the bar with Erin, chatting, as the light fades outside. It is the relief of being out of the house, talking to someone else, stepping away from the constant worry he has for Corinne. Not that he'd change things, not for anything, but he wishes he could figure out how to help her. It's nice to have a friend to talk to. Still, he ought to get going soon. Another pint and he'll be struggling.

They chat a bit more about Erin's court case, the woman on trial for the death of her daughter.

'It's just so sad,' Dom says. 'I mean, maybe it's something to do with the fact that I'm about to become a parent, but I just can't understand how you could ever hurt your child. It's mad to me, it's just inconceivable. God.' He shakes his head. 'Poor kid of ours is going to be spoiled rotten if I've got anything to do with it.'

Erin doesn't say anything, traces a shape in a patch of spilled liquid on the tabletop.

'I know,' she says eventually, 'it's a horrible case. Awful. It's been hard writing it up, to be honest. Glad it's over now.' She looks suddenly very sad, and Dominic feels bad. He hadn't meant to upset her, knows only too well how harrowing court cases like that can be. He tries to change the subject, starts to tell her about overhearing Alison in the office.

'She was on about some deal, it was weird,' he says, but Erin isn't listening. She's staring at him, her head resting on her hands.

He stops talking.

'Penny for your thoughts?' he asks her.

'Oh,' she looks suddenly vulnerable, her blue eyes big in her face. Dominic thinks of Andy ignoring her in the office, of the things she must have had to listen to in court. He doesn't know why people want to hear that stuff.

'You OK?' he says, raising his eyebrows at her over his pint glass.

She shakes her head as though clearing water from her ears. 'Yeah,' she says, 'Just remembering something, that's all.'

43

London

Dominic

The taxi splashes through the wet London roads as Dominic makes his way home from the bar. The city looks darker tonight somehow, there is something menacing about the slick hiss of the pavements. He glances at his watch; it is later than he thought. He's had too much beer, he should have stopped after the first one. It had just been such a relief to be sitting out in a bar, talking to someone else, making conversation that didn't revolve around doll houses or IVF. Dominic winces at his own thoughts. He shouldn't think like that. The alcohol is making him mean.

The taxi drops him off outside their building. Dominic sees a figure in the downstairs hallway, waiting at the window, and panics when he sees it is Corinne. Why is she down here?

Corinne's feet are bare and her skin when he touches her is freezing. Goosebumps cover her arms, the hairs on her flesh standing on end.

'What are you doing?' he asks her. 'Why aren't you in the flat?'

'I can't go back in there, Dominic.'

Her eyes are red; she is holding something in her hands. He stares at her in confusion and she wordlessly thrusts it towards him. The sight of it pushes everything from his mind.

She is holding a little doll. It has a beautifully painted face and long brown ringlets, is clad in a red velvet dress. There is a giant hole in its stomach, cutting through the plastic. The edges of the hole are jagged and sharp.

'What the hell is that?'

Corinne begins to cry. He takes her in his arms; it is later than he realised, gone eleven at night.

'Where have you been, Dominic? Where have you been?' She is crying hard now, her breath speeding up. 'Look at this! Someone left it in the sink. Someone is getting into this flat. I told you! *I told you!* We need to call the police.'

'Slow down, slow down. Start from the beginning.'

She takes a deep breath.

'I came home. I was going to make dinner. I thought I'd do a risotto. I … I needed a knife so I looked for the big silver one, the one your mum bought us and … and –' She covers her face with her hands. 'I found her there. Lying in the sink. Someone cut her open with the knife, it's nowhere, it's not here. They've taken it with them. Oh God.' Her voice becomes a wail. They stare at the doll together. Its plastic eyes stare back. Dominic takes a deep breath, tries to think. Corinne is frightening him, her eyes are wild.

'Do you want to stay down here while I go check the flat?'

'No!'

He takes her hand. Together they climb the stairs to the flat and go inside. It is empty; there is nobody there. There is no sign of any breakage – whoever got in came through the front door.

'The knife's missing,' Corinne says again. 'The big kitchen knife. They've used it to cut Beatrice then taken it.'

Dominic's heart is beating fast. He checks the flat twice, goes in and out of the tiny rooms, locks all the windows and slides both the bolts across the door. He'll call the locksmith first thing in the morning.

'We need to work out who would do this,' he says. He is finding it increasingly hard to think straight, the combination of the Peroni and now this is making his head feel painful.

There is a space in the knife block. One of the set is definitely missing. They had a set from his mother, she'd given them a load of kitchen stuff when they first moved into the flat. He opens the cutlery drawer, searches through it just in case. It is definitely not there.

He swallows, looks at the body of the doll. It stares back at him blankly. 'We need to call the police.'

Corinne is holding his hands tightly. 'I'm really scared, Dominic. I don't want to stay here tonight.'

He looks at her. Her eyes are huge in her face; she looks like a hunted animal.

'We can't go anywhere tonight,' he tells her. 'It's gone midnight. We'll get the locksmith out first thing in the morning, and we'll work out what to do. Whoever it was has gone, they're not here.'

'Please, Dominic,' she says. 'Please don't make us stay here tonight. They might come back.'

He sighs, runs a hand through his hair. Maybe she is right. There is a Travelodge on Gray's Inn Road. Perhaps they should go there.

'All right,' he says. 'All right. Grab some things and we'll get a taxi to somewhere cheap for the night. I can't drive, I've had too much to drink.'

Corinne goes into the bedroom. He hears her scrabbling around, the thud of the wardrobe door as she gets her overnight bag out. Beatrice lies on the table; he can see the wood of the surface through the hole in her stomach. Dominic shivers, and picks up the phone. His fingers dial the three digits: nine, nine, nine. His eyes dart around the flat as he listens to the voice on the end.

Then

I can feel myself becoming less and less patient. At night my apartment gets too hot — I push back the sheets, scratch at my chest. It feels as though bugs are crawling across my skin, nipping at me, reminding me that time is running out. Slipping away. I pick up my mobile, think about calling his phone. That would get her thinking, wouldn't it? But I make myself stop, put the phone down on the table, stare at it until the green light goes off. I lie back down, stare up at the ceiling. I think about being in the garden, wriggling through the fence, wanting to press my face against the window and merge through the glass. I imagine my body pushing through into their living room, the windows shattering around me, cutting my limbs and my flesh like hundreds of tiny knives.

I wish I could sleep, let my body relax. I'd have a drink to take the edge off but I don't drink much any more. When I was at school, some of the older kids used to make me — they'd pass me the vodka bottle, watch as my lips unpursed and the liquid wriggled down my throat. I didn't like it. That's what she reminded me of the other night, all big eyes and weak stomach. Her hair was all over the place. She couldn't even walk in her heels. I took a photograph, thought I might upload it to her Instagram account. It made me laugh a little bit, then I panicked and pressed delete. I can't mess this up.

I'm at my best when I'm planning, when I'm thinking of ideas. Mum is too, now that she's busy her voice is brighter when we speak. Some of the ideas work, and some of them don't. My best ideas come when I've had a good long session of remembering — remembering how bad I used to feel, the splash of the cold water in our old flat, the sour smell of Mummy when she hadn't washed.

The way the kids at school looked at me. The way the grass felt against my knees in their garden. The day we got to go inside. That day really got to me, I think. It changed things. It made me see how big the difference was, between what I had and what I deserved.

I put my hand into the child's high chair yesterday, felt the hot sweaty flesh of its fingers. One of them curled around mine and I jumped backwards, felt my breath catch in my throat.

'Let go,' I said, but it just clung tighter, and its eyes stared up into mine like it really liked me. Trusted me. That child really shouldn't do that.

44

London

Corinne

The police are here. They take a horribly long time to arrive and we have to wait in the flat, listen to the ticking of the clock. At last two men appear at the door, one of them in his early forties, the other looks barely older than Lucy. He has a twisted cauliflower ear; I can't stop looking at it, at how ugly it is.

'So, do you want to run us through what happened, Mr and Mrs Stones?' the elder one says. 'I understand there's been a break-in?'

'We're not married,' I say then, and a look of hurt flashes across Dominic's face. I reach for his hand, feeling instantly ashamed; we aren't married because we can't afford it. I don't know why I felt the need to say that. I suppose I feel cross with him, cross that he wasn't here tonight, that he was out with Andy while I was going through the horror of finding Beatrice all on my own. Cross with him for not changing the locks when I wanted him to. Cross with him for only now starting to take me seriously when I've been trying to get through to him for weeks.

'I came home,' I say, my voice shaking a little, 'I was going to make dinner, I was just about to – to chop a pepper and – and I found her. I found Beatrice, that's the doll–' I gesture stupidly at her ruined body on the table between us. 'She was in the sink, with a hole in her stomach. My knife is missing, our big kitchen knife. I think they used it to cut her open.'

The younger policeman is staring at the doll, a look of revulsion on his face. I feel impatient. That isn't going to help now.

'And where were you at this time?' the elder policeman asks Dominic, his pen poised in the air.

There's a tiny pause.

'I was out,' Dom says, 'I was with a colleague in a bar. Just an after-work drink.'

The man nods. 'Someone can vouch for that?'

I frown. Where is he going with this?

'He was with Andy,' I say. 'He's his friend from the paper, yes, he'll vouch for it. That isn't the point here. Someone's been in the flat,' I say, my voice rising. I can feel panic building in my chest.

Dom squeezes my hand gently but I ignore him, carry on speaking. 'I don't know how they got in, nothing's broken, nothing's been moved. Just this, just Beatrice.'

The older policeman is taking notes, his pen moving swiftly across the page.

'And you say one of your knives has gone?' He directs the question at Dominic, not me. He thinks I sound hysterical, I can tell.

'Yes,' I interrupt. 'The big silver one, it's gone, it's definitely missing. I'm telling you, someone is using this as a threat. This is my doll, she belongs to me.'

304

I want to cry. The horror of it all is sinking in, the air in the flat feels tight and oppressive. Dom's eyes are slightly bloodshot, as though he's had too much to drink. I feel like screaming the place down.

The younger policeman picks up the doll and his colleague snaps at him.

'Put that down, Mark.' He turns to us again, meeting my eyes this time. 'We're going to need to take the item for fingerprinting, if that's all right with you. Whoever did this will have left some sort of trace, we hope. Without that, with no sign of disturbance … well, it's difficult.' He looks between us, as though he's doubting me, as though he thinks there's more to the story. What does he think, we've had some sort of twisted domestic?

Dominic seems suddenly to come to. 'That would be great, Officers,' he says, and I can see they're relieved that he's speaking up, that he's corroborating my story.

'If you can keep us updated, that would be really helpful.' He glances at me. 'We're going to stay elsewhere tonight, my girlfriend doesn't feel safe in the flat.'

I stare at him, the blood beating in my ears. 'Oh, and you do?'

He takes my hand again. 'No, of course not, Cor. Calm down, I'm on your side.' He smiles awkwardly at the police officers. The younger one takes a pair of see-through gloves from his pocket, picks up Beatrice and deposits her clinically in a clear plastic bag. Her face stares out at me through the cellophane. I feel helpless.

'Did you see anyone around the property?' the elder policeman asks. 'Anything unusual?'

'I saw my neighbour,' I tell him. 'She was outside the flat when I got home but she couldn't have been inside. She doesn't have a key.'

'Does anyone else have a key to this place?'

'No,' I say. 'Well, just my sister. And my mum does, actually, I think. But nobody else.'

'And … this might seem a strange question, but do either of you know anyone who might want to do something like this? To threaten you?'

The younger one is speaking now, they seem to be taking it in turns. I shake my head. Dominic is looking at the floor, his face unreadable. I frown at him.

'Dom? Do you?'

He looks up, raises his eyebrows at the police.

'Nope,' he says, 'Nobody at all.' He pauses. I can see him swallow, the Adam's apple bobbing in his neck. 'I don't know who would do something as violent as this.'

'We'll need to speak to your neighbour,' the elder officer says. I give him Gilly's details and he scribbles them down in his little notebook. Dominic frowns at me.

'She might have seen something!' I say. 'She was outside the flat when I got home. Leaving me a note, she said.'

'She was outside your flat?' the younger policeman says, and I nod. He makes a note on his page.

'I mean, I don't think she did this!' I say hastily. 'But she lives just across the hall, so if anyone might have seen someone, it's her.'

'Yes, it's best that we speak to anyone in the vicinity,' the policeman says. 'What's your relationship with this Gilly? Are you on good terms?'

'Yes, we are,' I say. 'We've become friends.'

'And you met her when she moved into the building?'

I nod. 'Only a few weeks ago — well, actually, we met a couple of years ago but she doesn't remember, it was a coincidence.' Dominic frowns at me, as do the police. Quickly I fill them in, leaving out my mad thoughts, just saying that she came into Dad's office once to get a quote.

'Hmm,' the older policeman says, and I see the pair of them exchange a quick look.

'Honestly,' I say, 'Gilly's nice, she didn't do this. She's not who you ought to be looking at.' I pause. 'But I don't know who is.'

The police leave after that, taking Beatrice with them. I hold the older one's card between my fingers tightly, as though it is a lifeline. I stare at his name, printed on the front. DI Ellison. I hope he knows what he's doing.

'Come on,' Dom says, lifting my bag onto his shoulder. 'Let's get out of here.' He leads the way out of the flat, stumbles slightly at the doorway, his body slumping slightly into the frame.

'You always drink too much when you're with Andy,' I say. He doesn't answer me. I don't know if he's heard.

45

London

Dominic

Dominic wakes up from a terrible night's sleep at the Travelodge. His mouth feels furry from last night's beer, he looks over and sees that Corinne is already up, pacing the room like a caged lion. She pounces on him when he opens his eyes.

'We need to call the locksmith.'

He obliges, picks up his phone, Corinne hovering anxiously at his side in her navy pyjamas.

'Someone will be with you in about an hour,' the man on the phone says. 'Meet us at the property, it'll be seventy-five quid.'

He gives the guy his card details. Corinne is very on edge, which doesn't surprise him. He is pretty freaked out himself. Who the hell has come into the flat and knifed a doll in the stomach? Dominic shudders. They'd sat up last night after the police left, huddled together in the bare Travelodge room, discussing possibilities. In the middle of the night, Dominic had woken up in a cold sweat, thinking of the broken doll's plastic blue eyes, of them staring back at him accusingly from the table. He wishes he'd been there with Corinne when she found her. He should have been. If he had maybe none of this would have happened.

Dominic doesn't want to admit that he was out with Erin last night in the first place, wishes to God that the whole thing had never happened. Not that there was anything in it, of course, she is just a friend, but he hadn't mentioned it at the time and now it seems too late. It will make it sound worse, like it is something it's not. If only he could wind back the clock. Instead, he feels like the world is speeding up, as if events are happening faster than he can think, faster than he can process. At the centre of his mind is Corinne and their baby.

They get a bus back to the flat early in the morning. It is deathly quiet. It looks untouched.

Dominic tries to think clearly. He boils the kettle, the sound loud in the quiet kitchen. He makes them both hot drinks, coffee for himself and boiling water for Corinne. Neither of them have really slept.

Suddenly there is a knock at the door and Corinne jumps, spills her drink over the table. Dominic goes to the door, pulls back both bolts. It's the locksmith, a young guy armed with a briefcase of tools. He grins at them both.

'Morning all.'

Corinne says she will wait with the locksmith, wants to make sure it is all done properly. Dominic hesitates. He doesn't really want to leave her alone.

'Will you ring me when you get to the gallery, Cor?'

She nods. 'Yes. I'm going to take the Tube. I don't want to walk alone.' She swallows. 'I'm supposed to be meeting Mum and Ashley tonight, remember? It's the anniversary of my dad.' Her hand goes to her throat. 'We were supposed to mark the occasion.'

Dominic nods. 'Of course, shit, I'm meant to be picking your mum up. Do you still want me to do that? Do you still want to go?'

Corinne nods. 'We have to go, Dom. It's what we always planned to do. I want to take flowers to the grave.'

'OK,' he says. 'You're right, you should. We shouldn't let this – this thing scare us. I'll drop your Mum off at the cemetery then pick you up from the restaurant afterwards. I don't want you coming back alone late at night. We can come home together, work out what to do.'

He puts his arms around her. Corinne's heart is skittering against his chest, like a caged bird. As they embrace he catches sight of the fridge behind her, the shiny white surface with the grainy image attached.

'Is that—?' They break apart, and he picks up the scan. In spite of everything, even though the locksmith is right next to them fiddling with the locks, Dominic kisses Corinne, a huge smile breaking out over his face.

'I can't believe it! Wow, Cor. When? How?'

She's smiling too, her eyes teary. 'I know. I'm so sorry, at my appointment yesterday, the nurses just asked me if I could have a scan while I was there, and you were at work already so I thought I'd just have it, surprise you. Amazing, right?'

He nods. There is a lump in his throat. He feels a thud of guilt. He can't believe he forgot the appointment. 'The appointment? Oh God, Cor. I'm so sorry. I completely forgot.'

He has to turn away from her, terrified she will be able to see the guilt on his face. 'I am so, so sorry. I can't believe you went alone.' He feels like crying.

'Hey,' she says softly, taking his hand. 'Don't be silly, you've had lots on at work and we'd already done the home tests. I thought it was just a routine check-up. But the nurse said I should have an early scan. That's all. You'll be there for the next one. The big one is at twelve weeks!'

He nods. 'Of course I will.'

'I wanted to show you last night,' Corinne says. 'But then, well.' They both look at the tabletop, thinking of Beatrice's slashed body, the torn crimson folds of her velvet dress.

He kisses her forehead and then leans his own against it. 'It's amazing, really amazing.'

He can see the edge of her smile. 'It is, isn't it?'

'I love you, Corinne,' Dominic says. He leans back and rubs her cheek with the back of his thumb. He fastens the little picture back onto the fridge, marvelling at the blurry shape as he does so. It is a brilliant feeling.

'I'll pick you up tonight,' he says. 'Make sure you're safe.'

'Thank you.' She smiles at him, a proper smile this time. 'You're the best.'

As he stares at the picture sitting under the bright red heart magnet, he feels a sudden shudder, thinks of her standing at the sink last night, finding the mutilated doll. Guilt shivers again down his spine. *I'm not*, he wants to whisper. *I've let you down. I should have been here.* But he doesn't say anything, he just kisses Corinne, pulls her familiar warm body tightly against his. It's partly cowardice keeping him quiet, he knows, but it's also a form of protection. Corinne and their tiny baby need to be kept safe from everything right now. And he's going to make sure they are.

46

27 March 2017
The day of the anniversary

London

Ashley

Lucy hasn't put a toe out of line since the police brought her home. She sits on the sofa with her brother, helps Ashley in the kitchen, goes to and from school without complaint. Her high heels stay on the rack, her eye make-up in the tin.

'It really scared her, didn't it?' James says to Ashley. He is putting on his tie in their bedroom, standing in front of the mirror. Ashley is up early with him. Holly woke at four and after Ashley had calmed her down there didn't seem to be any point going back to sleep. She called the doctor's surgery when it opened at seven and asked for Doctor McPherson, hoping to find out why the blood test results are taking so long.

'I'm sorry, Doctor McPherson isn't in this morning,' the receptionist had told her, the sing-song of her voice too bright in Ashley's ear. 'I'll make a note of your call.' Ashley had hung up, sighed, stroked Holly's blonde hair with the ends of her fingers. Today is the anniversary and she feels a sense of weight on her shoulders, a pressure behind her eyelids. She has a lot to do before she can get to the cemetery tonight. James is looking at her expectantly, waiting for an answer. One thing at a time, that's the way to do it. She nods.

'I think it did scare her, yes, which is a good thing, I suppose. It really scared me! I think she frightened herself.'

'Has she mentioned anything else to you?'

Ashley shakes her head. 'No. I've asked. She says the older girl has gone quiet, she hasn't been able to get hold of her since that night.' Ashley shudders. 'Little bitch. She won't even tell me her name. I think Luce is secretly really hurt by it, more than she lets on.' She sighs. 'I've been thinking about sneaking a look at her phone, looking on this Instagram thing to see if I can work out who it was she was talking to. I don't like the thought of her putting herself out there online like that. Sharing stuff with this weirdo girl.'

James nods. 'It was seductive, I suppose, for Luce. Imagine, at that age. Someone older paying you attention. Taking you out. It's a big deal.'

'The internet's a dangerous place,' Ashley says. 'I just keep thinking – what was this girl's intention? Why befriend her at all? It's weird. And then to just leave her like that, alone on the street? Unconscious? It's really odd, James. Creepy.' She pauses. 'It's almost like …' She shakes her head, doesn't want to say the words aloud.

James turns around, tie in place. He reaches for his jacket. 'Go on. Almost like what?'

Ashley looks at him. 'It's almost like she left her for dead.'

The room seems to chill slightly. For a moment, Ashley and James stare at each other and then Benji shouts for some juice in bed; the spell is broken.

'Ashley!' James says. He forces out a laugh. 'Don't be so dramatic.' He comes towards her, circles his arms round her waist. 'It was some older kid who bit off more than she could chew, that's all. Panicked when she saw the state Luce got into. She probably wasn't much older herself.'

Ashley nods her head against his chest. 'OK. OK. Sorry. I just feel like there's something weird about it, something not right. Do you think it was this girl making phone calls to the house, trying to get hold of Lucy and hanging up when she got me instead?' She sighs, shivers despite the sun crowding through the window. 'God, James. When I think of the police at the door like that … How close did we come to losing Lucy for good?'

James looks her in the eye. 'We didn't though, Ash. We aren't going to lose her. I promise. And the calls?' He shrugs. 'Well, could be her, I suppose. She doesn't sound particularly mature.'

Ashley remembers the laughing, the horrible sound of it echoing down the phone. She wants to say more, to tell James how worried she feels, but she keeps her mouth closed. He has bigger things on his mind at the moment.

He is straightening up, looking at himself again in the mirror. He looks nervous and Ashley goes to his side. Today is the day. His boss Daniel is making a decision: James will find out whether he keeps his job.

'You look wonderful.' Ashley reaches for her husband's hand and they stand like that, side by side, looking at their reflections in the floor-length glass. Now both of them look nervous.

'I've told you, I'm here for you,' Ashley says. 'As long as you're honest, as long as you tell me exactly what Daniel says. No more secrecy. No more lies.'

'I never lied to you!'

'Evasion of the truth then.'

He nods, blows out his breath. 'OK. OK. I need to go. Thank you, Ash. For supporting me. For believing in us.'

She kisses him, knowing that he means it, that she means it too. His cheeks are damp, freshly shaven.

'I love you, James. No matter what. Remember that. And go fight. You can do it!'

She grins at him, waves him off from the window, mentally praying that he comes back with good news. The room is quiet when he leaves; she makes their bed, pulls the sheets taut across the mattress. The children aren't all up yet, it is still early, but Benji will be rocketing around in his room. He is full of energy at the moment, the only one who is. Holly has had another dose of the medicine from the doctor, settled down into sleep again. Ashley had stared at her baby's closed eyelids for a while after she'd stopped crying, as though she could look inside her daughter's mind, see the nightmares for herself. She hates the thought of her baby being scared, even in dreams.

The telephone rings as Ashley is on the way downstairs to make a start on the breakfast and pour Benji some juice. She pauses. Perhaps it is James, maybe he's forgotten something.

Ashley runs down the stairs, feels her socked feet slip slightly on the polished wood and grabs the rail. Breaking her neck, now that wouldn't do. She picks up the phone.

'Hello?' She waits. Nobody speaks. There is a strange sound, sort of a squeak, then silence. It is happening all over again.

Something inside Ashley snaps.

'Whoever this is, stop calling here! Just fucking stop it!' she shouts into the phone, and she slams down the receiver, bangs it down again and again until the plastic begins to crack. She stops, slightly out of breath, rests her forehead against the cool of the hallway wall. Before she can cry, she quickly dials 1471, expecting the usual voice telling her the number is ex-directory, but to her surprise it methodically lists out a number she knows better than her own: her Mum's.

Relief courses through her, and then guilt. Mum. It's just Mum! Thank God. Ashley cringes. Must have been a bad connection and she'd screamed those awful words down the phone. What is wrong with her? She is so tired.

She presses 5 to return the call, but the line is now engaged. Perhaps she's called Corinne. She hopes she's not telling her sister about what she shouted. Her face flushes with embarrassment and shame. There's a thud upstairs, a patter of feet and the sound of the toilet flushing; Benji is up. Ashley opens the cupboard and gets out the orange juice for him, starts laying out the bowls for the children's cereal. She takes a small scoop of coffee granules from the jar and crunches. She's sure her mum will call back.

47

27 March 2017
The day of the anniversary

London

Corinne

The locksmith is really kind. He gets everything sorted then hands me a brand-new set of keys for the flat. I grip them tightly – finally. What I've been wanting for weeks. The door closes perfectly, locks easily, I've checked.

'There you go,' he told me, 'All done for you. Only person who'll be able to get into this flat is you. And your partner of course.' He smiled at me, nodded his head in the direction of the fridge. 'Couldn't help but overhear your news. Congratulations!'

'Thank you!' I say. It's the first time a stranger has said it. It feels wonderful.

He smiles and leaves, gently shutting the door behind him. I don't want to stay in the flat so I grab my trench coat from the back of the door, tuck the new keys carefully into my handbag and go downstairs. I'm too early to go to the gallery really but I want to get out of here, I don't want to be in this flat for a second longer, even now the locks are changed and I know nobody else is inside. I cannot get the image of Beatrice out of my head. I think back to the policemen, of Beatrice in their clear plastic bag, a specimen to be studied. My beautiful doll now an item in their custody, proof of someone's horrid act of violence. I want to go back to the police, tell them about everything else: the horrid pink bootees nestled in the cradle with that note. The rocking horse, the chimney pot, the little door ripped from my doll house. The dead rabbit, splayed for me to find. All of it. Dom doesn't want me to, he's worried they won't believe me. But I'm going to persuade him tonight, when I'm back from dinner.

We sat up last night in the horrible Travelodge room, trying to think of people who would do this to me.

'I don't have any enemies,' I told him. 'Really I don't. This is a threat, Dominic. It isn't me being crazy. Think about everything that's happened.'

He hadn't met my eyes properly, kept glancing away from me.

I'd leaned forward. 'You do believe me, Dom, don't you? You believe that this was in the house when I got home.'

Silence.

'I didn't do it myself, Dominic!'

He'd woken up at that, grabbed my hands. 'I know, shh, Cor, I know. I wasn't suggesting that! God. I was just thinking, is all. I was just trying to figure something out in my head. Why didn't you tell me about Gilly knowing your dad earlier?'

I shrugged. 'I didn't really have the chance.'

'And you were by yourself when you came into the flat?'

I'd stared at him. I couldn't believe he would even consider that I would do something like this myself, that I would be making it up.

I didn't sleep all night.

Out on the street outside, the light feels very bright after the dimness of the flat. The road is quiet, bathed in sunlight. I pull out my phone and text Dominic. *Locks all done!* I don't feel like being near our building, not after everything that's happened in the past twelve hours, so I head to the Underground, thinking I'll get the Tube to Highbury and Islington and then walk down Upper Street. I can make the most of the sun for a bit until I need to be in the gallery at ten.

The Tube is very busy; I know getting on is a mistake the second I'm through the doors. I thought it would make me feel safer than walking alone but when strangers brush past me I tense up. When a man leans close to me as I'm in the ticket hall I imagine his hand around my neck, pressing into my glands while his other hand reaches for my purse.

I can't wait to get off.

My coat is too hot and I feel sweat start to pool underneath my arms. A big, heavyset man jumps on just as the doors are closing at Finsbury Park; he has to force them back open with the tips of his fingers. I wince. He squeezes up against me, pulling an apologetic face, and I take a deep breath, try to turn my head away so that I am not pressed up against his chest. The train rocks on the tracks and he is thrown against me again. I feel a pain in my left arm near my wrist; it is trapped between the man and the wall of the carriage but this isn't an ache, it's a needling pain, as though something sharp is cutting into me. There is no room to move so I can't work out what's causing it, can't look down. I give a little yelp as the pain comes again, stabs into my skin. The big man I'm pushed up against frowns. I ignore him. It hurts! Perhaps my gold bracelet has come loose. The clasp of it is sharp, finely cut. It was a gift from Dominic. I don't want to lose it.

When we finally reach Highbury and Islington I get off, gasping a little, relieved to be out of the busy carriage. Immediately, I feel for my bracelet but it is fastened tightly on my wrist where it always is. The pain in my arm has gone but when I lift an arm to swipe my Oyster card it is there again, this time sharper. I jump at the sensation. What *is* that? Have I left a safety pin in this coat?

Outside it's still nice and sunny; I stand by the grassy roundabout for a few seconds, letting the sun warm my face. When I move a hand to my stomach, the pain in my wrist pricks me again; I frown, puzzled. With my other hand I pat the sleeve of my left arm and instantly there is another, sharper pain further up on my forearm. My fingers feel something very sharp; there's definitely something stuck in this coat. I shrug it off, ease my left arm out of the sleeve.

I'm bleeding. I realise with a shock that there is a long, vivid scratch trailing up from my wrist bone and a small trickle of dark red blood snaking its way out. I blot it with the end of my scarf then shake the coat out in front of me, hoping to dislodge whatever is inside. I gasp. It's not stray pins – it's glass. Tiny shards of it fall onto the grass in front of me, glinting in the sunlight like minuscule knives. Frantically, I keep shaking, ignoring the strange looks from passers-by, and when I think it's all out I walk shakily down the high street, lean against the wall of a coffee shop, oblivious to the people tutting as they try to move past. I hold the left sleeve of my coat up to my eyes.

The lining has been ripped, there is a hole up by the shoulder. The little shards of glass have been pushed through so that they fell down to my cuff, gathered together by my wrist, ready to cut into my flesh. I look around me, feeling sick. How could they have got there? This is my trench coat, the one I always wear – I had it on the day before last. The hole is neat, the edges crisp as though it's been made with scissors. Someone has done this on purpose.

'Spring daffs, only a pound a bunch!'

The sound of the flower seller cuts through my consciousness. I look up; it's a little stall on the edge of the street, and the short, balding guy at the front of it is waving bunches of daffodils in his hands, calling out to passers-by. He has seen me staring and I try to smile at him, try to look as normal as I can even though my brain is racing, thinking about the hidden glass, imagining fingers going through my kitchen drawers, taking out our scissors, snipping a deft hole in the lining of my coat. Hands shoving the glass in, taking care not to cut themselves. Who? *Who?*

'Interested, love?'

I stare at the brightly coloured petals shining in the sun, but all I can see is the glass, the deadly shards left for me to find.

'Maybe later,' I tell the man and I start walking away, feeling a bit unsteady. I'll go to the gallery early, at least

I'll feel safer there. My arm throbs. The flower seller looks disappointed when I move off. I attempt a nod when he catches my eye. I'll come back; I can get some daffodils on my way to meet Ashley and Mum after work, they were always Dad's favourite. I can leave them at the gravestone.

I walk down Upper Street, my hands across my stomach, my coat folded carefully over one arm, held away from my body as though it's poisonous. It's not cold without it; I'm wearing a woollen dress today that comes down past my knees. I wanted to look nice, I wanted to feel special today for Dad. Twelve months. Sometimes I cannot believe it. It will be good to do it properly, mark the occasion.

I call Mum from my mobile as I walk towards the gallery. I'm not going to tell her about the glass, of course I'm not, she'll panic – but Dominic's picking her up later and I want to make sure she hasn't forgotten. I wonder how she is coping with today so far. I think of her, cowering in her house, unable to tell me how she really feels. I put a hand to my forehead. Everything is so horrible. I just want to get through today, remember Dad properly. I want to do it right.

Mum's home phone rings and rings; she doesn't pick up. I frown. She hardly ever goes anywhere; she's usually rattling around the house. Still, it's a nice day. Perhaps she's in the garden. Dom will get her later on.

I put my mobile back in my bag, wait anxiously at the crossing opposite the gallery. I can't stop looking around, staring at the people on the streets. *Is it you? Has one of you been in my flat?* My eye catches sight of a woman coming out of Lullaby, the baby shop on the other side of the road. She's heavily pregnant, her stomach stretches

322

out before her and she's carrying lots of bulging lilac bags, emblazoned with the shop's distinctive logo. I avoid this shop normally, used to avert my eyes whenever I had to walk past it.

The lights change and I cross the road, still with my coat held gingerly across my right arm. The blood on my wrist has dried, I can feel the hard crust of it on my skin. I pause outside the baby shop. I can see a sales assistant hovering by the door, smiling at me hopefully. I dither awkwardly. I've had such a bad night. Perhaps this will help. When I walk in I feel weirdly nervous. The sales assistant smiles at me warmly. Rebecca, her name badge says.

'Welcome to Lullaby! What can I help you with?'

For just a moment, I stand still, breathe the shop in. I have imagined this in my dreams; choosing a pram, picking out little bootees, the perfect teddy bear. And now I'm finally here.

'It's my first baby,' I tell her, 'I haven't bought anything yet.'

'How exciting!' she squeals; her joy is infectious and I let myself smile, allow myself to relax for just a minute. She tells me I can leave my coat and my handbag by the till while I walk around and I put the coat down gratefully, surreptitiously feeling it between my fingers as I do so. I can't feel any more glass.

She walks me round the store and, as we go up and down the aisles, I feel better and better, more and more happy, safe in the brightly lit shop. *I'm going to have a baby! I'm going to be a mother.* When it comes down to it, that's what matters. Whoever is doing this to me can't take that away from me. I won't let them.

48

27 March 2017
The day of the anniversary

London

Ashley

Ashley has got the dinner ready for the children, laid everything out as she normally does. All James needs to do is put the fish fingers in the oven; she's guessing he can manage that, whatever the outcome of today is. She looks at the clock. Quarter to four. She had been hoping to see her husband before driving to Hampstead, is desperate to hear the news. But she can't cancel tonight, she has to go see Corinne and their mother, go visit the grave together and have dinner afterwards. It's what they said they would do on the one-year anniversary. It has always been their plan.

Ashley shakes the Birds Eye fish fingers out onto the oven tray, sets out three plates, three forks, three knives. Adds the bottle of ketchup, the salt and pepper in their little china pots.

'Will you be home soon, Mummy?' Benji is in a funny mood, clingy and a little bit tearful. He has been playing

Grandmother's Footsteps after school in the garden with Lucy, making the most of the first sunny day of the year. She kisses the top of his head.

'Yes, darling, I'll be back tonight. Daddy and Lucy are taking care of you this evening, remember? And it's fish fingers and chips for dinner!'

Lucy comes into the kitchen, wearing an old T-shirt with Minnie Mouse on it. She looks like a child for the first time in months and it inflates Ashley's heart.

'Come on, Ben,' she says to her brother, 'I'll play racing with you until Dad gets back.'

'He should be here,' Ashley says, glancing at the clock again, thinking of James in the boardroom. Maybe he's with Daniel right this second. Her stomach twists with nerves. She feels like time is speeding up; Lucy can watch Benji for a little while but she can't leave Holly under their care too. She is too little, the risks are too high.

When the clock reaches five, Ashley gives up. She has to go. She takes Holly over to June's, armed with her little bag of spare nappies, change of clothes, the medicine the doctor gave them. Her daughter screams all the way there, her cries filling the car. Ashley glances at her watch. She feels terrible leaving Holly for June to deal with but she has to get to the cemetery and James is still not back from the office. She daren't call him in case they are mid-meeting.

June waves away Ashley's apologies, shakes her head when Holly's cries continue.

'There now, someone's in a bad mood, hey? Poor little love. Has she been like this all day?'

'She's been like it for weeks now,' Ashley says, proffering the little bottle of medicine. 'I thought it'd been getting better but today she's a mess.' Ashley pauses. June is looking at her sympathetically and she feels a sudden lump in her throat, swallows hard to quash it down. 'Here's the medicine, you know what to do if she wants to sleep. It'll settle her down. I'm so sorry to leave her like this, June, really I am. I'm all over the place at the moment – I came to drop her off on the wrong day the other week, and now I'm descending on you unannounced! I'm so sorry.'

June places a comforting hand on her arm, shakes her head. 'Not to worry, I love having her here. Anytime.'

Ashley smiles in relief. 'Thanks, June. James should be round to collect her soon, he's just been delayed at work and the thing is I've got to be in Hampstead – we're having a memorial for my father tonight.' She tries to say the words matter-of-factly, like an adult, not wanting the older woman to hear the tremor in her voice. But it seems June understands; she puts a hand on Ashley's shoulder and smiles at her.

'You get on,' she says. 'Don't worry about this little one, I'll settle her down and then when that husband of yours gets here he'll take her home. You concentrate on your family, on remembering your dad. I'm sure he'd be honoured.'

She raises her eyebrows when she says 'husband of yours' and Ashley hesitates – she ought to tell June that she was wrong, that James hasn't been playing away at all. She looks at her watch – she has to go. She'll sit down with June next time, they can have a good laugh about how silly Ashley has been.

Kissing Holly's hot little cheek, Ashley feels her daughter's hands clinging on to her, her fingers curl around Ashley's hair, her jacket sleeve, the beginning of her collarbone. She starts to cry again, as though she cannot bear for Ashley to leave. June smiles.

'Don't worry,' she says. 'She'll be fine once you're gone. She always is! Now be off with you.'

Ashley hesitates, can feel her heart twitching as her baby cries. But she has to get on. She needs to be with Corinne.

Ashley disentangles herself from Holly, thanks June again and hurries back to the car. She has told Lucy to call her as soon as James gets back. Her mobile is safely ensconced in her pocket, she will feel it if they ring. Her stomach churns. *Oh, please God.*

49

London

Corinne

I've bought too much!

I panicked when I got to the gallery because Marjorie was already there and I haven't told her yet that I'm pregnant. I was going to hustle the Lullaby bags to the back room and hide them before she saw, but I had five of them and it was a struggle to get them through the door.

She came towards me as I huffed and puffed, and I started to try to think of excuses but she peered inside the first bag and I saw the expression on her face. She knew, I know she did.

'Marjorie—' I said, but she must have heard the panic in my voice because she interrupted me.

'Corinne, you're pregnant?'

I didn't know what to say, it seemed ridiculous to lie.

'I know I should have told you,' I began, 'but it's really early days—'

She was laughing. Marjorie was actually laughing! The nervous words died on my tongue as she smiled at me, took three of the heavy bags from my reddening fingers.

'Oh, Corinne,' she said, 'that's really wonderful news.'

I was so surprised that she was being so nice that for a moment I forgot what had happened, I forgot the glass in my coat and the horrible night in the Travelodge and I became for a second what I am – an excited, hopeful, soon-to-be mother. Marjorie helped me unload the Lullaby bags and stored them in the back room.

She was being oddly kind, I'd never seen her like this before. I stared at her doubtfully as she started to rummage in the bags, looking excited. A thought occurred to me. Perhaps she sees it as a convenient way to let me go? She's never seemed to like me much. I watched her hold up a little white bonnet and I suddenly hated myself for the thought; what's happened to me? I never used to be so cynical. But then I saw the cut on my wrist, and I felt a spurt of anger – I know what's happened to me: a dismembered doll in my kitchen and glass in my coat. I knew I needed to call Dominic but Marjorie was holding up a little pink Babygro now, her eyes bright.

'So cute!' she said. 'Look how tiny it is. Pink – you're having a girl then?'

'Well.' I shrugged, embarrassed. 'Actually I don't know. But that's what I'm hoping for. We haven't found out.'

'Got a name yet?'

'Not yet!' I said. 'But plenty of time!'

I remember Dad and I used to spend ages coming up with names for all the dolls he bought me. Belinda,

Emilie, Alicia, Lucille. Beatrice. I shiver. We've got to go back the police, chase them to take action. Judging by how long they took to arrive last night I'm not convinced they'll do anything fast. I'm worried they weren't taking me seriously enough yesterday, got the wrong end of the stick with the Gilly thing. I'm going to make Dom listen, especially after the glass. My mind spools back, remembering the mangled rabbit on the bonnet, the violence of it. The blood matting its fur, the blood trailing down my own arm. What if it was personal? What if this whole thing has been about as personal as you can get?

I'm not going to take no for an answer any more.

'You must be so excited, Corinne,' Marjorie said to me, and then she put her arms around me, gave me a happy little cuddle, which was very unlike her but actually very nice. I wanted to cling to her, bury my face in her cardigan, but instead I just stood there and smiled, trying to pretend I was OK.

That was this morning. It's late afternoon, now, I've almost made it through the day. Dom still hasn't called but he texted earlier to say he was on the way to get Mum and to check I was OK. I didn't mention my coat or the cut on my arm; he'd only worry more, or make me go straight home. And I have to go and see Dad tonight, there's no way I'm not going. Whoever is trying to hurt me won't know where I am if I'm not at the flat, I haven't told anyone about Dad's anniversary. Except for Dominic, of course. The only other people that know what today is are his old colleagues, but they'll all be at the memorial dinner at the RIBA. For a moment, I picture the scene and wish

I could be there – smartly dressed men in suits raising a glass to Dad's memory, to his success, his cleverness and his charisma. And an empty space at the table where he should be. I blink, quickly. No, it's better that we have our own private time to remember, away from all the fuss. *Home is where the heart is.*

I'm meeting them both in an hour at the cemetery gates. As if reading my mind, the gallery phone rings and it's Ashley on the line. 'I'm here already, the traffic was on my side! Got the flowers?' she says. 'Dom is dropping Mum off here, right?'

'Right, he should be there soon,' I say, glancing at my watch. 'I want the flowers to be fresh so I'll get some en route, I saw a guy selling daffodils this morning so thought I'd get some of those.'

'Perfect, thank you,' she says a little breathlessly. 'I've made reservations for us at Taprinska. We can have steak! Dad's favourite, so he'd definitely approve. I'll just meet you in the cemetery? I'm going to go up now and just sit with Dad for a while.'

Before I can reply she's hung up. Thank God we wiped all the paint off, it would be so horrible for her to have to see the gravestone like that. I wouldn't wish it upon anyone. I shudder, remembering. I don't want to tell Ashley about Beatrice, I don't want to upset her today.

Checking the time, I'm relieved to see it's only ten minutes until we close the gallery. Dominic and Mum must be on their way. He'll be annoyed later that I haven't told him about the coat straight away, but I want to tell him in person, want to see his reaction. I'll sit him down, tell him everything I'm feeling. Force him to come to the police with me tomorrow morning. Tonight is about Ashley, Mum and Dad and our immediate nuclear family, small as it is. A year is a milestone. A time to remember. We'll sit and have a proper meal, and talk about Dad, and raise a big glass of wine to his life. Well, I'll probably have tonic water.

finding it must have been, feels so guilty for leaving her alone in the flat. He pulls out his mobile to call her, tell her he is in Kent, but the screen stares blankly back at him – of course, there is no signal here. Never is.

He can almost see Mathilde's house through the trees at the end of the road; he drives the car the last few metres and pulls in, his tyres crunching on the gravel. There are no lights on; it doesn't look like she's in at all. The idea strikes him as odd, Corinne says she hardly ever goes out. He should have called her first but she is expecting him at this time. Perhaps she is just waiting to go.

Dominic looks at his watch. His headlights shine onto the dark windows of the house; they stare back at him blankly. He goes to the front door, knocks twice. There is no answer. He wonders how Mathilde has dealt with this day, the anniversary of her husband's death. It must be incredibly tough for her down here, all on her own in this house. Dominic always remembers Richard as such a big presence, always the centre of attention. To lose that kind of energy around you must be very strange. There were times when Richard's need to be in the middle of things grated on Dominic slightly – just little moments, ones that he would never and has never mentioned to Corinne. A flash of something in his dark eyes when the conversation moved away from him. A witty retort that left Dominic in the dark. He wasn't the sort of man Dominic felt he could keep up with, and at times he worried that Corinne would notice the differences between them – her shining father versus her local journo boyfriend. Still, it hardly matters now.

Dominic is about to go round to the side door of the house when something makes him pause. There is a sound, a very faint thudding sound, quiet, but unmistakably there in the silence of the countryside evening. Something about it makes him feel uneasy. He turns back towards the house. It is totally dark, but Mathilde has no neighbours, the house is isolated. Could the noise be coming from inside? On instinct, Dominic approaches the main front window of the house, the one that looks into the sitting room. The curtains are open; he steps gently onto Mathilde's flowerbed, his feet sinking into the soft soil. He stares through the window, his eyes adjusting to the darkness.

He catches sight of something then, and for a moment he thinks he must be wrong but then he looks closer, presses his face right up to the glass, and what he sees sends waves of horror straight through his body, over and over like a horrible electric shock. Mathilde isn't out. She isn't out at all.

51

London

Ashley

Ashley is walking to the graveyard, her black heeled shoes tapping on the pavement as she hurries down the hedge-lined road to the leafy Hampstead cemetery. Her mobile rings and she scrabbles desperately in her pocket for it, pulls it out with a shaking hand.

'Ash?'

'James?' Her heart is in her mouth. Her fingers are tightly clenched. She wants him to tell her quickly, get it over with, and, mercifully, he does.

'Ashley, it's all right. They're letting me stay. They're going to keep me on.' Ashley feels as though her knees might give way. She stops still and clutches the phone, taking a huge, shuddering breath. *Thank God. Oh, thank God.*

'Ash? You there?'

She finds her voice. 'Of course, oh, James, that's so wonderful. I'm so pleased.' She has tears in her eyes, wishes she could be with her husband, hold him close to her, kiss him. She closes her eyes, feeling the warmth of the sun on her eyelids. The evening sun is oddly bright for the time of year, casting a burning orange glow as it dips slowly below the horizon. It is beautiful; the first warm day of spring.

'I love you,' she tells James. 'I have to go to Dad's grave, but I'll be home later. We'll celebrate, OK? I'm so relieved. And I'm proud of you.'

'Me too,' he says. 'Thank you for trusting me, Ashley. It means a lot. Now go be with your family, the kids and I will be fine. I'm going to drive to June's and pick Holly up now.'

They hang up. Ashley can feel waves of relief crashing over her. She takes a deep breath, thanking God that James trusted her at last, that they are going to be all right. How horrible it must have been for him, not knowing how to tell her, not knowing what would happen. She still can't quite believe he let it all get so out of hand in the first place, but she knows that she wants to be there for him, to support rather than condemn. He is her family, her partner. He's the man she loves.

Ashley puts her phone back in her pocket, switches it to vibrate. At the entrance to the cemetery, she pauses, looks at her watch. Corinne won't be here for a while. She pushes open the black iron gates; she can sit by the grave, take half an hour to herself with her dad.

She can't believe it has been a whole year, a year since his body finally gave in to the cancer, since Corinne closed his eyes in the hospital room. Some days it feels like a lifetime, some days it feels as though it was yesterday. It has always seemed ridiculous to her that a man such as

337

her father could succumb to something like cancer – it didn't fit with his whip-smart brain, his endless ability to problem solve.

Ashley is wearing black; her best coat and suit. It's one of her only outfits that hasn't been ruined by the children, most of what she owns has been lost over the years to glitter and glue, snot and saliva. She smooths a hand over her skirt and, as she does so feels her mobile begin to ring again, the vibration shuddering through her jacket pocket.

Her heart leaps as she glances at the screen: blocked number. James wouldn't ring from a blocked line. *Please, not again.* The last thing she needs tonight is another silent call. She hesitates, standing in amongst the headstones, the slightly swaying trees that dot the cemetery. The phone vibrates again in her hand and she quickly presses the little green button.

'Hello?' Her voice is hushed, she feels somehow guilty for speaking loudly in the quiet of the cemetery.

'Mrs Thomas? It's Doctor McPherson here, I'm calling from the surgery. How are you?'

Ashley breathes out. Of course – doctors' numbers are always withheld.

'Fine,' she says, pressing the phone to her ear and resuming her walk through the graveyard. 'I'm fine, thank you.'

'Well, Mrs Thomas, Ashley, I won't beat about the bush here – we've had Holly's blood test results back in and I'd be keen to have a word with you.'

Ashley freezes on the spot. The graves around her feel suddenly too close, as though they are closing in on her, hemming her in.

'Is everything all right?'

There is a pause.

'Everything will be fine, Mrs Thomas, but I would like a quick chat with you as soon as possible. The results are a little unusual, you see. I'm sorry they've taken a bit of time to come back but I ran them past a few people, wanted to be sure.'

'I ... What do you mean? What's the matter with her, what's the matter with my baby?'

'I'd really rather discuss this in person, Mrs Thomas. Is it possible for you to come to the surgery? As soon as you can?'

'I'm − I'm in Hampstead,' Ashley says. 'We're − my father ...'

'Ah.' The doctor's voice is clipped, firm. He knows their family history, knows about Richard's death. Ashley thinks he attended the funeral, it is all a bit of a blur but she has a vague recollection of clasping his hand as they said their goodbyes, before the crowds gathered in the old house for the wake.

'Is Holly all right?' Ashley's voice is urgent, loud. She has given up speaking quietly.

'Your daughter is not ill, Mrs Thomas, she is in no immediate danger. I would, however, request that both you and your husband come to the surgery first thing in the morning, I can book you in for eight-thirty. I would rather explain this in person.'

Ashley swallows, confused. What can be so important that she cannot be told over the phone? And if it is so serious, shouldn't she be with Holly now? Making sure she's all right? Her mind floods with scenarios − leukaemia, blood clots, all manner of terrible diseases take shape in her brain.

'Please,' she says, 'please can you tell me what's wrong with her? I'm her mother, I need to know.'

'I will go through everything in the morning,' the doctor says. 'Please try not to worry, but do come see me, as soon as you can. Thank you, Mrs Thomas.'

Before she can say any more, the line goes dead. Ashley stands still, her mind racing. She thinks of her baby girl, screaming and crying, the huge wide blue of her eyes. She will die if there is something wrong with her. She will not bear it. *Your daughter is in no immediate danger.* Is it her imagination or was there something unusual in the doctor's voice, something cold, almost accusing? It seemed to contain none of his usual familiarity, none of the normal warmth.

There's a rustle in the trees behind her, at the side gate to the cemetery and Ashley turns around. Nobody there. The sun dips behind the church and the cemetery is plunged into gloom, the trees dark shadows against the sky.

Ashley makes her way down the familiar gravel path leading to her father's grave, her thoughts spinning. Ought she to go visit the doctor now? The surgery won't be open. Should she ring James? Her footsteps echo on the stones. As she rounds the corner of the church, she sees a figure, standing alone at the gravestone. She frowns; the girl is too blonde to be her sister, and too tall. She is holding something in her arms, wrapped tightly in a blanket.

Ashley picks her way through the mounds of earth until she is right beside the woman. The blonde is staring at the gravestone, holding herself very still. Ashley feels awkward. Perhaps she's one of her dad's old colleagues? Bit young though. She clears her throat.

'Excuse me?'

The woman looks up, straight into Ashley's eyes. Her eyes are cold and blue, like chips of ice in her face. Her blonde hair hangs down her back in a golden stream. She's beautiful, and oddly familiar.

'Sorry,' Ashley says, 'I just … This is my dad's headstone, I was just coming to put some flowers down.'

There's a silence.

Ashley clears her throat. 'Did you – did you know him too?'

The girl is staring at her. There is a strange expression on her face. She shifts the bundle in her arms. Ashley frowns. It looks like it could be a baby or an animal, but it's completely covered up. Maybe she's protecting it from the sunlight?

'What are the chances,' the woman says. Her lips are painted with a thick gloss, her teeth are bright white. 'This is my dad's headstone too.'

Ashley stares. She must have misheard her. 'What? Sorry, I—'

'It's so nice to finally meet you, Ashley,' the girl interrupts. 'How's Lucy doing?' She shakes her head, a quick little movement from side to side. 'I'm sorry about all that. Didn't quite … go to plan.' She gives a little tinkling laugh. Her eyes don't leave Ashley's face.

'What?' Ashley says again. She can't think what else to say, cannot understand what this woman is saying. How does she know about Lucy?

341

'Sorry, how rude of me!' The girl steps forward, so that she is even closer to Ashley, they are standing on the soil of her dad's grave, directly above his body. Ashley can smell the woman's perfume, it smells like thick vanilla.

She lifts the bundle in her arms so that she is gripping it with only one hand, and stretches out the other towards Ashley. Her nails are small and round. Her hand is perfectly still but the bundle in her left arm stirs slightly, begins to move.

Now

Ashley's face is a picture. I want to keep it in my mind, suspended in my consciousness for ever, with all the other pictures of her I have collected in my mind over the years. This is the best one yet. I can almost taste her surprise.

This is the release of it all, the end of the years of waiting. The adrenaline is electric. I've been up since five but I'm not tired – I was awake before the light, packed everything I needed into the car, checked and double-checked. Then I picked up the keys off the hook, including his with the stupid little football key ring, and I closed the front door. As I drove, I threw them out of the window, one by one, pulling them off the key ring and tossing them into the open air. The wind swallowed them up. I didn't look back.

And now it is worth it. It is worth what I had to do earlier, the horror of it, the way her elderly body twitched on the ground as I wound the rope round and around. I wasn't expecting her to know about me, about what happened with Mum. It put me on the back foot a bit, but I'm here now. I'm ready. I smile at her. It begins and ends now.

I look once more around the graveyard, checking to see if anyone else is around. It's deserted. They've cleaned his headstone, it glistens in the gloom. The trees are dark and, for a moment, I think I can see her, the little girl crouching in the darkened garden, and I narrow my eyes at myself. Pathetic. I'm not going to be that girl any more.

'I didn't introduce myself properly,' I say. The baby is heavy in my arms. 'I'm Erin. Your sister.'

52

27 March 2017
The day of the anniversary

Kent

Dominic

Dominic rushes to the front door of Mathilde's house and begins to throw his weight against it, over and over, ramming his shoulder against the lock until it gives and springs open. The air rushes out of his lungs as he pushes open the door to the sitting room, steps forward into the gloom. The sight in front of him is worse than anything he saw in his news reporting days.

Mathilde is lying curled in an S shape on the cold wooden floorboards, her arms and legs tied with rope. It cuts into her thin wrists. She has been banging her joined hands onto the floor, trying to get his attention. Dark red marks are blooming either side of the ties.

'Jesus fucking Christ.'

'Dominic …' Mathilde's voice is weak, like that of a child.

Dominic's first instinct is to call the police, but he can't bear to leave her tied up for even a second longer, the sight of her fragile arms encased in the bonds makes him feel physically sick. Mathilde is wearing a purple cardigan he remembers Corinne buying her last Christmas and brown, old-lady shoes; she looks like a broken bird. Her face is pale, her lips dry. Her eyes are closed but, as Dominic steps forward she opens them, looks into his.

'What happened to you?' Dominic says, but as he sees Mathilde's tiny chest begin to move, sees her start to try to answer him he stops her, brushes the question aside. 'Never mind, God, don't try to talk right now – let's just get you out of here.' He crouches down, touches Mathilde's hair. It is soft, like feathers. Mathilde's lips are moving; she is trying to speak.

'She …' Mathilde says. 'Erin …'

Dominic twists his head; in the shock of seeing Mathilde he hasn't even checked if she's alone, if there is anyone else lurking in the darkness of the house.

'What? Who did this to you?'

Mathilde's eyes are on his, as though she can read his thoughts as he wildly looks around the room.

'She's gone,' she manages. 'There's nobody here. It was Erin, Dominic. She's Richard's daughter.'

Dominic's brain feels sluggish, slow-moving. Erin? It can't be. Erin is his friend. She's his colleague. She wouldn't do this. Mathilde coughs, and Dominic feels a jolt of fear as he sees the way her body shakes. There is no time to piece together what Mathilde is saying, the only thing that matters in this instant is Corinne. If Erin has gone, he must find Corinne. He needs to know that she and the baby are safe.

'All right,' he says, trying to think quickly, willing his brain to snap into action. He wants desperately to stay calm. He can't panic Mathilde any more than she already is.

'All right, Mathilde, all right, we're going to sort this out, we're going to get you up and I'm going to call the police.' He keeps his voice soft, quiet, controlled. Mathilde is moaning slightly, a low, painful sound that breaks Dominic's heart. He reaches into his pocket, grabs his car keys and uses them to loosen the ropes on her wrists. They are not tied as tightly as he'd first thought, after a few minutes he is able to ease her left wrist out of the rope, followed by her right. She gives a little cry as they are released; he sees tears prick her eyes.

'Hush now, nearly there,' he says, as though talking to a child. He moves on to her ankles, forces his way through the thin tie that knots them together. The rope is fraying, he has to pick it apart with the metal of his key. It seems to take forever, all he can hear is the sound of his breathing, ragged and fast. Mathilde's feet are horribly swollen, he winces at the sight of the elderly flesh pouched around the rope.

'There!' He has done it. Mathilde's legs jerk apart and she lies still for a moment, her body rising and falling, rising and falling. Dominic puts his arms underneath her, helps her to a sitting position. The floor beneath them is unforgiving and hard.

The skin on her face looks almost translucent.

'Dominic,' she says. 'Dominic, thank you. Thank you so much.'

He stares at her. Her lips are deathly pale but she looks unhurt, he can see no blood, no sign of any injuries save the welts on her arms and legs.

'Mathilde,' he says, 'what happened to you? What did she do to you? We need to call the police.' He glances down at

346

his mobile. No service. 'Where's your phone? I need to use your house phone.'

She raises an arm, points to the kitchen. Dominic pushes open the door, snaps on the light in the kitchen. There is a bottle of cleaning fluid on the side, the lid discarded next to it. A half-drunk cup of tea lies cold by the sink. He looks around wildly, sees the phone. His stomach drops. The cord dangles uselessly down, the white plastic shorn to reveal stumps of copper wire. She's cut off the line.

He has to get to London. Back in the sitting room, Mathilde's teeth are chattering, she is shaking her head. She reaches out a hand, grips his arm.

'It's been cut,' he says. The words sound hollow in his ears.

Mathilde tightens her grip. 'She left hours ago, Dominic. There's no time.' He feels her nails dig into him, can sense the urgency in her touch. Wordlessly, he puts his arm underneath Mathilde's shoulders and gently lifts her up so that they are both standing. Her body is so light, she feels almost weightless in his arms. His mouth has a metallic taste.

Together, they half walk, half stumble down the driveway to Dominic's car. He checks his phone again, his heart hammering in his chest. Still no signal. The police took so long to arrive last night. He'll call as soon as they hit the road. Dominic switches on all the lights in the car, checks the vehicle just in case. It is empty. Cold air whistles through the open doors.

He helps Mathilde into the back seat, lifting her gently so that she can lie down. She closes her eyes, briefly, and Dominic sees how much pain she must be in. How long has she been a prisoner in her own house? How long has she lain on the cold floor?

He starts the engine, swings the car towards London. His body feels as if it is on autopilot. He talks through the steps in his mind: drive, get reception, call the police, find Corinne. The words are on a loop in his head; he is trying desperately to squash down the panic that is threatening his insides. Erin? Young blonde Erin who sits in a desk chair, typing up court stories and flirting with Andy? How can this be happening?

Sweat breaks out on Dominic's forehead. What kind of man is he? He hasn't been paying attention to Corinne, hasn't been taking the threats seriously. As embarrassingly naive as it sounded – especially as he was a fucking journalist – he'd had no idea what humans really were capable of, until he'd found Mathilde. Bad things didn't happen to people like them, that's what he'd secretly thought when he'd heard the horrid stories, read the dark news pieces. The arrogance of his belief makes him blanche.

53

'I don't know what you're talking about.' Ashley stands firm on the grave, staring at Erin, wishing she wasn't on her own. 'I don't know who you are. My dad didn't have another daughter.'

Erin shakes her head. Her arms move back to hold the bundle in both hands. The blanket is still covering it completely. Whatever is inside is not making a sound.

'You're both the same, you and your sister. Privileged. Blind. But then, why would you care? You had it all. And you know what I had? I had nothing. I had a father who kept me a secret. I was a disgrace, an embarrassment, a weird little kid who no one wanted. Have you any idea how that feels, Ashley?'

Her arms are looped around the bundle and she is scratching at her arm, dragging her perfect nails up and down the skin on her wrist. Ashley sees the first spots of blood begin to appear, bright scarlet on her flesh.

'I'm sorry,' she says, 'I don't know – I don't know what you mean.'

Erin laughs. It echoes around the cemetery, bouncing off the graves.

'You wouldn't. Living in your little bubble, your happy family. You never gave a shit. None of you did. You didn't grow up like I grew up.'

Ashley's mouth is starting to dry up, her stomach beginning to twist.

'I grew up differently,' Erin says. 'You grew up living, and I grew up watching. Inside, outside. You see how it works? I spent my life staring through the windows as you and your sister had the life I wanted, the life I deserved.' She narrows her eyes. 'It was like torture. You grew up with a family home and a father and a fucking state-of-the-art doll house. And now you've got it all over again, you've got the kids and the house and the husband. I'll never have any of that.'

'I—' Ashley says, her mind sticking on the mention of her children. 'We didn't—'

Erin sucks in her cheeks, spits saliva onto the ground.

'I didn't have a life,' she says bitterly. 'I still don't. All we ever had was money, and then he robbed us of that too. So then we had nothing. I had nothing, no one but a mother who was losing the plot and a full-time job watching you.'

She looks down. Ashley hears a flicker of emotion in her voice when she speaks again. 'You think I don't know you, Ashley, but I do. You and your sister were all I thought about. I never had friends. I was sneaking around, seeing things unfold.' She grins suddenly. 'Why do you think I'm so good at it now?'

She looks at Ashley, puts out a small pale hand and touches the sleeve of her black coat. Ashley flinches, jerks her arm away before she can think what she is doing.

Erin's mouth twists.

'See,' she says. 'None of you want me. Not then, not now. I just wanted to get to know you, Ashley. I wanted to be involved. I've always been left out. It isn't fair, it's never been fair. He's just as much mine as he ever was yours. He's my dad. And he hated me.'

Her eyes are beginning to glitter with tears; she reaches up, wipes a hand across her face as though cross with herself.

'Still, it's over now,' she says. 'Your time is up. Perfect childhood, perfect life. Funny how things work out. My mother had nothing. I had nothing. He left us. He pretended we didn't exist.'

She looks down briefly, runs her eyes over the gravestone. 'Richard Hawes. Family man. Ha. Nothing was ever enough for him. Not even you two, in the end.' She smiles, her features twisting.

Ashley opens her mouth. The words won't come.

'I – I'm sorry,' she says. 'I don't ... I don't know what to say. I didn't know, I didn't have any idea.'

She watches as Erin begins to scratch at her arm again, like an animal. Ashley's mind twists in circles, trying to gain control of what is happening, what she is being told. Perhaps it is best to play along.

'Would you ... would you like to go somewhere, talk?' She tries again. Her heart is beating far too quickly and her armpits are wet with sweat. She has no idea if the girl is telling the truth, does not know what to think. But she doesn't want to be here any longer, alone in this graveyard. She doesn't feel safe.

Erin's head is bent, but, as Ashley takes a small step backwards, her head snaps up.

'I don't think so.' She steps closer, puts a hand on the blue blanket that is covering the shape in her arms. Slowly, she pulls it back so that a face appears, that of a sleeping child, a child with blonde curls and dark lashes. Ashley screams.

54

Dominic is driving as quickly as he can, revving the car up and down in fits and spurts. Mathilde is lying in the back seat, her wrists shining raw and red in the flashing headlights of the M25. Cars zoom past them, their engines loud.

He's just got off the phone with the police. He has told them to check the cemetery and the flat, explained who Erin is and what she has done to Mathilde. Corinne is in danger. He knows she is; he can feel it.

'OK, sir, we're going to get some people out now,' the DI had said, his voice crackling through the speakerphone in the car. 'Someone will ring you with an update as soon as we can. In the meantime, try to stay calm. We'll need you to bring the victim you have there to the station as soon as possible.'

Dominic is trying as hard as he can to be gentle with Mathilde, even though his heart is racing and he wants to scream at the top of his lungs. His body feels as though it is straining against his seat belt, he wants to get to Corinne so badly. He's tried her mobile, Ashley's mobile, and the flat phone consistently since calling the police, but there is still no answer.

The police haven't called back. It has been almost twenty-five minutes – what the fuck are they doing? He pushes the accelerator harder, his mind not focusing properly on the road ahead. Suddenly, a car looms in front of them, his brain clicks and he slams on the brakes.

A whimper echoes from behind.

'Sorry, Mathilde, sorry.' He pulls back the speed and rubs at his face.

'Dominic?' Her voice is thin, reedy, almost unrecognisable. 'When did you last see Corinne?'

He swallows at the question and looks into the rear-view mirror. In the darkness she is only a shadow, a tiny shape curled on the seat. 'This morning.'

When she doesn't reply he glances back again; lights from the car to the side of them reflect in her eyes, staring out of her face like marbles.

'Mathilde? Can you tell me what happened?' he says. 'Can you tell me what happened today?'

'She came to the house,' Mathilde says. Her voice is so quiet, he has to strain to hear her above the sound of the motorway.

'It was this morning, early. There was a knock on the door. I was in the kitchen, I was cleaning out the cupboards. Spring, and all that. It was a nice day today. And, with the anniversary, I wanted a distraction.'

Dominic nods. 'So you let her in?'

Mathilde shudders. 'Not at first. I opened the door,' she says. 'I still had the sponge in my hand and when I opened it, the blonde girl – Erin—' she shudders '—Erin said she knew me. She said she had something to tell me. I thought she had me confused with someone else. When I said she was mistaken, she got a hold of my arm. She had …' She pauses. Dominic waits. 'She had a knife. A big kitchen knife, and she came into the house. Just straight in, as if she owned the place. She looked around the house, all of it. For ages. I had to go with her, she was holding a knife against my throat.'

Dominic feels sick. He tries to keep his eyes on the road, overtakes the car ahead of them. It is so dark outside now.

'Then she forced me into the sitting room,' Mathilde says. 'She tied me up, she kept the knife by my throat the whole time. I couldn't struggle. I think she'd have killed me.'

'Did she tell you who she was?' he asks. How much does Mathilde know?

'She told me I was a stupid old woman, that I didn't have a clue about anything. She looked like she hated me. But she was wrong. I knew by then.'

Mathilde's voice breaks.

Dominic takes his eyes off the road for a second, stares back at Mathilde. In the dark he hears her crying.

55

27 March 2017
The day of the anniversary

London

Ashley

'Holly! Give me my daughter!'

In one quick movement Erin opens her arms. Holly falls, her body hits the ground with a sickening thud and there is a cry that stabs Ashley's heart. She looks oddly floppy, as though she is a puppet with the strings cut. Her leg has twisted underneath her. Ashley lunges for her daughter but Erin steps forwards and Ashley sees the flash of silver by her side. Shock pulses through her. She's holding a knife. The long blade glints in the half-light and Ashley ducks, desperate to touch Holly but Erin is on top of her, she is grabbing Ashley by the neck and twisting, pushing her down to the ground. Ashley cries out in pain and falls to her knees, hitting the cold earth. Erin steps on Ashley's hand, crushing it into the dirt. The pain is exquisite. Beside them, Holly's howls fill the air. Ashley is trying desperately to work out if she is seriously injured, whether she has hit her head. Her head is turned sideways at a funny angle. *Please God, no.*

'You think you got off so easy, don't you, Ashley?' Erin hisses. 'Your Lucy was a pushover. Pathetic. Shame the police arrived when they did. Guessing she looked quite the slut, lying on the street with her legs apart.' She laughs, harsh and cold. 'Guess it runs in the family.'

Ashley is gasping. Her head is very close to the stone of the grave. She can't move. The knife is at her neck. Holly's cries are getting quieter. She is losing her energy. 'How did you get Holly?' she gasps. 'Tell me. Tell me now.'

Erin suddenly removes her foot from Ashley's hand, lifts the hair on her scalp so that Ashley is face to face with her, they are looking at each other right up close. Erin lowers the knife, smiles.

'You gave her to us,' she says.

Ashley's skin is stretched tight over her head, Erin's fingers still tangled in her hair. It is an effort to speak. Erin's words force their way into her brain.

'What?'

'That's right,' Erin says. 'You handed her over three times a week, Ashley, because you couldn't quite find the time. Let's hope Mummy took care of her as well as she used to take care of me, hey? I have to say the medicine came in handy tonight, although let's face it, she might not have needed it if she hadn't been staying with my mother. Enough to give anyone night terrors, I'd think.'

June. Ashley closes her eyes. The shock is visceral, like a punch to the stomach. Memories come back to her, of her handing Holly over, the small spurts of relief she used to get when June would reach out, gather the baby towards her, shut the front door behind them. She has been giving Holly to June for months. June is this girl's mother, and Ashley has trusted her with her baby. She is the worst mother in the world. *What have they been doing to her daughter?*

Erin is shaking her head, frowning. 'The thing is, I think Mum might have been a little lax with the medicine bottles lately. You see, what's good for an adult can be – well, it can be poison for a child, wouldn't you say, Ashley? Especially one as young as your Holly. And Mum's been on some pretty strong medication for a long time now. Keeps her on the straight and narrow – well, if that's what you'd call it. I must say I'm impressed with her; she plays the part brilliantly.'

The thought slams into her. The blood test. The doctor's tone. Ashley can feel her insides going cold, as though a hand is squeezing her heart. As the realisation begins to dawn on her, Erin starts to laugh. 'Don't feel bad, Ashley. That little bottle you've been giving her kept her nice and quiet for me all the way here. What a shame you couldn't deal with your daughter without drugging her more than we already were.'

'You … my baby …' Ashley is staring at Holly's tiny shape on the ground, willing her daughter to scream, cry, whimper – do anything to indicate that she might be alive. She is no longer making a sound.

Erin is still speaking, her eyes bright in the darkness, almost as though she is talking to herself now. 'Mum quite likes you, I think. Considering how well she's managed the retired schoolteacher role. I don't think she's ever even been inside a school. She certainly never came in mine.

Too busy running after my dad.' She smiles to herself. 'Perhaps you brought out the best in her. I never could.'

Erin looks up, as though remembering where she is, that Ashley is there. She reaches out, touches a hand to Ashley's cheek. Her fingers are freezing. 'It's a relief to do this, Ashley,' Erin says. 'The last few months have been … tiring. Frustrating. Working with a load of stupid journalists isn't exactly my idea of fun.' She smirks. 'Still, at least Lucy knows how to have a good time. That kid can be wild.' She winks. 'Your husband's face was great when she got into my car. You're lucky I'm a safe driver. Some people aren't.'

Ashley makes a sudden movement, tries to wriggle out of Erin's grasp. In an instant, the knife is pressed against her cheek and she stops, lies still.

Erin laughs. 'I wouldn't struggle if I were you. Your sister buys quality kitchen knives. Good and sharp.'

Ashley has no idea what Erin is talking about. Her head is in so much pain, her hair held taut. She cannot think of anything to say, is desperately thinking of an escape route, how to protect Holly. How can she stop this? How can she make Erin stop?

'You're not very strict with Lucy, are you?' Erin says. 'You want to be careful, Ashley. Young when you had her, weren't you? Around my age, I used to think.'

Ashley's head is spinning. Perhaps she should keep her talking. Perhaps someone will come by. She sucks in her breath, tries to speak.

'Erin,' she says, her breath coming out in a hoarse whisper. 'Erin.'

Erin loosens her grip on Ashley's hair, ever so slightly.

'How did you … How did you do this? How did you know about us?'

Erin smiles. 'I've always known. It's something we've been working on for a while, Mummy and I.' She looks down at the headstone. 'Ever since Dad died, really. I thought it was time. Enough waiting. I wanted to show you. You've spent long enough playing happy families, don't you think?'

Ashley nods mutely. She cannot take her eyes off the silver of the blade. Her eyes dart between it and the bundle that is her daughter, lying prone in the graveyard under the blue blanket. Is there any blood?

'So I set it up,' Erin says. 'I got the job at the *Herald* with Dom, let the paper do a write-up on our old house to keep everyone quiet. It's not like we ever got to live there once your father finished with us, he made sure of that. We had no money. But you'd be surprised how many doors the de Bonnier name can open, even when the money's gone.' She pauses.

'After that it was easy. You've got better taste in men than your sister, Ashley, that's for sure!'

She grins, loosens her grip on Ashley a little bit more. Ashley shifts slightly. She is still on the ground, Erin crouched over her. Her legs are beginning to go numb.

'I stole Dominic's keys,' Erin says, 'so I could get into their flat. That was the fun part, messing with Corinne. None of you believed her!'

She chuckles, flips her blonde hair over her shoulder. It glistens in the moonlight. 'I wanted to play around a bit, you see. Have some fun of my own. Games are different when you're older, aren't they? And I never had dolls.'

She smiles widely.

Ashley says nothing, does not meet Erin's eye. She feels as though she is going to be sick. *Let Holly be OK, she thinks to herself, just let Holly survive. I don't care about myself.*

'But all good things must come to an end,' Erin says. 'It's a shame really. I was hoping to find Corinne here tonight. You know she was his favourite?' She widens her eyes at Ashley. 'Dad loved her the most. It was obvious.'

Ashley finds her voice. 'What do you mean?'

A flicker of something passes over Erin's face.

'I used to watch from the garden,' she says. 'I hid in the shadows, watched through the window. All through the years when she was at home, moping about the house without a boyfriend. Dad talked to Corinne for hours. Hours and hours. They used to play chess. And he made her that doll house, it was for her really.' She pauses. 'I was so jealous. It hurt so much.'

Ashley's body gives an involuntary shudder. Can this be true? Erin has been watching them her entire life?

'It's true,' Erin says, as though she can read Ashley's thoughts.

'After I was born Dad turned me away. Mum took me to see him, she thinks I don't remember, I was only six, but I do. He gave me a little navy coat. The only gift I ever got. But it didn't work. It wasn't enough to keep us away. He didn't want to know about me. He already had his perfect family. He'd gone too far this time. Too much greed, too used to having his own way. But he messed up. He didn't want us. He wanted you. Apparently.'

There is a sudden shriek from above them, the call of a bird. Erin looks up suddenly, sees the darkness of the sky.

361

Ashley watches her face harden, her lips tighten. Panic blooms in her chest.

'Got to be careful of memories,' Erin says, as she yanks Ashley's hair and lifts back her other hand. 'They're dangerous.'

Her dad's headstone is very close now, she can see tiny blemishes in the stone, what look like black specks of paint hidden in the grey.

Ashley thinks then of her children, pictures Lucy sitting at home, Benji drawing endless solar systems on the kitchen table. James must have realised Holly isn't at June's, she hopes he has had the sense to ring the police. She imagines his panic, just after his good news at work, and tears spring to her eyes. She can taste blood on the inside of her mouth.

The last thing Ashley sees before Erin grabs her head is her dad's name, engraved on the stone. *Architect.* Her forehead slams into the gravestone. *Husband.* Blood drips down her forehead. *Father.* Her vision begins to blur.

'This is for my mother,' Erin shouts. And then it is dark.

56

27 March 2017
The day of the anniversary

London

Dominic

'Knew what?' Dominic asks. 'You knew who she was?' He glances at the dashboard, at the judder of the speedometer stick. Faster, faster. Still no word back from the police.

'I knew she was his. I knew she was Richard's daughter. It was when she looked at me, I saw it in her eyes. She has his eyes, Dominic.'

He swerves, hears the beep of a horn beside him. He is slipping over towards the central reservation. He takes a deep breath, straightens up the car, shifts to fifth gear and presses his foot down towards the floor.

'He – Richard had an affair?'

Slowly, Mathilde shifts herself upwards to a sitting position, he sees her wince in pain, her features caught in the headlights of the cars that fly past them.

'It was so long ago, now, just over twenty-five years. The children were little. They loved their father so very, very much. And so did I. Lord, I thought the sun rose and set on that man. For the most part, anyway. He was so clever, Dominic, so good at making you feel like the only person in the room. When he shone his light on you, it was like no one else mattered.'

Dominic thinks of Richard holding court at the dinner table, of his voice echoing through the house. Always ready with a smile, a laugh. What really lay beneath all that?

'But it was that house,' Mathilde said. 'When he started working at Carlington, everything changed. He hid it well, Ashley and Corinne never noticed. They never knew a thing, he never admitted it, you see. Never came clean.'

She pauses. Dominic doesn't speak, can focus only on keeping his eyes on the road and his mind on her words.

'But I saw them once,' Mathilde says. 'He and June de Bonnier. I saw her when I came to Carlington, I'd come to find Richard. It was Ashley, she'd been sent home from school for something, I forget what, and I needed him to come home. So I went to the house, and I saw that woman.'

Her teeth start clacking together, she is shivering despite the warmth of the car. Dominic's mind is running backwards, remembering the day at Carlington House. June de Bonnier, leaning on his car, taking tablets from the little packet in her hand. Her words come back to him with a jolt. *This house nearly ruined me.*

Mathilde is still talking. 'He denied it, of course. Straight away. And I never saw enough, I never had proof. It was just a glimpse as I walked across that lawn, they were up against the wall of the house. But he said I was wrong, that nothing was happening. And I was too far away, I could never be sure. So I turned the other way.' Her voice breaks.

'As long as he came home, I looked the other way to protect my girls.'

'And you knew about Erin?'

There's a silence in the car. Dominic twists his head quickly to look at her and sees the glimmer of tears on her face, shining down her cheeks.

'I'm sorry, Mathilde …' he starts, but she shakes her head.

'No,' she says softly, 'I didn't know about any child. Not until I saw her. When I saw her today I knew. She could never be anything other than Richard's. Those eyes … I can't believe he covered it all up.' She puts a hand to her eyes. 'We weren't enough for him, me and the girls. It was always more, more, more. More money, more success, more validation from the outside world.'

Dominic glances at the clock, flicks his indicator to overtake again. His phone stays resolutely silent. Where are the police?

'I think he might have left me,' Mathilde says, and her voice changes slightly, takes on a tone of almost wonderment. 'I think he might have done it for her. For June. I think he might have loved her. Either that or he just liked the challenge. He always did crave those.'

Dominic shakes his head. She sounds as though she is talking partly to herself, is lost somewhere deep inside her mind.

Mathilde is leaning forward. 'But he couldn't do it, he couldn't leave his girls. He wouldn't leave our babies. So instead he left her, and Erin, and now—' She suddenly lets out a sob, puts a hand to her mouth.

'Oh God,' she says. 'Oh God, Dominic. I need to get to my children.'

'I know that!' Dominic says, and he pushes his foot even lower on the floor, swears as another driver comes too close on the right of the car. He is driving way over the speed limit, as fast as he can. They are on the outskirts of North London now; they are almost there. The cemetery is the best place to start looking.

'I feel so guilty,' Mathilde says suddenly.

'Guilty?'

'I knew who June was. I saw her, once more, not long ago in London. It was the night I came for dinner with Corinne. I recognised her instantly, she was outside the restaurant. Gave me the shock of my life. I should have said something, I should have told Corinne, but I didn't, I just went home. Perhaps if I hadn't been such a coward …' She trails off. 'I had no idea about Erin, but if I'd known.' She stops. 'I don't know what I would have done if I'd known.'

'You couldn't have known!'

'I never wanted the girls to know,' Mathilde whispers. 'I never wanted them to find out what kind of man their father really was. They loved him so much. That's why I never told them, held it together.'

Dominic exhales. 'And then he died,' he says.

Mathilde nods. 'And then he died. And I thought it would be a secret, something I would just hold on to, and actually I was relieved because I'd done it, I'd given them the very best idea of their daddy that a pair of girls could have.'

She takes a deep breath, wipes her eyes with her hand. 'Not that he deserved it. He left me with a mountain of debt, Dominic. I had to sell off a lot of his things, including the girls' doll house. It broke my heart every time Corinne asked about it but I could never tell her what had happened.'

Dominic frowns. 'You sold the doll house?'

She nods. 'Some man made me a huge offer, said he was a collector. I had no choice. I felt terrible lying to her, but I was terrified of her finding out about how much trouble Richard had got us into. It's shameful, I know it is, but … I had no choice, Dominic.'

Dominic runs a hand through his hair. Could Erin have the doll house too? Is there any point telling Mathilde about the little parts of it Corinne has found? It will only scare her more. He thinks to himself how planned this whole thing must have been, how chillingly thought out. Erin's behaviour is psychotic – the pretence, the lies, all of it. How could he have been so stupid?

They are almost in Hampstead; they are getting very close. Dominic sees the tail of headlights as they round the bend and feels dread sink into his stomach. He changes gear, feels his hand slip with sweat on the stick.

Mathilde gives a moan as she sees the traffic. Behind them, a car horn sounds. The air in the car feels tight and stale. All Dominic wants is to reach Corinne, feel the warmth of her, trap their baby between them. The lights of the vehicle in front of him seem unreasonably close; there is another line of cars snaking out before him like a ladder. Reluctantly, he moves the car into third gear, second, first, his foot lowering to the floor as he squeezes the brake pad. The clock on the dashboard flips over, the red lines watching them both like slitted eyes. Mathilde looks at him, and her question sends an icy dagger of fear straight into Dominic's heart.

'What if we're too late?'

57

27 March 2017
The day of the anniversary

London

Corinne

I'm late to meet Ashley. We had a rush of customers right at the end of the day, and Marjorie was getting stressed out. Normally, I'd just leave but I felt bad. She'd been so lovely to me about the baby. So I stayed, helped her cash up, then ran to the Tube, taking the alleyway between the banks. I haven't got the flowers – by the time I left the guy with his stall had packed up and gone home. It's colder now, I've had to put my coat back on. I shook it out again before I left, turned out the pockets in case there was any more glass lurking inside. I tried to ring Dom but it just went to voicemail; I don't know where he is, I hope he's with Mum. I wanted to tell him how kind Marjorie had been too, how unexpected her reaction was.

I get on the tube north towards West Hampstead Station. I manage to get a seat and try to relax, ignore the jolts of the carriage as it trundles along the tracks. It's no quieter than this morning, and as we go further, the train becomes even more packed, so that by the time it pulls into the station I am completely surrounded. I feel a little bit sick but at least I'm on the way now, I'll meet Ashley and Mum at the graveyard and we'll go have a nice dinner together. I hope they're not annoyed that I'm late. Maybe it's been good for Ash to sit with Dad on her own for a bit, she never gets any time to herself. Always rushing around after the children.

I step out of the Tube carriage, sling my bag over my shoulder. I'm down the wrong end, I turn and make my way down the long platform to where the escalators are, dodging around the crowds. As I look up I see a girl, waving at me, her blonde hair shining in the underground light as she cranes her neck to catch my eye. She's wearing a fluorescent yellow scarf, it's very bright, and she's smiling, a big wide smile like she knows me. I stop, thrown, trying to remember how to place her. As I get closer it clicks: Dom's work. Of course, it's the girl who rescued me that awful day. It's Erin.

I groan inwardly. I haven't got time to have a conversation now, I'm already so late. But she's really smiling at me, as though she's happy to run into me. She's already moving towards me.

'Corinne!' she says, and I smile back at her, even though I want to get up the steps, feel terrible for keeping Ashley waiting. She was so kind to me though, I remember her sharing the gingerbread man, looking after me while I panicked and cried. I'll have to be polite, just for two seconds. I behaved embarrassingly enough that day.

'Erin,' I say. 'Hi, how are you? This is a coincidence.'

'Is it?' she says. I blink, wrong-footed. For a moment I think I've misheard her. I smile uncertainly. That's when

I notice her eyes; they are slightly off, there is something strange in her gaze.

'Are you OK?' I ask her. I wonder briefly if she might be a bit drunk. I take a step backwards, glance at the exit tunnel, at the people going up into the fresh air.

'There's something I need to tell you, Corinne.'

I stare at her. It can't be what I'm thinking. He wouldn't do that to me.

'There's no need to look so worried,' she says, and I feel a flush of relief. I'm being ridiculous!

'I'm in a rush, actually, Erin,' I say, but she interrupts me, places her well-manicured fingers on my arm. I look down. There's something red on the back of her hand.

'Have you cut yourself?' I say then, and that's when she starts to laugh, a horrible, high-pitched laugh that makes the hairs on the back of my neck stand on end.

'No, Corinne, I haven't,' she says, and she brings her face close to mine, so she's looking right into my eyes. 'But thank you for your *concern*.' She says the last word sarcastically. She's being very weird. What's wrong with her?

'I've got to get on, Erin, Dominic is waiting for me,' I lie. I try to move past her, towards the escalator, but she steps quickly to the right, blocking my way.

'Oh yes, Dominic,' she says, nodding her head up and down, too fast. Her movements seem jerky now I'm up close to her, almost manic. She gives me another smile. 'I've got pretty close to Dom recently – did he tell you? Friendly, if you know what I mean.' She winks.

I instantly feel sick.

She raises her eyebrows, reaches out a hand towards my face as though she would cup it in her fingers. I flinch, back away from her hand. There's definitely a smear of blood on it, wiped across the pale white skin. The sleeve of her black jacket rides up slightly, exposing her wrist. And that's when I see it: a watch, far too big for her, circling her bone. The strap is navy and the face is a brown oval with tiny golden hands. I'd recognise that watch anywhere.

I stare at it, and she sees me looking and grins, a horrid, slow, grin that shows her perfect white teeth. A woman pushes past me, pulling her son along by the hand, tutting because we're in the way, but I can't move, I can't do anything but stare at the watch, my dad's watch, at the little brown face of it glinting on Erin's wrist.

'Where did you get that watch?' I touch it with my fingertips, feel the cool glass face and then the cold, clammy skin of her wrist.

'Dad's watch? That's what I've been meaning to talk to you about, Corinne,' she says. She circles the watch round and around her wrist, it's bigger on her than it even was on me. The leather goes round and around, the skin underneath reddening. The gesture is eerily familiar, it's exactly what I used to do when he let me try it on. Dread starts to thud through my body. Every muscle in my body is urging me to run, to get away from her, but I am frozen, hypnotised by Dad's watch.

I swallow. 'Tell me what you mean.'

'Our dad said he was going to leave you, Corinne. Did you know that?'

The words hit me like a knife in the stomach.

'Our dad? What are you talking about? You're lying.' There's a roaring sound and the next train is beside us, a stream of people starts to disembark, clutching their briefcases, their buggies, their bags of shopping. None of them so much as looks at us, standing close together, our eyes locked. It's too loud, I can't hear anything apart from the Tube. Erin waits, her head cocked to one side. The big orange clock on the station sign behind her flicks over: I am beyond late now. Ashley will be worried.

The train pulls out of the station. Erin shakes her head. 'I'm not lying, Corinne. Your dad told my mum we'd be a proper family. He promised us everything. I should have had that doll house.' She looks away from me briefly, at the dark mouth of the tunnel. 'I got that in the end.'

'My dad never left us,' I say. 'He never did anything wrong. He loved Mum. I don't know who you are. I don't know what you're talking about.'

She shakes her head, tuts under her breath as though I'm a naughty child.

'My dad wouldn't have had an affair,' I continue, and, as I say the words, I cling to them in my head, cling to the truth. It has to be the truth. It just has to be.

'You ought to be careful with Dominic,' Erin says then. 'Men are all the same.' She pauses, narrows her eyes at me. 'Do you really think Dominic is with Andy every time he goes out?'

I cannot look away from her. My heart is beating beneath my coat, far too fast. I think of the shards of glass falling out of it, of what she's said about the doll house. I don't feel safe. I need Dominic. Where is he?

A wave of sickness rolls around my stomach. I'm not sure how long I can stay calm, I'm trying so hard, for the baby. Breathing in, and out, in, and out. I want to catch somebody's eye but everyone is glued to their phone, there's a teenager fiddling with her headphones to my right, a group of tourists studying the Tube map on the wall. One of the Underground attendants is further down the platform but he's not looking our way, he's looking at the railway tracks, tapping out a beat with his foot. No one is going to help me.

'I don't believe you,' I say, because I can't, I can't believe her, I can't believe that Dominic would lie to me, and I can't believe that my dad would have done this. To my mother. To us. To me.

Erin twists her wrist, looks down at my dad's watch.

'No?' She shrugs. 'Oh well. Have it your way. Your sister believes me, I think. Not that she'll be much help to anyone now.' She gives a half-smile, tosses her blonde hair over her shoulder. Her blue eyes burn into mine. She leans in to me, her breath right up against my cheek like she is going to tell me a secret.

'He loved you the most,' she whispers, curls her mouth upwards in a grin. 'I knew you were his favourite. Oh, he loved Ashley.' She nods. 'Of course he did. But not as much as you.' Her eyes search mine, as though looking for a secret that I don't have. 'That must have felt nice.' She sighs, a flicker of disappointment crosses her face. 'It's a shame you won't listen to the truth. We might have been friends. I'm not a bad person, Corinne. I'm just trying to make things right.' For a moment I see it in her eyes – a flash of humanity, of some great sadness that is hidden just beneath the glassy exterior.

I hesitate, then make a sudden movement, try to dart past her. Her hand flies out and she grabs my arm, jerks me back towards her. I cry out, the pain travels up to my shoulder. Her nails dig into my flesh.

'Come on, Corinne, we're only chatting,' she says. 'Don't go making a scene, will you. No one likes a drama queen.'

'You're insane,' I gasp, my breath coming in short pants. 'You're totally insane. None of what you're saying is true.'

'It is though,' she says, and she looks amused now, she's laughing at the way my breathing won't slow down. 'It's all true. Dad was quite the family man, Corinne. So much so that he had two! I didn't like being the daughter he ignored.'

I look behind her desperately. Should I call out?

Erin sees me looking, moves her foot slightly so that her boot is on my toes. My eyes water.

'Time is up now, Corinne,' she says, and the amusement is gone from her face. 'You and Ashley have had your fun. How do you think it felt, watching you from the sidelines? Seeing you have the life I deserved?' She presses her boot down harder on my foot. 'It didn't feel good.'

'I … I'm sorry,' I whisper, 'I didn't know, I didn't—'

'No,' she says, 'you never bothered to look. You took it all for granted, didn't you, your perfect little life, your perfect father. You had it all.'

Her mouth twists. 'But now you don't, do you, Corinne? Now he's in the ground, and there's no one here to protect you.'

58

Erin's grip is vice-like on my arm.

'Did you like the gifts, by the way? Had to pay your mum quite a lot for that doll house.' She smiles at my shocked face. 'Didn't she tell you? She took the money for Dad's things fairly easily, when it came to it. Don't think she knew who was buying them.' She shakes her head. 'I had to hire someone to do that because I knew it would look odd, a twenty-year-old buying antiques. Still, she needed the cash.' There is a pause. Erin tilts her head to one side, an odd smile on her face. Her eyes are fixed on mine. I can't look away.

'She probably didn't tell you about the debt, did she? Another secret of Dad's. That's what happens when your husband has pissed off the de Bonnier family.' Erin laughs.

The ground feels unsteady beneath me, as though I might lose my balance. Her words cut into me like tiny knives.

'Word gets around. The work dries up. By the time he died he'd lost us almost forty thousand pounds and the rumours were starting. You only have to look at Carlington to know he didn't do the job he was supposed to do. Used the cheapest materials, never finished what he started because he knew he had Mum wrapped around his finger. Not such a great guy, after all, but no one saw through him.' A look of disgust crosses Erin's face.

'She never would have done anything but lap up his lies so he took our money, cut corners on the property, put the rest straight into his bank account. He blackmailed my mother for years; kept her hanging with the idea that he might come back to us as long as she never went public about what he'd done to Carlington. That's why she'd never sell the house until now, now that he's dead. Not much chance of him coming back to us now, is there?' She pauses. 'Not that there ever really was.'

'No,' I say, 'you're making this up. You're making all of it up!'

She just carries on, as though I haven't spoken at all.

'That was a lovely doll house, wasn't it? Really beautiful.' As she speaks, her eyes sparkle, and suddenly I know why she looks so familiar, why I felt like I had seen her before when we first met. Her eyes remind me of Dad's.

Time seems to slow down.

Suddenly, as I am staring at her it is as though something clicks in Erin's brain, she sets her lips, shakes her head.

Her grip loosens slightly on my arm and I spot my chance; I yank myself away from her, use all my strength to push her to the side so that her body hits the wall of the platform, collides with the dirty white tiles. Then I am shoving through the people, my face wet with tears, desperately trying to reach the exit. I can hear her footsteps coming behind me but I don't look back. I bang into the man in front of me and, before he can say anything I am past him, threading in and out of the people on the platform like a grass snake.

I turn around and I can't see her. I keep moving, my arms stretched out before me, brushing aside mothers and fathers and families who clump together on the platform. A group of schoolchildren all wearing matching blue blazers make a huddle underneath the station clock, the black electric sign with the orange writing which says the next train is in one minute.

My breath is coming in pants and I scrabble for my phone, yank it from my handbag as I move, but I can't call anyone because there's no signal and so all I can do is keep going, my thoughts turning over and over, and all I can see in my mind's eye is the watch, the big face of it telling me the truth, *because why would she lie* and then I twist my head and I see a flash of yellow and then I feel them, the hands on my shoulders, like angel wings, and I turn around and we are grappling, her arms are so strong, her palm hits my cheek and I'm clinging on to the end of her scarf like it is a life rope. As I pull, it tightens around her neck, bringing our faces right up close, pressing our skin together, her cold cheek icy against my own.

Her mouth is close to mine and I think she says something, something about her mother, and we're too close to the edge and my boots are slipping and then shadowy

59

27 March 2017
The day of the anniversary

London

Dominic

He sees the blue lights before he hears the sound of the sirens. They're rounding the corner to the cemetery when the ambulance roars past, the flashing lights engulf the car for a second and Mathilde lets out a horrified moan.

'Dominic!'

He watches as though in slow motion as the ambulance stops outside Hampstead cemetery, as he had known it would. Two police cars block the iron gates. Without speaking, he screeches to a halt behind them. They are too late. It is everything he feared.

Mathilde is whimpering like a wounded animal in the back seat.

'I think you should stay in the car, Mathilde,' he tells her. He gets out, closes the door, forces himself to put one foot in front of the other, over and over until he's by the gates. He cannot see inside.

A policeman steps forward, illuminated in the flashing blue lights. 'Sir, I'm afraid the cemetery is closed temporarily, please don't come any further.'

Dominic is about to lose his temper completely. Nobody has called him back, not one of these officers has spared a thought for him, driving at breakneck speed to get to his family. And now they're telling him he can't go inside?

'My girlfriend's inside!' He roars the words at the officer, feeing a tidal wave of rage and grief welling up inside his chest. The policeman's face falls; Dominic sees him putting the pieces together, sees him reach for his walkie-talkie but Dominic doesn't care any more, he just needs to know.

Someone is coming. Dominic is going to throw up. The policeman puts out an arm to him and they both are forced to step back as three paramedics come out of the cemetery, carrying a figure on a stretcher between them. Dominic's vision starts to blur.

'White female, found on the floor, multiple head injuries,' one of the paramedics is saying to a policeman, who is reporting the information into a clip on his shirt. 'Serious blood loss, victim found unconscious but breathing.' They are moving quickly, opening the doors of the ambulance. Dominic steps forward. The walkie-talkie crackles again. 'Second victim, baby girl, head injuries, critical.' The cemetery gates open again and more paramedics come out, carrying something small, something tiny. Dominic feels sick. It's not possible.

The ambulance doors open and a flood of white light gushes out, illuminating the figure on the stretcher. Dominic's heart gives a massive jolt. The blood is everywhere, but the familiar face is still recognisable. It is not Corinne. It is Ashley.

380

60

27 March 2017
The day of the anniversary

London

Ashley

There are shapes all around her, they shift and twist like a kaleidoscope as she tries to make them out. She doesn't know where she is. Somebody who looks a bit like her mother is sitting on a fold-down chair with a man she doesn't recognise, a man wearing white. Everything feels very loud, and they are moving too fast. There is a terrible pain in her head; when she tries to lift herself upwards somehow it doesn't work, her body doesn't do what it's supposed to. Her baby. She needs her baby. The man in white reaches out to her, puts a hand on her arm.

'Try to keep still, Mrs Thomas,' he is saying, and she wonders how he knows her name. The figures around her are so fuzzy, fading in and out. Something is attached to her arm. She thinks they might be in a vehicle. The school bus? Are the children here? Maybe that man isn't a stranger at all. Maybe it's James. Where is James? She hopes he's put the fish fingers on. Another thought keeps rising in her mind. Her baby. There is something wrong with her baby girl.

'Ashley.' A face looms before her. She tries to smile but there's something wrong with her mouth, it tastes funny, metallic and strangely wet. The pain in her head is so bad, it feels like it's getting worse. Why is her mother here? Her eyelids feel very heavy. She's at home again, in their old house, and her parents are sitting on the sofa. They've got their arms around each other but there is something wrong, her Dad's face is slipping and sliding, it's melting onto the floor. She needs to clean it up, there'll be a mess.

'Can you hear me, Ashley?' She wonders what she is supposed to say. Why are they going so fast? It is making her feel sick. Has she been sick already? Her brain feels like it is clouded in fog. She cannot remember what has happened. It's something bad. She thinks it's something bad.

The man wearing white says something to the man driving the vehicle and they seem to go a bit faster. Ashley closes her eyes again. It is too hard to keep them open. As she starts to lose consciousness, a face flashes into her mind. Blonde hair, piercing blue eyes. That face. It makes her feel frightened. It makes her feel like she is going to die.

61

27 March 2017
The day of the anniversary

London

Dominic

The police cannot find Corinne. Where the hell is she? He had tried explaining to the paramedics, but they kept saying that Ashley was alone with Holly in the cemetery, that there was no sign of Corinne at all.

'No!' he had shouted, 'You don't understand – you aren't listening to me! This girl, the girl that did this – she's still out there, she's looking for my girlfriend. You've got to find her.'

Dominic had stared at Ashley, at the blood blooming from her head as the paramedics stretchered her into the ambulance, helped Mathilde into the vehicle with her. They moved with worrying speed, their actions quick, urgent. Holly is put into a separate ambulance, it leaves immediately, screeching down the road.

'You'd better come with us in the car,' one of the policemen had told him, as he watched the ambulance doors slam, the blue lights pull away. Ashley's hair was matted to her skull, the strands thick with blood.

He thinks of James and the children. They must know Holly is missing. Has anyone called them yet?

He tells the police what he knows. The officer in the passenger seat starts radioing the local stations, passing out the alert as they follow the ambulance towards the Royal Free Hospital. Dominic feels helpless, he phones the flat over and over again, praying that Corinne will pick up. He has tried the gallery, the mobile, but the gallery phone rings out and her mobile goes straight to messages.

He can't keep his thoughts straight. A tiny part of him is hoping against hope that Corinne is safe, that maybe she didn't come to meet Ashley at all. He hates himself for being grateful that it is Ashley hooked up to the machines – he loves her too, she is like family – but Corinne is his life. He cannot believe the injuries on Ashley's head. He thinks of Erin and feels sick.

The police car speeds through traffic lights, bounces slightly as they turn the corner of St John's Road. Dominic shuts his eyes. *Where is she?* The radio in the front seat begins to crackle and a voice comes over it, speaking to the officer behind the wheel. Dominic sits forward in the back seat, every muscle in his body straining to hear. But there's no need; the words come through startlingly clearly.

'10-78, fatality at West Hampstead Tube station. Young woman under a train. They're sending the crew out now.'

Dominic feels the floor of the car begin to shift. Cold fear clutches at his heart. He opens his mouth, but it's already happening, the police car is braking, beginning to turn around.

62

The train officer is directing everybody away, his outstretched hands fielding off the angry commuters. Pigeons scatter in the air like terrible shadows as the people are herded from the station, shunted out into the Hampstead streets. Barriers surround the station entrance; blue lights highlight the scene. Whispers catch Dominic as he dodges through the crowds, *Did you see it, did you see what happened? It's the driver I feel sorry for …*

There is a cluster of police huddled around the top of the escalators; the metal barrier separates them from him, he can see their mouths moving but their words are indistinct. Dominic pushes through, faster and faster. No matter how quickly he moves, it feels as if everything is in slow motion, as though he got out of the police car hours ago rather than minutes, as though his whole life has been leading up to this moment, this terrible day. In his mind's eye he sees Corinne, her eyes shining as she told him about the scan, her face a picture of happiness. That was only this morning. How can this be happening?

He is at the front of the barriers; a man in a fluorescent jacket is speaking into a radio; as Dominic approaches, he steps to the left, moves to one side. The police officers guide Dominic forward, one of them puts a hand on his shoulder, but Dominic's heart has stopped in his chest. Standing behind the man in the fluorescent jacket is a woman, clutching the ragged remains of a bright yellow scarf. She sees him at the same time as he sees her.

63

London

Ashley

She is drowning, she is deep below the surface. Shadowy shapes swim around her, they fade in and out. For a while she had struggled to breathe, had tried to get to the fresh air, but now she thinks she might give up. It is too tiring, she is finding it too hard. Is it really so bad to stay down here? She's been trying so hard for so long.

Someone is touching her, pushing something sharp into her arm. It hurts and she tries to cry out but nothing comes out of her mouth except bubbles. The darkness around her crowds closer and closer. Her dad would be cross with her for giving up. He told them never to give up, even when they were children he used to say that. But for some reason she doesn't think she has to do what her dad says any more. She doesn't believe him like she used to.

She still feels like she is moving but things are smoother now, like she is gliding rather than bumping in a vehicle. A lot of people are talking but she has no idea what they're saying. She isn't sure whether she cares. Perhaps she'll stop listening soon. It's quieter down here in the dark. Ashley would so like a break from it all sometimes and now here is one. It would be nice to finally take it. Her head hurts a lot.

64

27 March 2017
The day of the anniversary

London

Dominic

Corinne is wrapped in a silver aluminium blanket, her face deathly white. The sleeve of her coat is ripped and a bruise is forming on her cheekbone, blossoming purple in the strange half-light of the emptying ticket hall. She is standing alone, holding the remains of the yellow scarf, the police to her side, staring straight at Dominic. Their eyes are connected like lightning across the room.

The relief Dominic feels is visceral; it punches him in the chest and he feels his knees slip slightly, his feet lose their grip on the ground. For a moment the feeling is so strong that he can't move, can only stand there while it washes over him. Then he is rushing forwards, he is yanking aside the barrier and he is holding her in his arms, both of them are crying, pressed against each other even though the police are all around them, and someone is shouting their names.

Dominic can't speak. All he can do is hold her, whisper into her hair.

'Thank God,' he says, over and over. 'Thank God I've found you. Thank God you're alive.' He touches her face, and that's when she begins to cry, the tears begin to pour from her eyes as though they will never stop. She's saying something, he has to hold her shoulders and step back to make out the words.

'She fell,' she is saying, her voice wet with tears. 'She fell. Erin is dead, Dominic. She fell onto the tracks.'

65

London

Corinne

She's dead. The image replays, over and over in my head, while Dominic holds me, while I sob and shake against his chest. He is stroking my hair; I can feel his heartbeat thudding against my own.

Her hands on my back. The scarf around her neck. The roar of the train, the sight of her falling, down onto the tracks, the millisecond where I saw her face, saw her scream before the train slammed into her, before her body disappeared in the screech of the brakes and the rush of red. So much red.

I can't stop picturing her face, the swing of her hair and her piercing blue eyes. My father's eyes. Gone forever. The ambulance men are clustered all around me, trying to get me inside the van. I don't want to go.

'Corinne,' Dominic is saying, he's holding me tightly, in amongst the crowd and the faces and the horrible bright lights. A policeman is coming towards us. I am terrified someone will drag me back down there, back into the tunnel. Dom's telling me something, his mouth is moving but I'm not listening, I can't hear him, it's like my mind has frozen and all I can hear is the roar of the train, the sound it made when it hit her.

'Ashley,' he is saying. 'We need to go to Ashley.' I finally focus on his words, and when I understand what he's saying it jolts me back into my body, I can feel the cold of my hands in his and the chattering of my teeth, the sounds come back as though someone's turned the volume back up.

'We need to go to hospital,' he says. 'You have to get checked out, you're in shock and you've got to think about the baby. Ashley is there.' He pauses. 'We need to go now.' The paramedics step forward. This time I let them take me.

*

I grip my sister's hand, feel her gold wedding ring cold on my skin. Her head is heavily bandaged and her eyes are closed. They've tidied her up but part of her hair has been cut away to make room for the stitches, thick black lines that lace her scalp. Holly is in the children's ward, the emergency department. We aren't allowed in.

A nurse comes into the room, smiles uncertainly at us all, clustered around the bed. It's a fake smile, it doesn't meet her eyes.

'How is she?' I say urgently.

The nurse checks the bandage on Ashley's head, adjusts her pillow slightly so that her neck lolls to the side.

I stiffen. My whole body is aching but I don't care about myself any more. Ashley is so pale.

'She's lost a lot of blood,' the nurse says. She cannot meet my eye. The door of the room opens and James comes in, joins me silently at the side of the bed. The only sound is the whirr of the monitors, the beeping of her heart.

*

There's a lot of time to think in the hospital, although I try hard not to. I spend most of the first day having tests, sitting with my legs apart while they poke around inside me. The baby is healthy; despite the struggle on the platform, physically I am unharmed save the bruise on my cheek, the place where her hand collided with my bone. After the tests I go back to Ashley's room, sit down on the plastic chair by the bed. That's when my thoughts start to spiral.

It's as though I am holding a looking glass up to my childhood, magnifying all of it in horrible detail. Dad putting his arms around Mum, sitting opposite me at the chessboard, knocking my pawns over one by one. All of us on holiday, walking along the seafront in Cornwall, collecting cowrie shells on the beach. Dad at work, Ashley and I waiting for him to come home, throwing ourselves at him like miniature missiles when he walked through the door. His face in the hospital room, the people at the funeral. People who adored him, people who are toasting his name tonight. Were they there then, the others? Was she there in the crowds, her blonde hair unnoticed in the mass of mourners? None of us will ever know.

Ashley is unconscious for almost two days. I don't leave her side except to go to Holly, who is attached to machines, breathing with the help of a ventilator. The sight of the wires connecting to her tiny chest makes me cry, I bury my head in Dominic's jumper, whisper prayers that I don't think I believe.

I know they're keeping the press away; Ashley has a private room at the end of the corridor, away from the main ward. I imagine the journalists swarming outside, the things they must be saying about her, about me. About our family.

Dominic comes in and out, brings me food, says I need to keep eating for the baby. James is with me, most of the time, but the children stay away. He doesn't want them to see her like this. Not unless the time comes when they have to. Both of us are praying that doesn't happen. Our desperate thoughts fill the room like balloons.

*

It's Tuesday morning, the grey dawn light is filtering through into the hospital room. We are finally allowed in to see Holly. Her blue eyes stare up at me and she reaches for my hand. I burst into tears. All her hair is gone, there is a scar across the back of her head where she hit the ground, and one of her little legs is strapped up from where it twisted beneath her. But she is going to be OK. They have run test after test, confirmed that the results from the doctor are conclusive: high levels of prescription drug in her body, built up slowly over a period of time, adding to the medicine given to her by the doctor. The specialist told us that the overdose Erin gave her was actually a good thing, it helped cushion her fall because her body was in a near-coma state at the time. I close my eyes as he tells us, imagining June and Erin forcing the liquids down Holly's throat, wondering what lengths they went to to make her comply. No wonder she screamed at night. No wonder her body was floppy. Dominic takes my hand, squeezes it. The doctor gives us five minutes with Holly then ushers us out, back into where Ashley lies mute on the bed.

The room smells of the lilies that Mum left here, the air is warm; they leave the heating on all night. I sit down. The relief of seeing Holly alive makes my body feel exhausted, my limbs ache with tiredness. *Soon you'll have a baby cousin*, I think in my head, *so you just better get well, Holly Thomas. There are too many people who love you and my baby is going to need a playmate.* I can feel myself drifting off, clench my jaw to try to stay awake.

I wake up with my head on Ashley's bed. Someone is holding my hand. I raise my head. Her eyes are open.

'Ashley!'

The nurse bustles back in, and this time when I look at her the smile is real, it reaches all the way to her eyes and I sit up straight, allow myself the first flicker of hope.

'She's a fighter!' the nurse says, and then I feel it, the soft pressure on my hand; Ashley is squeezing my fingers.

'Oh my God,' I say, and I start to cry, I lean forward and I weep with gratitude, because I am so lucky, I am so relieved that my sister is awake. The tears drip down onto my dirty wool dress, soak into the fabric.

'You're watering the baby,' the nurse says, and I smile through my tears.

Ashley is squeezing my fingers again. I lean forward. She's saying something, the words coming out in a whisper. I try not to look at the swell of her head, the dark flowers underneath the bandages. The scars will take a while to heal.

'It's all right,' I say softly. 'You're going to be OK.'

'Holly,' she says, 'Holly.'

I squeeze her hand 'Holly's OK, Ash. She's in the ward next door. The doctors have told us she's going to make it.'

She closes her eyes. I start to panic again but then she opens them, and they are full of tears. I lean forward, lean my forehead against hers. Our hearts beat as one. When I sit back, she gives me a weak smile, and I sit there with her, hunched on the bed, my face close to hers, until James comes back in, brings me a drink. His face lights up when he sees Ashley and I smile as he hurries forwards, grips her other hand.

'James,' she says, the word coming out quietly, and at the sound of her voice he lets out a sob and bends down, puts his arms around her body as best he can.

'Thank God,' he is saying, his voice muffled against her chest. 'Oh Ash, thank God.'

I leave them then, I stand up quietly and let myself out of the little white room. Outside, the hospital corridor is silent and calm, and I stand there for a minute, outside the door, breathing in and out. My neck still hurts from where the scarf twisted around it but I can feel the muscles in my back beginning to unwind, to loosen themselves gradually. It feels as though they have been clenched for a very long time but I know I have to try now, I have to try to relax. I touch my stomach. My family are safe. It is over. I look up and down the corridor. It is deserted. I push down the voices in my head, knowing it is time for me to go.

66

One week later

London

Dominic

Over the next week, they all have to give statements: Corinne, Ashley, Mathilde and James. Dominic spends two hours in the bare white room of Finsbury Park police station, talking to DI Janson, the younger officer who came to the flat the night they found Beatrice.

'Did you know Erin de Bonnier's history, sir?'

'No,' Dominic says, 'I didn't. She was my colleague. We were … we were friends for a while. But she never told me anything about her past.' He looks away from them when he says that, down at the scuffed floor of the station. There are track marks on the linoleum, as though someone has dragged something across it. There is no point mentioning the night in the bar. What purpose will it serve now?

'And her mother,' the officer consults his notes. 'June de Bonnier?' He shakes his head. 'We've got a search party out. The house is deserted. I doubt she'll last long. The papers have really gone to town on this one. Lot of medication papers found in the house, seems she'd been on treatment for depression and psychiatric issues for years. Can't say she's much of a threat now, mind. Looks like her daughter had her fairly under control. S'pose you gotta feel sorry for her, really. Poor old biddy with a daughter like that. I'd almost class her as a victim.' He raises his eyebrows. 'Classic case of manipulation.'

Dominic stares at the man's ear; it is twisted, ugly. He feels a flash of anger at the officer's unprofessional tone.

The media are already all over the story; Corinne has refused to read any of it, avoided looking at the pictures, the screaming black headlines. The de Bonnier name is mud. All of the details have been reported: Erin's mental health issues, Richard's debt, the story behind June and Carlington House. Their kitchen knife is found halfway along the Jubilee Line, thrown by the force of the train that hit Erin. The only thing the police don't find is the doll house, it is never recovered in the search of Erin's flat. Perhaps she destroyed it.

In the weeks that follow, Dominic stares at her desk sometimes, at the empty seat, the blank space where her computer used to be. The sight makes him shiver.

67

London

Corinne

The dreams are the worst. They go on for weeks. They can't find June, she is nowhere, she is gone. The police are still looking, but they aren't as worried as I am. She's elderly, they say, she was under her daughter's control. I'm not so sure. Almost every night Dominic wakes me, I find myself thrashing in his arms and he holds me close, repeats the same words to me over and over again.

'You're safe, Corinne. You're safe. It's over.' But it's not over. Every night, I lean silently into his chest and close my eyes, try to push away the image of her face, her bright yellow scarf, the shock in her eyes. The shock in my own. I put my hands on my stomach and I feel it grow, and I know that my baby is in there, and that she is safe, and that that is down to me. And only then can I sleep.

Epilogue

It's Dad's birthday today. I've got a bunch of butter-bright roses ready to take to the grave, yellow was always his favourite. In spite of everything, I still want to go, even if no one else wants to come. I can't explain it, apart from to say that he's still my dad. Even though he lied, even though he stole money, even though he cheated. He's my father. He was the only one I ever had.

It's hot, the first boiling day of summer, and the gallery is calm and quiet. I like this because it means I can keep very still, holding myself in position, a china doll surrounded by paintings. I am humming quietly, potential baby names spinning in my head. Gilly is coming over tonight with her partner, we're going to decide on a name once and for all. She's been a real friend to me over the last few months, after everything. I'm glad she got her happy ending. We talked about it all, and when the press hammered on the door, when my morning sickness came, when the media attention made me hole up inside the flat she was there with endless cups of decaf and trashy magazines. She knows about Dad, of course, about what he did. I told her I bet she's glad they didn't use his firm, that they might've been even worse, but she's too kind to agree, she just gave me a cuddle.

'I'm not glad about anything, Corinne,' she said. 'I'm just so sorry this happened to your family.'

Anyway, she and Graham are coming later, they're bringing little Tommy, and we're all having dinner. I'm thinking about what to make for them when the little bell of the gallery rings to announce a visitor. I look up, my fingers halfway through writing the curve of a pound sign. A woman walks in, slowly, carrying a handbag. She wanders over to the left of the gallery, gazing at the newly commissioned prints on the wall. Her back is towards me; I cannot see her face.

'Let me know if you'd like any help,' I call, conscious of Marjorie in the back room, and I go back to writing the price tags. I'm nervous about this afternoon. None of us have been back to the cemetery since it happened, but the doctor thinks it might help with the nightmares. Memory replacement, she called it. It's a two-step process, apparently: *confabulation and repression*. C and R, she said, and I nodded like I'd told her the truth.

I put a hand on my rounded stomach, feel it's reassuring solidity. Not long now. Soon we'll be a proper family. It is becoming too warm in here, the gallery windows are sealed tight and I can feel my toes sticking together, rubbing against each other in my sandals. My swollen ankles strain against the leather.

'Excuse me?'

I look up. The woman is standing in front of me, resting one small hand against the counter. The other hand is curled up, as a child hiding a secret. When I see her face, my blood runs cold.

It is what I have been terrified of for four months, as the police trail has gone cold and the officers have gradually lost interest. I've watched the posters tatter in the wind and rain, the media coverage lessen, the stories about us be replaced by new horrors. Everyone has been forgetting. Everyone except me.

I open my mouth to scream but the sound doesn't come out. The woman in front of me opens up her fingers and that's when I see it, she's clutching a little object in her hand. A shudder goes through me, moves its way through my body until I am shaking all over. How has she got hold of it? As I stare down at her hand, the woman smiles at me, a horrible smile as though she's testing me, waiting to see how I'll react.

My heartbeat accelerates and sweat breaks out all over my body, beading my forehead and dampening the underside of my arms. My maternity dress starts to feel hot and tight and as I do a terrible sense of dread comes over me. Even though I've never met her, I know who this woman is. And she knows me.

Instinctively, I wrap my arms around my stomach. I need to say something, to ask her what she wants, but somehow my voice won't come, my tongue sticks to the roof of my mouth and I can't find the right words to begin questioning her. A slow sense of inevitability begins to build in my mind, as though some part of me has always known this moment would come.

I can hear Marjorie behind me in the stockroom, faintly, moving around, unpacking, stacking. She's listening to the radio; I can make out the soft hum of politicians squabbling, their voices talking over each other impatiently. I want to run to the sound, hide behind Marjorie whilst my mind tries to keep up with what my eyes are saying is true.

The woman hasn't moved, her hand is still open on the desk between us, challenging me to say something; her head is tilted to one side and she's showing her teeth, small stumps in the darkness of her mouth. The little rocking horse is between us, lying in the flesh of her palm. It mocks me for my silence.

'You need to leave,' I say, my shaking voice echoing in the quiet of the gallery, praying Marjorie hears me, recognises the panic in my voice.

She shakes her head, a teacher to a child, and turns away. I catch sight of her figure in the mirror opposite; the glass reflects her shape, bounces her back at me again and again so that she is everywhere, darting between the paintings like a black sprite. As I watch, she twists her head backwards, gives me a quick smile.

'Thanks,' she says. 'I think I'll come back another time.'

The little bell jangles again and she's gone. I stand and stare at the street, which already is deathly empty. My breathing is loud. I gulp air and crush closed my eyes until black shiny dots dance behind the lids. *Think. Think. I have to call the police. But I can't. But I have to.*

'Corinne?' Marjorie is calling from the office doorway.

I open my eyes and stand straight, about to turn to face her, but then I see it, she's left it there by my discarded pen. It is rocking gently as if a tiny hand is pushing it back and forth, back and forth. It is just like the last time. I open my mouth. And then I scream.

Marjorie comes running in. 'What's the matter? Who was that? Bloody hell, you scared me half to death!'

I am gasping. My thoughts are racing. They never found her. They never found the doll house. No one else could have known but her. I see it then, and I can't believe I haven't seen it before: the shuffle of her footsteps, the flash of her grey hair, her weathered old face, always near me, always just out of reach. Watching me, waiting. On the stairs in my building, walking past me in the park. She wasn't under her daughter's control. It was the other way around. Panic skitters through my body and I moan, putting my arms across my stomach.

'Marjorie,' I say, 'Marjorie!' My breathing is strange, distorted. The pressure in my head is building, mounting behind my eyelids.

She stares back at me. Since the accident she's been really kind, she's helped me get back to normal, one day at a time, turned the media away from the door until it all died down. She shielded me from the worst of the aftermath. I go to her, grab hold of her hands. She looks confused.

'What's the matter? Corinne? Come on, deep breaths, remember, like I showed you. In and out.'

I'm trying, I'm sucking in air but I can't calm down, I can't stop staring at the rocking horse moving, the sway of the little wooden rails. How else would she have it unless she knew? In my mind I am piecing things together, I am bent over as though the weight on my shoulders is physical.

'Marjorie,' I say again, 'they've got it wrong. I don't think Erin was controlling her mother, I think her mother was controlling her. Oh my God.'

'June de Bonnier? Is that who was just in here? Corinne, you need to call the police!'

I am frozen to the spot. It is coming, it is building up inside me. The thing I have never been able to tell anyone, not the police, not Ashley, not even Dominic. The thing that keeps me awake at night, the real reason I have nightmares.

Guilt.

I don't answer her. I race to the gallery door, slam the bolts across the top. Marjorie is staring at me. She comes towards me, puts a hand on my shoulder.

'All right, all right. Try to keep calm. We will call the police but the woman isn't dangerous, she was being manipulated. She's nearly seventy, Corinne.' She pauses. 'Didn't you read the stories? What would she want now?'

I look up at her. I know what June wants. It's the same thing she's always wanted, and I've made it so much worse.

It is the day of the anniversary. Erin and I are on the tube platform at West Hampstead Underground station. Her scarf tightens around my neck. We are right on the yellow line, my boots are beginning to slip. I hear the sound of the train approaching, I pull myself forward and we are both standing still, we are panting, our faces close together. She's staring at me. I think of my baby. She opens her mouth to speak and that's when I do it: I reach out and I push her into the path of the oncoming train.

'Revenge.'

The handle of the gallery door begins to turn.

Acknowledgements

This book would not exist without the support, encouragement and ideas of my agent Camilla Wray at Darley Anderson, who never stopped believing in me and whose editorial help was invaluable. Similar thanks go to Celine Kelly, whose incredible insight is very much appreciated. Thanks too to Naomi Perry, who did a stellar job of looking after me last year during Camilla's maternity leave – I finally found someone who shares my love of red pandas! The whole team at Darley Anderson are superstars and I'm lucky to be on their books.

A huge thank you to my wonderful editor Charlotte Mursell, who has made this process so smooth and enjoyable for me, and who is a great champion of all her HarperCollins books. Thank you to Victoria Oundjian and Lucy Gilmour at HQ for taking a chance on my book; I am so grateful. Thank you to Anna Sikorska for designing such a wonderfully creepy cover and for being the one to put my name onto a book jacket, which has always been my dream. Thank you to Alex Silcox for a great copy-edit and for catching all the things I missed, and thanks to all at HQ; you are all wonderful and I'm very proud to be published by you.

I feel lucky to know such talented, creative publishing professionals, but even luckier to call these people friends: special thanks go to the brilliant Helena Sheffield for your work with the bloggers and your friendship – you always go above and beyond. Thank you to the beautiful Sabah Khan who organised publicity for the book, I owe you a LOT of rainbow-coloured flowers. Thank you to Eloise Wood for reading a draft of this book and being a constant supporter and an excellent advice-giver too.

Thank you to the Doomsday Writers – you know who you are and I couldn't have done it without you, and I hope I never have to. Thank you to the kind authors who have read and quoted for my book, and to Kate Ellis, Kate Stephenson and Natasha Harding for your support too.

Thank you to Donald Winchester, who was one of the first agents to show interest in my writing, and to all of Team Avon and Helen Huthwaite at HarperCollins, the best bunch of colleagues anyone could ask for who publish amazing books with incredible passion and make my day job such a pleasure.

Thank you to my girlfriends for your encouragement and enthusiasm throughout this process; I promise never to put you in a crime book unless you come out on top.

Thank you to Alex for being my voice of reason, and for keeping me calm when I think I can't write at all. You are an amazing supporter and I love you.

And finally, the biggest thank you to my family – to my brothers Owen and Fergus for reading countless drafts and answering all my incessant WhatsApps – you are my favourite people on the planet. Thank you to my dad for building me a doll house, then reliably informing me which parts of the book made no sense (especially geographically – not my strong point) and for putting me in touch with helpful people too who know more about architecture than I do. Thank you to my lovely grandma for digging out my old short stories, encouraging me and making me smile. And finally thank you to my mum; there are no words for how much you have championed me and this book and I love you so much and am so grateful. Thank you.

Q & A with Phoebe Morgan

1. What is your favourite thing about the writing process?

I love the moment when characters begin to come to me and I start itching to get them down on paper! Often I will notice a small detail in my everyday life and make a note of it on my phone so that I can put it in a book someday, and I love the exciting feeling of starting a brand-new book with fresh ideas and thoughts which will work their way into the plot. Also, let's be honest, I like *having* written – when I have the finished product and can hear what readers' think!

2. How long did it take you to write *The Doll House*?

It took a few months of writing almost every day to get the first draft down. At the time I was working several other jobs and so my time was quite limited, but I made myself write 1,000 words a day until I had a reasonable manuscript. I then sent it off to agents, and the one I signed with helped me polish the manuscript before we sent it out to publishers. That took another 6-9 months – there was a lot of re-writing but I felt as though the book got better each time so I'm incredibly glad I didn't give up!

3. What drew you to writing in the psychological thriller genre?

I love to read in this genre so when it came to writing my own novel it felt like the natural choice. I am absolutely fascinated by people – their secrets, their childhoods, what makes us who we are – and I wanted to explore the darker side of family in this book. People can be so nuanced and there will always be strange currents hidden under the surface of everyday lives – fiction allows me to explore those!

4. Who are some of your favourite writers?

My absolute favourite authors are Maggie O'Farrell and Liane Moriarty, and more recently Sally Rooney. They all have a wonderful command of language and Liane Moriarty is an incredible plotter – her books never let me down. I also love Liz Nugent for psychological suspense novels, and Sabine Durrant. I'll drop everything for one of their new releases! There are so many brilliant books out in the world at the moment and I firmly believe there is room for everyone – I love trying new writers and discovering another voice. My to-be-read pile is somewhat out of control, it must be said …

5. Are you a plotter? How much planning do you do before settling down to write?

No, overall I'm not a plotter. I like to start writing and see where the story takes me – which means there is usually a lot of work to do post-first draft, but I prefer it that way. I find it quite difficult to meticulously plan a storyline, and often even when I think I know where a book is going, it might change midway through – I might get another, better idea or I might find one of my characters starts leading me in a new direction (it's almost as if they have a mind of their own sometimes!) I do a lot of self-editing and re-reading, making sure everything hangs together well, but the thought of planning before writing makes me panic! I think all writers either do one or the other – and I prefer to take things as they come and then go back over the manuscript once I've managed to get a long enough word count. A draft is much less intimidating than a blank page, no matter how terrible it might be to begin with!

6. Do you enjoy the editing process?

I do! I work as an editor myself (as well as being a writer) so it's a process that I really love. It's always a real privilege to receive feedback on my book, whether that is from my agent or my editor, and I feel lucky that they've taken the time to do so. It can sometimes be tricky when there are things you disagree with – but fiction is so subjective that there is never really a wrong or right answer. It's about working together to make the novel the very best it can be, and for me it's largely a really enjoyable process. It's amazing how much difference a fresh pair of eyes can make to a manuscript – sometimes it just takes another person pointing something out and it can make a huge impact. When you're writing every day and in the midst of your novel, it can be hard to see the wood for the trees after a while so you do need an editor to help guide you through.

7. Why do you think people like to read psychological thrillers?

I think a lot of people enjoy the escapism that thrillers bring – that total absorption in another world, that edge-of-your-seat feeling (which I hope you all had throughout *The Doll House*!) and the fun there is to be had in trying to guess who is behind it all. When I'm reading a psychological thriller, the rest of the world truly does disappear, and I become completely caught up in the characters, turning the pages at breakneck speed in order to get to the end. I sometimes find I have to force myself to put a book down, so that I can make the reading process last longer – it's just so enjoyable! I think readers like to explore the darker side of life, and reading is a safe way of doing so because once you've finished the book you can put it down and have a nice, calming cup of tea!

8. Why did you want to write about sisters in *The Doll House*?

I don't have any sisters, I have two lovely brothers, so I've always been interested in sisterhood and it felt like an exciting theme to explore in my book. I think there can be so many complex emotions surrounding siblings – jealousy, rivalry, love – and I wanted to take the idea of two sisters having very different lives – one able to have children, one not – and then add in the third element of Erin. Having children is such a personal decision for a woman and I wanted that to play a large part in the book too. I hope you all like the end result!

9. What advice would you give to anyone wanting to write their own book?

Go for it! It was always my dream to write a book and I'm so glad I did. Getting published is not always an easy journey – it wasn't particularly easy for me – but the key really is persistence, grit and determination. You only need one agent and one editor to like your novel – and nowadays there are other routes so you don't always even need that – and finishing a manuscript is an amazing feeling. Even if it takes you years, and you're juggling all sorts of other elements of your life while you write, you can do it – and even if you write a book that doesn't get picked up, you can always write another! Make the time for yourself and for your writing – you won't regret it.

10. What are you writing next?

My next psychological thriller, *The Girl Next Door*, is publishing in April 2019. It's about a married couple living in a small Essex village, whose lives are shaken to the core when the body of a teenage girl is found in the field behind their house. I've so enjoyed writing it and I can't wait to see what everyone thinks!

Website: www.phoebemorganauthor.com
Facebook: @PhoebeMorganAuthor
Twitter: @Phoebe_A_Morgan
Instagram: @phoebeannmorgan